Every Mother for Himself

Also by the same author:

Come Again

EVERY MOTHER FOR HIMSELF

Ed Jones

Ringpull • *Manchester*

Published in Great Britain in 1995 by Ringpull
an imprint of Fourth Estate Limited
6 Salem Road
London W2 4BU

A catalogue record for this book is
available from the British Library

ISBN 1 898051 13 5

Interior Design by Sandra Green
Typeset in 11/12.5 Melior by
Palimpsest Book Production Limited,
Polmont, Stirlingshire
Printed in Great Britain by Clays Ltd, St Ives plc

For B.G.

'*T*urn over.'

Nurse Jones obliged. Somewhat gracelessly.

It's difficult for a woman in her position to retain her dignity. On a desk top.

'How's this, Doctor?'

'Um, not quite – ah yes – perfect. Thank you, Nurse.'

Doctor Divine heaved a contented sigh, sank back into his senses and gave himself up to the pleasure of penetrating a woman he hardly knew.

It was a mark of achievement to the doctor, this aerobic indiscipline, and registered on his personal successometer in much the same way as the registration of his brand spanking new, tornado-red Volkswagen Golf GTi (16v).

An excellent start to the day, was the way he thought of it. Brisk, like a morning constitutional. As bracing as a draught of country air.

A tonic.

Gleefully he looked down on her, surveying the scene of his triumph, luxuriating in the sheer carnality and taking in the texture of the skin round her abdomen. No, not her abdomen – he regretted the term – *the soft skin of her vulnerable underbelly*, that was more like it. ·

There she lay before him, face up on the desk, her great unruly mop of black hair splayed out, even covering the telephone. What was she? Twenty-two? Twenty-four at top. Young anyhow. And there she was – recumbent. Supine. Stark naked. Exposed. Denuded. Bare. He was inside her. He, Doctor Nicholas Divine, physician, owner of a nice new apartment in the city centre, driver of a new tornado-red Volkswagen Golf GTi (16v) . . . he struggled for a moment to find another suitable epithet and, finding none, returned to the matter in hand.

She was *at his mercy*. She was lying; he was standing. She was starkers; he was dressed. She moaned and he

1

buffeted. He drank it all in as he heaved: her breasts, her young flesh, the delicate mottle, the smooth freshness of the skin round her clavicle – er, collar bone – dammit! No technical terms, *please* . . .

He tried to concentrate.

But ended up thinking about golf, how badly he was playing lately.

Then he was thinking about work and his life in general. The bits that weren't so victorious. There were things in his life right now that niggled him intensely. But sex wasn't one of them, no. Sex was one of the good things in life. Yes.

Actually he was bored, though he didn't admit it as such. Rather *it* admitted *itself* and showed up in all kinds of ways: the way his Practice annoyed him; his impatience on the roads; and of course his extravagant sex drive.

Slap, grunt.

He was broke too. No control over his finances.

This morning's orgy was his reward for putting up with the shit. Slap. And there was plenty of shit to put up with. Grunt.

He might be pushing forty, but he could still push it up in the morning. He was still shagging away. Damn lousy Manchester Practice. It seemed to attract the scum.

He stared down at her now and watched her bosom heave. Or, rather, wobble. She was clutching the sides of his desk to steady herself and moaning aloud. He wished she could be quieter and in a clumsy effort to communicate this to her took hold of her hips and squeezed, dug his fingers into the flesh. But the telepathy failed and Nurse Jones was only encouraged in her agitation.

Doctor Divine winced.

And Nurse Jones gave vent.

He curled his toes anxiously and tried to finish off. But he could only picture the dowdy visage of

2

Mrs Temperance scowling across the antiseptic stillness of the waiting room – and the muffled whimper
of malpractice wafting past the waiting patients.

Concentrate! Get it done quickly . . .

He looked down on her as on the vanquished. She
was his. Squirming and his.

He was *having his way with her*. He concentrated
on the fact of her nudity, offsetting it against his own
clothedness.

Damn it she's making too much noise. He shook his
head. Just finish now. Come on, quick!

*She is lying face up on my desk and I can do whatever
I like with her.*

He was trying to see it as a scene in a film.

She's sprawled. Spread-eagled . . .

He had to block something out. He tried *not* to think
something.

She's sprawled – spread-eagled . . .

Scrawny. She was scrawny.

But her skin was nice.

He strained and stretched and tried to think only of
the pluses.

Like her age. And her skin – well, most of it. Her
pretty face. She did have a very attractive face.

But her face was screwed up now and had momentarily lost its charm. There were heavy purple blotches
under the eyes and other bits of her flesh were wobbling
in time with the breasts. And the noise!

'Jesus!' He said it out loud.

Nurse Jones froze.

Doctor Divine was panting and realised he was
soaked in sweat.

'You done?' she asked.

He shook his head. 'Shh! . . .' he hissed. He didn't
mean it to sound quite so reprehensible.

As she let her head fall back, a slight curl at the corner
of her mouth betrayed her irritation.

He stood his ground, waiting for his breath to return

3

before commencing what had to be the final assault. But he knew now for sure that the pleasure wasn't mutual. The spell was broken. There could be no further suspension of disbelief.

It was impossible to stop, however. He was determined to relieve himself. He needed to get the business over with, so he bit his lip and resumed his poking and grinding, his dry grinding.

With an expletive he reached for lubricant which he knew would besmirch his desk top and stole a glance at his watch.

Ten minutes? Can't have been!

He began pummelling in earnest.

He screwed up his eyes and made an enormous effort of concentration – trying not to imagine Mrs Temperance coming through the door to discover them. (With his evil eye he saw himself as she would: his shirt tail dangling, the back of his hairy thighs exposed, his socks visible above the crumple of his dropped trousers.)

Then he blocked it out. All of it. And beamed down on his penis and the uterus he was probing. The cervix he was nudging.

No, the pussy . . .

He called up other lovers, younger, more voluptuous, women who wanted him, who called out his name in ecstasy. He visualised and fantasised, stretched, strained and shook.

And . . . finally . . . almost . . . don't picture Mrs Temperance now . . . think of naked . . . pussy . . . she's enjoying it despite herself . . . she loves it . . . she's going to come . . . I'm coming . . . yes! . . . now!

And then those few seconds of just being, of throbbing and . . . Oh! . . . Got to stop!

Ouch! And panting . . .

And Nurse Jones lying on his desk, still spread-eagled, her unruly mop in rebellion, her breasts limp and her neck craned, looking to see if he's done.

At last.

He reached for a tissue and adjusted his testicles.

As he washed his hands he heard her gathering her airs and graces. He turned towards her and smiled warmly, although he didn't feel warmly towards her.

He felt relieved.

'Thank you, Nurse.'

'A pleasure, Doctor.'

She was smiling nicely too, thank God.

He sauntered over to his desk to mop up the mess.

'An excellent start to the day,' he remarked jauntily. As he mopped he added, 'You're a very slippery customer.'

But Nurse Jones was no longer smiling. She was standing there expectantly.

'Oh yes,' muttered the Doctor, 'I almost forgot.'

Nurse Jones didn't return this smile either. In fact she looked downright unfriendly.

A few moments later she rolled up the sleeve of her creased uniform and presented the inside of her forearm, while he prepared a syringe from a glass ampoule.

*J*ed hated the bed almost as much as the nice quiet Northern seaside town where they lived.

The bed was so damn *frilly*.

There was something about the decorations in the bedroom that infuriated him too, something suffocating about all those fringes – the bloody house was dripping with them. It was as if some disease had infested the place, and the windows, lamps and sofas, even the damn bed, had sprouted ornamental fungus. There were tucks and ruffles dangling in the remotest corners, and everywhere the eye settled there was edging and flounce.

5

He had bemoaned the bedroom design in the pub that night, persisting to the point where his wife, Charity, had taken his hand and said, 'Hey lighten up'. He was embarrassing their friends.

Damn *trimmings*. Why were they so offensive?

Now Jed and Charity – Mr and Mrs Green – were sitting up in bed reading. That is she was sitting up. He was slouched, sulkily back, staring blankly at his novel, *Steppenwolf*, cursing the interior design.

A collection of *Penguin Modern Classics* was one of his cultivated eccentricities. He rather enjoyed the grave panelling of the covers and the hint they gave that there were hidden depths to his being. On the surface he might be a businessman – not a very glamourous one at that – but in his soul he was a bohemian revolutionary.

At least, he used to be.

All that was left of the dream these days was a faint philanthropy, a *Pretenders*' album he never listened to, and a dogged determination to vote for the opposition party in a constituency that hadn't changed hands since the days of the Regency.

He always said he was a Socialist at Heart. This had nothing to do with collective ownership of the means of production or revolutionary movements of oppressed peoples (although he had been a member of the Anti-Apartheid Movement in the old days), it meant, rather, being faithful to his wife, running an honest show work-wise, and hating the Royal Family.

Tonight he felt oppressed by the bedspread. Fringed with peach valance, it was all the more depressing for the fact that it matched the rest of the house. The rest of his life.

He was drowning in bland pastel shades and winceyette sheets.

He rather liked that word, 'winceyette', and toyed with it for a moment. It had a faint air of royalty that made it seem utterly repugnant. It reminded him somehow of Princess Diana's haircut, or one of those vile, finicky, pseudo-genteel pink and glass buildings that seemed to have infested the town centre recently.

He was living a winceyette nightmare.

'Shall I turn the light out?'

Charity's voice interrupted his moody meditations.

'You may as well,' he muttered eyeing the fancy lampshade as if it were leprous.

'Cheer up, it may never happen,' she chirped.

Jed stubbornly remained in his reading position as the nightmare of modern bedroom design was engulfed in gloom.

'Whassa madda – baby can't relax?'

He hated her baby voice. It usually meant – oh no!

Suddenly his wife was upon him, reaching straight for his manhood.

His heart sank. 'I'm fine, honestly.'

'Mmm – relax,' she whispered, wrapping herself around him.

This was the last thing he needed. He had planned to go to the bathroom and relieve himself onto the face-cloth as soon as she nodded off. Somehow, lately, he hated the prospect of sex with her and was depressed by his inability to refuse it directly.

'I'm busy tomorrow,' he tried.

'Shh,' she soothed, kneading and smoothing.

There was a slight and unwelcome uprising. If only he didn't get an erection just because he didn't want one!

In desperation he put his hand on hers and pressed, trying to counter her manipulations.

Why did he feel so *inhibited*? Yes, that was it – he felt shy of her, his own wife. It was the same choking claustrophobia he got from the bloody wallpaper, for God's sake.

Now, owing to the treachery of his own biology, she

had been encouraged to 'Go On Down South' as she called it, having mistaken his vague restraining gestures for passion.

In six years of marriage, he had entirely failed to communicate to her that he was indifferent to 'Oral Communication in the Home Counties' (as he called it). She was very adept his wife, being an ex-nurse, but for some reason the activity left him cold.

So, after a respectable pause and a civilised display of gratitude, he took hold of her shoulders (somewhat manfully), pulled her level, kissed her and, taking a deep breath, returned the compliment – until his neck began to ache and his mind to wander.

Charity took an age to reach her orgasm, so he had time to reflect as he nuzzled and sucked and gently incited.

As he did so the trivial irritations of the evening gave way to the underlying malaise: his whole livelihood was in jeopardy. His business was on the verge of bankruptcy. It was probably too late to save it. He should have acted sooner. It was his own fault for burying his head in the sand.

He felt his wife's hand on his head.

'Gently,' she whispered.

'Um, sorry.'

'It's OK. Umm, that's nice . . .'

He was overcome by a wave of guilt. He had married and sworn to love and look after this woman (albeit within the terms of an equal and honest relationship). She was hard-working (though underpaid), organised, loving – and oblivious to the danger they faced. There she was stretched out before him, vulnerable and trusting. Here he was staring humiliation in the face.

He loathed himself.

He thought about the house, *her* house really – she was the one who loved it. They might lose it if the worst came to the worst.

8

He was choked up now and and decided to concentrate on giving his wife a decent orgasm. At least he could still do something.

As soon as he began to concentrate she began panting in earnest and quickly went into spasm.

Then he 'did his dos' inside her.

Instead of onto the face-cloth in the bathroom as usual.

When she was asleep Jed wondered whether he loved Charity any more, or whether he just felt sorry for her. He pictured a new life on his own and rather liked what he saw. Which was a new apartment – perhaps on the Riverside Development – with modern, what was it, 'minimalist' interior design and a sexy young woman.

But then he thought about the state of his business again and experienced a sinking sensation. He pictured his wife in the arms of another man – or rather the bed of another man – and entirely abandoned the fantasy.

After that he spent a restless night going back and forth over stony ground.

'**C**areful mate, they're caught . . . these are six hundred quid trousers.'

Jed was pushing his way a little drunkenly through the old iron stile, Eddie was clutching his trousers trying to hold Jed back.

Jed shook his head. 'Six hundred quid for a pair of trousers?'

'Careful, you'll rip them . . .'

'Why the fuck are you wearing six hundred quid

trousers in the middle of the countryside?'

'This isn't the middle of the countryside, mate. This is my back garden.'

'Boll-ocks.'

'And I never wear anything *but* six hundred pound trousers.'

They were strolling through idyllic scenes half a mile down the road from Eddie's sleek, isolated bachelor home in the heart of the West Pennine Moors. You could just make out the roof of the house over the trees in the distance.

'What if you get cow shit on them?'

'I have them dry cleaned.'

Eddie was Jed's accountant. They had been friendly for some years now.

The stile negotiated, Eddie passed Jed the hip flask of whisky and said, 'How's suburbia, by the way?'

'Same as always.'

'Just like you, then, init?'

Init. Eddie's trendy-speak.

'And how's that beautiful wife of yours?'

Jed shrugged. 'Same.'

'Let you off duty, did she?'

'Fuck off.'

Eddie laughed, 'Semi-detached from life, that's you, mate.'

It took Jed a few moody minutes to formulate a reply to this witticism – 'Well you're wholly detached from responsibility' – by which time it was too late to say it.

Anyway, this evening Jed had to indulge Eddie because he had come on serious business.

He needed his £20,000 back.

He knew Eddie would be against it.

He was waiting for the right moment to ask.

They were sat on the old railway bridge now.

'I love this bridge,' Eddie said.

10

'It's quite an old one,' Jed said, blandly.

'I got thirty grand off the price of the house because of it.'

'That's a good basis for a love affair.'

'I kicked off about express trains passing half a mile away but you can't hear a thing from the house.'

There was a train coming a little way off down the track.

Eddie said, 'Lie on the wall while the train goes under the bridge. It's a good buzz.'

Jed said, 'No way!'

The wall was a low stone wall, quite wide, probably dating back to the age of steam trains.

'Come on,' said Eddie, lying down. 'Where's your sense of adventure?'

Jed shook his head. 'I haven't got one.'

Eddie tutted. 'You've got no sense of fun, either.'

'You're pissed.'

'No holding on . . .'

Jed stood back, saying, 'Don't come crying to me if you kill yourself.'

At that moment the train thundered by underneath giving them both a fright, the noise was so loud.

The bridge shook. Eddie screamed along to the noise and ended up holding on.

When it was over and Eddie had straightened his trousers, he said, 'If you'd lived a bit more dangerously you wouldn't be bankrupt now.'

'I'm not bankrupt!'

'Not officially. Not yet.'

Jed sighed heavily and kept quiet.

On the way back Eddie boasted about his latest girl friend – Vicky – fifteen years his junior. Rich father. He described her as 'a savage' in bed.

'The posh ones are the randiest,' he declared.

Jed wasn't really listening.

'Vicky's got friends you know.'

'I should hope so.'

11

'Randy friends.'

Despite himself, Jed exhaled wistfully. 'Girls will be girls.'

Eddie shook his head. 'Yeah, but boys don't seem to want to be boys.'

'I'm not a boy, I'm a man. And I'm married.'

'So are Vicky's randy friends.'

Jed gulped some Scotch.

It was one of Eddie's minor ambitions to induce Jed to commit adultery, probably so he could make a move on Charity whom he thought ravishingly beautiful and far too good for Jed.

'What we've got in mind is a little weekend away . . .'

'Forget it,' said Jed.

'Just the four of us . . .'

'You enjoy trying to unhinge me, don't you.'

'I'm trying to *oil* your hinges, mate. Open you up a bit.'

'When will you get it into your head? I'm faithful.'

Eddie smiled to himself and let go one he'd been working on. 'You know what you are – and I mean in life as in love?'

'Oh yeah?' Jed couldn't wait.

'Anally retentive.'

Jed hooted. '*Anally retentive*! That's a new one.'

Anally retentive, in life as in love.

It wasn't the most sophisticated business in the world, selling assorted novelty knick-knacks to the seafront traders but over the years it had provided a stable, and at times generous, living.

Jed had made a decent whack selling mobile phones when they first became popular (one of Eddie's tips), but soon everyone was selling them and he'd had to expand his activities.

His greatest business achievement came in the early Eighties when, in an unusually rash move, he followed a hunch and bought up a whole stock of 'boob caps' –

12

hats with plastic breasts on them – which a manufacturer had failed to sell.

The idea took off. The town was invaded by an army of drunken tit-heads and Jed made a small fortune.

Ever since then Eddie had tried to persuade him to sell his business and invest everything 'in Gibraltar', but Jed had refused, suspecting that Eddie's offshore business practices were at least unethical and possibly illegal.

Then English people seemed suddenly to stop taking holidays and business took a plunge.

In desperation Jed took a gamble and bought another stock of caps from the same manufacturer – who had since taken to drink.

The caps had a cock and balls on them and entirely failed to impress the few tourists who still had the money to get drunk.

Eddie seized the opportunity to tell Jed he was a 'dickhead' and that it was time for him to 'sell up and move offshore', adding, 'By which I don't mean drowning yourself in the estuary'.

Finally, after an unsuccessfully late attempt to jump onto the portable fax bandwagon, Jed took his cheque book in hand and placed twenty grand – his last disposable twenty grand – at his friend's mercy.

'Are you sure you wouldn't rather invest in another load of bollocks,' Eddie asked when he'd finally won over Jed with the promise that the investment he was making was 'entirely safe.'

'Entirely legal, you said.'

'Yes, mate. Entirely safe.'

'Eddie!'

'Don't be a dickhead all your life, Jed.'

Anally retentive: The desire of the honest businessman not to become an abject gambler. Or a crook. Or both.

They were back in the house now.

13

Jed had successfully steered the conversation to business but still hadn't asked for his money back, even after all that Scotch.

'You're fucked, you do know that?'

Jed could tell Eddie was getting philosophical. 'Thing's aren't good, Eddie.'

'Fucked by a load of bollocks. Mind you, you're in good company. The whole thing's fucked. The whole country's fucked. The whole *world's* fucked.'

'You should have been a poet, you know that?'

More whisky was poured and drunk.

'It's too late for you now, though mate,' continued Socrates. 'Even if the world survives, you're fucked.'

'Cheers for the vote of confidence.'

'You still think there's a chance don't you?'

'Um . . .' Jed couldn't admit it in words.

'You know something? That investment you made with me is the only thing you have of any worth. Apart from your attractive wife of course.'

Now. Had to be.

'Eddie, I . . .'

'And she is very attractive.'

'Yeah, yeah. I know.'

'Pity you've dropped her in the shit.'

'I haven't dropped anyone in the shit!'

'Hey that's an idea, why not withdraw your forty grand and buy a load of hats with shit on them. A good symbol of the times that'd be.'

Jed blinked. '*Forty* grand? What forty grand?'

'Oh didn't I tell you? You've doubled your money. Congratulations.'

Jed was dumbfounded.

'And before you get ideas, it's not enough to save your business, so forget it. I forbid you to withdraw it.'

Half an hour later Jed had decided to take a risk and leave his money where it was. Eddie said it would be worth 'fifty' in a month. So Jed thought

14

he'd hang on for a bit and *then* use it to rescue his business.

The accountant settled back in his chair and looked at his friend with pop eyes.

'What's up?'

I've got something here you might like.' Eddie seemed on edge slightly. He dug into the pocket of his jacket and produced a small silver box, opening it to reveal some fine white powder.

Jed blinked. 'Talcum powder?'

Eddie laughed, not realising that Jed knew what it was, or at least suspected.

'Cocaine. "Finest pharmaceutical".'

Jed was still shocked to hear it named. Not to mention embarrassed. He knew he would have to prove his terminal frumpiness by refusing it.

In silence Eddie laid out two 'lines' on the glass table, producing a gold American Express card to chop it up and organise it. 'That'll do nicely,' he joked at last, looking up with his famous smile which to Jed at that moment seemed like a demonic leer.

Jed waved a hand. 'I've got to drive.'

'You've drunk half a pint of Scotch, this'll sober you up.'

Jed shook his head and managed to sound reasonably casual. 'No, really . . .'

Eddie didn't seem that disappointed.

He rolled up a twenty pound note and sniffed both the lines himself – one up each nostril – and appeared to go into a trance, while Jed tried to stop his eyes boggling at the spectacle.

Jed felt like he had just seen his friend peel off a latex face-mask to reveal a pulsating, shrivelled *Dr Who* monster with a green nose and peevish little eyes.

Jed topped up his glass and drank with relish to his own steadfast lifestyle. He would survive. Eddie had turned to drugs. It was his friend Eddie who was going to crash, not him.

15

Then Eddie opened his eyes and smiled, topping up his own glass. 'I don't usually bother,' he declared. 'It was a present. It's an occasional thing.'

Jed tried not to look sanctimonious. 'Sure. Everyone does it, these days. Cheers.'

They both drank deeply.

'Tell me,' said Eddie, after what Jed thought was an awkward silence. 'And I want you to be honest with me. Do you still find your wife attractive after all this time? I mean, sexually. You still get it on?'

Jed smiled. 'Yes,' he said, 'Of course.'

Eddie smiled too. 'You know something, mate. I think you must be one of the last truly good men around.'

'Cheers,' muttered Jed, raising his glass, which was nearly empty.

*O*nce the home of the local gentry, the dignified stone building, named *Newfoundland* sometime in the Victorian period, was now a State-run rest home for the elderly, charmingly located in the sand dunes a few hundred yards down the beach from the dingy grey billets of Pontins holiday camp, next to the sewage outlet for the town.

Consequently the fascinating and mysterious flotsam of the adjacent beach – the knotted wood and twisted clumps of seaweed and jellyfish – lay in the company of myriad gnarled and shrivelled nuggets of human faeces.

The dunes themselves were an unofficial dump for local traders and anonymous litterbugs so that the scent of the sea, perfumed by the effluence of the seaside metropolis, was often enhanced by the reek of rotting rubbish.

A lot depended on the direction of the wind.

*　　*　　*

Edith was the day-nurse at *Newfoundland*. She was thin as a sweet-pea plant and as shaky as a drunk.

Her age was a matter of some controversy.

There had been a discrepancy in her retirement date in the nineteen sixties and now no one was sure what it was, not even the Department of Social Security, which, in the end, supported Edith's assertion that she was fifty eight – even though she looked to be a hundred and fifty eight.

She was generally thought to be somewhere in between.

'I'm as old as my tongue and I've outlived my teeth, God rest their souls,' Edith said the morning of the day she poisoned Mrs Crotchley.

'We should cut off one of her legs and count the rings!' laughed Lilly, the largest and jolliest of the residents, giving Edith a friendly nudge that nearly knocked her off her feet.

When she'd collected herself, Edith smiled as if she could hear and coughed the hacking cough that always seemed as if it would turn her inside out.

'Poor dear,' Lilly said when it was over. 'She's only a mop with a hair net on.'

Edith was still pretending she could hear.

Lilly pulled her nearer and spoke into her hearing-aid. 'I said, you're only a mop with a hairnet on, aren't you dear?'

Edith said, 'Oh!' put her hand over her mouth and giggled like a girl, then coughed all over again.

Lilly looked as if she might say something more, but then flopped back into her chair and fell silent. Like everyone else at *Newfoundland*, the jolly old giant usually sat round in a trance, deranged by tranquillisers, staring at day-time TV.

Still coughing away, Edith shook her head and happily went back to her work, which consisted largely in dishing out tranquillisers.

Like many of the residents at *Newfoundland* Edith

17

had lost her husband in the war and had never remarried. Now the old day-nurse looked on the residents of *Newfoundland* as her family.

She loved her work. 'I wouldn't give it up to save my life,' she used to say.

'We're not worried about saving your life! We're more worried about ourselves,' replied Mrs Crotchley one day, the sourest and most superior of the residents, her bitter-thin lips taut and serious. 'It really isn't good enough.'

There was a general murmur in Edith's defence among the residents.

'Leave her alone, you silly old bag,' Lilly said. 'She's only a mop with a hairnet on.'

There were one or two shaky nods.

Edith hadn't heard a thing but nodded with the majority and coughed until she had to steady herself on the back of Lilly's chair.

'Lord knows,' said Mrs Crotchley watching Edith splutter, 'There are no standards, anymore. Really, no standards at all. Are there, Tink?'

Tink, short for Tinkerbell, was Mrs Crotchley's tiny, evil-smelling Yorkshire Terrier, which at the slightest hint of attention from its austere owner, panted energetically, jumped friskily up, and sometimes emptied his bladder.

'Nobody's complaining. She does her best,' Lilly said, groping for Edith's arm, pulling her closer (a little too roughly for Edith's balance) and repeating into her hearing-aid, 'No one's complaining, dear.'

'We've all given up complaining,' said Mrs Crotchley, holding her frantic dog a safe distance from her lap, just in case.

This conversation, apart from being a ritual exchange, with Mrs Crotchley taking an unpopular position and the rest of the house disagreeing, was the longest conversation of the week.

The morning room soon returned to peace: Tinkerbell

relieved himself against the chair leg; the hypnotic weight of medication pressed down upon the assembly and the babble of daytime TV enveloped the scene, leaving Edith free to make a cup of tea.

The well-worn, well-meaning old day-nurse left a trail of cigarette ash wherever she went, including in the sterilisation unit, and she had an unfortunate habit that she'd picked up in her factory days, of spitting on the stone floor in the hall and scraping it with the sole of her shoe. But her simple Christianity, her kind smile and emerald eyes acted as a holy shield, protecting her from evil. She was well-loved by everyone.

Except Mrs Crotchley.

And anyone who was about to be given an injection by her.

The sight of Edith's trembling hand clutching a syringe, clumsily squirting fluid at the ceiling as she prepared to jab it in your arm (or elsewhere) was a sight as awe-inspiring as any of the devices invented by the English to defend the Empire. The way she smiled sweetly and said, 'Come along dear,' as she shuffled towards you brandishing the oversized instrument was as chilling as anything from Poe. (She was too shaky to use the standard size syringe which she described as 'fiddly'.)

On the whole Edith's duties were kept to a minimum and, if it were honestly told, the tranquillisers kept the workload manageable.

Charity – 'Mrs Green' – the manager at *Newfoundland* – suffered the most.

She was forced by her heart – or by her lack of having the heart to do anything about Edith – to bare the brunt of the ever increasing workload. She fell back on her own early experience of nursing and nursed her nurse along with the rest of them, while all the time falling behind on administration.

Things were a mess.

19

The whole place was falling apart. The cold wind of privatisation had blown much of the budget and most of the staff away as the centre was run down in readiness to be sold off as a profitable enterprise and, like everyone else in the service, Charity had become disheartened.

Small things kept her going.

That morning, Edith tottered into Charity's office on the ground floor of the historic building and teetered in front of the paper-strewn desk.

While the old woman composed herself it occurred to Charity with some relief that the old nurse might be about to hand in her notice.

'I just want you to know, dear,' Edith began at last, 'That your kindnesses have not gone unnoticed. You've been very good to me. I don't know what I'd do without it – without you, I mean, dear . . .'

For a moment Edith seemed to be about to add something to this homily, but then faltered, smiled once again and turned to leave with a deep queasy cough.

'Erm, Edith? . . .' Charity felt the need to say something.

Edith half turned. 'Yes, dear?'

'Thank you.'

'Oh! . . .' Edith raised her arm to fend off the compliment. 'Thank *you*, dear. Thank you for everything,' she said, shuffling away. Then she called back over her shoulder, 'I'm just going to give Mrs Crotchley her injection.'

'I'll do that . . .'

'No, dear. It's fine. I've "got the situation under control".'

Charity watched the old woman shamble across the ornate entrance hall giggling to herself, then spit on the stone floor and wipe it with her shoe.

*M*rs Crotchley passed out following her injection.

She was sitting down at the time, so Edith assumed she'd fallen asleep and left her there all morning.

There was some relief on the top table at lunch-time when Mrs Crotchley failed to appear and the smell of cabbage was for once unspoiled by the rich fragrance that Tinkerbell was only too pleased to waft about the place with his stumpy tail.

Edith reported that Mrs Crotchley was asleep.

'Let sleeping dogs lie,' said Rose, the busiest and most robust of the residents, and no one was sure whether Rose was referring to Mrs Crotchley or her dog. 'And I'll have the extra chop.'

'That bloody dog's gone senile,' said Lilly, towering head and shoulders above the rest and nudging her neighbour to emphasise her point, nearly knocking the poor woman off her seat.

Tinkerbell had only been allowed into *Newfoundland* in the first place on the understanding that he would die shortly of old age. Somehow he'd lingered on.

Five minutes later, Rose – her plate now piled high – happily cut a robust slice of lamb, dunked it in ketchup and was about to plonk it onto her tongue when her fork-hand was arrested a few inches short of her mouth by a terrible sight.

Mrs Crotchley was standing in the doorway, naked but for a pair of old-fashioned lace camiknickers. There was a great whoop all round before the poor afflicted woman demonstrated that she'd parted with more than respectability by vomiting over her beloved Yorkshire Terrier and stumbling dangerously back down the corridor shouting something about a plague of insects.

Tinkerbell seemed rather to enjoy his vile shower and proceeded to run about the dining room shaking himself energetically.

21

Rose sprang into action – or rather, bustled.

Rose and Mrs Crotchley were old enemies, both having been employed by the same family firm in the old days. In those days Mrs Crotchley had been a 'staff' employee and had looked down her nose from the dingy upstairs office on Rose, a 'works' employee and an active trade unionist considered to be a trouble causer.

But in the heat of emergency this ancient antagonism was forgotten as Rose roundly pursued Mrs Crotchley about the house, finally wrestling the poor raving woman into submission over one of the beds in the first-floor dormitory.

Rose was so shocked at the condition of her old adversary that she called her 'dear' several times and personally took charge of subduing Tinkerbell while the invalid was put to bed and the doctor was called.

There was a moment when Tinkerbell was cornered in the entrance hall when Rose considered letting the wretched thing out of the front door and onto the road to die his overdue death under the wheels of a merciful car, but as other residents arrived on the scene Rose recovered her humanity and gave him a vigorous bath instead.

Doctor Haggarty, whose rugged face was buried in a mound of folded wrinkles and who refused to believe that drugs could be improperly administered, even by Edith, prescribed rest.

'She probably suffered some kind of turn,' he said when Mrs Crotchley described what she'd felt.

'I assure you I've been poisoned,' Mrs Crotchley said groggily.

Edith, who was hovering by the door, was caught in the act of slinking off by the doctor's glance and stumbled guiltily, unsure whether or not to hobble for it.

But Mrs Crotchley's self-diagnosis was wasted on the doctor who generally expected old people to suffer turns and behave like vegetables. Or just die.

'Keep an eye on her. If she shows further signs of

delirium or complains of chest pains let me know. Otherwise,' he instructed the poisoner, who was doing her best to look like a professional again, 'keep her in bed.'

Edith and Doctor Haggarty were natural allies. They both, though for different reasons, felt it necessary to administer large quantities of trance-inducing drugs: Edith to save labour; the doctor because it is a central tenet of modern medical philosophy that the prescription of quantities of mind and mood altering chemicals tends to increase the flow of crates of fine whisky between pharmaceutical companies and the doctor's surgery at Christmas, and can even lead to a build-up of invites to medical seminars in far-off exotic locations.

'It was quite deliberate,' croaked Mrs Crotchley looking as fiercely as she could at the terrified Edith.

The doctor was just crumpling up the furrows of his enormous brow, which generally gave him inspiration if words failed him, when in marched Rose (having locked Tinkerbell in the cleaning closet upstairs).

'Now then, what appears to be the trouble?' she asked.

The doctor began to pack his bag ready to make a swift exit.

In her experience as a trade unionist Rose had developed a keen and dependable distrust of all the professions. Since her retirement she had come to despise especially the medical profession, viewing all doctors as kin to Josef Mengele.

'Please *do* give us the benefit of your vast experience and expertise,' she said.

'Humm.' Something inside the great man resounded.

The truth was that, even though he would never have admitted it, the doctor was scared of Rose. She was a potential trouble causer, always critical, always spouting nonsense.

A further problem was that Rose's condescending manner brought out the worst in the medic. He couldn't help it. When she was around he became rude and

23

surly where normally he was mild-mannered and polite.

After a pause in which both Mrs Crotchley and Edith expected the doctor to implode, and during which the man's brow almost folded in on itself and disappeared altogether, Rose said simply, 'Well, doctor?'

'She appears to have had some kind of turn,' he declared and realised, under the stark light of public inquiry, that the diagnosis wasn't the most sophisticated he'd ever formulated.

'Funny how many of us have our little turns, isn't it doctor?' Rose replied.

'Hum. Yes,' he mumbled doubtfully. 'I suggest you confine her to her bed and . . .' The doctor stopped himself and winced, realising his mistake.

Rose drew herself to her full height which was not very great, being more a question of width really. 'We most certainly *won't* confine her to her bed. Confine her to her bed, indeed! Hurrumph' She turned to Mrs Crotchley, who seemed to shrink into the pillows. 'Don't worry dear, we'll leave you there until your *legs* seize up and when you get *depressed* we'll give you a *stronger* sedative and when you wet the bed we'll diagnose *senility* . . .'

By this time the doctor's ancient leather bag was packed, or at least he'd managed to stuff everything in it, so he made good his escape with Edith following as best she could in his wake.

'Oh, well, have it your own way. But don't come crying to me if she pops it,' he threw over his shoulder as he tramped down the stone stairs, careless of whether or not offence was taken.

'I'm quite convinced I've been poisoned,' repeated Mrs Crotchley when she and Rose were alone.

'I think we've heard quite enough from you for one day, thank-you-very-much,' said Rose sternly tucking in her brittle old enemy.

'I ought to be making some kind of report about this,'

warned the doctor, back in Charity's office on the ground floor.

Edith, slumped in the wicker bath chair in the corner, normally so hard of hearing, let out a kind of muffled yelp at this.

'If it *was* a negligent administration of drugs, that is?'

Charity took the hint. 'Actually, no. We . . . checked the supply and . . . everything appears to be in order, after all. Didn't we Edith?'

Luckily for Edith the doctor didn't look at her. She was a simple, honest Christian and even though she managed to stop the denial coming out of her mouth, God seemed to be shaking her head.

'Humm. As I thought. Some kind of turn.' Doctor Haggarty hated paperwork. Reports infuriated him. He could go home now and drink fine Highland whisky instead. 'Keep up the good work,' he resounded as he disappeared through the ornate, tiled hall. 'Keep it up.'

'You should have told him the truth, dear,' said Edith, when he was gone, the emerald in her eyes shining. 'One little lie leads to another.'

It was a terrible thing for Rose to find herself in agreement with Mrs Crotchley for once.

Rose blamed excessive administration of tranquillisers for the state of apathy that existed in the house and tended to see the medication as a conspiracy against residents by management, if not a conspiracy by the government itself.

'There are far too many conspiracy theorists about,' was Mrs Crotchley's usual rejoinder whenever Rose spoke her mind on the subject.

But Lilly's was the general view: 'Edith knows what she's doing, don't you dear? Even though she *is* only a mop with a hairnet on.'

The truth be known, Rose had always been too fond of Edith herself to press the matter. But things had changed.

It was obvious that Edith could no longer do her job properly.

So while Mrs Crotchley was still laid up, Rose called an emergency meeting of residents with a plan in mind.

Immediately afterwards she led a small group of dazed residents, on whose behalf she presumed to speak, into Charity's office.

'We've come directly from an emergency meeting which was convened on the grounds of health and safety,' announced Rose, 'to which Edith wasn't invited to attend . . .'

Planting her feet firmly apart, Rose folded her arms under her huge bosom causing Charity to realise the gravity of the situation.

'It was unanimously agreed that it's about time Edith took a rest.'

Charity sighed and looked at the small group with regret. 'It probably would be sensible. Someone might have been hurt.'

'Somebody *was* hurt, dear!'

Charity was wringing her hands. 'I'll speak to Edith. See what she says.'

Rose seemed to inflate slightly, 'No, dear. The feeling of the meeting was clear. Edith must go.'

Charity looked to see if the rest of the group were in agreement but found their expressions impossible to read.

'But . . . what will she do? Where . . .'

'The meeting was quite clear on that point, too,' said Rose.

'Oh?' said Charity. She might have known.

Rose was beaming suddenly. 'It was agreed that Edith should retire and take up immediate residence with us here at *Newfoundland*, where she belongs.'

Some time and not a little bureaucracy later, a new nurse arrived at *Newfoundland*.

She had a great unruly mop of black hair and something

of a twinkle in her eye which Rose instantly took to.

Rose was alone in the office, shifting through some papers when the new arrival knocked timidly on the door.

'Come in,' sang Rose.

'Hello. Er. . . are you. . . in charge?' the young woman asked, a little surprised.

'Not officially, dear,' replied the old trade unionist with a friendly smile.

'I'm the new nurse. I'm new to the area.'

Rose could tell from the strong Manchester accent.

'Ah yes. Nurse Jones, isn't it?'

Charity didn't like his old friends, so Jed went to the wedding alone.

He was glad to get away. He would stay the night in Manchester on his own.

It turned out to be a drag.

So he drank too much and danced – or tried to avoid dancing – and smiled at jokes he didn't find amusing until his face ached.

It occurred to him how he'd changed.

Even *he* didn't like his old friends anymore.

Eventually, he got talking to a friend of the bride called Virginia, who was big, bold and drunken. Or rather she got talking to him. She was some kind of journalist with a local paper.

In his light-headed condition Jed had to admit that there was something attractive about her – her flashing eyes and her protuberant blouse, probably. She had red bobbed hair and a very wicked wit.

She entertained and flattered him.

A fatal combination.

'You'll have to excuse me,' she said, after making some crude remark, pressing his arm and leaving her hand there a little too long, 'I was educated in a convent.'

She had that kind of dirty laugh that lets everyone within a radius of a hundred yards know that she's talking dirty, and sparkling, biting teeth. She kept leaning over him as she spoke, far too close for social comfort and laughing that laugh. (A her her her huurr!)

Next they were dancing, Jed looking like he urgently needed the toilet.

Then, to the delight of the elderly revellers, the DJ played *The Birdy Song* and Virginia laughing ran off the dance floor to the back of the hall.

Jed followed.

Then it started. She said: 'You and I could get married.'

Jed wasn't sure what to say, or even if he'd heard correctly. '. . . Um.'

'We could get married, have a quick honeymoon and then get divorced.' A her her her.

She gave him a certain look, which, unwisely and against his principles, he returned. He felt a twitching, too, which caused him to accidentally say, 'Do you want another drink?'

She looked a little puzzled. So did he. He wasn't sure why he'd said it.

Jed had to stoop slightly as he stood up. What was he doing? He was drunk. But he wasn't that drunk he didn't know what he was doing!

Their conversation went off for a while when he returned from the bar. Jed had sobered up a little. He found he was making all the conversation. Virginia was sitting there just looking at him and he gained the distinct impression that she wasn't listening to a word he was saying. She just fixed him with her eyes. That gaze. Those teeth. Eventually he dried up and an awkward silence fell. (Actually it was *Tie a Yellow Ribbon Round the Old Oak Tree* playing at about thirty decibels.)

28

Still there was that look. Which bored into him.

The next thing, she nodded her head at the door to the entrance hall and stood up.

'Follow me,' he thought he heard her say.

After a pause, during which time he felt he was turning to stone, he followed. He didn't even want to. Not morally anyhow.

He was getting out of his depth.

When he arrived in the entrance hall Virginia was at the foot of some stairs leading up to the balcony of the old church hall. With a flourish she turned round and walked up.

Again he followed.

At the top she was leaning against a wall, out of sight of the revellers. He swam over and instead of kissing her, as he was probably supposed to do, he stood next to her against the wall.

He felt torn in half.

'You're an obstinate one, aren't you?' she said as she crushed him against the wall.

She swallowed the words 'I'm married' as they came out of his mouth.

She ground herself against him in an unholy fit of lust and presented her breasts to him vehemently. With a feeling of fear, and at least in part to push her back a little, Jed slowly reached down and put his hand first on her thigh and then up her skirt, to her crotch – albeit, as he said to himself later, touching her through both her tights and, presumably, her pants too. She ground him some more. Into the wall. And (through his clothes) squeezed him so hard he almost yelped. When he withdrew his hand – he needed it to protect himself in the Home Counties – she rammed him and banged him with her hips so hard he thought he would bruise his spine on the ornamental woodwork. When he pushed her gently away – or at least when she realised he was trying to do so – she stepped back, gave him a sultry look

29

and lay back in her finery on the dusty wooden floor, signalling for him to join her.

Just before he took the plunge he glanced over the balcony. Down there pious worshippers of a different age had knelt and now joyful revellers revelled. He felt a stab of remorse. He was losing his unblemished record of fidelity. The ferocity of the grappling had been utterly at odds with his desire which had been little more than curiosity really.

As he lay on top of her, feeling hot and faintly nauseous, the last traces of lust drained away.

He rocked and wobbled away for a few moments and then found the courage to say: 'You're going to ruin those clothes.'

'Who *cares*!' A her her her.

He was marooned for a while longer.

'There are better places to do this sort of thing,' he tried after a suitable pause (and some lip-crushing kisses.)

She stopped and looked at him. 'You're right. We'll go to one of them. Tonight.'

'Um.'

Then they were dusting each other down and straightening their clothes ready to re-enter the old world of the party.

Over the course of the next hour or so Jed managed to persuade Virginia that he had to return to his wife that night but that he would 'contact her and arrange something'.

It was a messy business because he had intended to stay the night with some old friends but he was worried now in case she followed him there.

'Oh, I know, don't ring me I'll ring you?' Virginia said.

'We'll meet again, don't you worry,' he insisted.

Then something in him decided to give her Eddie's address, to make her feel better.

If she wanted to write she could write 'care of' at

Eddie's office. He didn't want her to have his address, not even his address at work. She might turn up. In his madness he changed his name slightly too, to Green*house*. Eddie would understand (only too well). He told himself that she wouldn't even remember him in the morning, let alone write.

It worked anyhow. She believed him. He could tell because she gave him that look and when she smiled one of her teeth winked at him.

'We'll have a *rendezvous*,' she said. 'We can *conspire*.' A her her her hurr.

He drove home drunk. Which was stupid. On the way he stopped the car to relieve himself onto his chamois leather.

*I*t was agreed that while Jed was at his wedding, Charity and Eddie would have a night out on the town.

Jed was all for it.

Eddie and Charity were good mates, albeit second-hand, and had established a risqué banter that was easy and entirely without invitation – at least as far as Charity was concerned. Eddie, like most men, was incapable of preventing at least part of this innuendo lodging in his heart and germinating, no matter how obvious it was that they were strictly at play.

They decided to eat in and go out later to a club Eddie knew.

After they'd eaten, Eddie produced his little metal box.

'I don't normally bother,' he said, 'but a doctor friend of mine gave me some for my birthday. It's "finest pharmaceutical" – very pure – quite safe in small doses.'

'Cocaine?' said Charity with a mixture of fear and curiosity. 'Isn't it supposed to be addictive?'

'Very,' replied Eddie. 'Like alcohol. Perhaps a bit worse. So if you take a lot of the stuff every day you're going be in trouble.

'Humm.' She looked doubtful. 'Has Jed tried it?'

He gave her that grin of his. 'What, the king of the swingers? He took me to an orgy afterwards. I couldn't stop him. He was wild.'

She smiled.

'But you're more sensible than him, aren't you?'

She was definitely tempted. 'How much are you supposed to take?'

'Just a bit. You sniff it. If you feel OK take a bit more.'

'Doesn't it hurt your nose?'

'Your nose goes numb.'

A few minutes later they took a bit and then a bit more. Charity liked it. You could taste it dripping down your throat at the back. It wasn't anything like as overwhelming as she'd thought. In the end they took quite a lot, went out to the club and danced like crazy.

Between times, in a corner of the club at a dark table, they sniffed conspiratorially and continually, the mounting effects disguised by the noise and the heat.

By now Charity was feeling very good indeed and Eddie was feeling horny. The drug made Charity want to hug Eddie – she did so several times. It was all perfectly natural, under the influence.

It was when they got outside and sat in Eddie's car that the cumulative effect really hit them. Eddie produced his little box but Charity refused this time.

She blew through her lips and took a deep breath. 'Phew . . . I've had enough. I'm really going now.'

'Just sit back and enjoy it,' said Eddie helping himself.

'I am,' breathed Charity.

Eddie put some of Chopin's soft piano pieces on his turbo-charged car stereo and Charity began to moan aloud. She felt like her body was the piano.

'I could get to like this,' she muttered in between moans.

Eddie felt good too. Very good indeed, and for him the feeling was indistinguishable from randiness. He assumed it was the same for Charity. Certainly sounded like it was.

He wanted to make love to her all night long. He was sure she felt the same. He could feel it rising up in them both as they sat there writhing with pleasure. He looked over at her, she had her eyes closed and was letting out those damn sexy little moans.

'What shall we do now?' he said, hardly able to contain himself.

'I don't know. Anything.'

He sat there with bated breath. He had to say something.

'I suppose . . .' he breathed (nervously for him), 'I suppose it's impossible for us to make love?'

Charity looked at him. Her expression changed. Her response was instant and her voice deadly serious. 'Yes. It's absolutely impossible.'

Eddie realised his blunder. He was thunderstruck. Reality swept over him again.

'Oh my God, I'm sorry.'

She was silent.

He felt horribly exposed. He didn't know what to say. 'Jesus, you're my best friend's wife! I'm sorry. It's the effects.'

'It's no big deal, Eddie. Forget it.'

But Eddie couldn't let the matter drop. He kept going on about it all the way home – about how he loved Jed and respected Charity – how she was very beautiful and he was carried away by the drug, going over it again and again, saying that he'd confess his indiscretion to Jed in the week.

When they got back to the house for coffee it was the same all over again: Charity saying it didn't matter. In the end she pretended to be tired and Eddie went to go, still apologising.

When he got to the door he stopped and his tone became more serious.

'It doesn't change anything, does it? About "Gibraltar", our little "arrangement".'

Charity shook her head and smiled. 'Of course not.'

'Have you said anything to Jed, yet?'

She grinned. 'We have an open, honest relationship – so I haven't said a word.'

'You should talk to him soon.'

'I refuse to start talking about business at three o'clock in the morning! Especially when I've had cocaine.'

Eddie grinned. 'It's supposed to be the businessman's drug.'

'I'm not a businessman.'

'You soon will be. Businesswoman.'

'Not necessarily. Jed might not go for it.'

'Huh. We'll just have to rub him up the right way, won't we?'

She laughed. 'Go on. Go away.'

He grinned. 'Would you like one last sniff?'

'Get out, you bad man!'

Charity found now she was alone the effects of the drug were still quite strong. She slipped into the bath and began to masturbate.

She found herself fantasising about Eddie.

But before she had time to finish off she heard the front door open and close.

A few moments later in walked Jed.

'I thought you were staying in Manchester!'

'Na. There wasn't really room. It was only a small house. I didn't fancy sleeping on the floor. Having people puke on me all night. How was it with Eddie?'

'Fine.'

34

He stood there awkwardly, waiting for her to quiz him on the details of the night, preparing to slither around the subject.

Instead she said, 'Jed. I'm horny as hell.'

Jed thought of his chamois leather and wondered how to reply.

 *J*ed was sitting in his dusty unit with a job lot of dickheads and obsolete fax machines, contemplating financial ruin.

The phone rang.

He wondered whether or not to answer.

The dilemma was that it might be an order, although you wouldn't put your shirt on it. It was more likely to be one of his creditors or, worse, the bank.

If he could just survive for a few more months, things might pick up.

The phone rang itself out.

He pulled open a drawer in his desk, took out a bottle of whisky and stared at it.

The phone rang again.

'Bastard!' Jed swept the phone off the desk. 'Fucking bastard!' he shouted and stood scowling at it.

Then he heard a faint 'Hello?'

Shit. The receiver was off and someone had got through.

In confusion he picked it up. 'Hello? Sorry, I . . . the phone fell off the desk.'

'Mr Green?'

'Uh . . . Who's calling?'

'It's Mr Verity of the Nat West.'

Fuck. 'I'm afraid Mr Green isn't here right now, can I take a message?'

'Oh. Who am I talking to, please?'

35

'Oh . . . I'm just a friend . . . an employee.'

'I wasn't aware there *were* any employees.'

'Shall I get him to phone you, when he gets back?'

'Where's he gone?'

Jed was getting cross. 'He's out on business.'

'Oh, well that'll make a change.'

'. . .!'

'It's Mr Green speaking, isn't it,' said Mr Verity. It wasn't a question.

'. . . I think the best thing is if I get Mr Green to phone you as soon as he gets back.'

'You're a lying little toady, Mr Green.'

'Sorry?'

'I said, you're a lying little toady.'

Jed suddenly recognised Eddie's voice, which he'd stopped disguising. 'You fucking dickhead!' There was a loud laugh on the other end. 'I've got enough stress to deal with!'

When Eddie got his breath back he said, 'You know I'm sure you're losing your sense of humour.'

In despair Jed resorted to breathing heavily through his nostrils.

'How long are you going to keep up this charade?' Eddie said.

'As long as it takes.'

'Oh, not long then.'

'Eddie, *please*!'

'You can't keep running away forever, your sins will eventually catch up with you.'

'I haven't committed any sins.'

'Really?' There was a pause. 'There's a letter addressed to you here – at least I think it's you – "Jed Greenhouse". Shall I open it?'

'. . . No!' More casual, 'No – no leave it. I'll . . . come over and get it. I was just coming over anyway.'

Before Jed left, he put the bottle back in the drawer. He was feeling a bit drunk now anyway.

*   *   *

'That was quick.'

Jed was at Eddie's office now.

'I don't hang about.'

Eddie sat there looking smugly at him. Jed was trying not to blush.

'Well?'

Jed looked puzzled.

'What did you want to see me about? You said you were just coming over.'

'Oh – yes.' Jed reached for his briefcase with a flourish. When he'd fumbled it open he said, 'Shit, I've left it at back at the unit – tut – sorry.'

When he looked up Eddie was brandishing the letter.

The envelope was bright pink.

'Oh, is that that letter?'

'Yes. That's that letter.' The debauched accountant didn't move.

'Oh cheers.' Nonchalant.

Eddie could hardly contain himself. He made Jed lean right over the desk to take it off him.

'Thanks,' Jed said as casually as possible slipping it into his briefcase.

'Oh, aren't you going to open it?'

'Nah . . . I'll look at it later.'

'It might be something from the tax office. They do use pseudonyms and pink envelopes sometimes . . .' It was the best fun Eddie had had for ages.

Jed had to say: 'It's not what you think.'

All Eddie did was make that certain face of his. He *knew*. He was flattered that his friend had trusted him enough to include him in his debauched adulterous plans – for that was certainly what they were.

And at last. No one could be faithful forever, however good-looking their wife.

Eddie was a Cheshire cat. 'I'm glad to be of service,' he mewed.

'It's not what you think,' Jed tried again.

'Oh, I don't think anything. I'm your accountant.'

Jed scuttled out as soon as he could.

When he had driven a short way up the road he parked up and opened the letter, feeling, despite himself, a twinge of sexual excitement.

This was the letter:

Telephone number . . .

Dear Jed,

                                    Act.

                                          Virginia.

When Jed had adjusted his trousers, gone through a few possible scenarios in his head, rejected them all as impossible and decided that at least he could have a few lively fantasies, he thought: 'Jesus, thank God I didn't give her my number!'

He destroyed the note, tearing it into tiny pieces, getting out of the car specially to put it in a litter bin.

'"Act" – what the hell else do I ever do?'

Saturday night, when Jed and Charity were reading in bed, she said:

'Have you seen Eddie lately?'

'Eddie? . . . Yeah.'

'Did he say anything to you – about when you went to the wedding?'

There was something about the way she said it that put Jed on his guard.

'Why? Have you got something to hide?'

'He said he'd tell you.'

'. . . He did mention something,' Jed lied.

He was embarrassed – she knew something he didn't.

He hated that. His guilty conscience throbbed. Surely Eddie wouldn't have mentioned the letter! . . . It was impossible . . .

'Did he tell you he tried it on with me?'

Jed was relieved and at the same time shocked. And jealous. Shit, he was jealous!

'. . . He mentioned *something* about it, yeah.'

'Well, either he did, or he didn't. What did he tell you?'

Jed tried not to splutter. 'That he'd tried it on with you.'

'Anything else?'

'Er . . .' He tried not to make it sound like he was guessing. 'That you turned him down(?)'

'Anything else?'

'No, not really.'

'Not really?'

'No – nothing.'

After an embarrassed and fairly tense silence, Jed asked in a slightly wobbly voice: 'You didn't want to . . . with him then?'

Charity pulled a face. 'No I did not!'

Jed's jealousy was relieved. (Mostly.)

She turned off the light.

'What the hell do men ever talk about?' she said.

Jed found himself suffering from an aching erection. The jealous kind.

He lay there for five minutes. It had been so long since he'd started anything.

In the end he had to. The face-cloth wouldn't do.

It was the best sex they'd had in a year.

Afterwards Charity said: 'I'm going to ask Eddie to make a move on me again.'

*N*urse Jones was a fraud, but to keep up appearances she had learned the rules and regulations more thoroughly than most legitimate nurses.

She saw straight away that procedures at *Newfoundland* were lax and that the law was being broken in numerous small but significant ways and that resident care was not all it should have been.

As soon as she saw it she knew the dressing on Mrs M's foot was dodgy. She removed the dressing and found that the poor old woman's foot was full of maggots.

Obviously the dressing had been neglected in the preceding chaos. Mrs M was one of the 'less troublesome' residents – suffering only rare outbreaks of lucidity before relapsing into long periods of mute oblivion. She was supposed to have been removed to a specialist geriatric centre some time ago, but the geriatric service was in a state of chaos too.

There weren't the facilities here, there weren't the facilities there, so here was Mrs M and there was her foot.

When she had finished retching, Nurse Jones realised the danger: it was obvious that the doctor would have to be called and that he in turn would feel compelled to report the neglect to the appropriate authority.

There would be an inspection of the premises.

The maggots were inside the foot itself, under the skin, so before phoning for the doctor, she fought her nausea and, with a pair of tweezers and a bowl of hot water, picked the larvae from the sore, one by wriggling one. She did well – she was only sick twice.

There was nearly a stir in the morning room when the news leaked out.

'It's a bloody good job she's a cabbage,' said Lilly. The jolly giant was trying to raise morale.

The other residents couldn't help but smile – except

for Mrs Crotchley, who after her poisoning had become all the more outspoken. 'Well if you ask me there's no great surprise in it,' she remarked. 'Personally I wouldn't be surprised it we were *all* full of maggots. The standard of care really is appalling.'

'Yeah, well standards of *dress* aren't what they used to be either – people keep stripping off and flaunting themselves!' Lilly taunted.

Whereupon Mrs Crotchley patted Tinkerbell fussily and with taut lips kept her peace.

Edith, now retired and ensconced at *Newfoundland*, missed this exchange. She was watching the maggot plucking.

'You don't have to watch you know,' said the young nurse when she saw that Edith was upset.

'I beg your pardon?'

'It's not a pretty sight. You don't have to watch.' Louder.

'I'm afraid it's all my fault, dear.'

Poor Edith's eyes were wet and she seemed all the more shaky suddenly, so that even without coughing she was forced to steady herself against a chair.

'It's not your fault. The whole bloody service is in chaos, things like this happen all the time.'

It wasn't clear whether Edith had heard.

'I'm afraid I've been very selfish, dear,' she said sadly.

When Doctor Haggarty arrived and saw Mrs M's foot, his eyebrows hovered dangerously above the ploughed field of his forehead.

His head swivelled towards Nurse Jones, but thankfully as he looked at her his anger was distracted by the soft freckles on her nose and the calculated twinkle in her eye.

'Humm,' he resounded. 'Humm.'

He rummaged in his prehistoric leather bag.

Then with another threatening look at Nurse Jones

41

(this one successful), he produced a pair of tweezers.

Then he rummaged in Mrs M's foot.

'It's just as well the old maid's insensible,' he rumbled as he ferreted about in the gore.

Nurse Jones exchanged a glance with Edith who was hovering by the door.

After a few tense moments the doctor seemed to find what he was looking for. The 'Humm' came from deep within his furrowed being as he held up to the light a tiny speck of something that Nurse Jones had obviously missed. He folded his face into a squint.

There was a long, professionally leaden pause.

'Enjoyed fishing did she?'

'. . . Sorry?'

The enormous tweed-covered man peered over his glasses at Nurse Jones.

She did her best not to look like an impostor and twinkled for dear life.

'You cleaned up this wound did you?'

'Yes.' Gulp.

'Where did you train, Nurse?'

'. . . Manchester.'

'Um-hum.'

She waited.

'Humm.' He was turning the tweezers from side to side as he spoke, giving her an occasional sideways glance. 'Bit quiet for you in these parts, isn't it?'

'I've retired,' she quipped.

'You're not running away from anything?'

'Only a sordid past.'

The great man smiled.

'I like the fresh air,' she added.

'Humm. You'll need a good dose of smog after a fortnight in this God-forsaken town.'

The young nurse laughed. (Charmingly.)

'I need some peace and quiet,' she said.

The doctor chortled and glanced at Edith who smiled vaguely. 'That's the last thing you'll get here.'

Nurse Jones began to relax.

The doctor looked at her again. Especially the freckles on her nose. He eyed his find once more. It was only small. 'Well, you did a very good job of cleaning it up.' He threw the speck onto the floor. 'She'll have to go to hospital, of course.'

'Yes.'

'And I'll have to – report the matter.'

'Yes.' Twinkle, twinkle.

He was packing away. 'I'll do it first thing tomorrow. Should give you time to get things ready. You're new aren't you? It wasn't your fault. I'll mention that.'

'Yes. Thank you.'

'Well, good day,' he boomed and made off with the bag that did for black leather what his face did for skin.

With the doctor departed, Nurse Jones, Charity and Rose – hindered by a small but well-meaning posse of the more able-bodied residents – tackled the worst of the shambles.

The young nurse directed the operation: beds were shifted; the medical room was rearranged; the kitchen was cleaned; and miraculously they managed to get the lift working.

Next day the inspection passed off without a hitch.

When the Inspector had gone, Rose came up to the new young nurse – now known to all as Miranda – with a look of pure admiration. Her bosom proud, she beamed as she spoke. 'Welcome to the family, Miranda.'

The young impostor's eyes shone.

 At first Charity hadn't known what to make of Miranda with her foul mouth and her great unruly mop of black hair, but after the incident with Mrs M's foot they became firm friends.

Charity had never met anyone like her before.

For one thing she used foul language as if she were a man and for another she treated having sex like eating pizza.

Super Supreme with Spicy Sausage.

Not that Charity was a prude, she used to be a nurse herself, but there was something new to her in Miranda's attitude.

They were soon giggling away together, talking about men and sex and . . . almost anything really.

'If you don't mind me asking,' said Charity the evening after the Inspector called, 'Do you sleep with all the men you go out with?'

'So long as they're fit,' Miranda grinned.

Charity was fascinated by her.

'It's usually pretty shit though if I'm honest. I haven't had a decent shag in ages.'

'I know what you mean,' sighed Charity.

'You're married aren't you?'

Charity nodded. 'The sex goes off after a while.'

'Yeah – two weeks.'

They both laughed.

Miranda said: 'I usually get obsessed with a guy for a while – I mean totally obsessed. I'd do anything. Then I start hating them – start slagging them off in public – being really horrible to them . . .'

Charity admired Miranda's honesty. She wondered if she could ever hate Jed.

'It was very intense between me and Jed at first.'

'How long you been married?'

'Nearly seven years.'

'Shit, no wonder you're bored.'

44

Charity was a bit hurt by this. 'I'm not *bored*. Just . . .
I don't know . . .'

'Some of the excitement's gone?'

'Um.'

'That's bored.'

Charity had to admit it was true. 'I would like to try
something a bit different.'

'Some*one* a bit different you mean.'

'No, no not really. Just something . . .' Charity shrugged,
she genuinely didn't know, 'a bit different.'

Within a very short time Charity began talking
with real openness. It felt as if her other women
friends had been conspiring in some way to keep
her from looking at what was really happening in
her life. She hadn't bothered with her friends lately
anyhow. She'd been too busy; it had hardly seemed
worth the effort.

Miranda was a refreshing breath of foul air.

The next night Charity and Miranda decided to go for
a 'girls night out on the town' and strode down the prom
arm in arm. The light from the illuminations mirrored
the lager-induced glow inside them both.

Charity felt like she was back in her early nursing
days. In those days she drank with the best of them
and slept with a few men, but found the experience
largely uninspiring. Even though the men (all three of
them) had complimented her on her skill at performing
fellatio.

They were sitting in a hotel bar near the pier when
Charity recounted this.

Miranda said: 'Urh. I don't blow *no*body's horn, me.
Fuck that!'

Charity, who was knocking back her third bottle of
Pils at the time felt that she had gained some sort of
credibility. Here was something with which she could
actually shock Miranda.

Miranda asked: 'Do you like it? Honestly?'

Charity stared straight ahead for a second. Then she

had to tell the truth. 'No. No, I can't stand it – but I'm told I'm very good . . .'

They both guffawed, Miranda blowing a raspberry in the process.

They were getting one or two looks from other people in the bar by now.

'Actually I don't mind doing it to Jed.'

'I bet he doesn't mind either.'

'Oh he loves it,' Charity grinned. Then she became morose. 'I don't know what's wrong with him lately. He never starts anything. Might be stress or something. But . . . the funny thing is he . . . you know . . .' she made a shy little gesture with her right hand and nodded her head instead of finishing the sentence.

'What, he likes having a good old wank?'

Charity blushed, looked over at the bar to see if anyone had heard and nodded. She lowered her voice. 'I mean, it's nearly every night!'

'What, you mean he's lying there like that while you're being jigged up and down, pretending not to notice?'

They laughed at Miranda's mime.

'No – he goes off into the bathroom when he thinks I'm asleep. I wondered what was going on at first. Then I looked through the keyhole one night and there he was.'

'What like that?' Again the comic mime.

'Onto the face-cloth!'

'Urrh! . . .' Over the laughter Miranda managed to say, 'Remind me never to wash my face at your house!'

And so it went on.

After her fourth bottle of Pils Charity declined another.

'We haven't even started!' Miranda moaned.

'I'm finished,' insisted Charity.

Miranda had another four bottles and seemed hardly to bat an eyelid.

Eventually they rolled home.

46

When Charity got in, Jed was reading. He was still struggling through *Steppenwolf* and was sepulchral on the bed.

That night it was Charity who went to the bathroom at midnight.

Next morning Jed was woken by a recorded delivery letter slapping the side of his face.

'I think it's from the bank,' Charity said. 'A policeman delivered it.'

'What!' Jed was too groggy to appreciate humour at that hour.

Then, with a 'lazy bones!' Charity was gone.

Jed decided to eat breakfast before ruining his digestion for the day by reading the letter from the bank.

After breakfast he ruined his digestion for the day by reading the letter from the bank.

Basically it said: 'You'd better phone us you bastard, we know you're avoiding us.'

Jed paced around the house for half an hour, cursing the lampshades and the borders, thinking about his £20,000, or £40,000 as it now was.

Until palpitations caused him to act.

Muttering away he phoned Eddie at work.

He wanted his money.

When he got through, Eddie's secretary sounded distinctly odd.

'Who's calling?' she said. Normally she recognised him straight off.

'It's the Sultan of Oman.'

'Is that you, Jed?'

'Yeah. Is the Great Gatsby there?'

'Jed, Eddie's been arrested.'

If he'd have been a character in a cartoon, he would have broken out in cracks and collapsed into a dusty pile on the carpet.

Instead he said, 'Oh fuck.'

*E*veryone outside her immediate circle considered her vile.

Everyone else – including her political party, the ladies from the charities she patronised and business associates of her husbands – thought her a thoroughly worthy woman.

To the one camp Mrs Prior-Pointment appeared pert, chilly, unbending, austere, mannered, prim, formal, priggish – and these are the respectable epithets. To the other she was steadfast, resolute, dependable, loyal, firm, balanced, dedicated and, above all, staunch.

The fact that there were so many warring opinions about the woman in the first place was testament to the fact that there was nothing neutral about her. She was a public woman of the highest order.

Slim (bony), fine-featured (gaunt) outspoken (vicious) and elegant (rich), she was the unofficial leader of the local constituency party. She held no official post, but if local papers wanted a comment on some issue and the MP was out of town it was to Sylvia Prior-Pointment that they naturally turned. She was considered the embodiment of the party's principles in the local area.

And so she was.

The Prior-Pointment household, like the woman who ran it, was orderly.

The house itself was tall, impressive, Victorian and red-brick. The windows were dark, imposing and far too grand for net curtains. The rooms were dark, imposing and far too gloomy for living in.

Any children unfortunate enough to visit the house suddenly found a strong, unexpected desire to behave themselves and talked in hushed tones, preferring to stay close to the adults.

In the vast and ancient garden, to where children were usually shooed, the poor things found themselves stifled by the canopy of the dark, imposing trees through which no ray of light penetrated. They

48

would slink cautiously about among the rhododendrons, aware of strange smells, or crouch, gazing in awe at the hideous shapes suspended in the black water of the stagnant pond – surely not fish.

And they never played in the imitation rococo summerhouse, suspecting it to be haunted.

There were three residents in the house.

One of them seemed permanently to live, or rather linger on, in the semi-darkness of the musty old drawing room, wrapped in a bale of tartan blankets, her thin, lumpy, nylon-coated legs forever propped on an ancient leather pouffe. She was a decrepit old woman who sat munching her jaw at nothing, never spoke and was rarely spoken to.

This poor lump of tartan and bones was Mrs Prior-Pointment's mother-in-law, whose presence in the fusty room was taken (and given) as living proof of the daughter-in-law's compassion, commitment and loyalty to the eternal ideals of The Family.

A burden bravely borne.

The man of the house, Mr Arthur Prior-Pointment – often not *in* the house but tending to be in Gibraltar on business, or on the golf course doing business, or simply on the golf course, or in the golf club-house, or in the public house – was also a well-known local worthy.

He was a well-groomed, shiny-headed, good-humoured, whisky-drinking businessman, the complete opposite of his wife. He was warm – she was cold; he was extravagant – she was thrifty; he laughed aloud – she smiled thinly; and he got pissed while she held coffee mornings, though not *at* the coffee mornings.

If you met them separately – Arthur in the lounge bar of the Royal, Sylvia at one of her charity functions – and later learned the two were wed, you would, depending on which camp you belonged to, either marvel at the mystery of the ancient rite of matrimony, its heavenly powers, its magical harmonising properties, the sheer potency of the institution – or you'd smell a rat.

'Sylvia? It's John. John Stingham.'

Mrs Prior-Pointment was rather taken aback.

'John, hello.' She tried not to sound disappointed.

'Sorry to phone so late.'

The good woman was expecting a call from her husband who was in Gibraltar. The phone hadn't stopped all night but still no offshore call from Arthur.

Even though it was an honour to be called by the Minister of the Environment personally, she still felt dismayed.

But it didn't show in her voice.

'We're always open for business here, John, you know that.'

Her disappointment showed in her almost-Roman nose, the thin end of which twitched slightly, but there was no one there to see that. Only her mother-in-law. Who just sat there. As always. Munch munch.

It was definitely a pleasure to be on first name terms with the Minister though. Very nearly enough to cheer one up. 'It's about the press conference, isn't it, John?'

'I presume you have everything under control.'

'It's good of you to take a personal interest, John.'

'It *is* rather a crisis.'

'Nothing, John, that a little common sense won't repair.'

'I think it may take rather a little more than that I'm afraid.'

'Nonsense, John. The Party will survive.'

'Yes yes. The Party will survive. Of course. We're rather worried, however, about . . . the particular Minister.'

'Ah. The particular Minister.'

'Quite.'

It was a crisis for the party. The government of the day was conducting a campaign against working-class women bringing up children alone and claiming state support. In order to do so it was necessary at the same time to call for a return to 'traditional family values'. Given that the 'traditional family' no longer exists, it was a ploy necessarily fraught with difficulty.

The party to which Mrs Prior-Pointment belonged was the party of government and the Member for her area had been caught with his trousers down. Which might not have been so bad had he not been in the company of a known prostitute at the time.

'I'll be discussing the matter with the ladies' caucus before the press conference in the morning, John.'

'Of course. I just wanted to let you know that the press conference could make all the difference.'

'Yes, John. The girls and I are very well aware of the importance of the press conference.'

'That's why I was phoning.'

'Thank you, John. For phoning.'

'So we can count on the ladies, can we?'

'Oh you can always count on the ladies, John.'

'. . . To support the particular Minister?'

'To uphold the principles of the party, John, yes.'

The crackle on the line was probably electronic.

'It's national coverage, Sylvia.'

'Yes, John.'

The Minister seemed reluctant to ring off, unsure that he had made his point.

'Goodnight, John.'

'Yes. Yes. Goodnight. And good luck.

'Thank you, John.'

'And give my regards to Arthur.'

'Yes. Of course.'

If he phones.

The preliminaries, in the form of a discussion of the latest news on grandchildren and the health of absent friends, were lavishly conducted.

Then came the fundraising update, which was easily dispensed with to the satisfaction of all. Then . . .

'Today is ladies' day.' declared Mrs Prior-Pointment, her almost-Roman nose pointing out the significance. 'The *baton* (pronounced in the French) of national wellbeing, usually so secure in the hands of the men (dramatic pause) has been passed to us . . .'

There was a clinking of china coffee cups in lieu of applause.

'. . . And for once, proper order shall prevail.'

'The girls' had gathered in the Prior-Pointments' sombre red-brick castle for their 'war cabinet', as Mrs Bullmore called it with her pinched, chinny smile.

The men were nervous and wanted to interfere. The local party secretary had telephoned several times that morning, but he was told in no uncertain terms that the ladies would inform him of their view when and only when it had been formed.

'There's been far too much shilly-shallying, lately,' declared Mrs Bullmore, her chin pushing ever upwards as she spoke until it jostled for position with the imitation crystal chandelier. 'I remember Profumo. In those days a man was a man. That is – he still made a mess of things, but when caught out, he acted honourably and immediately. There was no question.'

The fact that this assertion was untrue had no bearing on the proceedings.

'It's about time we ladies had our say,' agreed Mrs Strutting, with a nod of her pinkish perm. 'If it were up to us it would be quite simple and straightforward.'

'My dear, it *is* up to us,' chinned Mrs Bullmore with a

staunch grin at Mrs Prior-Pointment. '*That* is what this meeting is all about.'

There was a stunned silence while the ladies took this in.

'Girls, our day has come.' Mrs Prior-Pointment's face was gaunt with meaning. Today was the day that her dedication to the eternal ideals of The Family was to be rewarded, her life's work consummated.

'If only Arthur were here to see it,' she kept thinking.

She wanted to telephone the apartment in Gibraltar to tell him to listen to the World Service. But something was stopping her.

'He's probably terribly busy on the beach,' she thought and vowed that she wouldn't let her husband's failure to contact her interfere with her enjoyment of the occasion.

'We must be decisive,' declared Mrs Bullmore, now angling her jaw to offset her pearls. 'We need to send a clear message to the Party and to the nation. Family Values are Family Values. We must practise what we preach.'

As they cleared up the coffee things, Mrs Strutting ventured into the dismal recesses of the drawing room to replace the silver teaspoons in the military chest, whereupon she remembered about old Mrs Prior-Pointment whose knobbly old legs were propped on the ancestral pouffe, as usual.

'Dreadful all this, isn't it, dear?' she remarked sighing excitedly.

There was a twitching and what Mrs Strutting took to be an expression of indignation amid the pile of tartan and fine wool.

Munch munch munch.

It was difficult to believe the old woman had once been such a powerful and respected figure.

Mrs Strutting nodded her damaged pink strands. 'Dreadful.'

*   *   *

They drove to the press conference in Mrs Prior-Pointment's unpatriotic, but extremely reliable Honda Legend.

Only the three of them attended the press conference: Mrs Prior-Pointment upright (rigid) in the driver's seat, pointing the way with her almost-Roman nose; Mrs Bullmore seeming to occupy the whole interior of the car from the passenger seat; Mrs Strutting in the back doing her best to keep the draught from upsetting her perm.

Their neatly ironed and fabric-softened clothes were fine and delicate, expensive and carefully planned, though not quite well-fitting: light woollens, plaid, nylon, polyester and cottons, lightly coloured, overlaid by heavy tweed and gabardine.

The overall impression was not designed to be high fashion, rather to be ordinary, respectable and decent. And probably in the context of the bridge club and the charity function it did, inconspicuously, achieve just that.

But in the busy streets of the town and amid the bustle of reporters at party headquarters, the clothes, the brooches and pearls, powder and pan-stick, talc and perfume and their self-consciously stately airs created the impression of something rather larger than life.

Perhaps Mrs Bullmore had overdone it with her hat. Maybe the large mustard check of Mrs Strutting's coat was a little too much beneath the pinkish halo. Whatever it was there was an undeniable unearthliness about the triumvirate as they bustled through the *mêlée*.

Something of the strangeness struck the three women too, as they were buffeted by the storm.

The violence and rudeness of the journalists, the urgency of the whole thing appalled them. Despite their age and experience, the harshness of the world seemed odd to them and clashed awfully with their clothes.

As the various press agencies vied for control of the situation, the three women took their seats and assumed the air of generals at a military parade.

Most of the reporters felt a slight chill at the sight, unconsciously reminded of their school days (not in most cases all that long ago).

Within a few moments, silence fell.

'Thank you,' said Mrs Prior-Pointment in the most patronising manner, after which even the hardiest of the hacks found themselves entirely unable to interrupt.

'A senior member of Her Majesty's Government (she began), a member of this party, has disgraced himself. The ladies (and other party members) of this constituency, on whom the Member depends for his seat, will find it impossible to ask the ordinary people of this area to place their confidence in someone who has disgraced himself and his Family (the capital letter was audible) in this way. His behaviour threatens the credibility of the party locally and consequently the government itself. We are forced therefore to call on the Member to resign.'

And that was that.

The lingering silence was broken only by the local party secretary who was hunched in the corner. The grimace that accompanied his involuntary ejaculation appeared in the pages of several newspapers the next morning.

Mrs Prior-Pointment said a firm 'Good morning' and the three women marched out.

The Member for the area announced his resignation within a quarter of an hour.

On the way back to Mrs Prior-Pointment's cavernous red-brick home they listened to the news on the car radio.

'There'll be no more shilly-shallying now,' declared

Mrs Bullmore victoriously, her chin set in the style of Napoleon.

'You really were very good indeed,' giggled Mrs Strutting in the back of the car, apparently careless of her perm which now resembled spaghetti with attitude.

But Mrs Prior-Pointment was distracted.

She was wondering if Arthur would hear the various broadcasts. Would he phone to congratulate her, or even for that matter to tell her off?

She was withdrawn throughout the victory tea party. The ladies had to make do with the everyday china and many of them were gathered around Mrs Bullmore quietly speculating about the morale of the leader who most certainly 'wasn't herself'.

There was an item about the press conference on the national television news that night, but Mrs Prior-Pointment watched it in taut silence.

Still no word from her husband.

Nor did he communicate with her that weekend.

When he failed to contact her on Monday the good woman finally gave herself up to a foreboding and resolved to act on a feeling she had about the ancient writing bureau in her husband's study upstairs.

The bureau was locked and, after an agony of indecision and a frantic search for the key, Mrs Prior-Pointment completely lost control of herself and opened the thing by forcing the lid with a screwdriver.

It was typical of Arthur that the bureau was in disarray. There was no proper order to anything. There were all kinds of documents relating to business in Gibraltar, and some unruly piles of paper relating to Columbia and the Argentine.

All very businesslike in a unbusinesslike sort of way.

She began to regret her violence on the lock.

As she was closing the thing back up, or trying to, she discovered a small compartment.

She froze, except for her almost-Roman nose which twitched terrier-like.

It might well have done.

Inside she discovered a letter which began, 'Dear naughty boy'.

*T*here was no visiting until twelve noon.

Jed had to mill anxiously about town for a couple of hours.

He tried phoning Eddie's to speak to his girlfriend, but it was only the ansaphone. 'Uh . . . Hi Vicky. It's Jed – Jed Green – I . . . heard what happened, I was phoning to see if you're OK . . . if there's anything I can do.'

He wondered if she had his number and decided she might not and left it.

By the time he joined the bedraggled queue of visitors at the detention centre Jed had drunk too much coffee, been arrested himself a number of times and sentenced to several terms of imprisonment.

He kept thinking he was walking into a trap.

That his money was involved.

Next minute he was feeling smug and self-satisfied, believing he had always known Eddie's games would come to no good.

Then he'd start worrying again.

Eddie in a bloody detention centre!

He shuddered and began to wonder how to present himself to his old friend. He didn't want to look on him with pity written all over his face. Eddie would most likely be miserable and feeling sensitive, but he didn't want to bluster away too cheerfully either.

In his business suit he felt conspicuous among the other waiting people.

The queue began moving and he was shown through into a passage by, he assumed, a prison officer.

He walked somewhat self-consciously past a series of cubicles with glass screens.

Then he heard a 'Yo!'

Yo! Trendy to the last.

'Eddie!'

'How y'doing?'

'Huh. Pretty shocked, actually.' Jed sat down.

'Don't worry, it's nothing.'

Jed almost laughed. *Nothing*! 'Er . . . How's Vicky? – How's she taken it?'

'She left me at the weekend. She must have had a premonition.' The grin. 'It was over.'

Jed looked at him. He assumed the joviality was a brave face. 'I'm sorry.'

Eddie shrugged.

'What have you done?'

'I haven't *done* anything.'

'No, no, of course. What are they *saying* you've done?'

'I've been charged in connection with a series of company frauds I know nothing about. (Shrug.) There're trying to connect it with stuff in Gibraltar.' Because of Jed's face Eddie added, 'But they won't. It's impossible.'

'Umm. What have you told them?'

'Not a thing.'

Jed frowned.

Eddie said, 'You don't tell them anything. You keep *stumm*. That way you don't drop yourself in it.'

'I thought there was no right to silence anymore.'

Eddie's face was a picture of scorn. 'Not according to *them*, but if you've got brains you still keep *stumm*.'

Jed doubted very much whether in Eddie's position he could 'keep *stumm*'. He felt sure that if he was arrested he'd want to confess immediately to everything they wanted him to.

'I'll be out in a couple of days. I'm on what they call a "lie down".'

Jed said: '?'

'They're holding me so I can't go and warn anybody who might be involved. They'll see if anyone calls me up, or does anything suspicious while I'm away.' He shrugged confidently. 'Which no one will.'

Jed swallowed. Had he said anything stupid on the ansaphone? He'd left his number. Fuck!

Then he found himself wondering if Eddie *did* know anything about the series of company frauds and whether his own money had been involved. Eddie must have read his mind.

'You're in the clear, Jed.'

'Oh I'm not worried about that.'

'Good. Don't be. Your money's safe. And legal.'

'Yeah, yeah. Fine.'

Jed badly wanted to ask if he could get hold of his money, in cash, quickly. Preferably today. He really did need it. To keep up the fight to save his business.

Instead he asked. 'Is there anything I can do? Anything you need.'

Eddie's smiled. 'Actually mate, there is something, yes.'

Jed was pleased. 'Anything.'

'I've got to raise the bail. By Wednesday.'

'Yeah? What – how much?'

'Seventy-five grand.'

'*What*!'

Jed listened. It was all he could do to keep his mouth closed.

'Seventy-five grand's nothing.' Eddie flapped his hand, as if at some poor joke. 'It's gunna take a couple of days to organise that's all.'

'Um.'

'Thing is, the most liquid asset I can get hold of right now, includes your forty . . .'

59

Forty. Jed noted the figure with a twinge of disappointment. It was supposed to be fifty by now.

'I've got to cash it in. It's a shame. It was doing well.'

Jed blinked. 'Don't worry, it's fine.'

'You don't mind?'

'No problem.'

'You're a pal, Jed.'

Jed shrugged.

'You're a good man,' Eddie said. 'And . . . if you don't mind . . . I'm gunna need to borrow it for a few days. Weeks really. Until I get organised.'

'Oh. OK. Sure. Anything.'

Shit.

'**P**ick me up at eleven, we can go for a coffee. It'll make a change,' Charity said one morning.

Yet another morning after a night of sex that Jed would rather not have had.

They were sitting in the kitchen, Jed's favourite room in the house. It was the least frilly. It had a nice solid wooden table and a reassuringly quarry-tiled floor.

'I'm busy this morning.'

'I thought you said it was quiet.'

'Yeah, well, I've got an appointment at ten-thirty.'

'Who with?'

'Eddie. He's been released.'

'Oh, I forgot to tell you, he phoned this morning, while you were snoozing. He said to say sorry but he's going away for a couple of days, possibly weeks. He'll call you when he gets back.'

Weeks?

Jed was already trying to think up another excuse.

She was getting ready to leave. She was always first these days. 'So pick me up at eleven.'

'I've got things to sort out. Honestly.'

Charity fixed him with a look. 'Hang dog' he called it. It always got him. 'Are you avoiding me?'

'Of course I'm not avoiding you.'

'We never do anything together anymore.' She let it hang there. Dog-like.

'You're the one who's been going out with Nurse whatever-it-is – Miranda – every night.'

'It's not every night.'

'Well.' His look said 'almost'.

'Twice.'

'Three times.'

'Three times.' (Meaning: So what?)

'Three times this week.'

'I asked you if you wanted to come.'

'I don't want to go on a "girls night out". I'm not a girl.'

'What about all the other nights? When we sit round bored . . . or I do. You bury your head in a book.'

He slumped. 'I'm not avoiding you. That's stupid.'

'So come for a coffee with me this morning.'

He sighed.

She pulled a face. 'You don't like my company anymore.'

That got him.

The problem was, it was true.

He pictured the scene. They would go into town. She would get distracted by a boutique, drag him in to look at clothes – or worse, home decorations – ask his opinion on articles he thought poncy (clothes or furniture) and he would hum noncommittally, too embarrassed to express his real feelings. She would be hurt and go quiet. A ghost would follow them to the tea rooms, poison the coffee and turn the cream cakes sour. They would be strangers.

'I'll pick you up at eleven,' he said.

61

'Leave it if you're busy.'

'No. It can wait.'

'It's not a duty.'

'I want to come.'

'I want it to be something you enjoy.'

He laughed. As a child would, caught out lying. 'I'll enjoy it.'

She sat down opposite him, looking tired suddenly. She put her elbows on the table and her chin in her palms.

Jed's heart sank. He knew what was coming. All he wanted was a digestible breakfast.

'You don't love me.'

'Of course I love you!'

'Doesn't sound very convincing.'

'I'm not convinced of anything until I've had a bowl of Alpen in the morning.'

The attempt at humour failed.

'When was the last time you kissed me?'

Oh my God. 'Last night. We made love for God's sake.'

'You didn't kiss me last night. I kissed you. I waited to see if you would. And you didn't.'

'Of course I kissed you or maybe there was someone else there. I'm sure I kissed *someone.*'

There was a sulky silence.

He resented having been put to the test.

All he had to do was be nice to her – physically – kiss her and hold her for a few minutes and everything would be alright. But he was immobilised, choked up and angry.

Then the silence became worse than the loathing.

'Come here,' he said softly, moving his chair back to make room for her to sit on his knee.

She refused to move.

'Come on, come here.'

She shuffled round. Petulant. He was sure there were tears lurking.

She plonked herself on his knee.

He said: 'I don't know why I didn't kiss you. I'm sure I did. I mean as far I knew we were kissing each other . . .' He shrugged. And said it. 'I love you.'

He'd said it – he may as well make it convincing.

'I do. You're my wife. All this is for you.' He loosely indicated the surroundings.

She thawed a little, looking at him again, albeit doubtfully.

He was required to go on.

'There's a lot going on at work. I mean not-a-lot, but it's getting on top of me. It's pissing me off. I'm not paying you enough mind, I know, but . . . I get . . . locked inside . . .' He was embarrassed. It was the sort of thing he'd said a thousand times before. And meant it a few.

The tears were just sitting in her eyes as she looked at him.

Even he began to thaw a little. To feel a little of the love that had been so strong. So long ago.

Or was it pity?

He looked at her. Did he love her?

He kissed her anyway. And squeezed her.

She held him, limply and reached for a tissue from the box on the table.

Proper tears had been avoided.

He was relieved.

She said: 'I'm sorry. I get scared. I get it into my head that you don't love me. Then everything shows it . . .'

It was inevitable. She had to say it:

'I want children – we've been waiting years. It'll be too late one day . . .'

They were the sort of things she'd said a thousand times and meant it every time.

He listened and then told a few more 'sweet lies'. About how they were just waiting. For God-knows-what he didn't know, but they were waiting.

She went to work reassured.

Mostly.

'I'll pick you up at eleven,' he said as she went out the door.

'Only if you want to.'

'I want to.'

 *T*he office in Jed's unit seemed particularly depressing that morning.

He hated lying to his wife.

Everyone did it, he knew, but he thought himself different – not *one of them*. To him it was loathsome and repulsive. He had a basic urge to be honest and do the right thing and an even more basic urge to conceal his real feelings and lie about everything. From the real state of his business to his lack of sexual desire, it was all secret.

'It'll be too late soon, leave her while she's still young enough', Eddie unhelpfully advised when consulted. Which was rarely.

It was alright for Eddie to talk like that. He was different.

But the thought of children *was* sobering.

Actually it made him want to get drunk.

He felt such dread at the thought of having children that it made him doubt his intentions towards her. Why was he scared of the thought?

Because it would tie them together.

It would make the decision he couldn't make for himself.

To stay with her. Stay put.

The morning's conversation had shaken him more than the hundreds they'd had before, coming on top of everything else.

He thought of Charity sitting on his knee, nearly

64

in tears. The thought that he was stringing her along
made him feel sick. He pictured the sex they'd had the
night before. That was the proof, surely, that it was all
wrong, how he dreaded the sex.

His heart sank.

He pictured her getting older.

Surely it would only get worse.

He was pacing about the office cubicle now, taking
breaths to calm himself.

He sank into his chair, opened his draw and removed
the whisky bottle.

He was racked with guilt anyway.

The extra guilt over a morning drink would only be
a top up.

Even so, as he put the bottle on his desk he hesitated.

He was drinking in the morning, which was a sure
sign of alcoholism. But it wasn't every day. He hadn't
had anything on Tuesday. And it wasn't every night.
Well not a lot every night. Just enough.

To stop this pain.

Fuck it. It was only lately. Because of the stress.

He poured a shot into the coffee mug. Splashed it
from the tap to 'dilute' it.

It wasn't that he ever got *drunk* in the day. He just
liked to warm himself.

Then he was back in his chair.

Feeling a little warmer.

Now he could look at this morning's scene with
equanimity.

Did he, or did he not want to be with his wife?

He pictured staying with her.

The sex.

Children.

The sex.

Getting old with her.

Becoming entombed in a frilly mausoleum.

The sex.

That feeling of being unable to breathe.

65

Of being unable to express his lack of desire.

The sex.

He stared at this picture of their relationship for a few moments, held it up to the light, indulged in the unsavoury aspects, until it hurt.

He formed a picture of her, sitting on his knee, crying, telling him she loved him and needed him and felt a sickening wave of pity.

What was he doing to her? Staying around, because he was afraid to go. While her womb dried up, along with his heart.

He was being cruel.

He would leave.

He pictured leaving.

She had a job. She would survive.

She could start again.

She still had her looks. Didn't she? He couldn't be sure. Not any more.

Everyone else thought so. (Eddie.)

She'd meet someone.

She'd have children.

Live her own life.

She'd survive. She'd be better off.

He sighed.

Does it always just go off?

Was it just that she was getting older?

Would a young woman retain the attraction longer? Always?

Would he want a young woman?

He didn't *know* any young women.

He shook his head. It didn't matter. If he was to leave he would leave to face the consequences.

He would stand alone.

It would be a relief. Easy. Easier than staying and hurting Charity, hanging on to her until she was too old to start again.

He reached for the bottle. Just one more.

Then eat some mints, so she won't smell it. At

eleven.

Jesus, what time was it?

Better make it a quick one.

Screw, splash, clunk, over to the sink, splash, gulp – *ghahh* . . .

Where was he?

Oh yes. Standing alone. To face the consequences.

He put pity behind him and fell into fantasy.

It was as if an angel had descended, swooped among the litter and dust of the unit and slid through a crack in the office door. She was hovering behind him, massaging his shoulders, whispering things to him.

Sweet things.

Things with no definite form. Warm, secure sensations.

He would get a flat – an apartment – somewhere. Nowhere in particular – modern, but not poncy.

The angel was there too. Whispering to him. Being gentle and nude. In his dim imaginings, she was a strange distorted combination of women from his past, especially the bold drunken Virginia (now gentle and serene), but also a woman he saw regularly at a bus stop on his way to work. And others. Aspects of women he had met rolled into a hazy erotic fantasy.

He became aroused. Dreamed a creamy, purring dream.

The phone rang.

He stared at it and accidentally projected into the illibidinous straits of his financial future.

He felt a stab of horror.

Fuck. He'd go broke.

And Charity would be with someone else.

Someone successful. (Eddie.)

Each ring of the phone tormented him. Hurt his head and pierced his heart. Gutted him.

Fuck, he'd be broke!

He reprojected.

Some kind of bedsit. Angelless. Dank.

67

He pictured the jealousy he'd felt when Eddie made a move on Charity.

He put that in the bedsit.

He saw Charity in a happy family setting, gloating, patronising.

He was already there – shivering in some tiny room, pursued by creditors. He'd end up drinking, getting bitter.

Out on his arse.

The phone stopped.

Left him with the quiet, dreariness, of the office.

Which suddenly seemed cosy. What he had seemed cosy and warm.

He needed his £40,000.

Now.

He picked up the phone.

Eddie. Where the fuck is he?

His secretary.

'Sorry Jed, he's away. I don't know where. Came in here with a new woman on his arm. Honestly – you're all the same you men. OK, yes, I'll give him a message. Phone you as soon as he gets back. Or calls.'

Jed stood up with his teeth bared. Picked up the litter bin and hurled it with all his force across the dismal little office.

The angel had taken flight.

She was on Eddie's arm.

He flopped into his chair.

What had it all been for?

*T*hat was the morning Jed first set eyes on Miranda.

She was in Charity's office at eleven o'clock.

He was sucking an Extra Strong Mint.

Charity was on the phone and hardly gave him a glance.

'Hiya, Jed,' smiled Miranda, guessing his identity.

'Ah, Nurse Jones, I presume?'

'Have you come to take up residence?'

He grinned. 'I feel like it.'

It was his first smile of the day.

There were more to come.

'You're taking me out,' she announced from under her unruly mop.

He caught a glimpse of her soft freckles as he took in the words.

Charity was still on the phone. She looked harassed.

Jed glanced from one face to the other, trying very hard not to compare them.

'She fucked up,' said Miranda.

The words 'fucked up' momentarily sent Jed into a trance.

'Hello?' Miranda was comically waving a hand in front of his face, grinning. 'Anyone in?'

'Yeah, yeah. Sorry, I er – "Fucked up"?'

'The Inspectorate are sending over a surveyor. She can't go out with you. You and me are going into town on an errand.'

'Oh.' He tried to sound disappointed.

Charity was listening in as best she could. She put her hand over the mouthpiece. 'Sorry, darling . . .'

'Oh . . . it's OK.'

'You don't mind?'

He shrugged. Casually. 'No. It's fine.'

He was driving.

'So you're the woman that's been keeping my wife

out late, getting her drunk, are you?'

'I try my best.'

'You're doing quite a good job.'

'She said you might come one night.'

'I might. Keep an eye on you both.'

'You don't need to. There's not a lot of trouble a girl can get into round here.'

'You sound disappointed.'

'I fucking am!'

Jed laughed. It was his first laugh of the day.

They were on their way into town, in Jed's none-too-cheap, none-too-flash Rover.

'You're from Manchester, aren't you?'

'Man-ches-tor.' She spent a minute instructing him in the correct pronunciation of the city's name.

Jed said, 'If you don't mind me asking, what are you doing here? I mean it is a bit dull.'

'You mean: "What's a bad girl like me doing in a nice place like this?"'

'No – no I . . .' he saw her grin. '. . . Yeah. It's not exactly swinging.'

'Boring as shit.'

'Yeah, boring as shit.'

She laughed. And imitated him. 'Shi*t*. With a "t".'

He blushed. 'Fucking shit, with an "F.U.C.K.I.N.G."'

'The sea-front's not bad.'

'Do you think?'

'Well – it's not good either.'

He smiled, to express sympathy. 'Well?'

'What?'

'What's a bad girl like you doing in a nice place like this?'

She grinned, hesitating.

'You don't have to tell me.'

He waited.

'It's a secret.'

'Yeah, sure. Sorry.'

He wasn't sure what to say now.

There was a moment's silence. Then Miranda looked at him, tutting theatrically. '*N-o* – now you get all curious and ply me with questions about my secret.'

He laughed, a little unsure of himself. 'Oh, ha. Er – what do you mean "secret"?'

There was something about the conversation now that was unsettling. Not unpleasant, just unsettling.

'I mean secret secret.'

'"*Secret secret*"? Never heard of it. What sort of secret's that?'

'It's the sort of secret that requires a hostage.'

Not 'not unpleasant'. Fun.

'A hostage?'

'Um-hum.'

He wanted to say 'What, you mean "you show me yours if I show you mine?"'. Instead he said, 'A hostage?' again. It was more his style.

She said: 'I'll show you mine if you show me yours.'

He hooted. 'I was going to say that!'

'Beat you to it.'

He had to negotiate a confusing right turn.

'You can't tell where you're supposed to be going,' he said as a tram nearly crushed them.

'Well?'

'I haven't got any secrets.' He was thinking about Virginia.

'Don't lie!' she laughed. 'I *know* you've got secrets.' She was thinking about the face-cloth in the bathroom. 'Come on. Mine's worth it.'

He was a little flustered. 'I really can't think of anything.'

'Nothing at all?' she coaxed.

'Not really, no. I've never done anything that bad.'

'O-oh. You're no fun.'

'Sorry.'

He was surprisingly disappointed. And he really

wished he hadn't said 'Sorry' Made him sound really
stupid.

'You're not going to tell me, now, are you?'

'No,' she said and looked out of the window.

*T*he errand was run in one of those
superstores with no staff.

Conversation returned when Miranda
told Jed that they could 'clear the bloody
place out no problem', telling how she
was always getting into trouble for shop-
lifting when she was younger, and other
anecdotes from her past.

From which Jed learned that she was brought up in
a miserable block of flats in Macclesfield and had a
drunken father who beat her mother and made her
childhood miserable. She had escaped at the earliest
opportunity to take her chances alone in Manchester.

What secrets she might have Jed could only wonder.
Personally he wouldn't have let out what she'd volunteered already.

'So where are you taking me for lunch then?' she
asked with a twinkle.

Over lunch, Jed learned that Miranda had had a
hard time in Manchester and a lot of men trouble.
He'd never met anyone like her before. She may
as well have come from Mars. In turn he admitted
some of his financial difficulties. He told her that
the cheque he would write for lunch would probably bounce, which was a lie but seemed to impress
Miranda.

When the wine was drunk and the coffee ordered
she sat back and said: 'So come on then, play the
game.'

Jed realised that what had seemed impossible an

hour ago – telling this stranger, who was a friend of his wife, that he'd felt up a woman at a party – didn't seem so impossible after all.

'There *is* one thing,' he admitted.

'Of course there is.'

'But you have to go first.'

She folded her arms across her chest (*under* her chest), grinning wickedly.

'I see. And why's that?'

'It's very secret.'

'A secret's a secret.'

He hesitated. 'Yes, but you have a certain advantage over me.'

She seemed pleased.

'Ah. Now this *is* getting interesting.'

He was surprised. 'Is it?'

'You're naughtier than I thought,' she said.

'You don't know that.'

'Well, in terms of the game we're playing, the only advantage I could have over you at this stage is that I'm a friend of your wife. Therefore it must be something – *extramarital*.'

It was his turn to sit back and fold his arms across his chest. Under his blushing face.

'Not necessarily,' he pretended.

'Not necessarily perhaps,' she challenged, 'but very likely.'

He couldn't afford to be too flippant. *Must remember she is a friend of my wife*. He wished she wasn't.

'Ladies first,' he said, weakly.

'Alright.'

'It'd better be good.'

'I'd better choose carefully then, hadn't I?'

'Choice of sins, eh?'

She laughed. 'I'll say.'

He was riveted. And there were rumours in the Home Counties.

'I slept with a man for money.'

73

He blinked.

A smile escaped repression.

And spread.

He nodded. 'It's a good one alright.'

'I thought you'd like it. Men usually do.'

'You've played this before?'

'It's my favourite.'

Rumours were turning to hard news.

'Is . . . that what you're doing here?'

'Sort of. I had a spot of bother. Not a lot. Just a bit.'
For a moment she looked a little uneasy.

'What sort of "bother"?'

She shook her head. And smiled. The smile said:
'Your turn'.

He sat back. He wanted to sweat. 'Well mine's not
as juicy as that.'

'No, but it could possibly cause more trouble.'

'Um.'

He swallowed.

She sat back. 'It's hard to trust a woman who's slept
with men for money, isn't it?'

He blinked again. ' "Men"?'

She stopped.

'You said "men". In the plural.'

She considered a moment and shrugged. 'Well then.'

He sat back again. 'Humm – does your – *employer*
know the full extent of your experience? It's a very
comprehensive CV.'

'Well, let's put it this way: . . .' she hesitated. 'No.'

They laughed.

He breathed more easily. 'Well I must say that makes
me feel safer.'

'O-oh.' Disappointment. 'I don't want you to feel
safe. It's a risky game. That's the fun of it.'

'Huh.' Not for him.

She was still waiting.

'It's not much, I told you. Not compared to . . .'

They looked at each other.

He couldn't say it.

'. . . No, well not compared to you.'

'Well wake me up when you're ready.'

He took a breath and then the risk. 'I – got off with a woman at a party.'

Her lips were pursed in anticipation.

'Yeah. And . . .'

He shrugged. 'That's it.'

'Wh – *bollocks*!' She said it so loud they both thought people in the restaurant had heard.

'You'll have to give me more than that. Did you shag her?'

'No.'

'*No*?'

'We kissed. Well, she kissed me.'

'What, on the end of your dick?'

That really made him splutter. 'No. On the balcony of a church hall.'

'Is that *all*?

'Yeah.'

'You didn't feel her up?'

He looked into his coffee.

'You *did*, didn't you?'

'Only . . .' He didn't really know how to talk about it. It was the first time it had ever been aired.

'Come on, tell me the details. "Only" what?'

He sighed. He was trembling slightly. 'Over her clothes.'

'Sorry – you're muttering.'

'Over her clothes.'

'What, her tits?'

'No – yes . . .'

He put his head in his hands. It was too much. He was crushed by what he'd said, wanted to unsay it, yet he felt ecstatic too.

She said: 'What – down there,' and made a comical gesture with her face.

He had to stop it. 'Come on, let's go.'

75

'O-oh. That was just getting interesting.

'You're too much. You really are.'

'You're not the first man who's said that.'

He did his best to retain his composure while the waiter fussed over the bill. Then they were out in the street, which seemed impossibly bright. Shoppers and holiday makers hurrying about. Cars, dust, stupid novelty trinkets everywhere. (Not his either.)

Miranda at his side.

'It's not easy being married is it?'

'No. No it's not.'

'Have you always been faithful?'

'Yeah. Apart from a grope. *That* grope.'

'You could hardly call that unfaithful.'

'Thanks.'

Then they were back in the car and Miranda talked of the difficulties she had with guys. How they always ended up wanting her more than she wanted them – making demands she couldn't meet. How she'd always wanted a man who'd just be there when she wanted him to be there and not ask questions.

'I don't ask for much,' she laughed.

Jed was transported.

He listened in awe and wanted to be there when she wanted him to be there and not ask questions.

He never got a word in edgewise all the way back.

He just listened.

Hung on the words.

She poured it out.

Tales from another planet.

But nothing about – that, her revealed secret.

He just had to wonder about that and wish he had further secrets to swap for details.

They landed.

His none-to-cheap, none-too-flash Rover crunched on the gravel courtyard of *Newfoundland*.

'I don't know why you drive a shed like this,' she

said as they pulled up. 'With your money I'd have got
– I dunno, something nice.'

'This used to be nice.'

'Na. I mean something – *nice*.'

He laughed.

She got out. 'Don't go grassing me up now!'

'Likewise . . .'

Slam.

She was gone.

He sighed, closed his eyes and realised he was in
some pain.

'**S**ylvia?'

'Arthur(!)'

'Sorry I haven't phoned, dear.'

It was a little awkward. Mrs Bullmore
was sitting there and Mrs Prior-Pointment could tell from the jutting of her
lieutenant's considerable chin that the
sturdy woman was listening intently, despite the air
of nonchalance.

'I've been worried, Arthur.'

'Sorry dear, I've had my hands full.'

Despite having rehearsed speeches, Mrs Prior-Pointment was stuck for words. She'd been waiting for
Arthur to phone for over a week now.

He said, 'I heard you on the news, dear. It was on
the World Service. Very impressive.'

'Oh.' Despite herself Mrs Prior-Pointment was cheered
by this. 'I thought you might have missed it.'

'Served the bugger right. Miserable old dog.'

She hesitated. 'I rather thought you might have
sympathised with him.'

'Certainly not!' A hearty laugh. 'He got everything
he deserved. I was proud of you.'

She was on the verge of tears suddenly. 'I was thinking . . . I rather thought . . . I might come out for a week . . . next week.'

There was a moment's hesitation.

'Sure. Sure, why not.'

'I can get a flight for Monday.'

'Monday's fine.'

She blinked in disbelief.

(So did Mrs Bullmore who'd heard nothing about any flight.)

She had worried about nothing. Surely.

Since discovering the frightful letter the dutiful wife had done her best. She'd forgiven and denied, reasoned and excused, disavowed and negated.

'Naughty boy' did not after all necessarily refer to Arthur. It could have been somebody else, a friend. It could have been a joke, by a male friend. It could have been a silly mistake. Some silly woman with a crush on him. It was of so little consequence he'd put it in the old drawer and and forgotten it. How could he have been expected to explain a thing like that to his wife? It would have been embarrassing, to both of them, and silly. It *was* silly. The whole thing was silly. She was being silly.

But more evidence, to support the case for the defence, was required.

She had needed the reassurance of his jovial voice.

Over the years his convivial, carefree attitude had been a source of annoyance to the doyenne of sobriety, but in waiting – longing – for the phone to ring she realised with a flush of emotion that his gaiety had always been a source of comfort.

She felt sure that just the sound of his voice would allay her fears, yet she had feared it too. What if he were cold? What if the tone of adultery were somehow discernible?

She had waited uncomfortably. The evidence against was flimsy and circumstantial. But she needed certainty to settle the matter in her mind.

And then the phone had . . .

Finally . . .

Rung.

And . . .

Of course, she had been foolish. She would be there with him on Monday.

He was a good man.

How *could* she have *been* so foolish. She felt like a girl.

Then his voice again, 'Oh – no – wait a minute. Monday. I forgot. I'm flying to the Canaries for a couple of days next week.'

It was a slap across the face.

'. . . I have to leave on Tuesday. Probably be away until Friday, at least.'

'That doesn't matter, I can wait for you in Gibraltar, I could do with a break.'

'Well, I'm back in England the following week. Probably. There are one or two things to sort out . . .'

There was silence at home and abroad.

Then his voice, deep and sincere. 'Sorry Syl.' He was using her pet name, 'Things are a little hectic right now. I'll be back soon, then we'll have a proper holiday, eh?'

She wanted to stamp her feet and cry like a girl. Instead she said, 'I could get a flight tonight.'

He became a little cooler. 'Please yourself dear. It hardly seems worth it. I'm at a meeting this evening. And all day tomorrow.'

'That's not like you. Evening meetings . . .'

'I told you – things are a *bit stiff*, right now.'

The dutiful wife's mind cut the word 'stiff' from the record.

It was a rout. He, had not supported the case for the defence at all. Now for Mrs Prior-Pointment it would be either submission or confrontation. Confrontation usually took the form of silence, so there wasn't a lot of difference.

79

Mrs Bullmore was fidgeting, minding her own business, though her chin was still listening intently.

There was a submissively confrontational silence which felt to the wife like impotence, during which the poor woman sieved the impressions of the last few moments and measured them against a lifetime's experience.

In the space of a few moments an entirely new man had flickered into being before her. A trickster.

Possibly. It was only a fleeting impression.

But, in those few green and sickly seconds, the worst-case scenario dropped into place.

He had another woman, who lived in Gibraltar.

Why else didn't he want her to go?

Council for the defence huddled busily. They had more to defend than the mere man, after all – there was an institution at stake. He didn't want her to go because he was going to the Canaries, because he had his hands full.

She wondered grimly how often she had been put off visiting Gibraltar before, only without the benefit of a 'Dear Naughty Boy' to sharpen her wits.

But she didn't really like Gibraltar.

She always felt like she was . . .

She never really felt welcome.

Oh, God.

'How's mother?' he said.

She made him wait before replying, 'She's the same.'

'Oh *good*.'

She knew that somewhere, beneath the surface, he must have detected a seismic tremor.

Mrs Bullmore rustled a page of *Woman's Realm*.

'We'll go away soon. Just the two of us, eh? Somewhere tropical,' Arthur said.

'. . .'

'Take a look at some brochures.'

'. . .'

'You're tired, I can tell.'
'. . .'
'You must rest. Have a break from doing good and do yourself some good for once.'
'. . .'
Pause-wise it was like a Pinter play.

But in the end she couldn't help herself and spoiled the effect. 'When – *exactly* – *will* you be coming home?'

'Oh, a week Thursday, no later.'
'. . .'
'Give Mother my love.'
'. . .'
'Goodbye.'
'. . .'
Click, burrrrrr.

She said goodbye as if they were still connected for Mrs Bullmore's benefit, then hung up. She was unsure how to present herself. She wanted to be alone. With her husband.

'Everything alright dear?'

'Oh. Yes.'

'You don't sound very sure.'

'Oh . . .' Mrs Prior-Pointment shook her head to say she didn't want to talk about it.

'You didn't tell him about your appointment.'

Since the press conference when the ladies had called for the resignation of the disgraced MP (or 'Flown in the face of common sense' as the Minister for the Environment put it), Mrs Prior-Pointment had been highly honoured by the Party. It was thought by central office that if the good woman was brought closer to the party-proper she might in future use her influence more responsibly.

She had been appointed head of the quango responsible for selling off Elderly Services in the local area and overseeing the whole thing thereafter.

She hadn't even mentioned it to Arthur.

81

'It's a very important position. It couldn't have happened to just anyone, dear. Especially not after you gave them a black eye at the press conference.'

Mrs Prior-Pointment nodded modestly, despite her distress.

'Doesn't Arthur approve of you working?'

'Oh, he's been nagging me for years to get a "proper job". He doesn't approve of charity.'

'Good lord, really?'

Suddenly the dutiful wife was in tears.

You could have knocked Mrs Bullmore down with an embroidered handkerchief. She didn't know what to do, or rather it was so long since she'd had to do it that she'd forgotten how. So she mumbled 'dear dear', and sat, dithering, on the arm of the chair next to her friend.

Neither woman was used to emotional display, but Mrs Prior-Pointment was utterly distraught so Mrs Bullmore steeled herself, or tried to unsteel herself, for once.

The taut entanglement was sufficiently awkward to sober up the sufferer.

'I'm so sorry,' spluttered the leader as she pampered her eyes and fussed around in her handbag.

Mrs Bullmore probed clumsily for a few moments, but had to make do with platitudes.

'I'm a little tired', 'I really do need a break', 'Arthur's very busy', 'It's absolutely nothing'.

From which the first lieutenant deduced that her friend's husband was having an affair with a woman in Gibraltar. She resolved to rally the ladies immediately, which would require considerable making of phone calls and considerable wagging of her considerable chin.

That evening Mrs Prior-Pointment was calmer.

Cold even.

She spent the evening in the drawing room with

Mother who seemed to have detected something and was giving the daughter-in-law occasional malevolent sideways glances. Munch munch, munch munch.

This was nothing more than the old woman's usual habit, but there was something irritating about her tonight. The shrivelled old woman, sunk in tartan, seemed particularly pathetic.

Annoying.

Why?

Was this how she would end up herself?

A useless burden?

No.

Poor Mother. It wasn't her fault. She wasn't a burden.

She was Family.

The phone rang.

The good woman answered it in the other room.

'Mrs Prior-Pointment?'

'. . . Yes?'

It was a man.

He was very impertinent.

She couldn't quite take it in. Some accountant. Eddie Someone. About her husband's investments in Gibraltar. He demanded to meet with her urgently. What did it have to do with her? He would explain what it had to do with her when he saw her face to face.

Her heart was still in her throat when she replaced the receiver and returned to watch television in the crypt.

She didn't like the sound of this Eddie who-ever-he-was.

What on earth was going on.

Gibraltar?

*A*s the tranquillisers administered by Edith had worn off, so the temperature at *Newfoundland* had risen.

With rotund, organisational support from Rose, Miranda went to work with those residents who under the old regime had mummified. She walked them, coaxed them, sympathised with them, bullied them and tended to their needs until they were comparatively gymnastic.

Without drug-induced comas to keep them going, the demons Bed-wetting and Incontinence almost died out completely.

One or two of the residents suffered unpleasant withdrawal symptoms but quickly recovered their spirits as their general health improved. Residents long thought to be senile were now chatting happily away and getting about (albeit shakily).

It was a bit like the last scene of Sleeping Beauty, only more chaotic.

And there was no handsome Prince.

And the food wasn't as good.

And they didn't have most of their lives ahead of them.

But at least they could remember the past more clearly.

Recovery wasn't universal, but even the worst cases seemed improved. Perhaps it was just the jolly atmosphere.

What was universal was the way the residents took to Miranda with her unruly sense of humour and laughing eyes. They all wanted to confide in her and spoil her with little gifts, bony squeezes of the hand, conspiratorial winks and smiles.

They were all waiting in the morning room for a residents meeting to begin, when Mrs Crotchley confided her secret of thirty years.

84

Mrs Crotchley was explaining to Miranda (for the third time that week) that she was used to higher standards, that in the old days she had been the Company Secretary at the Prior-Pointment factory, and that really and truly she had expected more from *Newfoundland*. But all things considered she was too old now to move, so she had resigned herself to her poor station and the inferior society.

Miranda was nodding and smiling and hardly listening when the old woman pursed her bitter-thin lips, drew herself closer and let out her 'little secret'.

'You mustn't tell anybody. It's not something I've publicised. In fact, nobody knows at all. Not a soul.' Here the old woman looked over her shoulder furtively. 'I'm a Prior-Pointment myself, dear.'

'A what?'

'A Prior-Pointment.'

'What's a one of them?'

'It's my maiden name. Surely you've heard of them dear? As in "Prior-Pointment", the firm I told you about – where I was Company Secretary?'

'Oh,' said Miranda vaguely.

Lilly was calling for Miranda to go over to her where she sat towering head and shoulders above the now shrunken Edith.

Mrs Crotchley ignored Lilly, 'My father owned the company,' she went on.

Miranda said, 'Oh,' again.

Lilly wasn't giving up. 'Don't get her too excited! She might strip off and start cavorting again!' she shouted.

Mrs Crotchley looked peeved. She held on to Miranda's arm and said, 'Don't say a word, dear.'

Lilly was in a wicked mood and told Miranda, when she finally got away from Mrs Crotchley, that in the old days when Lilly had worked at the Prior-Pointment's factory, Mrs Crotchley had skulked in the little upstairs office, looking down her nose at all and sundry, never having a kind word to say of anyone.

Miranda asked, 'If she was Company Secretary what's she doing in a place like this? I mean . . .'

'Company Secretary! Her! She was nothing more than a miserable typist,' said Lilly. 'And I'll tell you what, it was a disgrace. She's a Prior-Pointment herself – her father owned the company, but because she was only the daughter of the family she never got a penny. She was just expected to marry herself off.'

Miranda looked across at Mrs Crotchley who was fussing over her little dog.

Lilly went on, sounding outraged on Mrs Crotchley's behalf: 'When her husband was killed in the war they gave her a job as a typist. She was so ashamed she never told anyone she was a part of the old family. She was paid a pittance too. Everyone knows she had to scrimp and save. "Genteel poverty" some people call it. Poverty's poverty, I always said.'

'Poor thing,' said Miranda.

'Oh, they bring it on themselves. She was snooty to us all her life. She could've made friends with us, but she preferred to look down her nose.'

Lilly groped round the table for her cup of tea and knocked in onto the floor.

'Why do you pretend you can see?' Miranda asked her.

'Oo, they'd have me out of here before you could say "guide dog" if they knew,' said the huge old woman gaily.

'Everybody knows!'

'Nonsense. It's a secret,' laughed Lilly. 'Nobody knows I'm blind, do they?' she asked of the general assembly.

One or two of the residents nodded their heads doubtfully, one or two others giggled.

'You wouldn't get me out of here. Not unless you had a bloody pulley that could lift two tons.' Here

86

Lilly leaned over to Edith who was always at her right hand these days and spoke into her hearing aid. 'I said, No one's moving me out of here unless they've got a pulley that can lift two tons . . .'

Edith giggled. And coughed.

'You could get help,' said Miranda.

'I don't want help, thank-you-very-much.' Lilly was indignant. 'It's not as bad as you think, going blind. I mean, if you looked like me, would *you* miss looking in the mirror!'

For the third time since they'd met, the enormous old woman, sombre now, recounted the misfortunes she'd survived over the years. Her husband crippled in the war; her two daughter's emigrating (one of them only as far as Luton); her youngest girl run over by a tanker that went out of control in the street where they lived; and her only son shot in Ireland in '72.

'I've already died three times over,' Lilly said and Miranda gave her hand a squeeze. 'I even forgot how to laugh for a few years.'

There was more: 'Here, give me you hand.' Lilly was grinning again now. 'I've got a plate in the side of my head, feel it? And a plastic hip. And I've got pins in my knees. And I'm *covered* in scars from my operations – hernia, gall stones, hysterectomy . . .'

Miranda said, 'You're the bionic woman.'

At which – even though she'd never heard of the bionic woman – Lilly let out a great, jolly laugh and nudged Edith who, when she'd recovered from the blow, whooped and put her hand over her mouth, even though she hadn't heard a thing.

Jed was staying in bed later and later in the mornings.

He heard Charity slam the front door, start the car and then listened to her drive off with some satisfaction.

He settled back down under the covers and let the thought of Miranda seep into his still sleepy mind.

There was a knock at the front door.

He answered it in his dressing gown.

It was Miranda.

'Hiya. Has she gone?'

'You've just missed her.'

'I was gonna get a lift. But I'll just have to come in for a coffee and be late instead, won't I?'

They went into the kitchen.

He sat at the solid wooden table, she leaned against the working top with the sun shining straight through the window, making a halo of her hair.

After a few minutes of talk and coffee-making, Miranda sighed. The words she spoke were very carefully worked out:

'You know what would be ideal? What would be ideal is a man who was already "tied up". Because he wouldn't demand too much of me. He'd be a bit older because then he'd get really horny if a young woman offered herself to him – and he'd know how to satisfy me. Preferably he'd be married to make it even safer for me. I'd come and go as I pleased, calling him up occasionally, whenever I wanted uncomplicated sex and we'd do it during the day so we wouldn't have to do all that waking up in the morning together shit. I'd come. And I'd go.'

Jed was nearly coming.

Then she slowly took off all her clothes. Right there in the kitchen, instructing him to look at her while she did so. When she was naked she stretched her arms up luxuriously and said: 'Now you tell me what to do,' and Jed was on the very verge when the phone rang and his train of thought was disturbed.

Shit. His fantasy was ruined. He was back in the bedroom, alone with his troubles. He threw back the bed covers and trudged to the phone.

It was a surprise.

'Eddie, you're back! Where the fuck have you been?'

'Have I woken you up? Some of us have been at it for hours.'

'No, no, I've been up for ages.'

'Look, I'm at my office. I need you to get down here as soon as you can. Could you come immediately?'

'Huh. Very likely.'

'You're out of breath, what's wrong?'

Despite being alone, Jed blushed. 'Er, nothing, I'm fine.'

'You won't be when I've finished with you.'

'What do you mean?'

'Just get down here.'

'Are you in trouble again?'

'No mate, I'm in the clear.'

'What then?'

Eddie's voice was strangely urgent. 'I'm waiting.'

'OK.'

*C*harity was there.

'What! . . .'

Jesus, they're having an affair.

Eddie pointed at a chair. Next to Charity.

Jed tried to stop his voice wobbling. 'What's going on?'

'Sit down, mate.'

Jed looked at his wife, but she was made of marble. He throbbed with jealousy.

Eddie opened a drawer in his desk and took out a letter.

'What's that?'

'It's the end of world as you know it.'

There was still no response from the statue of Charity.

'Stop fucking around.'

'The bank have recalled your loan.'

Jed blinked. He knew what that meant. Which was the end of the world as he knew it.

Eddie opened the letter and quoted: 'Dear slippery customer, you're broke!'

'Fuck off, give it here.'

The spell was broken, Charity stood up and spoke. 'For God's sake Jed!'

'What?' Jed was trying to read the letter.

'You're bankrupt! You've been bankrupt for months!'

'Only now it's official,' put in Eddie.

Charity was pacing the length of Eddie's gaudy metal blinds.

'I'm not bankrupt – things could pick up.'

'Not now the bank have pulled out, mate. It's impossible.'

Jed took this in for a few moments while his teeth chattered to themselves.

'Why didn't you tell me?' Charity said.

'I told you things were difficult!'

Jed glared at Eddie, his eyes saying, 'What the fuck is *she* doing here?' He didn't say it out loud, because it was an equal and open relationship and they had no secrets from one another.

Eddie shrugged. 'You wouldn't listen.'

'He never listens.' Charity again.

Jed's arm, with the letter at the end of it, flopped into his lap. That was enough. This was what he'd been waiting for. 'I want my money Eddie. Today!'

Eddie opened his drawer again, took out an envelope and threw it onto the desk with a disdainful flourish.

Jed opened it. It was was some kind of document.

'?'

'The document verifies the loss of your forty grand. It states that the whole thing crashed. There's nothing

90

left of it. The bail thing was just a cover, mate. I was trying to buy time . . .'

There was a pain in Jed's toes as his feelings tried to flee. They must have bounced back up his legs causing him to stand up.

Before he knew where he was Jed was shouting abuse and squirting tears over Eddie's shiny black desk top.

He really let go.

It all came out, while Charity watched in amazement.

Everything from Eddie trying to fuck his wife and being a miserable, drug-riddled dirty old man that no woman ever stayed with longer than two months, to the time Eddie borrowed a fiver off him and never paid him back, despite his supposed riches and so-called financial sagacity.

He went red in the face and cursed and swore and snot came out of his nose and he didn't wipe it away. He even kicked Eddie's desk, nearly breaking his toe.

It took a full minute-and-a-half of lyrical retching before he realised that Eddie had taken another envelope (a large jiffy bag) out of his drawer and was waiting to hand it to him.

Panting, Jed slumped miserably back into his chair. Eddie threw the envelope into his lap and Jed opened it sulkily.

As he did so hundreds of wads of notes tumbled out.

Eddie said, 'Fifty-five thousand pounds. Cash. Used notes. All yours.'

As he handled the bundles, Jed could hardly take in the meaning of what was being explained to him by Eddie and Charity.

It had been inevitable that he would have to declare himself bankrupt.

He would not, as a bankrupt, be able to trade for two years.

Eddie had seen it coming for a long time.

91

The money would not have held off the creditors for more than a month or two and it would have been swallowed up with his other assets.

The document stating that his money was lost was legal, at least as far as creditors were concerned. Other than that it was a fraud. But safe.

Eddie had despaired of getting Jed to see reason and had approached Charity to see what she thought.

She had agreed with his plans, wholeheartedly.

Throughout the exposition Jed burned with embarrassment. All he could think of were the insults he had heaped on his friend. He was grateful Eddie didn't mention any of it.

As he listened he pulled himself together.

During a pause in the narrative, in which Jed became aware that he was supposed to say something he muttered an 'I'm sorry – I didn't mean it, I . . .' and shrugged.

Eddie could afford to be generous. 'Most of it was true, mate, I'm a thoroughly despicable character. But I've got your best interests at heart.'

Jed was crushed by the magnanimity.

Eddie said, 'Blow your nose on a twenty-pound note and forget it.'

Jed grinned stupidly and looked at Charity.

'We'd have lost the house,' she said. 'We still might.'

'She's right, Jed.'

A vision of frills, fringes and flounce danced before his eyes.

He almost laughed, but shook his head instead. 'Sorry, I just wasn't expecting to go bankrupt when I woke up this morning.'

'I dunno why not,' said Eddie.

They sat there for a few moments.

Then Eddie went over to the blinds, let in some daylight and said, 'Right, that's the easy bit over with, shall we tell him the rest?'

Charity returned to stone.

*R*ose came into the morning room, bustled importantly and clapped her hands. It was time for the resident's meeting to begin.

'Come along ladies,' Rose sang. 'And we *are* all ladies in this house, aren't we?'

'More's the shame,' shouted Lilly, 'I miss a bit of nookie.'

Mrs Crotchley blenched at this. 'Language, Lilly, really! Let's at least preserve a minimum of decorum.'

'Oh! Listen to the streaker everyone . . .'

Rose began organising people.

When she saw Miranda chuckling away with Lilly, Rose called to her and, with a wink, firmly patted the chair she had placed next to her own. The old trade unionist was jealous of Lilly's friendship with the young newcomer, whom Rose looked upon as her comrade in the struggle to organise life at *Newfoundland*.

Miranda gave Lilly's hand a final squeeze and joined in the preparations, largely a matter of moving chairs around and pouring tea.

There was a near disaster with the teapot as Lilly, in combination with Edith and Mrs M, blundered into the coffee table.

Lilly had lately formed an alliance with Edith and Mrs M. (Mrs M had returned from hospital now with her foot in a big clean bandage and her head in heaven.)

The three women all had mobility problems: Edith's legs seemed to have failed altogether since her shock over Mrs M's foot; Mrs M was wheelchair-bound; Lilly was blind.

So Edith would clutch at the handles of Mrs M's wheelchair to steer while Lilly took her arm, whereupon the three became one moving unit.

And woe betide anyone who got in their way – or woe betide their shins.

'See no evil, hear no evil, speak no evil,' joked Lilly about herself, Edith and Mrs M, just before they crashed into the table and nearly upset the teapot.

When she was feeling cheerful Mrs Crotchley referred to the trio as 'The Terrible Trinity'. When she wasn't she just muttered miserably to Tinkerbell about some residents being more suited to geriatric units.

'Pull yourselves together everyone!' Rose huffed. 'This is *not* the Christmas whist drive! . . .'

In the new atmosphere the retired trade unionist found she was no longer master of the situation. Chaos ruled, meetings were nigh on impossible to organise, the whole democratic structure of residents meetings, painstakingly nurtured by Rose over time, seemed likely to collapse under the strain of the new 'sobriety'.

Rose wondered sometimes whether things had been pushed too far and perhaps residents were better off drugged up after all.

But no, the struggle had to go on.

Rose climbed unsteadily onto a chair and shouted to get attention:

'Ladies! I think you're all being *very rude indeed*. This is the first time we've ever had a member of staff at one of our meetings (here she nodded proudly at Miranda) and I think we should demonstrate some basic common decency.'

'That'll be the day, won't it Tink?' said Mrs Crotchley to her dog who had just lifted his leg against the chair.

Rose's pronouncement did have some effect. Mainly it embarrassed people. Within a few moments a degree of order was achieved and the meeting was able to begin.

When Miranda had been formally introduced and the minutes of the previous meeting read, Rose began the meeting proper with a specially prepared announcement: 'I suppose you all know *Newfoundland* is to close, shortly.'

As a dramatic device it worked a treat.

Even Lilly was stuck for words. All you could hear was the plop of a pair of false teeth as they fell from someone's gums.

Rose was exaggerating. She had learned from Miranda that the government had set up a body locally to oversee the privatisation of Elderly Services in the area. Rose said she was determined to use the news to 'knock some sense into them'.

Miranda was about to say something when Rose winked slyly at her causing her to sit back in her chair in amused bewilderment.

Only Mrs Crotchley seemed unmoved. Her look of cynical resignation was the same as always.

Rose allowed time for the implications of her announcement to sink in: that what residents needed most of all under the circumstances was firm and experienced leadership to guide them and regular, well-organised meetings to keep up with developments.

With her arms folded militantly under her bosom Rose was about to speak, to explain the real situation, when Lilly beat her to it, speaking and acting at the same moment:

'Right, well we'll have to do something about it then won't we!' As she spoke Lilly gave Edith a shove, to stand her up. 'I said, we'll have to do something before it's too late, dear!' she said into Edith's hearing aid. 'Come on everybody, we're not going to take this lying down!'

Edith clutched at the handles of Mrs M's wheelchair. Lilly was up.

For a few crucial seconds Rose was dumbstruck.

'We're right behind you Lilly,' shouted one of the women as everyone else stood up. They had no idea where they were going, but there was a feeling of going to do something important, so they began to gather up their handbags and cardigans and to follow as The Terrible Trinity blundered towards the door.

The residents had been angry for some time over the drain of meagre resources from the centre; they had simply been too drugged up to express it. Rose's over-dramatisation of the danger had been unnecessary in the present atmosphere. She realised her error too late:

'Ladies! Ladies I think you may have misunderstood – we need to do some *talking*.'

'*Talking*? What's the use in *talking*?' Lilly shouted, 'We want to be *doing* something. Come on everybody. We'll give *them* something to talk about.'

It was hopeless; Rose couldn't make herself heard over the clatter.

One or two of the livelier residents were doing an impromptu (if unsteady) hokey-cokey and people were talking, shouting and laughing all at once. Only Lilly, being the centre of attention, could make herself heard.

'Miranda you'd better get those folding chairs from the store-room – and someone had better get hold of the press, we're going to give them something to report.'

Rose saw her last opportunity to influence the course of events and seized it. '*I'll* deal with the press! (Goodness me.)'

As people left the room Mrs Crotchley approached Rose with a look of indignation that made her usual sour expression seem like a state of quasi-religious ecstasy. 'I really must protest in the strongest terms, stirring up trouble like this! You'll make matters worse and cause trouble for everyone.'

Rose was thunderstruck. Her confusion vanished. In the face of Mrs Crotchley's conservatism Rose found herself gripped by the clenched fist of revolt. She puffed to her full inflation and laughed in Mrs Crotchley's face. It came out as 'Harrumph!'

However, Mrs Crotchley's conservatism wasn't going to be repressed by a simple harrumph. 'You know very

96

well the centre isn't going to be shut down. It's simply a matter of a change of management . . .'

'My *dear*, the local authority are about to hand over the care of our lives to some unscrupulous businessman who'll squeeze every penny out of us he can!'

'That is not the same thing as the centre closing down,' insisted Mrs Crotchley with relentless logic.

But Rose was glad of the opportunity to air the rhetoric she'd prepared for the ill-fated meeting. 'And what may I ask do you think will happen when the business fails to make a profit?'

'Pshht,' was the best reply to that. Followed by, 'I think you're just causing a lot of trouble for your own reasons. As usual.'

It was a fine debate and, as there was some truth on both sides and the outcome would make little difference to the course of events, both women knew there was little point in continuing it any further.

So with a simultaneous *harumph* and *pshht* they went their separate ways.

Miranda came up to Rose with a grin. 'You did say you wanted to galvanise them into action.'

'Yes, dear, but I didn't want to start a revolution!'

*E*ddie said, 'So how are you going to spend the loot?' and winked at Charity.

Jed said, 'I'm going to hire a decent accountant.'

'You're going to need one.' Eddie took a passport from his inside pocket. He grinned at the look on Jed's face. 'You know I've always enjoyed shocking you.'

'You're having a field day.'

'Guess what?'

Jed was on the ball. 'You're doing a runner.'

'Correct.'

Jed was still shocked though.

'But – what about . . . (?)'

He didn't need to name them. The house, the business.

Eddie was nonchalant. 'Take a look at the passport,' he said, sliding it across the shiny, black desk.

It said, Doctor Nicholas Divine. '*Doctor*?'

'An old doctor friend of mine's starting a new life – gave me his old one.'

'He looks just like you.'

'It *is* me you dickhead! It's a forgery. His passport, my photo.'

'Who did that for you?'

Eddie sighed and looked at Charity. One of her eyebrows shut Jed up.

So he sat back in the black leather chair, sinking lower and lower as he listened. He wanted to interrupt and ask all sorts of stupid questions, but decided against it.

Eddie *was* in trouble. The game in this country was up. Eddie was 'taking the rap' for a number of mysterious people who would 'see him alright'. Everything in Gibraltar was safe, but the British operation was being abandoned.

At the end of it Jed said, 'I'm sorry.'

'What for?'

'Well. For you.'

Eddie laughed. 'Don't worry about me, mate. I'll be fine.' Jed must have looked doubtful because Eddie said: 'You're the one who's in the shit, not me. I'll have an extremely healthy bank balance at the end of it.'

Jed was stunned. 'But . . . you'll be . . . well . . . an outlaw . . .'

'So bloody what! At least I'll retire on a decent pension.'

'I don't call sneaking out of the country on a false passport "retiring on a decent pension"!'

98

'I do,' said Charity.

Jed turned on her at last. 'Oh I can really see you in a mud hut in South America! I don't think they have Laura Ashley out there.'

Charity ignored him.

'I think they do actually, mate. It won't be South America, either. And it certainly won't be a mud hut.'

Jed was choked with resentment.

Eddie was right. It was him who was in the shit.

He'd done everything the way he should have – legally.

All those hours of honest travail.

All that stress.

Eddie was just a common crook. Possibly a drug addict.

Jed was struck by a thought. He brandished one of the bundles of notes.

'Tell me honestly. Where did you get this money?'

'It's safe. It's not connected with all – with my trouble.'

'I said where did you get it? What was it invested in?'

Eddie looked at Charity.

She nodded.

Eddie sighed, deeply.

Jed said, 'It's drugs, isn't it?'

'No, mate.'

'What's all this looking at each other – there's something going on.'

'True, but it's not drugs.'

Charity said, 'It's been invested in some fairly unsavoury third world situations, that's all.'

'How unsavoury?'

'Oh you know, mate, the usual: death squads, political prisoners, that sort of thing.'

'We didn't think you'd approve,' put in Charity.

'I don't,' said Jed. 'Which countries, exactly?'

'The worst we could find.'

Eddie had to explain to Jed the first rule of foreign investment: the more horrendous the regime concerned, the greater the return on capital.

'Where the hell else are you going to more than double your money in six months?'

Jed eyed the money on the table, half expecting to see it dripping with blood.

Charity found the carpet very interesting for a while.

Eddie was defiant. 'Wait until you hear what your wife's got planned.'

'Oh, you've got it all worked out have you?'

Charity looked guilty. Eddie said. 'Yeah man.'

'We've looked into it carefully,' Charity said.

'What, since this morning?'

'We've been looking at it for a few weeks.' It was as if Charity was trying to tell him something with her hooded eyes.

Eddie said, 'We've sorted out some of the finer details this week.'

Jed was doubly puzzled. 'You've been away . . .'

Eddie was shaking his head.

Shit. He hadn't been away, he'd been spending time with Charity behind his back. There was ozone depletion and acid rain in Jed's stomach as he prepared an unfeeling face to receive the details of the plot. He chewed his lips as he waited.

Charity hesitated.

'Just take a deep breath and let it all out in one,' Eddie advised. 'I'll help.'

She did. Jed made fine adjustments to his expression as they went on.

'We buy *Newfoundland* when it comes up for privatisation . . .'

'Which is now . . .' said Eddie.

'And we run it as a business . . .'

'You even get to work there as a paid employee . . .'

'The figures are good, Jed.'

'They're very good, mate.'

100

'We'll actually be better off than we've ever been . . .'

The thing was, both Charity and Eddie knew that there was probably only one thing Jed hated more than the Royal Family and modern architecture – apart from his home town and Laura Ashley shops – and that was privatisation. Which accounted for the feeling the conspirators had that the poor bankrupt man might explode at any moment.

But as the two of them spluttered through their plan, Jed rather surprisingly found himself drawn to the idea.

It was entirely against his principles, of course. Possibly it was against any kind of common sense too, but . . .

There was a thought hanging there amongst the feelings of repulsion and humiliation, one that was hard to bring entirely into focus amid the chaos of his thinking – not because of its complexity, but rather because of its terrible and childish simplicity. He tried not to let it come into his mind.

He drew on the objections and concentrated on his resentment.

But, no matter what, the rogue notion continued to excite his intelligence. Or his lack of it.

It was this: Miranda.

Who worked at the centre where he might even get to 'work as a paid employee'.

It was ridiculous, he reflected, to be sitting there thinking, albeit vaguely and in no way seriously, that it would be a grand thing if he ended up as Miranda's employer, and even better, working there with her every day.

The whole thing was ludicrous.

'You wouldn't even get the kitchens for fifty grand,' he said suddenly. 'The building itself's worth a fortune.'

The conspirators, surprised that Jed was entertaining the idea at all, looked at one another, conspiratorially.

101

Eddie said, 'The authority will look at your – or rather, your wife's – application in a favourable light.'

'They'll make special arrangements for us,' Charity added.

Jed decided not to be surprised anymore.

But he couldn't help being angry, because he'd been tricked.

He huffed and puffed and tried to feel solid, dependable indignation. He wanted a pure, simple feeling to combat the crumbling inside.

Eddie said, 'It's one of the best business opportunities I've ever come across in this country. It's happening everywhere; you've got to get in there while you can.'

'Surely they'll get a better offer if it's that good,' Jed said.

'They'll accept your offer.'

'What makes you so sure?'

Jed detected more signs of plotting. There was a rat sniffing away on the corner of Eddie's desk, next to the executive *Game Boy*.

'Come on, what's going on?'

Eddie shuffled on his chair.

Charity said, 'The woman in charge of the sale of Elderly Services owes Eddie a favour.'

'It's down to her, mate. It's the way they do things these days. It's pretty corrupt really . . .'

'But legal,' Charity added. 'It's her decision at the end of the day.'

'What – sort of favour does she owe you?'

Eddie was deadpan. 'Her husband has certain business interests in Gibraltar. Corrupt ones.'

'It's Mrs Prior-Pointment, Jed,' Charity said.

'What! . . .'

There was probably only Mrs Prior-Pointment herself who had been more shocked than Jed by the news that her husband was involved in shady business ventures in Gibraltar when Eddie who-ever-he-was had taken the trouble to inform her of it.

102

'She doesn't want to drop her husband in it.' Eddie said. 'I think she loves him very much.'

Although he didn't know her personally Jed was Mrs Prior-Pointment's most fervent adversary, at least in word. Jed considered her the most despicable, vile and obnoxious specimen ever to have crawled out from behind an oversize posy of pampas grass and had spent many a local news broadcast pacing the front room cursing her and her party and the petti-fogging bourgeois values she and her party espoused. To hear him you might have thought that she had personally engineered his having chosen, against his better judgement, to become a business man in a smug Northern seaside resort instead of a bohemian revolutionary in Paris in the 1930s – or that she had personally decorated their house.

Any Socialist at Heart would rejoice to discover that such a woman – the doyenne of decency, the decorative symbol of respectability, the mascot, the edging and flounce of the enemy – was worm-eaten and rotten like the rest of them.

It was like a libertine discovering that Queen Victoria enjoyed taking it from behind while her husband went down on Gladstone and Disreali.

Not every Socialist at Heart would have been able to justify using the discovery to take over a state-owned service so as to run it as a business and spend more time in the company of a young woman he found fascinating, however. And to his credit, Jed didn't do so himself, immediately.

For now he sat there with an inane grin, causing the two plotters to believe that they had won.

Eddie said, 'It's every mother for himself out there, mate.'

 *T*hey took Eddie straight from his office to the airport in Charity's Mini.

Eddie and Charity sat in the front chatting, Jed stained the seat in the back with dank, dribbling resentment. On his knee, the money in his brief-case hummed a sickeningly beguiling melody.

At the flight check-in one of Eddie's goodbyes was awkward, the other wasn't.

Jed didn't know what to say goodbye-wise. 'Good luck,' sounded lame as it came out.

Eddie said 'Come 'ere!' pulled him forward to give him a hug, but Jed didn't know how and sort of held his head away feeling stiff and ungainly.

'Be brave, man,' grinned Eddie, shaking Jed gently.

'Umm.'

Jed and Charity had the number of another account-ant who would help them if they 'made the right decision' about *Newfoundland*. All they had to do was give him the word.

'Do the right thing, mate.'

'You mean the wrong thing.'

Eddie winked.

Then Eddie and Charity stood facing each other, their hands joined. Charity looked very sad and said, 'Thanks for everything,' and shook his two hands, adding a 'really, I mean it'. Then she kissed his lips and gave him a hearty hug.

Jed hated Eddie then. It wasn't jealousy, it was more all-encompassing than that.

Jed had taken the honest path and failed. Fucked up. Been humiliated by his best friend and his wife.

Eddie was the Scarlet Pimpernel.

'Send us a postcard, won't you,' Jed mumbled unskilfully, trying to break up the cosy twosome.

Then Eddie was gone. For good.

*   *   *

Charity suggested lunch somewhere near home.

Jed slumped in the passenger seat.

Neither of them said a word, which choked Jed up some more.

He felt pathetic. He was embarrassed at his earlier outburst and ashamed that he was considered incapable of conducting his own affairs sensibly.

He couldn't look out of the window directly for fear of looking like he was sulking and he couldn't look at his wife for fear that he would be utterly revolted by her, or, which was worse, that she would read his mind from the look in his eye.

So he stared ahead and indulged in glorious self-pity. He swam in swamps and crawled through slime-filled ditches. He ate worms and lashed himself with a thousand reproaches, telling himself he'd got his just desserts, that he should have known it was much better to break the law and invest in unsavoury regimes. How foolish he'd been to imagine that honesty paid off in this world.

He didn't indulge in gluttony over the fifty-five grand for fear of sobering the comforting drunkenness of his misery.

At the end of this dark tunnel of wounded vanity was a tiny pinhole of light which grew in intensity as he raged against Fate and Society.

As it grew he became all the more ashamed of himself. How pathetic a man he was to be thinking that among all this ruin he might soon be spending time in the company of an impossibly attractive young woman whom he didn't stand a chance of . . .

They were nearing *Newfoundland* now as they made their way into town. The mile after mile of silence had become unbearable. Jed wanted to break it. The problem was that someone had bricked up his wind-pipe. He attempted to say 'Where shall we go then?' but accidentally said: 'I'm sorry,' and shrugged helplessly, adding, 'I really don't know what to say.'

105

Charity said, 'How about telling me you still love me?'

Jed was saved from having to formulate a reply to this by a disturbance of some kind on the road up ahead, just outside, or so it seemed, *Newfoundland*.

'What's going on?' Charity said while Jed breathed a sigh of relief.

A line of cars had stopped and there were people in the road. Quite a few of them by the looks of things.

When the traffic had finished shunting and everyone had moved up as far as possible so that they were only a few inches from the car in front and it was impossible for anyone to turn round anymore, Jed and Charity joined the other curious onlookers who were getting out of their vehicles to see just what the bloody hell was going on.

Jed and Charity were probably only marginally more surprised than everyone else to see that the cause of the jam was a crowd of elderly people sitting on collapsible chairs in the middle of the road singing *We Shall Not Be Moved*.

'It's the residents!' said Charity whose first thought, which caused her to run on ahead, was that one of them had perhaps been run over.

It was a demonstration.

Jed realised it as he approached. He could see a couple of placards made out of broom handles and old crutches. 'No privatisation', one said, 'No sell-out' another.

(Rose had hastily made up the placards so as to give the demonstration some real meaning after her exaggeration.)

Jed smiled at the irony, had somebody tipped them off about Charity's plans? Did everyone in the world know? Had he merely been the last to know? He also smiled because he'd just caught sight of Miranda stand-ing to one side chatting with a very crotchety-looking old woman who was holding a small dog in her arms, shaking her head in ostentatious disapproval of the scene in the road.

Miranda looked as if she was having a grand old time.

Some photographer was there taking photographs and . . .

Then he recognised the journalist that was with him. It was the sound of her that did it. Sounded like she was laughing at some dirty joke

A her her her!

Jed froze then burrowed behind one of the cars. He had to pretend to tie his shoe-lace to cover his skulking.

He was still a little distance away, but there was no mistaking her. Virginia. What the fuck? . . .

A her her her *hurr*.

He turned about face and marched straight back to the car.

Jesus, what happens if Charity talks to her!

He dived into the front seat and crouched there like a frightened rabbit.

 *W*hile Mrs Bullmore and Mrs Strutting rallied the ladies' caucus in support of Mrs Prior-Pointment – which involved making a lot of phone calls to let every-one know that Arthur was in some sort of trouble and that the marriage was on the rocks – Mrs Prior-Pointment herself seemed mysteriously to blossom.

Arthur had (or so he said) gone to the Canaries and returned to Gibraltar and then returned to the Canaries and then returned to Gibraltar and then flown to Jersey and gone from there to the Canaries for a few days and then returned to Gibraltar.

Next Thursday had turned into *the following Thursday without fail*, which in its turn had become *any day now* for a fortnight, then *positively next Thursday without fail*, for nearly a month.

Twice, she'd phoned the travel agents for a flight. But twice, reason had prevailed.

She had her work.

And she knew now, from Eddie who-ever-he-was, that Arthur had made mistakes. As such he needed her now more than ever.

Poor Arthur had got himself into a spot of bother and had bravely sheltered the family. He must have been worried that she would desert him in his hour of need. She bitterly regretted her attitude on the phone after discovering the letter. He was a good man after all and a good husband.

The faithful wife took a good look at herself and her life and her marriage.

She returned in her mind to the early days and replayed the scenes of their courtship. How surprised she had been that Arthur had shown an interest in her. How flattered. How he seemed to understand, even admire her. How he made everyone laugh. How she had longed for him to come and see her.

How young they had been.

She remembered the first kisses.

The long walks and confidences.

Looking back even the weather seemed to have been better – they were kinder brighter days.

She remembered how one night at the tennis club he had taken hold of her hand and asked her to marry him. How handsome he had seemed in the red glow of the evening sun, as she remembered it.

She had loved him then with a girlish longing.

How shy she had felt. How scared she had been of him as a man. How powerful he seemed. How she wanted to give herself to him, yet feared it too, lived in terrible, heart-warming dread of the first night.

And then how kind he had been. How loving. And gentle. And patient. And firm. How beautifully it had turned out. How surprised she was at her own pleasure.

She adored him then with womanly ardour. How passionate they had been. How he taught her, awakened in her an interest in the world. They had gone everywhere together, read the same books and joined the Party, spending the long summer evenings together at the tennis club. Mixed doubles champions, 1957.

How pleased she had been that she was pregnant.

Then the children.

And Arthur's work.

(And his drinking.)

And his friends.

Then later, her work. Her charity work. The children growing up.

Somehow they had drifted. Slowly but surely it had all changed and they had become separate people leading separate lives. That too had seemed natural enough. Their duty, surely, to the family.

When the children had gone, she'd looked after Arthur's mother. Willingly, of course – dutifully.

But it was the early days that occupied the dreamer now.

The love and the closeness.

The passion.

To avoid the present, she roamed the plains of the past, searching for something long lost, feeling it as a loss.

She looked at herself in the mirror. How athletic she had been as a girl and as a young woman. She looked for the change and told herself it was superficial.

The longing for him to return to England was the longing to feel her old love and security.

As she waited for Arthur's return, she began to ache with a desire that quite startled her and coloured her nostalgia still further (not to mention her cheeks).

She lay awake at night and found herself revisiting intimate scenes from their past, passionate scenes so vivid and close that at times they made her tummy thump.

She went shopping for new clothes – something a little more elegant – and spent at least an hour choosing new lingerie. She flushed at the counter and left her credit card behind. Then she was called back. The woman said she had forgotten to remove the security tag and took the lingerie out of the bag to check. Mrs Prior-Pointment had the uncomfortable feeling that a man who was waiting in the queue said something to his wife about her. It was only a pair of silk camiknickers (with pretty lace and matching underskirt – very expensive). Was he laughing at her?

Was she being ridiculous?

Of course not. No.

Nevertheless she went back the next day and bought something slightly more conservative, plus a new negligee just in case, and spent a couple of days trying out the various items in front of the bedroom mirror, wavering between them according to her nerve.

The biggest change was to her spirits.

Despite the worry over Arthur's mistakes her spirits soared.

He was having difficulties in Gibraltar and it was obvious that his shielding of the family accounted for his strange behaviour and his to-ing and fro-ing from the Canaries. Her original suspicions (though understandable) had been silly and girlish.

She went for jaunts along the seafront when she wasn't working in the day and once or twice wrapped Mother in a few extra blankets and pushed her silently down the promenade to the old pier where the old matriarch would munch out at the estuary.

Waiting, waiting.

Mrs Prior-Pointment's work was dispensed with firmly

and efficiently, with a flourish even. Especially after the furore surrounding the demonstration.

Committees, known as quangos, had been set up by the government to sell off public concerns and oversee the running of the remaining services. Mrs Prior Pointment's quango was a fine outstanding example of such a committee.

The wily old politician had absolute power to hire and fire members, decide who to consult in matters of public concern, administer the budget, prepare the accounts and most important of all, had the power to decide her own salary and that of everybody else on the committee.

Yet, despite these democratic safeguards of her right to do whatever she (or the Party) wanted, Mrs Prior-Pointment was still concerned about the possibility of unnecessary and unwelcome attention being paid to the sale – made public by the demonstration – of *Newfoundland*.

She soon saw that the situation could be turned to her advantage.

She would make a spectacle of selling off *Newfoundland* to the existing staff, portraying it as a typical case of Government and therefore Party benevolence.

She felt certain her committee would see things the way she did, particularly in view of the fact that all most of them had to do was turn up to a meeting once a fortnight and earn themselves £4,000 a year – and that the next two most senior posts were occupied by Mrs Bullmore and Mrs Strutting.

Arthur announced that he was arriving Thursday.

On the phone Mrs Prior-Pointment, while trying to be warm and loving – romantic even – found herself tongue-tied and tormented. She wanted to say 'I'm *so* looking forward to seeing you darling, I've missed you terribly', and, 'What do you say we have

111

a candle-lit dinner for two at home (I'm sure Mother will understand)'.

Instead she said, 'At long last,' in rather a chilly voice, and, 'What time's the flight?'

To which he replied, 'Don't be cross, darling. I told you I've been busy,' and 'I won't be in until late. I expect I'll be tired.'

She found herself suggesting he take an earlier flight and he had to remind her again that he was busy and that there were things to sort out before he left.

She said she'd meet him at the airport and he said, 'Don't bother dear, I'll get a taxi.' When she insisted he pointed out the possibility of delays. She said she didn't mind that, she'd be glad to get out of the house. He pointed out that Mother would be left alone. She reminded him that Mother was a big girl now and spent most days alone in the house and then, at last, she managed an 'I've missed you'.

At which he softened and said, 'Yes, well it would be nice to have someone help me find a trolley.'

So then she just had to wait two days.

She was amazed at the difficulty she'd experienced expressing herself. Why had she said 'at long last' like that? As if she were his mother.

She became nervous.

The romantic scenes she had envisaged were suddenly uncertain.

Her powerlessness in the face of his voice on the telephone only intensified her desire to be loved and, accompanied by a fear not of rejection, but of camaraderie, the yearning assumed terrible proportions, became involuntary, at times consumed her.

For two days her whole being hung in the balance waiting for acceptance or approval. She needed more than just his kindly smiles and joviality, his friendly familiarity and calm reassurance, his gentle mocking of her foibles; what she required, with her whole soul, was hot, passionate sex.

112

Mother seemed to sense something and observed the wife's nervy preparations with what looked like contempt. She munched at the to-ing and fro-ing and especially at the camiknickers when she caught sight of them amongst the washing. But she got a bath and a change of clothes and taken for walks to the pier and the mobile hairdresser came to do both their hair.

Somehow the time passed and as the crisis approached the good wife became calm. Or at least numb.

She took his car. He could drive back if he wanted to. She was determined not to fuss over him.

She heard him before she saw him, his deep voice booming happily and laughing easily with a couple he'd obviously met on the plane, his shining head standing out above the crush. His hand appeared in a merry wave and his teeth flashed white against his sun-tanned face.

Her own wave fluttered primly for a moment before it was checked.

He looked handsome and well. She felt that her smile was stiff and she was aware suddenly that she would have to find some way of not behaving formally. She felt self-conscious in front of all these people.

She froze. She had no idea how to play her role. The gestures with which she usually felt comfortable did nothing to express her feelings, which were new and unfamiliar. She was Pinocchio trapped in a wooden body.

Then he was standing in front of her.

He dropped his suitcase, smiled happily and took her in his arms, giving her a big, bold hug and held her there so that her reaction – or lack of reaction – was of no consequence, her feet were hardly touching the ground.

And still he held her in a gigantic bear-hug.

She was overcome. Her emotions welled up and tears came to her eyes. There was nothing for it but

113

to bury her head on his chest and wait for him to guide events.

She was a child in his arms.

She didn't fuss. He put his own suitcase on the trolley and they made their way to the car. He took the car keys without a word and chatted happily away. She was pleased that she didn't have to say much and when she did he listened carefully and attentively and she didn't feel formal or stiff at all. His presence was so grand she felt like a cheeky bird hitching a ride on the back of a sun-tanned hippopotamus.

In the dark, under the lights of the motorway, she almost vanished completely, felt like a gorgeous firefly speck in the vast conurbation stretching on into the night before them.

She wanted to kick off her shoes and curl up with her head on his shoulder and place her hand on his leg as he drove. But no.

When they got back to the house he went and sat with Mother for what seemed an eternity. Must have been about an hour.

Then he ate some toast and they went to bed.

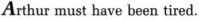

Arthur must have been tired.

He didn't notice the new negligee. They talked for a while then he curled up and went to sleep. Mrs Prior-Pointment lay for a long time, happy but yearning.

In the morning he was first up. He was dressed when she opened her eyes. There were some 'matters pending' business-wise so he suggested they eat out that night at an old restaurant that had been special to them in the old days.

The day passed in hunger.

That evening, before they left, Arthur spent more time

with Mother at the end of which the old matriarch was glowing and munching brightly.

On the way Arthur enquired closely as to the nature of his wife's new post, listening attentively to the minutiae of various committee decisions which the good woman was pleased to describe in probably a little too much detail. (Omitting anything incriminating regarding *Newfoundland*.)

Unfortunately the restaurant turned out to be a disappointment. Arthur was surly with one of the waiters over the wine menu and the food was second-rate, despite the price.

Conversation flagged as a result so that the poor tormented wife found herself talking unnecessarily and asking one or two questions about goings-on in Gibraltar for the sake of something to say. It was an area she wanted to avoid. She wanted only romance and, later, love.

She wanted to say: 'Arthur, can't we leave now? Forget the wine menu and the waiters, forget everything. It's a beautiful evening, let's walk along the front and then go home to bed and make love', and was on the verge of overcoming the dryness in her mouth when Arthur said: 'Darling there's something we have to talk about,' in such a way as to make her heart miss a beat.

'Yes?' she mouthed dryly.

He rearranged several of the utensils and adjusted the condiments. Mrs Prior-Pointment knew it was something important.

'Darling, I have to return to Gibraltar.'

'Yes, of course.'

'For quite some time.'

'Yes.'

He looked at her with what she took as a look of love.

'We'll be apart for some time.'

'Yes.' She tried to sound disappointed but brave.

She just sounded disappointed.

Arthur said, 'Do you find it terribly hard?'

'No. No, I think I've become accustomed to it.'

He looked straight at her. 'You can't be happy.'

'No. Yes. I mean, we have our separate lives. (There was something in his tone that was unsettling her.) I mean we survive. We do what we must.'

'Yes,' he muttered somewhat bitterly. 'That's just it. We do what we must.'

The waiter was standing there. Arthur ordered a large brandy. His wife shook her head.

They sat for a while in silence.

Mrs Prior-Pointment found herself trembling.

The brandy came and the brandy went. In two gulps.

Then he spoke. 'Darling I'm in difficulty business-wise.'

She nodded.

'And I don't want to make difficulty for you.'

'No.'

'Or for Mother.'

'Of course not.'

A thousand things crowded in on her.

She wanted to tell him that she would do whatever she had to for their love, that it was a sacred duty, a pleasure even, to suffer. She wanted to hint that she understood his difficulties. But she could do that later. She didn't want to appear untrusting, or interfering.

She was moved, too, that he wanted to protect her (and Mother).

He was a good man.

Made all the more good by his bravery in the face of difficulty. All the better for his fallibility, his humanity.

She wanted to offer to come with him, but she knew it was impossible. She would stay and look after Mother. She was independent and strong. So long as she knew he loved her and cared for her,

116

she would remain strong. She would do whatever was necessary.

'When must you leave?' she managed at last.

'Sunday evening.'

It was as if someone had moved the restaurant over a couple of feet to the left. She'd expected at least a few weeks.

It had to be bravely borne.

She went to say 'Well, that gives us two days, so darling, let's make them very special. I love you and I'll stand by you come what may'. Instead she burst into tears and sobbed hopelessly, causing Arthur (and the smart young couple on the next table) some discomfort.

Then she went to say, 'I'm sorry, darling,' but that made matters worse and she lost control utterly.

She pulled herself together in the lavatory.

They were silent in the car, apart from an 'I will be able to see you?' which made Mrs Prior-Pointment feel surprised how small she sounded, and an, 'Of course you will,' which made Arthur seem like the sky and the illuminations.

At home he again spent an age with Mother.

Then they were in bed.

As soon as he rolled in she snuggled up to him and he put a hairy arm round her.

She lay for a long time, waiting, moving as slowly as death, making tiny – no, smaller than that – molecular signals in search of a reply, in *need* of a reply. At fist her Lilliputian caresses were eliciting small encouraging squeezes which sent currents of pleasure ringing through her, then there was nothing for a while, then another squeeze.

He let out a small moan (or was it a grunt) and she placed her hand under his pyjamas, laid it on his belly and smoothed it lovingly. He squeezed her arm gently. She was aware of how long it had been, which made her stomach turn over.

117

Then she carefully removed her hand and slid it into his pyjama trousers, her hand resting on his lower belly, trembling lightly (and deliciously). She began a slow, teasing descent with her little finger, gently touching. Lower and lower. Cautious as a squirrel, light as summer. Holding her breath. Shivering involuntarily.

At which point he took hold of her hand, removed it from the region altogether and said, 'No, dear.' Followed by, 'It's impossible, don't.'

He removed his arm and made it clear that she was expected to move up now.

He curled up and went to sleep.

The next day it was as if nothing had been said about his going away.

They both pushed Mother down to the pier in her wheelchair. Conversation was bland and sparse.

Whereas only yesterday her wifely duty had seemed sacred and ethereal, today it loomed austere and demanding.

The words 'It's impossible, don't' chimed implacably, over and over.

What did they mean?

Was he trying to protect her still, so that their love would be bearable during the time of their separation? If so she should explain that she could and would and wanted to live with that pain.

But she called to mind the tone of the hideous pronouncement. The sound was not soothing and nurturing. The words had not been tenderly delivered.

Was he referring to their age?

Was there some medical problem perhaps?

She became a linguistic alchemist, trying to make gold from cold, poisonous lead.

Fools' gold.

By the end of the day she was exhausted. She hadn't slept well.

She hadn't slept.

Before she knew it they were in bed once again.

She waited for advances she knew weren't coming, lacking the courage to raise the subject.

She feigned sleep to avoid conversation whereupon he slipped downstairs to use the phone (she was sure). He was gone a long time.

The next day, the last day, Arthur left the house without his wife, to push Mother along the promenade.

Mrs Prior-Pointment sat in his study, her almost-Roman nose pointing at his briefcase as if it were the enemy. When she finally decided to examine the contents, she discovered it was locked.

Something led her to look in the little compartment of his old bureau.

It was a long shot, but she vaguely remembered there being a key. It was an old briefcase; it was just possible there was a spare key.

She had remembered correctly.

Or perhaps some psychic disturbance had caused nature to forge a spare key and place it there for her use.

It was the same colour as the metal clasp of the briefcase.

It fitted.

She was almost disappointed.

She both desired and dreaded to find something conclusive.

She therefore had mixed feelings when she found a photograph in one of the flaps.

Her hand had gone straight to it.

She knew what it was before she looked at it.

Despite the fact that the image would be forever etched on her memory Mrs Prior-Pointment felt curiously unmoved as she looked at it.

Arthur and some woman. In a cafe. She must have been half his age. Maybe even less. The young woman was staring into the camera. He was kissing her from

119

the side, looking comically sideways at the camera also. They looked drunk.

She wondered for a moment if it wasn't some dancer he'd met that night, or perhaps . . .

She turned the thing over.

The inscription was conclusive.

All the alchemists in the exchequer couldn't save her now.

'To the naughtiest boy in the world,' and a recent date.

She checked, coldly, to be sure she was sure.

The handwriting matched that of the letter.

Council for the prosecution sat down.

No further questions, your Honour.

 *J*ed put his fifty-five grand under the bed and went to court to declare himself bankrupt.

Then nothing much happened.

So he went for walks along the prom and sat watching seagulls and rain clouds, and women with children. And women without children.

He let the whole(sale) impression of the seaside bustle wash over him. He sniffed the air. Umm. Chips, doughnuts, beer, cigs, cheap perfume, aftershave, carbon monoxide and donkey shit.

It was no longer something Jed was a part of. He felt like a holiday-maker himself – a tourist in his own life. It was the first time for years he'd felt anything remotely resembling calm.

Sure the last few years of work had come to nothing. He was thirty – thirty-fucking-two – and bankrupt, but the feeling was still one of release.

He walked in the sand dunes on the estuary and even

smelt the sea as he kicked his way through the sand and litter. Must have been a freak of nature.

He drove to the West Pennine Moors, drank the mountain air and spotted five falcons on the hillside.

Twice during the first week he went out and got a video, pulled the sofa round in the living room, turned the lights off and plonked Charity in front of the television with a glass of wine. He even got fresh during *Aliens III*.

Sunday morning he made a big fried breakfast and served it to Charity in bed.

'You'll make me fat,' Charity said, flushing.

'So bloody what.'

The following weekend he rummaged under the bed, produced eight hundred quid and said. 'We're going shopping.'

He didn't bat an eyelid in Laura Ashley. Not even when Charity bought a new sofa of soft paisley design.

Charity, in her delight, nearly suggested having children. But didn't.

Saturday night, during a rest from love-making she judged it safe to say: 'So what are we going to do then?'

They fantasised for a while over how they could spend all the cash in a couple of months and then Charity repeated the question.

Jed climbed on top of her, bit her nipple and made her squeal. 'I always did fancy the life of crime,' he laughed.

So they called their new accountant and Charity invested her 'inheritance' as she and Eddie had planned.

Simple as . . .

Somehow Jed had been expecting it all to be a breeze.

It turned out to be extremely heavy.

The bank were suspicious of the 'failed' investment.

There were endless meetings of creditors and threats of bills that would make it impossible for him ever to get out of debt and at one point someone mentioned gaol.

Jed was summoned back to court following a meeting with suppliers and subjected to an investigation.

They challenged Charity's ownership of the house and tried to get them to sell it to pay off what Jed owed.

Charity cried every night for a fortnight.

Eventually a judge ruled in Jed's favour over the house.

There was an extremely nasty moment when the bank demanded to see the documentation regarding the 'lost' twenty thousand pounds again.

It was a full month before they heard anything.

When the documents came back, they spent another month worrying whether anything was going to come of it.

No one said: 'Oh, we checked those documents but they're fine, so don't worry.'

They just had to assume everything was OK.

One day Jed came out of his unit, where he'd been winding things up, to find the tyres of his none-too-cheap, none-too-flash Rover had been slashed and the windscreen broken.

His bitterness was soothed by the fact that he'd been ordered to sell the thing and the creditors were due the loot.

The whole process took months.

The plan had been for Jed to start work at *Newfoundland* as soon as the sale went through – which was remarkably quickly – but as his troubles multiplied he became listless and depressed and the idea was unilaterally dropped in favour of him skulking dismally around town and otherwise haunting the house.

In effect he became a househusband. A pretty bad one at that.

On days when he wasn't in court, or with his accountant or having the windows of his car broken, he drifted about amongst the edging and flounce – rearranging piles of magazines and hoovering.

He stayed in his dressing gown until noon, stopped shaving and for the first time ever bought pornographic magazines from a newsagent (a good distance away) and conducted lonesome afternoon orgies.

He still didn't get raging drunk during the day, just enough to keep the worst of his anger at bay. And never until noon, or half-eleven at the earliest.

Once or twice he went to *Newfoundland*, ostensibly to see how things were going but really to see Miranda who hardly took any notice of him. She did chat to him once but try as he might he couldn't extract from her the slightest hint that she'd ever had a conversation with him in which she'd admitted selling herself to men and he'd confessed to feeling up a woman at a party.

That woman.

Virginia.

Jesus.

Why the fuck did he ever do that?

What the fuck was she doing round here?

Please don't let her be living in the area.

When he went out now, Jed stomped up and down the prom, scowling at the women and children, resenting smiling faces, thinking how the children's tantrums served the women right.

Or he walked in the sand dunes and smelt nothing but shit.

One day he borrowed Charity's car and drove to the West Pennine Moors. This time he sat miserably in a pub, got drunk and decided he was going to go and play Eddie's little game on the old railway bridge.

So he staggered down the path, ripped his trousers on the stile and threw himself carelessly onto the low wall.

When a train thundered by underneath he shouted his anger at the overcast sky and lay there wondering what it would have been like to throw himself into the path of the train.

On the way back he ran the car off the road, so now one of Charity's fenders was bent and they couldn't afford to get it fixed.

Even Charity lost interest in sex at this point and the marriage reached an all time low. She was busy at *Newfoundland* and found Jed's misery increasingly oppressive. But it was an open and honest relationship, so she didn't say anything about it for months.

Then one night she gave him a lecture on pulling himself together. They were lucky to have survived at all. He looked a mess. He was drinking too much. She produced a hidden copy of *Men Only* and accused him of keeping secrets from her. If he was miserable he should talk about what was getting him down and stop feeling sorry for himself. There were plenty of people who'd suffered worse. And so on. And on.

At first Jed was angry, then embarrassed (especially at the *Men Only* bit) and then sorry. He cried and swore he would pull himself together.

That night he felt a strong urge to make love to Charity again, but she refused his advances saying she was tired. It was the first time he could ever remember her having refused him. He was almost sick with desire and became jealous that she was seeing someone.

He lay there for a while and in the end practically begged her for sex. She obliged. Afterwards he regretted it and apologised. She said it was OK.

He ached with desire for her after that but they didn't have sex again for weeks, during which time the housework got done thoroughly everyday and all the shopping and all the washing. He cooked a meal for her every night and masturbated furiously so he wouldn't feel compelled to try and screw her when she didn't feel like it. At least that was what he told himself.

He made a serious effort to stop drinking which was

nearly successful. Until he was notified of the date of the final hearing when the drinking started again, only more stealthily.

After everything was settled, Jed was ordered to pay off £60,000 from future earnings.

He was outraged.

Charity let him rage for a few days.

Then she admitted that things at *Newfoundland* were't going too well, not as well as they'd thought they would, very badly in fact.

His help was urgently required.

*P*rojected figures always look good.

Eddie's calculations had taken everything except Rose into account.

The figures were based on estimations provided by Charity, which in turn were based on the existing budget, which was the sort of budget that might have made Mr Bumble more inclined to hang Oliver Twist than smack him on the head with a ladle when he asked for more.

It is all very well to refuse to provide this and that 'luxury item' to residents when some faceless bureaucrat on some faceless committee cuts the budget every ten minutes so that faceless staff at the town hall can continue to pay themselves to sit on faceless committees cutting budgets.

It's different when you own the place and Rose is standing in your office every day with her arms folded under an uncompromising bosom demanding 'basic necessities' formally considered to be luxury items. Especially now she was a celebrity, a hero even.

Following the demonstration, there had been photographs in the local paper and even a mention of the episode on the regional television news. Rose had excelled herself with eloquent rhetoric, condemning the evils of privatisation and articulating the worries of vulnerable elderly people everywhere. In the home she was Churchill on D-Day, Lenin in October, Robinson Crusoe on Friday.

But surprisingly Rose had not opposed Charity's privatisation plan.

She knew an opportunity when she saw one. Within a few weeks of the 'staff takeover', under the wide girth of Rose's influence, the budget rocketed. Charity had been powerless to stop it.

Jed, was sunk in the paisley sofa staring blankly at *The Trial* by Kafka when Charity finally admitted things were going badly at *Newfoundland*.

He sat there for a moment and then cheerfully said: 'You want me to be the World Bank and introduce "austerity measures"?'

His heart felt like a piece of hard bone. Just the job.

The very next day Jed walked into *Newfoundland*, briefcase in hand, and set to work. He talked to all the staff, right down to the cleaners, inspected the books, and spent an hour making himself look important around the home.

Rose, suspecting something was afoot, stayed out of his way.

Jed suggested taking Miranda out to lunch to discuss the nursing arrangements and any other problems she might know of. Charity could hold the fort.

While Miranda changed in the new staff room on the top floor (she *never* came to work or left work in her uniform), Jed introduced himself in the morning room.

'I've always preferred men in smart clothes,' shouted Lilly, suggestively, nudging Edith in the ribs and repeating herself into her friend's hearing aid.

'How do you know what he's wearing?' Edith giggled.

126

'I had a quick feel as he walked past!' Lilly roared to a general whoopee.

Jed did his best to hold his own until Miranda beckoned him from the door.

Lilly shouted after them, 'I haven't had a chance to show him my scars yet – here feel this, I've got a plate in my head . . .'

Jed heaved a sigh of relief in the corridor.

Miranda said, 'You were lucky to get away with your trousers.'

They were about to enter the office to say goodbye to Charity when Jed caught sight of something through the glass of the office door that made him stop in his tracks.

A man.

Charity was sitting back in her chair with her head tilted at what struck Jed as a rakish angle and the man was holding merrily forth. The flush of Charity's cheek caused an unpleasant sensation in Jed's stomach.

He turned to ask Miranda if she knew the man but she had vaporised. He just caught sight of her disappearing back down the corridor to the morning room.

His indecisive lurching was interrupted when the office door opened and the man came out carrying a rather large briefcase, nodding as he went on his way.

In the office Jed accidentally said, 'Who the hell was that?' instead of 'Who was that?'

Charity grinned. 'It was my new lover.'

'He seemed to be having a jolly old time of it.'

'It's Doctor Haggarty's new partner. He's just moved into the area.'

'Looked like an old friend of yours.'

'Jealous.'

'I'm not jealous! I'm just . . .' He shrugged.

'Suspicious?'

'No!'

127

'It's allowed, you know. You're my husband. I'd be flattered.'

Enter Miranda.

'What was *he* doing here?'

'Do you know him?' Jed was first off the mark.

'No, . . . I mean, who was he?'

Jed said, 'He's the new doctor,' partly to see Miranda's reaction, which was just enough to make Jed certain she did know him.

'What did he say his name was?' she asked.

'He's not the new doctor,' Charity said. 'He's Doctor Haggarty's new partner. Haggarty's off for a week, that's all.' She added the detail for Jed's benefit.

Miranda went over to the window, presumably to get another glimpse of the doctor in the car park.

'What did he say his name was?' she asked again.

At that moment the doctor walked back into the office with only the slightest of knocks, tip-toeing comically.

'I forgot my pad,' he said, picking it up from the corner of Charity's desk.

There was half a thought in Jed's head that the man had left his pad there on purpose so he could come back for it later and see Charity. But it never really germinated because he was more interested in watching Miranda's reaction.

Miranda had swivelled round and put her back to the wall like a rumbled sniper waiting to receive a fusillade of bullets to the chest.

Jed watched for the doctor's reaction.

But as the man's glance took in the young woman at the window his expression didn't flicker. He left with a 'bye now' over his shoulder.

Charity was flattered still further as Jed joined Miranda at the window to watch him drive off. 'His name's Stayne. Dr Stayne,' she said.

'Hum,' hummed Miranda.

'Nice car,' said Jed.

It was a tornado-red Volkswagen Golf GTi (16v).

128

'**Y**ou've come up in the world,' mocked Miranda as they squeezed into Charity's mini.

'Yeah. Somebody broke the windows on mine.'

'Looks like someone's had a go at this one!'

Jed didn't want to talk about it.

'So what do you do when she's got the car?'

'I stay in.'

'What, houseboy?'

'Something like that.'

They set off, driving towards town.

He was trying to avoid being too friendly. He knew she would walk all over him if he tried to be jolly and he wanted to assert some authority this time. He even resisted the temptation to ask about the mysterious doctor.

They sat in silence until Jed couldn't stand it any longer.

'Where do you fancy?'

She sounded bored. 'Anywhere.'

'Same place we went last time?'

'If you want.'

He had to squirm for a while longer.

He was racking his brains for something original.

'Er . . . how about we get a couple of sandwiches and sit in the park. It's a nice day.'

She inclined her head and looked over at him. There was a slightly awkward manoeuvre on the road.

She said, 'How about taking me somewhere really special? Can you afford it?'

His hand waved itself. 'Yeah, sure. Do you know somewhere?'

All things considered he wasn't doing too bad a job of sounding nonchalant.

'I know somewhere.'

'Right, where is it?'

She sat back comfortably. 'Take a right here.'

He was in the driver's seat; she was at the controls.

They both knew it.

There was still a pile of cash under Jed's bed, though only leftovers now. It was a good job Jed had helped himself to a wad that morning. He must have had a premonition.

'Sure you can afford it?'

'I wouldn't have said yes if I meant no.'

The waiter fussed round, expensively. Jed said, 'Thanks' to him a few too many times.

They ordered and sat back, Miranda with a big grin which Jed struggled to keep from spreading. Until she said:

'So?'

'. . .?'

'Men don't usually take me out to dinner unless they want something.'

'Huh, it's nothing very interesting I'm afraid.'

She shrugged. 'So what is it?'

'Just what I said, I need to know about the nursing arrangements. We've got to make a few changes.'

'Oh, yeah?'

'Yes.'

'And?'

'That's it. I told you it wasn't very interesting.'

'Hang on,' her mocking tone, 'you mean to tell me you've brought me to the most expensive restaurant for fifty miles to discuss the nursing arrangements?'

'Yes.'

'I could have told you about that in the office with your wife there.'

He was embarrassed. 'Well, I haven't seen you for ages. I thought it would be nice.'

She looked at him like a schoolmistress over pretend glasses. 'Anything else?'

At last he let the grin crack his face up. 'N-o.'

She sat back. 'OK, so ask me.'

He explained about the over-spending, how Charity was too friendly with the residents, about his appointed role. How they were close to breaking point. She told him everything she'd observed about the way things were run.

When they'd covered most of the ground she said, with a wicked grin, 'Right, I'll have a pint of lager and then you can tell me the truth.'

Jed laughed nervously. 'What do you mean?'

'Make it lager and lime.'

While they waited for the drinks to arrive they sat in silence, looking at one another. That is, she looked at Jed and he held her gaze for as long as he could, then shuffled a bit and had another go.

But at least he held his tongue.

There were a few sips of lager (slurps on his side) before she spoke:

'So, what do you want to know?'

Jed blinked, 'I thought you were the one who wanted to know something.'

'Oh I do, but you're going to need a hostage, aren't you?'

Jed wasn't in game-playing mode. He needed warming up. He tried to say 'What do you mean?' again in such a way that she'd understand this. It worked.

'You know the score. What you have to tell me might be incriminating so you're going to need something incriminating against me.'

He swallowed and said, 'It always comes to this. I wish I had something to tell you,' and momentarily considered making something up. 'Unless you count buying a copy of *Men Only* from the newsagents.'

She sat there looking at him.

'I haven't been to any parties, either,' he said. 'Unless you count a meeting of the creditors, that was a bit of an orgy.'

She shook her head. 'Who said anything about sex?'

131

'Er, huh, nobody.' He stopped and took in the more serious look on her face.

One of her eyebrows arched, archly. 'Call me suspicious,' she said. 'But you go bankrupt one day, and a few weeks later your wife buys a business for tens of thousands of pounds – at a suspiciously low price.'

'It was an inheritance.'

When he said it, Jed realised it sounded far more convincing when your solicitor uses the word 'bequest' or 'legacy' at a formal meeting or, even more effectively, in correspondence. Miranda's brow seemed to sense the same thing.

Jed had something in his eye that needed attention. 'Some old uncle of Charity's died . . . in Switzerland.'

Miranda frowned. 'She said it was her aunt.'

'. . . Did she? Yeah, yeah, I forgot. It was her aunt.'

'She said it was her aunt from Jersey.'

'Yeah, yeah, she had a house in Jersey, too . . . as well as Switzerland. She was pretty bloody rich.'

'She left you all that money and you forgot her?'

'Hey, come on. We hardly knew them. She was very traditional. She wanted to leave the money to her family. There were only a few of them left.'

'You're definitely sure it was the aunt?'

Jed grinned, embarrassed. '*Yeah.*'

'Well that's *really* odd because Charity never said that to me at all. She said it was her Uncle from Switzerland and she never mentioned anything about Jersey.'

Jed blushed deeply and tried to say something. Miranda beat him to it.

'It's none of my business, but you really ought to get your story straight if you're going to get away with it.'

Jed called the waiter and ordered the bill.

'Cash, eh?' she remarked when he paid.

132

*T*hey were walking around the marine lake when the subject came up again.

Miranda had been chatting away about the men she'd been with since arriving in the resort town. How dull they were. She wondered whether there were any men in the area who just wanted to have a good time.

Jed wondered again about the new doctor.

'They all start getting serious after about two weeks,' she complained.

'You know *why*?'

'Cos they want a nice little wife,' scoffed Miranda.

'Because you're a very attractive woman.'

Both Jed and Miranda were surprised by this comment. She was caught off guard and laughed. 'Thank you.'

'They've probably never met anyone like you before.'

'You're right there.'

'They're never likely to again either, most of them.'

'You make it sound like a crowd.'

'I thought it was.'

'It's only three — so far.'

Jed laughed. 'I've only ever made love to three women in my entire life.'

'Serious?'

He nodded. 'That's a secret.'

'Why's it secret?'

'Charity thinks it's more than that.'

Miranda smiled and slipped her arm through his saying, 'I like you. You're dead honest.'

'You were calling me a liar before.'

'Yeah, but you're an honest liar.'

She tugged his arm gently. 'If anybody comes I'll move my arm, don't worry.'

He tried not to.

It was a little bit awkward like that. He had to put his hand in his pocket to give her something to link her arm through and then it was hard keeping in step. He wasn't sure whether to squeeze her arm in a friendly kind of way, or not.

It felt nice though. Very nice indeed. Not sexual, exactly. But warm and close. He felt like some kind of big brother.

The incestuous kind.

She said, 'So are you going to let me in on it then?'

He said, 'I can't.'

She seemed to think about this for a while.

It occurred to Jed that he'd just admitted that there was in fact something going on. She was bound to have spotted that.

She gave his arm a squeeze. 'I'll give you a good hostage. Something that'll make you feel dead safe.'

He sighed. And contemplated actually letting her in on the whole thing.

'If you're up to something you need someone who can help you. I've got a lot of experience operating scams.' She hopped on ahead slightly. Then she was walking backwards. 'I'll be your *special adviser*.' Now she was running on ahead. 'Buy me a coffee,' she called pointing to the waterfront cafe.

'You go first,' said Jed and her eyes lit up.

'What do you want to know?'

'Anything I can hold against you. And it had better be good.' He was stirring his coffee. Intently.

'So you've been that bad have you?'

'That's for me to know and you to wonder.'

She set her face. 'Look, I'm going to tell you something about me to make you feel safe, right? Even though I'd rather make you feel nervous – even though it's pretty bloody obvious what you've done from what I've seen and what you've told me already.'

Jed's face must have shown doubt.

'Do you want me to tell you what I think it is?'

She was going to anyway.

134

'Somehow you've managed to save up a lot of money on the sly while you were going bankrupt, probably in cash, and you've got some bent accountant to fix it up as an inheritance through some Swiss bank, or trust, or whatever it is they do out there . . .'

Jed pursed his lips, holding relatively steady. Then said, 'So what are you going to give me to use against you?'

Miranda grinned victoriously. 'I knew it! It's that mate of yours, he's the bent accountant, the one who got arrested. He had to leave the country didn't he? Charity told me about him.'

'What! What did she tell you about him?'

'No – not that he was bent! I mean *about* him. He's the one who got horny with her one night when they'd taken cocaine, and you got jealous and practically shagged her to death when she told you about it. Isn't he?'

Fuck-in-'ell!

Jed was blushing. 'Actually she never mentioned anything about the cocaine.'

'Whoops.'

'What the hell else does she tell you?'

'Oh, all kinds of things.'

Miranda was sparkling now. And thoroughly beautiful. He was powerless.

She said, 'I was right, wasn't I?'

'I'm glad you don't work for the bank.'

'I've got an eye for these things.'

He smiled. 'We got some forged documents . . .'

As he said it he saw a new look come into her eye. It was only a split second, but in that instant he didn't recognise her. He suddenly remembered she was almost a complete stranger, and wondered if he should just shut his mouth and leave it at that, but he went on anyway.

He explained as few of the details as he could and answered her ever more penetrating questions. As he

135

did so the impression of her as a stranger intensified and he noticed, or imagined, a new expression
on her face. She looked strangely vindictive for a
moment.

Or was he just being paranoid?

He wanted to trust her so he blocked out the impression.

At last the inquisition subsided and she sat back
saying, 'Fuckin'ell. It's really serious that, you know.'

'Na, not really.'

'You could get pure time for something like that!'

His neck was itching. She was talking.

'Someone I know did a fraud like that . . .'

Fraud?

'. . . Twenty-five grand's worth, I think it was. *Nine*
they got – years. I suppose it depends on the judge.
Could you fix a judge?'

He practically spluttered, 'It's not *fraud*,' and found
that for some reason he was shaking slightly. 'The bank
are quite happy. They sent the documents back. It's all
"legit". As good as.' It was the first time it had actually
sounded seriously criminal – as opposed to a dodge, or
a ruse, or a 'bit of a fiddle'.

He found himself backtracking on the story, as if the
safety of the whole thing depended on his making it
sound alright to Miranda. In the end he gave more
details away.

At the end of it she said, 'Sounds like you're in with
some heavy shit there,' which sounded terrifying to Jed.
'Does Charity know the whole story?'

'It was her bloody idea.'

'Really? I'm impressed.'

'Well her and Eddie's.'

'What, the coke fiend?'

'He's not a coke fiend!'

'Sounds like one to me.'

As they walked back along the path by the inky black

water of the marine lake, Miranda put her arm through Jed's again.

'Does sound like it's been done properly though,' she said, reassuringly. 'You should be alright. Plenty get away with it. Most people only get caught if someone grasses them up. We'll just have to be careful, that's all.'

We'll. He didn't miss that.

They walked in silence for a while. Then Jed said, 'I thought you were going to tell *me* something.'

'What do you want to know?'

'Anything. Oh yeah, who was that guy, the doctor? You know him don't you?'

'Um.'

He felt a bit jealous. 'I thought so.' He hardly dared ask. 'Did you – was he? . . .'

'Yeah, I shagged him, yeah.'

He was thoroughly jealous now. 'I can't really use that against you, can I,' he muttered.

'You could actually. He knows all about me.'

'What . . . sort of things?'

It took her a few moments to get it out. 'Like I used to be a heroin addict.'

'What! . . . I thought you were going to tell me something to make me feel safe!'

'I'm clean now. That's why I came here. Getting away from the scene's half the battle.'

He thought for a moment and then said, 'I can't even use that against you.'

'You could.'

'How?'

'I lost my certificate through it. I'm not a qualified nurse. *I've* got a forged document *too*.'

She ran on ahead.

'Come on it's freezing!'

Jed was quiet on the way back.

He was thinking what a fool he'd been opening his gob.

137

Miranda wasn't even qualified for the job and he knew there was nothing they could do about it, because . . .

Not that he wanted to do anything about it, far from it, but it made him feel uneasy because it symbolised how little power he had over her. And how much she had over them now.

But Miranda had managed to cheer him up with her chat by the time they arrived back and he shook off his regrets for the time being.

On the steps of *Newfoundland* she stopped him and looked about furtively.

'Don't grass me up, now,' she grinned.

'Likewise' would hardly come out of his mouth.

She stood looking at him strangely for a moment. Then she stood on her tip-toes, pulled him towards her, kissed him full on the lips and disappeared through the door.

*I*f she had, over the course of the past months, had a bolt inserted through her neck and been attached nightly to electrodes running from a lightning conductor, Mrs Prior-Pointment would have undergone less of a change.

Mrs Bullmore and Mrs Strutting noticed every shortening of her skirt, every application of blusher and new layer of foundation, each strand of newly blackened hair, every pound in weight lost. They even believed that one or two of the crow's-feet around her eyes had disappeared, though not everyone in the ladies' caucus agreed about this.

Talk, however, reached fever pitch when, passing in her car, Mrs Bullmore spotted a strange man going into the house. The first lieutenant was so surprised to see a man entering the Prior-Pointment household that she immediately parked just round the corner to keep an eye on developments and, her staunch jaw wagging at her in-car cellular telephone, related the news as it happened directly to the ladies' caucus.

About an hour later the man emerged, smoking a cigarette, and drove off in his car. Mrs Bullmore called at the house but failed to get an answer. Half an hour later she called back and was admitted. Despite considerable dropping of considerable hints the square-jawed lieutenant could not get the leader to allude to the mysterious visitor at all. So she noted the red puffy skin around the eyes, beneath a two or three-ply film of vanishing cream, and set off to confirm her reports that Mrs Prior-Pointment, poor dear, was having a sordid affair.

When Arthur had departed for Gibraltar Mrs Prior-Pointment had felt nothing.

On the doorstep she was chilly and, had he not swept her stiff body into his arms, she would have proffered her hand for shaking. She didn't see fit to go with him to the airport and he didn't ask her to go.

It wasn't until later that night when she looked at her watch as she was making a cup of tea in the kitchen that she suffered her first pang of real jealousy. It occurred to her that Arthur would be, at that very moment, arriving back at the apartment.

Before she realised what she was doing she pictured his little woman wrapping her arms around his neck and kissing him. She formed an image of warm lights, a little supper on the veranda, the view over the town, the breeze from the sea, the smell of the air and the calm of intimacy. There was a little flash of the bedroom and the bed, and the clean, fresh sheets pulled back in readiness . . .

She suddenly realised the terrible feeling of dread in the pit of her stomach. She fussed around the kitchen searching for distraction, but the image of Arthur's happy smiling face presented itself over and over, filling her with desire and disgust: his face, smiling at someone else.

After two days of increasing disquiet she decided to call a private investigator. Perhaps there was still some hope that she was over-estimating the importance of this young woman. She needed to know just exactly what was going on in Gibraltar.

So she waited and suffered for a month while the detective detected.

The mysterious caller seen by Mrs Bullmore was the detective coming to report his findings.

The man was an old friend of the family who had been disgraced and forced to resign from the police force many years previously. Mrs Prior-Pointment felt that he would be sensitive to the complexities of the situation and sympathetic to her plight, bearing in mind his own difficulties all those years ago. A mistaken belief which eventually cost her several thousands of pounds before the man was finally paid off.

But this difficulty was in the future.

For now Mrs Prior-Pointment had to swallow the news that, as well as keeping another woman in Gibraltar, Arthur was and indeed had been for some years involved in laundering money for a number of criminals ranging from common crooks – including some of the lesser figures in the Brinks-Matt gold bullion robbery – to mercenary armies and South American drug cartels.

Arthur's role in the whole affair, the detective told her, was 'the straight man', the legitimate front. His various ventures, including a holiday time-share scheme, were a cover.

The faithful wife was told that the business conducted in Gibraltar was mostly legitimate. The laundering proper took place in the Canaries and other resort islands and was overseen by other people –

'heavies' he called them (names and histories provided).

The enterprise was jointly owned by Arthur and one Doctor Divine, formally an accountant who had recently fled Britain. Arthur himself operated under an assumed name – probably to protect himself from his own associates if something went wrong.

The detective provided her with photographs of Arthur and his young woman in some extremely compromising positions, along with photographs of Arthur and Divine (who Mrs Prior-Pointment immediately recognised as Eddie who-ever-he-was) with various figures from the criminal underworld, a couple of mercenaries and a minor figure from the embassy of a small South American country.

The investigation had been fairly straightforward, the detective said, and conducted largely through his contacts with the criminal underworld. The organisation's activities were not difficult to discover, they were common knowledge in certain circles. The organisation was thought to be protected by people in high places.

Mrs Prior-Pointment interrogated the detective for some time on the nature of such organisations. The danger, she discovered, lay primarily in betrayal by some of the more dangerous elements involved. Jealousies and rivalries could be fatal. Suspicion would be rife. If one member were arrested for anything, no matter what it was, it would be thought that another of the members had become a 'stool pigeon'. That person would then be in grave danger.

'Your husband is playing a very dangerous game,' she was told.

Then the man presented her with his bill. There was an unmarked item which would have to be paid in cash the following day in respect of 'confidentiality'.

Mrs Prior-Pointment took the bill, promised the extra, showed the man to the door, wafted the cigarette smoke

out of the hall and went upstairs, where she lay on the
bed and cried and tore her hair.

She turned the fire of scorn on everything that had
separated her from Arthur.

She blamed Mother.

Arthur was badly brought up. Too much had been
expected of him. It wasn't right that a man should be
put under such pressure. Mother had driven him with
the desire for success and spoiled him so that there was
little hope of him ever living up to her expectations.

Mother had come to live with them. She was oppressive and demanding. A bully. It was no surprise that
Arthur hadn't been able to cope with life. It was less
surprising he had run away.

She realised with dismay that she had tried to be like
his mother herself; she had thought that that was what
Arthur would respect. Now he had another woman,
who was absolutely nothing like his mother at all.

The images from the photographs tore into her.
Sometimes she would give in to the desire to look
at them again and sit studying them until she lost
control of her breathing and felt she would die of her
suffering.

Her nights were filled with torment – a potent mix
of jealousy and insecurity. She lay writhing on the bed,
sobbing convulsively, grinding her teeth, consumed by
dread and, despite everything, a passionate sometimes
violent womanly longing for him.

Finally, when she had blamed herself and hated
herself and Mother to the point of exhaustion, she
would blame Arthur himself.

He was irresponsible, selfish, careless.

A fool. Inadequate. Weak.

But, when she thought of him, the photo-images
sprang to mind and, perversely, she found it impossible
not to want him.

He was irresponsible, selfish, careless – charming,

popular and handsome and she felt an overwhelming desire to make love to him.

She was revolted and compelled.

She wanted him to want her so that this anxiety would stop.

She stood in front of the mirror, naked and examined herself anew for defects, searched desperately for her womanliness. Was it really too late? Dieting was easy – food was impossible to swallow. She painted her face for hours on end and gazed into the mirror until her eyes stung.

Then one night during a thunderstorm, as she lay in bed listening to the wind and rain, trying to find a way to stop her feelings consuming her, she accidentally imagined that Arthur had died. She pictured the whole scenario: the funeral; the church service; the sandwiches afterwards – they would have salmon, a simple buffet, all her friends helping out. Everyone was very understanding and supportive, comforting her and sympathising with her. In her mind Arthur made a final, loving act of contrition from his death bed, told her that he had always loved her and that he had not meant to go astray and asked her to forgive him. She held him in her arms and he cried while she stroked his head. They kissed then and he was gone. Peace returned to her heart and she loved him serenely once again. It seemed a long time since she'd felt such serenity.

Then she saw again the mess of reality, felt the hatred of everything that had brought them to this.

She climbed out of bed, went over to the window and flung it open. She took deep breaths, held her arms out into the great warm blobs of rain and felt power, elemental and frightening, come into her.

The following morning at breakfast Mrs Prior-Pointment read the paper for the first time in weeks.

Mother's boiled egg winked impotently up at the old matriarch, who in turn munched impotently at

143

the younger woman. Mrs Prior-Pointment refused to acknowledge the appeal. She had fed Mother her last egg and soldiers, she would not go along with the game any longer.

Ten minutes later when Mrs Prior-Pointment had made a call from the upstairs study and returned to the kitchen, the egg was eaten, apparently of its own accord and Mother did not have egg on her chin. Indeed the old woman's jaw was steadier than it had been for some time.

'More tea, Mother?'

Mother nearly nodded.

Things were going to change. Forever.

'**N**o I will not pass you the tomato ketchup! You know very well I don't approve of ketchup on the table at meal times. It lowers the tone.' Mrs Crotchley went primly on with her dinner.

'Here you are, Lilly,' said Rose, helpfully. 'If you want to lower the tone of your lamb chop, you go ahead.'

'I'm trying to make it taste of something,' said Lilly.

Lilly groped for the ketchup, knocked it out of Rose's hand and sent it crashing into the condiments.

Mrs Crotchley sighed. 'I don't know why we can't put it in a little bowl and serve ourselves with a teaspoon – those of us that want the wretched stuff.'

Rose put down her knife and fork, significantly.

Mrs Crotchley knew what was coming; you could tell by the way her thin lips stretch-whitened.

Rose said, 'All those in favour of tomato ketchup on the table at meal times? . . .'

There was a clear majority of shaky hands raised.

'All those against?'

There were one or two tentative hands against, really

just fingers, but everyone knew that these were ladies who didn't want Mrs Crotchley's feelings to be hurt by an overwhelming majority.

For their trouble they received an impatient look from Rose and absolutely no sign of gratitude from Mrs Crotchley.

'Abstentions?'

Mrs Crotchley had not shown her hand at all.

'Really dear,' said Rose, 'If you're not going to take part in the democratic process there's nothing we can do.'

'What about the bowl suggestion?' said the dissenter.

Rose and Mrs Crotchley looked at one another defiantly.

Lilly spoke the answer that they both knew was coming:

'It makes too much washing up.'

Mrs Crotchley's answer to that was, obviously, 'Pssht,' which Tinkerbell took as a cue to try and scramble onto the table and waft hair into people's dinner.

Lilly was repeating to Edith that she liked ketchup because it made the food taste of something (to which Rose added 'What you mean other than dog-hair!') and taking an extra dollop for good measure when Jed came in armed with his briefcase, looking very smart and and busy.

He marched over to Rose.

Rose prepared her bosom sternly.

So far the old trade unionist had avoided Jed, or 'Mr Green' as she insisted on calling him. His briefcase in itself was enough to make her suspicious. Rose instinctively saw Jed as a threat to her leadership of the residents, a role she prized greatly.

Rose had during her working life always played second fiddle to the men. There had been opportunities for women in the trade union movement, of course, but the men always hogged the limelight. Her own husband, Jack, had been a leading light in her own organisation and despite her authority at home, Rose had always stood in his shadow.

She blamed her husband and men in general for her present predicament, for her poverty.

When the tide of history began to ebb after the great expansion of the sixties her union had been one of the first to suffer. Economic competition required new, cost cutting technology.

New technology required reorganisation.

Reorganisation meant sackings.

Sackings meant strikes.

Strikes meant trouble for trade unionists.

Sleepless nights, frantic days.

Swimming against the tide.

Under pressure to compromise the union had split.

In the heat of solidarity Jack and Rose refused to join the new ('scabs') union and fought alongside the men and women on the factory floor, the people of the town. Rose had been proud at the time, but she'd forgotten that since.

Their own wing of the union collapsed immediately following the defeat, based as it was on the will to fight.

When the town lay down to die, or, which was the same thing, sat down to drink alcohol, Jack went down with that ship too and was found dead on the kitchen floor, drowned in his own vomit.

He left only debts.

Rose could have stayed with the women but many of her good friends had vanished in the wake of the split. In the end she managed after a fight to get a place at *Newfoundland*.

It was an attempt to escape the past, but strangely she found herself in the company of Lilly and the others – who had also escaped the old town – and again found herself under attack.

The budget was cut time after time and there were constant rumours the place would be sold off, or close.

But with Rose's persistent efforts they had made small advances: the formation of the residents committee; the arrival of the new nurse and then . . . the demonstration that had turned the tide.

It was the first victory Rose could remember in twenty years and this time she had been at the helm.

There had been real achievements in the months since then: there were new curtains throughout; the morning room had been decorated; satellite TV had been installed; the food had improved; there was mayonnaise at meal times as well as ketchup; the top floor had been renovated and residents spread out into mostly single rooms (only The Terrible Trinity had chosen to stay sharing); and there were more heaters and new electric blankets. Even the residents themselves had been transformed since Nurse Jones had worked her magic.

'I wonder if I could have a word with you in the office,' Jed said.

Rose said, 'I'm eating lunch.'

'Yes, yes, of course. Afterwards. I'll be in the office.'

Rose stared at him.

'Yes . . . well . . . I'll see you later, shall I?' Jed said.

Rose went back to her lunch without another word.

Jed walked out of the dining room a little more awkwardly than he had walked in.

'Come in Rose. Take a seat.'

She didn't like his tone. She wasn't used to knocking on doors and being asked to sit down. It was more likely to be the other way round.

Rose resented the way he'd been huddled in the upstairs office with Miranda. Miranda was her accomplice and yet hadn't even spoken to Rose all week.

'If you don't mind, I'd rather stand.'

'Oh . . . yes, of course.'

It was a good ploy, Jed immediately felt awkward sitting behind the desk while Rose planted her feet firmly and rolled her arms into a great defensive barrier. It made it difficult to be informal and therefore difficult to be ruthless. The best modern managers know it's easier to stab someone in the back when you're on friendly terms.

'Would you like a cup of tea?' he tried.

'No thank you.'

'Ah. Right. I needed to speak to you about – the arrangements here at *Newfoundland*.' Shit he sounded like some kind of bank manager.

Rose decided to keep her plump lips plum shut.

'I don't know whether you know, but the centre is running into difficulties. Financial difficulties.' There was a fascinating stain on the desk. 'And we rather wanted to ask for your help.'

Plump plums.

'. . . There's been some considerable over-spending and – huh – we've come to the crunch really.'

'Yes, I see,' Rose unfolded and re-folded her arms. 'And who are you?' (They'd never been formally been introduced.)

'Oh . . . yes of course. Jed Green. My wife . . . Charity . . . Yes, well, pleased to meet you.'

He half stood up and proffered his hand.

She gripped a couple of his fingers loosely.

He more or less fell back into the squeaky chair. 'Yes, I'm afraid there are going to have to be some fairly . . . drastic cuts. Or else, I'm afraid the . . . centre may have to *close*.'

Rose stood waiting for him to finish and when she was certain that he was done she said, 'I see.' And waited.

Jed said, 'Yes.' And, 'Umm.' And then nodded.

Rose said, 'Is there anything else?'

'Oh, er no, no I suppose not.'

She left.

Jed felt like he'd made some kind of mistake, but he wasn't sure what it was.

He soon found out.

In the downstairs office Charity said, 'How did she take it?'

'Oh fine.'

'Did you explain that we needed her to help us?'

'Uh . . . Yes.'

'What did she say about the cuts?'

'Oh, I think she understood.' Jed was expansive. 'I told her we'd have to work together.'

'Did you explain about how we want to re-organise the budget?'

'Not in any detail.'

'But that was the whole point.'

'Well we can explain all that later. The main thing was to get the idea across that we're going to have to make changes.'

At that point Miranda came in. She looked at Jed with exaggerated horror. 'What have you done?'

'What?' Defensive.

'There's an "emergency meeting of residents" going on. And I'm not invited.'

Charity sighed pointedly.

Jed said something nobody understood.

*T*here was no need to call the meeting to order. They were all ears and hearing aids.

Generally these days the only disruptions to proceedings were Lilly repeating what was said to Edith and an occasional 'Pssht' from Mrs Crotchley as she disagreed with some faintly radical suggestion.

Rose cleared her throat and made sure her address was directed over Mrs Crotchley's head.

Histrionics were unnecessary. She reported her meeting with Jed word for word and though she said Miranda had been threatened with redundancy if she didn't co-operate, she confessed that this was only a hunch.

Closure.

Again that dreadful spectre.

Lilly started them off. 'What the bloody hell are we supposed to do, sleep under the pier?'

'Where *will* we go?'

'I ain't got nowhere.'

'There ain't nowhere.'

'They put you in a hospital if you've got nowhere . . .'

'Bloody loony bin, you mean.'

It was well-known that several residents from a rest home in Preston had been committed into psychiatric care when their home was forced to close. There had been horror stories circulating around *Newfoundland* ever since.

Rose let them simmer for a while.

There was considerable alarm.

Even Mrs Crotchley looked uncomfortable. 'I hope this isn't another of your exaggerations,' she said to Rose during the general hullabaloo.

'I wish it were, dear.'

'I'm not going nowhere, not for nobody. They'll have to carry me out,' someone said.

'They'd have a hard time carrying me out!' shouted Lilly, 'I'm fifteen stone!'

But no one was in the mood for laughter. There was real concern.

One of Lilly's friends stood up. 'It's a disgrace, treating old folk that way. If my Joe was still alive he'd have his shotgun out . . .'

Rose judged it time to speak her own mind.

She called order and said, 'Well, there only seems to be one sensible course. It's worked for us in the past; it's the only language people understand these days.'

There was silence (apart from a 'Pssht!' at the front) while the meaning of the words settled.

'It's a bit cold for a demonstration,' someone said.

Rose had expected a spontaneous eruption. Last time it had happened practically without prompting. Well, without prompting at all.

Now the whole assembly sat in silence.

Perhaps it was the fact that this time the suggestion was coming from Rose herself and lacked the authenticity of a movement from the floor.

Perhaps now they were living in relative comfort they feared that they had too much to lose.

Surely it wasn't just the weather.

Rose's experience prevailed: 'I think probably what they're most worried about is the heating. There's some suggestion of regulating the use of heaters in people's rooms,' she added shrewdly.

It was enough.

'Enough is enough,' declared Lilly, giving Edith a nudge and a shove to get her to her feet. 'Come on everyone. Make sure you wrap up warm . . .'

'I'll phone the press,' declared the instigator adjusting her bosom importantly.

Outside a harsh breeze was blowing off the estuary and whipping up sand from the road which made people's eyes water.

Things went badly from the start.

First of all it took a few minutes for the women to stop the traffic. Edith was almost knocked over as a car swept past blaring its horn angrily. This shook up most of them. After that they dithered for a few minutes, waiting for a pause in the endless stream of vehicles.

Then it was realised that five or six residents had decided to stay indoors and have a cup of tea instead, Charity and Miranda having accosted them in the hall and assured them that there was no threat of closure.

But eventually, sitting on collapsible chairs someone

151

had dug out of the old storeroom, the demonstrators settled themselves out on the tarmac and some reasonable good humour prevailed.

One of the held-up drivers became angry and shouted obscenities at them causing one or two more of the women to drift off. But there was a hard core who stuck to their guns, even when the irate driver drove by along the sandy pavement revving his engine aggressively and passing dangerously close to Lilly, Edith and Mrs M.

In the next car – now the first car in the line – a very large woman with a jaw line as impressive as Desperate Dan's was talking with great animation on her in-car cellular telephone, apparently describing the scene before her to someone with the enthusiasm of a sports commentator.

From an upstairs window, Jed was watching anxiously for the arrival of the press (in the form of Virginia). By his side several of the residents, led by Mrs Crotchley, were shaking their heads and worrying about the prospect of the demonstration making matters worse.

But Jed needn't have worried. The press didn't show.

They must have thought the story old hat.

Or perhaps they didn't want to encourage social insolence by providing the oxygen of publicity. Opinions were divided.

The police took the trouble, however.

On the first demonstration the one policeman who turned up to supervise the festivity had been a jovial fellow who had won the hearts and minds of the women, enjoyed himself, soothed the drivers and given everyone a good laugh. There had been a picture of him and Rose smiling together in the local newspaper.

Sergeant Filch was a different game of soldiers.

He was a very unhappy man with a particular dislike of demonstrators, but especially the female of the species for whom he reserved a warm, heartfelt loathing on account of his experience at Greenham Common where a woman, not unlike his mother, had kicked him in the testicles causing his colleagues to ridicule him in the face of the enemy and causing a lasting medical condition his comrades never found out about.

And there is nothing like a belligerent copper to inspire righteous indignation in the heart of the oppressed. Sergeant Filch's 'Right then, if that's the way you want to play it' was as inevitable as Rose's 'If you want to clear the road I'm afraid you'll have to make arrests'.

What was less inevitable was the fact that Rose's popular base should prove so flimsy.

The moment the two policewomen took hold of Rose's arms and led her into the waiting van the old trade unionist's mandate failed her.

There were a few 'oohs' and the windblown assembly disbanded looking very frail – as if Edith had been reinstated as nurse and administered an emergency dose of medication all round.

Lilly, Edith and Mrs M found their way to Sergeant Filch. Lilly said, 'They're going to close the place down. We've nowhere to go.'

To which the policeman replied, 'Just stand out of the road please, love, unless you want to accompany your girlfriend to the station.'

Lilly's head shook slightly as she realised the situation was hopeless.

'Poor Rose,' Lilly said as they joined the others shuffling back to the house.

'Lucky they didn't take the lot of us in.'

'What's going to happen to her?'

'They'll give her a good going over.'

'Don't be ridiculous.'

'Well she wanted trouble.'

'Something like this was bound to happen.'

'Hadn't we better phone the newspapers?'

'Let's go and ask Mr Green. He'll know what to do.'

There are many types of arrest. Some glorious, most dreadful.

Being arrested for a cause alongside a group of comrades with strong organised support can be uplifting. A demonstration against the arrest outside the police station itself works wonders. The police feel intimidated and are less inclined to dole out beatings and press unnecessary charges. The cops do their best to laugh off their discomfort at the commotion and to dampen the spirits of the detainees, but mostly they shuffle around looking embarrassed, getting rid of persons as quickly as possible. Released detainees then leave the station to cheers and celebration.

Being arrested alone, without organised support, is very different.

At first Rose was resolute. She had a nasty moment when she realised she was making a lone stand, but cheered up a little in the van with the nice woman officer. Her arrest would stir up public sympathy and she was looking forward to the coverage which would come when she was released.

She'd never been arrested before. She'd come close during the strikes and knew plenty of people who had but those arrests had generally been in the glorious tradition, though there had been cases where things had gone wrong and serious charges had stuck, or beatings had occurred.

They were nice enough to her at the station when the desk sergeant 'signed her up', as he called it, and then she was taken to a cell.

In the cell there was a hard wooden bed with a hard wooden pillow and horrible dirty tiles everywhere, like an old bath house.

The door closed.

She was alone.

And that was that.

154

She just sat there.

The emergency bell on the wall looked like it had been broken during the First World War and no one had got round to fixing it yet.

After two hours of hearing nothing she timidly knocked on the door for attention.

But no one must have heard.

She knocked louder.

Still nothing happened.

She was hungry and cold.

The dirty toilet in the corner kept flushing of its own accord.

She didn't like to use it, though she badly wanted to.

Where *was* everyone?

After about half an hour, she heard footsteps and the door opened.

An officer had a tray of food. He stood there and held it out. 'Food.'

She had to get up and take it off him. 'Er, is there . . . I mean, what's going on?'

'Don't ask me, love.'

She pulled herself together. 'I'd like to see a solicitor.'

'You've signed to say you don't require the services of a solicitor.'

'No I haven't.'

'It's on your charge sheet.'

He was going.

She hurriedly put the food down on the bed and went to the door after him.

Bang. Closed.

She knocked. A little frantically. '. . . Hello?'

The metal spy hatch slid back. 'What?'

'What's happening, am I being held?'

'It's too late to take you to court today, we'll have to hold you till morning.'

For the first time Rose was properly afraid.

'Tomorrow? Is there no way . . . surely there's no need.' She huffed firmly. 'I need to see a solicitor.'

'Sorry, love. Nothing I can do.'

Bang. The steel shutter shut.

'Er – hello?' she called.

She listened.

Again, 'Hello-oh?'

Were there footsteps? She wasn't sure.

The steel shutter slid back again.

'What now?'

'My phone call. I'm entitled to make a phone call.'

'You've made it.'

'No I haven't.'

'Says on the sheet you've already made your call.'

'It can't do.'

'I'll go and check.' Bang. Steel shutter closed.

Retreating footsteps.

A door banging somewhere further away.

Silence.

Rose waited.

And waited.

Until it dawned on her that the officer wasn't going to return. At which point she got up and banged angrily on the door and shouted, 'Hello?' at first sternly and then despairingly.

Then she sat on the hard bed and wept.

As Rose wept, the morning room at *Newfoundland* settled back down to its usual routine.

When the demonstrators returned to the house they besieged the office and Charity, aided by Miranda, did her best to calm them. (Jed was still skulking upstairs.)

In the end a few reassuring words did the trick.

Charity made an official announcement that Rose had been mistaken, the centre was not going to close down, but certain economies would have to be made. And, yes, the heating would be unaffected.

156

The group were deferential and one of the natural laws of late twentieth century group consciousness prevailed: the general tendency, in the absence of a crisis affecting them personally, for a group of people to sit down and watch TV.

At Lilly's insistence Miranda phoned the police station and was told Rose would possibly be released in a few hours when the charges had been considered.

Eventually, when he was trebly certain that the coast was clear, Jed came down sheepishly and volunteered to make a cup of tea. Charity and Miranda were in the office.

'Did you tell them you were going to chuck them out on their arse?' scoffed Miranda.

'She just took it all the wrong way. She didn't really listen.'

'They're terrified of the place closing,' Miranda said. 'They think they'll end up in a loony bin if we close.'

'That's where some of them belong,' Jed grumbled. 'That's where we'll all end up at this bloody rate.'

'Poor Rose,' said Charity. 'Shall we go and see her?'

'No way.' Jed was adamant. 'Let her learn from her mistakes.'

Charity was shocked. 'Jed, she's an old woman!'

'Well, she should behave like one. If she's going to go running out into the road every time she doesn't get her own way . . .' He stopped himself. But only because he saw that Miranda wasn't amused by his attitude. 'We're doing them a favour here,' he said. 'They should be glad.'

The kettle had just boiled when there was a knock on the office door.

There were two very stern-looking women rigidly standing there, framed by the glass door. One of the women had the jaw of a boxer and the other sported a coat with a large mustard check pattern and had pinkish hair that must have been arranged by static electricity.

'It's Tweedle Dee and Tweedle Dum,' giggled Miranda.

The woman with the square chin clutching a clipboard under her arm filled Jed with a feeling of dread, despite Miranda's joke.

'My name's Mrs Bulmer and this is Mrs Sutton,' she declared when she had gained admittance to the now crowded office. 'We've been instructed by the Inspectorate of Health and Safety (the capital letters stood out of their own accord) to conduct an impromptu (the "r" rolled like a red carpet from the tongue) once-over inspection of the premises in view of this afternoon's – *disturbance*.'

There was something disturbing about the pronunciation of the word 'disturbance'.

The looks of guilt on the three faces before her had the effect of increasing Mrs Bulmer's height by two inches at least (which was in reality achieved by a subtle re-adjustment of her Schwarzeneggeresque jaw.)

'Er, yes, of course. Nurse Jones will show you round,' spluttered Jed when he awoke from a momentary trance. 'I'm . . . sure you'll find everything in order.'

Mrs Crotchley was unusually chirpy that afternoon and indulged in several conversations.

She discussed the previous evening's episode of *Coronation St* with Edith, despite the fact that Edith hadn't watched it; she passed the time of day with Mrs M who had been dumbstruck since her return from hospital; and she was pleasant to Lilly as the old giant blundered about, challenging the sturdiness of the furniture. She wasn't even cross when Edith pushed Mrs M's chair over her corns.

There was a faint, bitter-sweet smile threatening to spread over her gums and she giggled at one of Lilly's crude remarks.

'What are you looking so bloody smug about?' asked Lilly. It was even visible to the blind.

158

Mrs Crotchley just shook her head vaguely and patted her little dog.

Then came the intrusion.

Miranda, Tweedle Dee and Tweedle Dum.

The two women took up a position in the centre of the room – or that is 'Mrs Bulmer' took up the centre of the room and 'Mrs Sutton' made do with the remaining space.

The overbearing woman with the clipboard jutted over the scene as she spoke her mind, seeming to address nobody and then everybody at the same time:

'Well I can't say I'm happy. I'm terribly glad the matter was brought to my attention by the demonstration on the road. Well done ladies! If it hadn't been for your magnificent stand – your sheer belligerence, the condition of the place would never have been brought to our attention. The whole situation is unsatisfactory. We may be able to force immediate closure.' The great woman took hold of her companion's arm. 'Come along dear. No time to lose.'

Nobody took the trouble to watch the two 'Inspectors' as they left the building.

At that moment the house, led by Mrs Crotchley, was too busy running around exclaiming that *Newfoundland* was to close after all and that all was lost because of Rose's trouble-causing. So nobody saw the two women walk through the car park, nip round the corner and climb into a very smart Honda Legend with green tinted windows.

In the driver's seat, waiting, sat Mrs Prior-Pointment.

There was a glowing exchange of significant glances and some triumphalism.

'You should have been an actress, dear,' giggled Mrs Strutting from her place in the back of the car.

'I did seriously consider it at one time,' said Mrs Bullmore with pride. 'I was told I was the wrong build.'

159

'How did they react?' asked the leader.

'Oh they were horrified,' mouthed the great chin.

Mrs Prior-Pointment was firm. 'That should stop their tomfoolery once and for all. We can't have people running out into the streets every time they're unhappy about something. Those days are gone.'

'And good riddance!' put in Mrs Bullmore, with a staunch nod.

'I'll telephone them in a hour or so and let them know that I received an order recommending closure, but that I was able personally to make the Inspectorate see reason.'

In the back Mrs Strutting was giggling away. 'We do have to be terribly clever, these days,' she said.

'Big changes are required in the way we do things,' declared Mrs Prior-Pointment as they drove off.

Mrs Bullmore grunted 'hear hear' to this.

'Yes.' Mrs Prior-Pointment sighed. 'And I'll be making one or two changes myself. I may as well tell you.'

There was a bristling and a patting of perms.

And another sigh from the leader before she announced: 'Mother is *going in* somewhere.'

'Good Lord, how dreadful!' said Mrs Bullmore with her usual tact.

'Yes,' said Mrs Prior-Pointment rather stiffly 'Yes. Arthur – er, that is, I . . .' (she had a tickle in her throat). 'It's time for a change. Mother will be happier in company. And I intend to spend some time in Gibraltar with Arthur.'

There was some more perm-patting. Mrs Bullmore had caught the leader's tickly throat.

'Now, shall we have tea somewhere?'

That night the ladies' caucus were made aware that Mrs Prior-Pointment was plotting terrible revenge on her husband and told to prepare for further bulletins.

And poor Mother.

160

*T*here's nowhere quite like a police cell.

Even in a nice quiet seaside town they are gruesome places. Rose was shocked at the violent obscenities scrawled on the walls and tried not to ogle. But there is only so long a person can spend in serene contemplation of a concrete floor and bronchial off-white pipes. In the end Rose read that 'Baz fucks all cunts' over and over until a mild state of hypnosis was achieved.

The only distraction, apart from the etched wisdom of the imprisoned mind and the abstract forms of dust and grime, was the spontaneously flushing toilet which constantly raised the question in the newcomer's mind: 'Will it continue to flush all night?'

Her anxiety was a splendid laxative and Rose ached to use the toilet. However the sliding steel shutter had the effect of a super-glued bottom bung two sizes too big. She hadn't seen or heard a living soul for two hours but she knew that the moment she settled on the seat, sure as buses going the other way, the door would open and all the lawyers in Chancery would assemble to watch her defecate.

And there was no toilet paper.

After two hours more of suffering, during which time Rose had replayed all the most crushing experiences of her life, occasionally pulling herself round with thoughts of the coming television coverage in which she would expose the abuse to which she had been subjected and the squalid conditions in the cells, she heard footsteps.

The steel shutter shot back and a newspaper was proffered by a uniformed arm.

A voice said: 'There's been massive coverage of your arrest in the evening paper.'

Rose grabbed the paper victoriously and quite forgot to ask for toilet paper.

161

She sat back on the bed excitedly turning the pages. It wasn't on the front page, which was disappointing. Nor page two. Maybe there'd be some kind of feature.

She found herself scrutinising the sports pages before she realised the cruel irony. There was no coverage.

She looked again. On page seven she saw a tiny article with no headline which said: 'An old woman was arrested today on Clifton Drive and charged with obstructing the highway.'

And that was that.

It was worse than nothing.

She gazed at the wall and spotted some grime that looked like a sneering face and realised again that Baz fucks all cunts.

Rose was desolate as she bedded down early for the night.

She managed to scrounge a couple of extra blankets from a sympathetic constable who made her a cup of tea and provided her with some toilet paper, albeit scratch-bottom variety, but her heart was full of bitterness which made the wooden bench all the more uncomfortable. The bed dug into her arthritic hip, the draught chilled her neck and the past cut into her heart.

In the dim light of the late evening her worries were amplified. Everything had been taken from her now and she was scared for her very survival.

Perhaps she would be thrown out of *Newfoundland* even if it didn't close down. Where would she go? Would they commit her to somewhere? Surely not.

She had nothing and no one; she was old and tired and alone. She was angry – they had no right to lock up an old woman.

It was the fault of that nasty Sergeant.

It was the fault of the residents who had abandoned her.

It was her husband's fault; he had been careless

162

and miserable and drunken. Why had they taken that ridiculous stand all those years ago? They had known it was hopeless.

She realised she had done the same. Repeated the errors of the past.

Why?

She turned over and over on the hard bed. Where was everyone? Surely she hadn't been forgotten already.

That was it. She'd been forgotten.

She was struck by the feeling that her life was over. The cell became a tomb and her heart darkened. It had all gone by so quickly. She wasn't ready. She was still full of life. She was afraid to die like this. It was miserable. She deserved better. Where were her friends? Did she have any real friends? The thoughts spinning around in her head disrupted her breathing.

Her heart was racing. It had been racing for hours. Perhaps she should demand to see a doctor?

But it was hopeless to bang on the door.

The man in the next cell had been doing so on and off for hours and the crashing and his cries of drunken anguish shook Rose and gave her a feverish impression that the world was dying with her.

She sat up. It was no good. She could wait no longer. Her bowls ached. It was time to use the toilet which had, mercifully, stopped flushing. She hesitated again, listening for a sound from the corridor.

Then nature took hold and sat her down.

She had just caused quite something of a stink and realised that it would be difficult to get rid of *sans* flush and without proper ventilation, and was about to cut herself with the razor paper when the cell door flew open and in walked an officer accompanied by Jed.

It was a moment before the intruders realised what was causing the smell and retreated apologetically, leaving Rose to blush furiously and wonder what Mr Green was doing there.

*   *   *

163

It was a couple of minutes before Rose realised she was about to be released.

'They've dropped the charges,' Jed was explaining.

'She appears to have gone into some kind of trance,' the desk sergeant joked as he waited for her to sign for her property.

'She's had a nasty surprise,' said Jed. 'Haven't you, Rose?' He was talking to a child.

She signed the form and refused Jed's arm when they came to the steps.

They were silent in the car.

Rose felt she was expected to thank Jed for the lift, or for having helped her in some way, but she would rather have drowned herself in the sewage outlet.

Jed broke the ice.

'I suppose I'd better warn you,' he said, 'You're not very popular at the house. We had the Inspectorate round this afternoon, after your little display. They issued an order recommending immediate closure.'

Rose stiffened. 'I hardly think the two things could be connected.'

'Oh they were. They announced it in front of everyone. They even had the nerve to thank the residents for bringing the state of the place to their attention. Though God knows what they found wrong. It was only because that dreadful woman, Mrs Prior-what's-its-name . . .'

'Prior-Pointment?'

'She intervened and saved us. She seems to have some clout with the Council.'

Jed stressed the connection between the demonstration and the threat of closure several times until he was certain Rose had taken it in.

Rose sat back in her seat and thought to herself that if it were true, her days as respected house representative were over.

'Don't worry,' said Jed, 'No one in the house would be tactless enough to rub your nose in it. They'll just be a little more careful in future. There was a meeting

164

this afternoon and it was decided to appoint me chair of the residents' committee.'

Shortly after the second demonstration, Jed experienced his first extended blackout, although he later had to exaggerate its length to cover up the real events of the 'lost two days'.

Since his last conversation with Miranda, or more specifically, since she put her arm through his by the marine lake and told him that he was taking big risks, then kissed him on the lips on the steps, Jed had felt restless and unsettled.

The second demonstration unnerved him. For a few hours – after the bogus inspectors had left and before Mrs Prior-Pointment had telephoned – he'd had to face the prospect of complete failure once more.

Charity was irritating him again. For months she had spurned him, now she was always touching him, looking to him for attention and he was again unable to respond.

Yet he was full of spunk. He was looking at women all day long – at bus stops, in the street, at Miranda. He was filled with longing which only whisky seemed to still. Dis-still.

He was looking for the door in the wall through which the hero of *Steppenwolf* had stepped. (Marked: 'Magic Theatre, Not for Everyone'.)

He wanted whatever it was those writers of existential fiction had depicted as a heroic, redemptive (debauched) alternative to bourgeois respectability. He wanted to become *The Immoralist*, or *The Outsider*. At least for the weekend.

One day, after a particularly depressing conversation with Charity which had begun 'You don't love me

165

any more', Jed was driving around in Charity's car, cursing away, working himself up into the mood for a good drink, when for the first time in his life the thought occurred to him that he could go with a prostitute. He was so aroused by the idea that he had to stop the car to adjust his trousers and catch his breath.

When he thought about it seriously he realised it would be easy to get away with. Easy.

Which caused trembling in his bones.

Fuckin'ell. His rage was instantly transformed.

The door in the wall opened.

He put the car into gear and revved the engine, but then stopped.

Where the hell do you *get* a prostitute?

Could you get a prostitute?

Of course you could. But he had to admit he had absolutely no idea how to go about it. He searched his memory banks feverishly. Massage parlour. You had to go to a massage parlour.

He pictured walking up to some kind of reception and not being able to look the receptionist in the eye. What if it were a woman? What if it were crowded.

His old self tapped him on the shoulder.

A prostitute? Not very *socialist*, buying someone. But he'd never really *been* a socialist, had he? He was a businessman for God's sake. May as well face it.

Humm. It wasn't very *sensitive*, either. He had always prided himself on his sexual sensitivity. Charity complimented him on it; he always made sure she had her orgasm. Going to a prostitute would go against everything he believed in. In life as in love.

A wet blanket descended.

Shit. He needed the rage.

He went back on his misery – pictured his efforts at work and at home and the years of his commitment. He replayed his persecution by the creditors and finished off with the picture of those meddling busy-bodies from the Town Hall, or the Health and Safety Inspectorate or

166

wherever they crawled out from to cut down people's dreams and throw everyone out onto the streets. He visualised Eddie on some far away beach.

There was rage and anger a plenty.

A prostitute would be his revenge. On them. On himself. On Eddie. He would do it. Now.

Not at a massage parlour though.

He remembered a comment of Eddie's about a certain area of Preston where women hung around on the corners and how it was always busiest there at rush hour, morning and evening, as the men came and went to and from work.

To Preston then.

Jed had seen something on television once about prostitution. The idea was, apparently, that the woman asked you if you wanted 'business' and you said yes and that was that.

He wondered what happened next.

Did you ask how much before they got in? If you didn't they might bump the price up at the last minute. He wondered vaguely if there weren't some statutory maximum price.

When he got to Preston he was disappointed to discover that he hadn't arrived in Babylon and the streets were not paved with vice as he had anticipated.

He decided the best policy would be to circulate for a while around the area that Eddie had spoken about. After twenty minutes of this he was on the verge of giving up and stopping to buy a paper and perhaps check out a massage parlour after all – not a very enthralling prospect – when he espied a figure standing just off the main road down a side street.

His heart leapt with excitement and fear. He jammed his foot on the brakes causing a dangerous situation on the road behind, then blushed furiously because the driver behind might have realised his intention.

Shit, he would have to go round the block.

167

He skidded round a few back streets and got stuck up a No Through Road and nearly wrecked his suspension on the sleeping policemen and eventually and breathlessly got back to the appropriate corner and there she was. Talking to another driver, leaning her arm on the roof, bending in through the door.

Double shit. He stopped the car a little down the road watching the exchange with envy.

She got in and Jed cursed aloud.

She got out again and Jed said, 'Oh my God.'

He thought how attractive she looked.

He took a gulp from a bottle he'd bought on the way then hid it under a coat on the back seat so as not to appear an alcoholic. He put an Extra Strong Mint in his mouth. Then he thought they might need the back seat of the car so he moved the bottle under his seat. He opened the window and wafted in air.

He was so nervous he could hardly breathe, and yet at the same time he was experiencing the most exquisite excitement.

She spotted him immediately. He nodded and turned down the side road before which she was standing and stopped the car. He saw her coming towards him in the mirror.

As she came round to the passenger side he realised the door was locked. He leaned over and the lock jammed because she opened it at the same time as he flipped the catch, so they had an embarrassing sign-language conversation about leaving the handle for a moment while he flipped and unflipped the catch and then finally she was leaning in.

'Business?'

'Yes. Er, please.'

She climbed in. 'Drive on.'

He hadn't asked the price, but obeyed her instructions.

'Take a left here, please.'

He was trembling.

'. . . How much is it?'

She explained the rates using terms like 'Hand Relief', 'Oral' and 'Full Sex'.

It seemed remarkably good value to Jed.

'I've never done this before,' Jed explained, though he had to admit it didn't sound very convincing.

'Have you had a drink, love?'

He nodded. 'Does it show?'

'Smells like a brewery in here!'

He smiled at her candour. 'Would you like one?'

'Have you got some?' She sounded surprised.

He groped under the seat.

'Oo, you've saved my life.' She took a long drink and held onto the bottle. '*Gahh*. Got anywhere to go?'

He shook his head.

'Take a left here, please.'

She was very polite.

'How far are we going?'

'Far as you like,' she laughed.

They stopped in a deserted industrial car park. She handed the nearly empty bottle back (it was only a half-bottle) and when he looked at her, close up like that, he realised she wasn't quite as attractive as he'd thought. Her face looked lived in.

By a family of five.

'What do you want?'

He decided on full sex.

Payment was in advance after which she said, 'Take your trousers down then.'

'Aren't you going to take your clothes off?'

'Full strip's extra.'

'How much?'

'A tenner.'

'OK.'

She fumbled with her clothes until she was undressed and he could see how pale and blotchy she was. He wished it was dark.

'Come on love, I haven't got all night.'

He eased his trousers down, feeling far from aroused.

She took hold of his cock and, before you could say gossamer, she'd fitted him with a condom, wiped the lubricant on his shirt tail and plonked the whole lot into her mouth.

Jed sighed and found himself having to fake pleasure as if he were at home.

She did a comic-book impression of being aroused herself and he found, rather surprisingly, that he had the beginnings of an erection.

As soon as this happened she sat back in her seat and said 'Come on then' and 'Can't you get the seat down?'

Charity's car *was* only a mini.

They had to faff around moving the seat back and, after some fantastically contortionate manoeuvring and a couple of false starts, Jed did manage partial entry, but sufficient penetration would have been impossible without an anaesthetic lumbar-puncture.

So she suggested hand relief or oral at the same rate as full sex because it was his fault he couldn't get it up.

He regretted her use of the term.

He opted for the hand relief and found that no matter how hard she pumped and pummelled and urged him on, telling him she hadn't got all night, he'd somehow lost the ability to ejaculate.

In the end they gave up.

'Maybe it's not for you love,' she consoled. 'Some people find it's just not for them.'

He dropped her back thinking how at least now he had something to tell Miranda but then realised it was too shameful for that.

He got another bottle of Scotch (a full one this time), bought a dirty mag from the garage and checked into a hotel to wank himself stupid, thinking, strangely enough, of the woman he'd unsuccessfully been with that evening. Then he drank himself to sleep staring at satellite TV.

170

The next day he started drinking in the morning, telling himself it was to relieve his hangover, and strolled, then staggered around Preston. He had intended to go back for a woman that night and possibly did except that he couldn't remember a thing that happened after about three o'clock in the afternoon.

He woke up at six o'clock the next morning aching, stinking and sick, sitting in Charity's mini wondering where on earth he was.

*J*ed and Charity were summoned to the office by Miranda.

'Right, you two in the visitors chairs, me behind the desk,' Miranda said and assumed a comic pose, looking at them over fake pince-nez.

'So. You've fucked up. What are you going to do about it?'

The couple's faces matched. Miranda tried not to laugh at the picture.

'Put it this way,' Miranda's impression of a city big-wig went on, 'you made an investment, dividends are negligible, so you either go down, get out, or make big changes.'

Jed and Charity tried not to look at one another but failed.

'Well, I can see you've given the matter great thought and discussed the options. It inspires confidence. Are you about to make an announcement to staff?'

'I don't think . . . I mean . . .' Charity couldn't finish.

'Oh, it's none of my business? It doesn't make any difference to me if you two fuck the thing up and I lose my job because you're too bloody stubborn to be honest with each other and admit that you're in the shit and maybe try and do something before its too late?'

They were stumped by her confronting them together. They were horrified, too, because it was true. Since Jed's arrival on the scene they hadn't mentioned the fact that nothing had improved financially, that the 'austerity measures' had made next to no difference.

Jed had to speak, 'I don't think this is necessarily the right time . . .'

Charity stopped him, nodded. 'She's right Jed, we haven't talked about it.'

'You *are* in the shit aren't you?'

Charity nodded again.

Jed flushed. 'Dog shit.'

'So what were you going to do about it?'

'We don't know,' Charity admitted it. 'You are right, we haven't talked about it.'

'Too busy being the happy couple, eh?'

Jed and Charity blushed. They all knew it wasn't true. It gave Miranda the edge.

'It's a good job I've got it all worked out then, init?'

Miranda had come round to the front of the desk and was looking down at them from what seemed like a great height.

She handed Jed a piece of paper she'd been holding. '. . .?'

'Congratulations, it's your certificate of nursing.'

Jed blushed and looked guiltily at Charity. Did she know? Had Miranda said anything about . . . *Shit* . . . Any minute now she might mention to Charity that she knows the whole story. He was suddenly reminded of the look on Miranda's face the afternoon they had spent together in the cafe by the lake, the impression of her as a stranger. Was she going to drop him in it?

Apparently not. Charity looked interested and surprised, she looked to be keeping an open mind. Miranda went cooly on.

'What's the main cost here?'

172

'Er . . .' Jed shook his head.

'Staff, init?'

Charity said, 'Yes, by far.'

'So sack them, all of them, even the kitchen staff. I'll train Jed up as a nurse. The three of us share the nursing duty . . . if we include Edith in the count it's the legal minimum. The rest of the work gets done by the residents themselves. We supervise. They can do it, I'm sure. It'll be hard, but you'll make pure money.'

'The *residents*. They won't, they couldn't . . .'

Jed was waved away by Miranda's hand.

'Leave the residents to me. All you have to do is double my pay . . .'

Miranda persuaded the residents that not only were they capable of the task, not only was it preferable to any other fate that might await them in some unknown psychiatric unit – or at the hands of relatives who'd already abandoned them – but that in 'looking after themselves, by themselves, for themselves' (as she put it) they would actually be better off both in terms of health and self-esteem.

She countered the main objection, that an uneven burden of work would fall on some, with reference to the basic tenets of Christianity. She even quoted Marx: 'From each according to her ability to each according to her means', although she didn't credit the author.

The only objection to Edith's partial rehabilitation came from Mrs Crotchley who pointed out that Edith had attempted to murder her.

It was all very easy to implement without Rose's chairpersonship of the residents' committee.

Rose sat back and watched the whole process with a withering eye and a huffing bosom.

Jed tried his best to include her. 'Come along, Rose, tell us what you think,' he would say during meetings.

'I don't think any more,' she replied. 'I've retired. You

can do things your own way. Just give me a job and I'll see it's done properly.'

'So you're not against, in principle?' Jed would try.

'I'm neither for, nor against, like the rest of them,' she would say.

One day Mrs Crotchley couldn't resist it. 'Really dear, if you're not going to take part in the democratic process there's nothing we can do,' she said with a cuttingly thin smile. Mrs Crotchley now took the minutes at the meetings.

Rose swallowed her chagrin and kept her political activity to a rugged defence of the right to have the tomato ketchup on the table at meal times. Even so within two weeks the ketchup was being served in little bowls with a teaspoon, despite the extra washing up.

Miranda said there were similar 'community projects' everywhere. 'It's the way they do things these days,' she said.

It was a necessary step if the centre was to survive as a business, but the way it turned out, Jed thought, was socialist.

At heart, anyway.

After (and during) the revolution in the arrangements at *Newfoundland*, Jed and Charity's marriage took a turn for the worse.

Under the new arrangements, the couple only got to spend every second night together at home.

Charity was amazed to find that she was disturbed by this. During the months of Jed's confinement in the house she had found his urgent caresses and clumsy advances pathetic and even mildly repulsive. Now he was busy at the centre in his business suit, clean-shaven, smiling, fending off the old women's good-natured taunts with his briefcase, she found she wanted to fuck his brains out.

At first she'd waited for his advances, but he'd

stopped making them. On the nights they slept together they still frigidly hugged the edges of the bed, and Charity began to feel very needy. For a few weeks she was too proud to break the mould, until, one night, softened by sheer lust, she snuggled into Jed's back before he went flannelling.

Jed responded by letting out an appreciative moan and went promptly to sleep.

Bastard.

The next night was Charity's 'night on' alone at the centre which frustrated her still further. She began to work herself up in a fury over his coldness. One minute he was pestering her for sex, now, as soon as she wanted it, he had turned cold.

She thought back to the bankruptcy, cursed him for not having had Eddie's nerve or imagination, cursed the business he had run and their bad luck. Blamed it all on Jed. But it didn't do any good. She still wanted to fuck him.

One night she bought a bottle of *Bacardi* and a video, turned the sofa round, plonked Jed down, got a little too drunk and shocked them both with the ferocity of her assault.

It was a wild, fiendish release of tension for Charity. She felt both lust and anger rise in her as she thrust herself at him and found it appropriate and satisfying to curse him and swear at him. For some reason she wanted to bite him and hurt him as they grappled. She ground her teeth and hissed and writhed and cut his back with her nails. Her shouts got louder and more obscene. She wanted him to respond and begged him to treat her 'like a slut'. When he obliged she got angrier still.

Jed loved it. (Apart from the fingernails in the back.) He almost forgot she was his wife and quickly adapted to the role in which he was cast, of demon lover.

First he had to suppress a stupid giggle.

When Charity saw this through the aching gloom she hissed: 'Don't laugh at me you bastard!' and slapped him hard across the face and spat at him.

The next ten minutes were the most obscene either of them had ever known and Jed wished it had been like that with the prostitute. There was spitting and slapping and cursing from the wife, and the husband tried with real anger to break her in two, which only increased the begging, the shouting and the swearing. It was as if they hated each other and the sex was an expression of malice and scorn. The climax was simultaneous:.raucous and shattering.

Afterwards they laughed and lay in one another's arms, though both of them were a little shocked and revolted by what had occurred.

The night after next they both wanted to try again and mechanically knocked and rubbed against each other for a while until they were done.

Afterwards they were both struck by the thought that somehow, somewhere along the line their love had died.

*R*ose was gazing from the window in her bedroom (where she now spent most of her time), when she was abruptly recalled from her melancholy cloud-watching by a sight she found difficult to credit.

In the car park, which her room overlooked, a very smart car had pulled up out of which climbed Mrs Prior-Pointment. The gaunt woman unfurled a wheelchair and was in the process of placing her elderly mother in it.

This must be their first fee-paying resident.

Surely not . . .

It had been obvious to Mrs Prior-Pointment as soon as she decided to take time off work to deal with Arthur that Mother would have to be looked after. At first, when the *Newfoundland* solution had presented itself she had dismissed the idea, but the more she considered it the more appropriate, indeed, progressive it had seemed.

Progressive because the trend in such places had to be towards private, fee-paying residents.

Appropriate because the whole thing had been set up as a result of Arthur's actions in the first place. When this thought occurred to her she wondered for a moment whether she was using Mother to get back at Arthur. But no, she decided that it was a multi-facetted solution to an ordinary practical problem. Mother would set an example for others to follow. They were political people, they always had been.

It would be, after all, very reasonable price-wise.

Despite her work to rule, Rose was the first on the scene.

The old woman in the wheelchair was clutching hold of a battered green holdall and refusing to let go of it, munching away and puffing angrily as Mrs Prior-Pointment (the younger) attempted to take it from her.

How on earth did you manage to organise this little lot?' she was saying to her mother-in-law.

Munch munch . . .

'Come along, I've got everything you'll need in the boot . . .'

Rose cleared her throat.

'Can I help you?'

Mrs Prior-Pointment looked unpleasantly surprised and abruptly stopped tugging at the old holdall, without letting go of it. She looked briefly down the considerable length of her almost-Roman nose at Rose.

'Erm. No, thank-you-very-much.' Then to Mother: 'Come along, dear, I'll take that now . . .'

Rose bustled stoutly over and took up a position behind the wheelchair.

'She's determined to take this scruffy old bag with her. It's such a mess.'

The old trade unionist inflated slightly. 'I think it's rather up to her, don't you?'

Mrs Prior-Pointment (the younger) straightened up with a glint of 'and who are *you* to interfere in my family's business' in her eye, when the old green bag unzipped itself and turned upside down, emptying it's contents onto the gravel.

Rose looked down and saw an impressive pile of neatly bundled bank notes, one of which had split so that sterling butterflies fluttered around in the breeze.

The younger Mrs Prior-Pointment grabbed rather inelegantly at the floating hoard, stuffing handfuls back into the old bag, still resting on Mother's knee.

'Now come along, dear!' she blustered, 'I'll take this and put it in the building society for you, that'll be the most sensible thing, won't it?'

There was a munching that even the casual observer (among whom Rose most certainly couldn't be counted) could see meant 'no'.

'It isn't safe to leave quantities of money lying round. It's silly when it could be earning you interest.'

It was time for Rose to act.

She moved round and placed a chubby hand firmly on the bag that had again become the subject of a tug of war.

'Why don't we ask the old lady what she wants to do?' said Rose and without waiting for a response she asked. '*Do* you want the money putting in a building society, dear?'

Both Mrs Prior-Pointment and Rose straightened up, one gaunt, the other stout, to watch the response, which was a munching in the negative.

'You'd rather keep it by you, wouldn't you, dear?'

There was a munching distinctly in the affirmative.

178

Gaunt and stout faced each other. Arms folded, nose almost pointing. There was an invisible conversation which might have been translated along these lines:

MRS PP: *Who* might I ask are *You*?

ROSE: Ah-ha, so, robbing your own mother-in-law now are you?

MRS PP: I know you, don't I? Didn't you work for Arthur? Didn't you run the union, and try to ruin the family business?

ROSE: You've spent your whole life pushing people around, thinking you're superior, now eat shit.

Before any proper exchange was possible, Charity appeared.

'Would you like to come in and see the room?' asked Charity.

'No thank you. I'm in rather a hurry,' Mrs Prior-Pointment said frostily, and, 'I'll come back tomorrow to check on things.'

Rose was sickened by this insensitivity and shoved the wheelchair speedily off with a great huff, nearly jolting old Mrs Prior-Pointment's head off in the process.

Mother didn't look too happy.

And the daughter-in-law didn't come back the next day as she said. Indeed she wasn't seen at the house for months, although she did telephone once or twice to check if there was anything the old woman wanted.

Motivated by curiosity (and the desire to oversee safekeeping of the battered green holdall), Rose appointed herself the old woman's minder. The first task being to help settle the newcomer into her room.

Mrs Crotchley was first on the scene, Tinkerbell nestled in her arms faintly wagging his knob of a tail.

'Well! . . .' she said.

Rose was a little surprised to see Mrs Crotchley's face so contorted and unfriendly. Then she remembered the old story about Mrs Crotchley being the daughter of the old family.

And again, 'Well! . . .'

Mrs Crotchley was advancing into the room, creeping towards the bed as if stalking some kind of prey. Tinkerbell seemed to sense something and gave a preliminary *wiff*!

Rose realised that the new arrival too, was behaving strangely, her beady little eyes flicking nervously about the room, her mouth munching double time.

As Mrs Crotchley added a 'So' to her 'Wells', Rose realised that old Mrs Prior-Pointment's eyes were darting back and forth between Mrs Crotchley and the old green holdall.

Mrs Crotchley progressed to more meaningful speech:

'So this is where you've ended up, is it? With the rest of us. How ironic. After all your efforts. Whatever could have *caused* such a turn? Surely *Arthur* hasn't turned against his *own mother*? After you did such a good job of muscling in and taking over. Well, well. My father's firm. Ha! Didn't do you any good in the end after all did it? Well well well . . .'

Rose gawped. Mrs Crotchley dribbled with spite, Tinkerbell croaked (he was trying to growl). Old Mrs Prior-Pointment watched her old bag with the eyes of a tiger.

So the old story was true.

Mrs Crotchley's own father had started the Prior-Pointment business.

The truth was that in Mrs Crotchley's day a daughter didn't count and while her brother (Arthur Prior-Pointment's father) had inherited the the firm, her own claim to the fortune had never been considered, not even by herself. Little Clarice was educated in ladylike behaviour in readiness to marry herself off. When her husband was shot in the war shortly afterwards, the family installed her in her lowly station, as office secretary.

And that had been that. She was never promoted. She was even sacked with the rest of them when the firm was sold off.

The old matriarch had of course married into the family – married Mrs Crotchley's brother (Arthur's father) – and lived in fine style ever since.

So now the poor old dog-lover, who for years had disclaimed her connection to the great family so that the busybodies in the works couldn't gloat over her misfortune, was able to sneer at the pathetic figure of the abandoned matriarch who was none other than her own sister-in-law. (It took Rose a while to puzzle out the exact relationship.)

'How terribly ironic . . .' Mrs Crotchley was still tutting.

As she watched the scene, Rose found that, despite the past, she was moved to pity the defenceless new-comer and in the heart of her own new-found isolation felt a certain kinship with the pathetic munching woman.

So as a gesture of sympathy and a snub to Mrs Crotchley, Rose picked up the green bag, winked at old Mrs Prior-Pointment who was watching eagerly, and placed it out of sight under the bed.

Old Mrs Prior-Pointment's eyes gleamed, secretly.

So did Rose's.

As other residents drifted into the newcomer's room to gawp at the famous old matriarch, an eerie silence fell as the meaning of the occurrence was mulled over – the imminent and final collapse of civilisation.

The silence was broken when The Terrible Trinity burst onto the scene with their usual grace.

'Well hello. How nice to see you,' boomed Lilly roundly and with warmth. 'What a nice surprise.'

At this moment Tinkerbell jumped from Mrs Crotchley's arms and ran about the room *wiff-wiffing* and, though nobody saw this, lifting his leg in the corner.

181

The unsteady threesome veered dangerously towards the bedside table. 'We're so glad to see you,' Lilly said.

The bedside table was struck and the glass of water went the way of all glasses of water in Lilly's presence.

Recognising Lilly from the old days old Mrs Prior-Pointment looked alarmed at first, expecting some kind of revenge attack.

But by the time Lilly had groped her way to the old woman's hand, taken hold of it, given it a friendly squeeze and continued her friendly expressions, referring to members of the newcomer's family as though they were old friends, said 'And do you remember old Mrs so and so . . .' several times, the munching old matriarch seemed to relax and for the first time in many months a little smile broke over her face.

Tinkerbell's frantic attempts to mate with the bedspread and then lick the old woman's face, seemed to add to the atmosphere of happy chaos. Until he was firmly restrained by Rose, at which point he let out a sudden pained whimper.

'I think it's time we all went downstairs for a cup of tea,' Lilly announced.

There was a bang and a crash as she turned round sending the bedside table the way of the glass of water.

Lilly's last instruction was, 'Mrs Crotchley, you can push our new friend's wheelchair.'

Mrs Crotchley's 'Pssht,' was drowned in the clamour.

Then she did what she was told.

Just as she always had.

When the crowd were gone Rose carefully placed the old green holdall in the farthest corner of the top cupboard of the built-in wardrobe and went back to her room to brood on the ironies of history.

*F*or Jed it was only a short paddle from the back streets of Preston to the muddy waters of obsession with Miranda.

The first frond of his desire for her – a sticky bud of fascination – under the potent husbandry of Miranda's damaged femininity soon became a dense and tangled briar of lust and lechery.

She nurtured the growth on purpose, but not necessarily consciously. She was too insecure about her job and her place in the world to trust to mere good work and *bon chance*. She needed Jed to need her.

Jed needed to feel something solid.

It progressed in stages.

When they were together, which was constantly in the weeks of the reorganisation at *Newfoundland*, Jed was soothed by a benign tranquillity.

After the meeting when they had finally agreed the changes, after Charity had left the room, she rested her hand on his and said:

'I want this to work out, you know.'

Jed was in ecstasy for days.

He began to organise sing-songs for residents and took those who could manage it for a walk along the prom and suggested a night out at the theatre.

She wanted it to work out, you know.

The night out was organised and paid for by Jed with the last of the money he had stashed under the bed. He obtained special group discount from the theatre and the local Round Table provided the transport.

At the theatre, Jed sat between Lilly (who didn't see a thing but said it was the best night out she could ever remember) and Miranda, both of whom took his hand during the show and gave it a hearty squeeze.

'You make me wish I was young again,' Lilly whispered.

Rose was the only able-bodied resident not to attend

the performance. She said she would stay and look after old Mrs Prior-Pointment for the evening.

Jed was very popular after the theatre visit.

In the van on the way back, as the lights of the illuminations flickered over their happy faces, Miranda sneakily held Jed's hand in the dark while all the old women, including Mrs Crotchley, sang for Jed, *You Made Me Love You*.

Jed had the feeling that Miranda saw him in a different light to other men in her life.

'I like the way you do whatever you want,' he often said to her and even partially meant it.

'I've never been able to talk to a man like this before,' she would lie.

She constantly cast him in the role of *confidant*, letting him in on the most intimate details of her sex life. Jed suffered the most appalling envy, while maintaining an air of calm worldliness, often expressing surprise at the inferior attitudes of the local Romeos who seemed inevitably to fall in love with her.

'They want you all for themselves,' he would say, 'Most guys are like that – especially round here.'

'Tell you what though,' she would say, 'He had a massive dick. I was hobbling the next day.'

Jed would throw his head back and laugh when really he might have howled like a dog.

But his advantage lay in their intimacy. So long as he didn't show her that he wanted her, or make demands that would scare her away, and was always there for her no matter what, she would gradually but irresistibly fall for him without even realising it, he reasoned.

'Reasoned' isn't the word to describe the process. It was more like *un*reasoning.

He wanted her, but there was no way he could have her. There was no way he would leave Charity for her. There was no way he could have an affair with her under Charity's nose. Yet at the same time he went about laying the foundations for an affair. There was a special part of his consciousness where this could take place, a part which he could, during the ordinary business of the day, bury out of even his own sight.

The flannel-wetting part.

The process increased his feelings of claustrophobia at home. He would curse his marriage now along with the decorations while knowing he wouldn't do anything about it. It was as if he was waiting for something *outside* to come along and solve it all.

At that time there was no one at *Newfoundland* who was bedridden, so for bed-bath training Jed lay on the bed (fully clothed) while she went through the correct procedure in the correct order. When she got to his 'tackle' as she called it, she made him hoot with her mime of washing him as if his cock were enormous. 'Make sure you do it like *this* and not like *that* (wanking gesture),' she said. 'Doubles the work.'

Neither of them mentioned that there were no men in the home.

Then it was his turn and she jumped onto the bed, guiding and chiding him until he arrived at her 'bits', when she said, 'Now, do you know your way around here, or do you want me to show you?'

He wanted her to show him, but said, 'I'm a married man. I think I know my way round.'

'It doesn't necessarily follow,' she laughed, then said, 'Basically you put the legs here,' and then demonstrated the wiping technique. When Jed was blushing deeply enough she exaggerated the action so that it became an impression of having a hearty wank, complete with noises that were so realistic Jed broke out in a sweat.

When she sat up, she said, 'God I feel horny now,' in such a way that Jed thought in all seriousness they were going to have sex there and then.

Often when he went back over the scene alone in the bathroom, he felt a stab of remorse, wondering whether he had blown it by not making a move, and kicked himself for having done an impression of a goldfish instead. But really he knew it was impossible for him to start anything and that he had to follow her lead. He reminded himself that she valued their friendship and told himself that sex would reduce him to the level of a local Romeo.

But then again, what about her speeches on 'the older man'? Had she really said all that, or had he imagined it? He couldn't be sure. 'An older man, who I could have sex with who wouldn't want to control me.' That was it. 'Preferably one who was tied'. Or was that his own embellishment?

He'd wring his memory to recover the details of conversations they'd had, analyse them for hints that she was falling for him, replay and rewrite them, then go out to get hot, steaming drunk.

Gradually he became her servant.

Whenever he could he ran her around in Charity's car, often dropping her off when she went to meet a man, sometimes even picking her up afterwards. On one occasion she phoned him in the middle of the night – when Charity was on duty – and asked him to come and rescue her from the clutches of a growling lover. He had to park outside and sound the horn, while she made a run for it. Afterwards they walked along the beach until morning.

Nothing was too much trouble.

Nothing was *enough* trouble.

One evening Jed was consulting a pornographic magazine in the bedroom at home when Miranda called.

After about half an hour of hostageless confession from her, which caused an inch of air to insert itself between Jed and the paisley sofa on which they were sitting, Miranda went off to the toilet.

When she'd failed to return after ten minutes, Jed went to investigate. She called him from the bedroom where she was sitting on the bed reading the magazine Jed had left there when he went to answer the door.

Jed's socks blushed.

'Have you got any more of these?' she asked with arched eyebrows.

'Na. Just that one Eddie gave me ages ago.'

'You liar! Come on, I love them. Where are they?'

Jed was shocked that Miranda could apparently share his taste in mags and showed her (part of) his collection. He was astounded when she leafed lustily through them saying things like, 'Look at her! She's really asking for it', 'Urrgh, look at that dog!' and, 'What *she* needs is a good fisting!'

There was a flurry of activity in the script writing department after that. Jed's imagination ran riot for weeks creating ever more perverse images and improbable scenarios for him to hurt himself with to the point of orgasm.

Fleshy, rotten chunks fell away from his already putrifying heart.

He cherished the very perversity of it all – even the new arrangements at the centre seemed perverse when he thought about them. 'Perverse socialism,' he called it once. It made him feel bohemian and revolutionary.

He began to feel drunk when he was sober.

*M*iranda and Charity decided to have a girls' night in to celebrate the success of the first months of the new system at *Newfoundland*.

Miranda agreed to bring round a couple of videos and Charity said she'd get the beer in. When she arrived Miranda had a big grin on her face.

'What's the matter with you?'

'I've got a couple of surprises.'

The grin spread to Charity's face. She was in the mood.

It was Jed's 'night on', so they knew they wouldn't be disturbed.

The figures for the period were good. Very good. Charity had been having a gloat over them before Miranda arrived. If things carried on like this they'd be laughing. Their worries were over.

Miranda knew things were going well, especially when her pay was increased again by a staggering fifty per cent. This, coupled with Charity's invitation to celebrate and Jed's week long sobriety had made her curious to see the figures for herself. She knew, however, she wouldn't get the chance.

'Here's to business,' toasted Charity when she had uncorked a bottle of wine. 'What's the surprise?'

'That's for me to know and you to wonder,' teased Miranda. 'Urrgh! What's this stuff?

'It's *Muscadet*. Speciality of Brittany.'

'Tastes like piss!'

She didn't have much trouble drinking it though while they watched the video.

When the film was over Charity said, 'I don't like crime films. Everyone always gets caught.'

'Only on TV'

'Do you reckon?'

'Course! You only get caught in real life if you're stupid, or if someone grasses you up.'

188

'I can't even watch *Columbo* at the moment,' sighed Charity. 'You know when he's just about to leave the room and the bad guy thinks he's done very well out of it, and then Columbo turns round and says "Oh just one more thing" and then asks a really awkward question? Makes me shiver.'

'You're just paranoid.'

'I feel like I've got reason to be paranoid.'

'Hey – it's only a fake nursing certificate . . .'

Charity nodded. She had no idea that Jed had let Miranda in on the whole thing. 'Yeah, just the certificate, yeah.'

Miranda raised her glass innocently. 'We're cel-e-bra-ting, re*mem*ber!'

'Cheers,' Charity said.

'OK, here's your first surprise.'

Miranda rummaged in the pocket of her jeans and produced a small fold of paper, opening it with care.

'Cocaine,' she grinned.

Charity's eyes lit up wickedly. 'Where on earth did you get that?'

'Oh, this rich guy I shagged last week.'

Charity blushed. 'It gives me this irresistible urge to masturbate.'

Miranda hooted. 'Don't mind me!'

She cut up the powder with Charity's new credit card.

'Just take a little bit at a time,' she suggested as she put out two lines and rolled up a tenner, shoving it up one of her nostrils. 'Here's to the new era,' she laughed.

There's nothing like cocaine to get you to open your trap.

'Do you ever wonder what it's all for?' said Charity some lines later.

I *know* what it's all for,' beamed Miranda from under her shaggy mop. 'My problem is I can't find anyone to do it with who doesn't want to marry me afterwards!'

189

'I don't mean that.'

Miranda nodded. 'You're on about having kids again.'

'I'm on about having a life.'

'I thought everything was going OK?'

Charity grinned. 'As soon as it gets alright I start worrying what it's all for.'

'How are you getting on with hubby?'

Charity sighed.

'That bad uh? Do you still want to try something a bit different?'

Charity grinned. 'Some*one* a bit different, you mean?'

'You said it.'

'You said it originally.'

Miranda coughed onto her nails and shined them modestly.

Charity lowered her voice. 'Shall I tell you a secret?'

Miranda's jaw dropped. 'Oh my God you haven't!'

'I haven't *done* anything.'

Miranda laughed. 'Why are you whispering then!'

Charity couldn't help but whisper. 'Well, you know that new doctor?'

'Y-*es*?' Grave.

'He phoned me and asked me out to dinner.'

'You didn't say yes!'

Charity was surprised, 'I thought you'd have been in favour.'

Miranda was trying to sound casual. 'He probably just wants a shag.'

'Well, exactly.'

'Oh my God. What have I done!'

'It's nothing to do with you. It was all my own work.'

'What the hell do you see in *him*?'

'I think he's charming.'

'Charming! I call that creepy.'

'He's obviously not your type. Too old for you probably.'

'You're not that much older than me!'

'No. Huh, I just act it.'

Miranda tried a different tack. 'I dunno – it's asking for trouble shagging someone that close to home.

'I haven't "shagged" him.'

'Not yet, you haven't.'

Charity grinned.

'You'll make Jed jealous.'

'It'll do him good!'

Charity tapped a finger on the side of her nose. Miranda took the hint and chopped up some more of the drug. Better drop it, she thought.

While she watched the operation, Charity chatted for a few more minutes trying to convince herself that the doctor *was* charming, trying unsuccessfully to get Miranda to say at least one nice thing about him. Then she said, 'To be honest I think Jed's got a crush on *you*.'

Miranda looked up. 'He's definitely got a crush on me.'

Charity grinned. 'I don't blame him.'

'Thanks.'

When they'd both had a good sniff Miranda announced that it was time for the second surprise of the evening.

She produced a video from her bag. 'It's the dirtiest video in the world.'

Charity rubbed her hands with glee. 'I've never seen one of those before.'

The phone rang.

'I'm a bad influence.'

'You're a good bad influence,' Charity giggled as she went into the other room to answer the phone.

As soon as she was alone Miranda pounced on the folder Charity had been reading before she arrived. It was there on the side and Miranda guessed immediately that it contained the figures they were celebrating. It took her a few minutes for her to realise how good they actually were. She felt a little peeved that her pay had only been increased by another fifty per cent.

191

She heard the phone being replaced and tossed the folder back on to the table.

'We're going to be famous,' announced Charity when she came back in. 'That was a woman from Granada TV – they're making a documentary. They want to include us in it . . .'

Miranda wasn't saying a word so Charity went on.

'. . . They're interested in the way we work – they've caught wind of it from somewhere.'

'So you told them to fuck off and mind their own business.'

'Course I didn't!'

There had been some kind of transformation. Charity was glowing.

'A few minutes ago you were worried about watching *Columbo* on TV in case he sniffed you out – now you want the whole world to poke their nose in!'

'It'll be good publicity. We might get some more fee-paying residents out of it,' said Charity.

Charity was already preparing some more cocaine. Rather clumsily.

'I'll do that,' said Miranda. She was going to have to talk to Jed.

When Miranda was done, Charity said, 'What about that film then?'

'I'm warning you, it's extremely disgusting.'

'Excellent!'

So the lights went off and the film went on and for the first five minutes Charity was really shocked.

'Oooh! You actually see it going in!' she said and 'Oh my God! I didn't know they came that big!' and 'Where the hell does it all go!'

Then even more surprisingly a few minutes later she found herself turned on by it. Then she got another shock: 'Jesus they actually come!' Finally she got into the spirit of the thing and started enjoying herself.

Miranda said, 'It isn't a proper film unless you see it going in and see it coming out.'

192

After another ten minutes Charity said, in a low voice, 'Miranda . . . *Do* you mind if I masturbate?'

Miranda looked shocked and said, '*I most certainly do!*'

Charity blushed and regretted having asked.

Then Miranda laughed and said, 'But you can have a wank if you like . . .'

Warning: Cocaine can seriously damage your moral well-being.

*I*t was Miranda who broke the news to Jed about the documentary.

Next morning she made sure she arrived at work before Charity. She found Jed slouched sleepily in the creaky old office-chair exhausted from a night of waking dreams.

'Excellent!' he said.

'I knew you'd say that. It's impossible, you'll have to put them off.'

Jed was amazed at her attitude. 'It's just the publicity we need!'

The Department of Social Security had announced that week that state funding for elderly people seeking residential care was to be cut. Not of course directly, but effectively through a subtle change in the law relating to the money made available to local authorities. This meant no new residents for *Newfoundland* unless they could attract private customers – a difficult task for a previously state run enterprise with its legacy of lower caste denizens, especially given the 'sensitivity' of those people affluent enough to afford private residence.

'Publicity is the last thing we need.'

'It's perfect. It couldn't have come at a better time.'

Miranda sighed plaintively. 'What about the fact that

the whole bloody thing's a big fraud!'

Jed got up and checked through the door's glass that there was no one in the entrance hall.

'Don't be daft. If we were going to be found out we'd have been rumbled ages ago.'

'Not to mention *Newfoundland*'s fully qualified staff! How do you know they're not setting you up?'

'I think you're being a bit paranoid,' he said, 'They'd be suspicious if we turned them down.'

Miranda knew it was hopeless. 'You're gunna get into trouble. You're getting careless.'

By the end of the week *Newfoundland* was in an uproar of excitement over the documentary.

It was blown up out of all proportion in the residents' minds. As far as they were concerned they were all to become TV stars.

Any lingering doubts in the minds of residents about the revolution in the management of the centre, in which they got to do all the work and Jed and Charity got to make all the money, evaporated under the iridescence of the divine light of the coming glory.

Sensing her moment, Rose stepped up the campaign for her rehabilitation. She had worked hard since her disgrace. If stealthily.

On her return from the police station all those months ago, she had found that her status within the house was zero and, what was worse, her role had been largely usurped by Mrs Crotchley.

So Rose kept herself to herself and in isolation worked out a strategy she thought rather clever.

Technically of course it was theft, and it wasn't without regret that Rose helped herself to her first handful of money from the battered green holdall belonging to old Mrs Prior-Pointment. Indeed the matter played on her mind for several nights as she tossed and turned uncomfortably on the coarse mattress of philosophical speculation.

Rose had always been a believer in the redistribution of wealth, not necessarily in exactly equal proportions, but she did believe firmly in the bulldozing of the mountain.

After some discomfort she came to the conclusion that it wasn't theft after all.

The money belonged to the residents in the first place.

Lilly, Edith and Mrs M and several other of the residents – even Mrs Crotchley herself – had worked for the Prior-Pointments in the old days and given the best part of their lives in service. Most had been poorly paid and many more had been cheated in the upheaval of the strikes and sackings.

The rest of the residents – working class women like herself – had suffered elsewhere.

And Rose wouldn't spend a penny of the money on herself.

No.

The money would be spent on little items con-sidered necessary by residents but now considered unaffordable under the new regime: a fan heater here, a new electric blanket there.

Each time she dipped into the bag – still out of reach in the top cupboard of the built-in wardrobe in old Mrs-Prior-Pointment's room – she wrote a neat little IOU and tucked it carefully into the tiny side pocket, telling herself that one day she would repay the money.

As each 'gift' was presented Rose said, 'I've managed to persuade the owners to squeeze a few pennies out of petty cash. Don't tell anyone dear, especially not Mrs Crotchley, you know what she's like over the budget.'

Under the new arrangements Mrs Crotchley was in charge of the residents' share of the budget, and the parsimony of her ways, legendary from the old days, was already causing trouble.

Rose knew her moment was coming. She could feel it in her arthritic hip.

In the days after the figures had been produced, Jed and Charity openly flirted with one another. The phone call from Granada TV brought them closer still.

They didn't get as far as making love, but there was unmistakable philandery.

During a rota-planning session Miranda had to say: 'Shall I leave the room while you two have a shag?'

But memories of their last sordid encounter prevented Jed and Charity actually going further – neither of them wanted a repeat of that scene – so they flirted around enjoying the cordiality, perhaps waiting for the opportunity to present itself. For the first time in months they behaved like friends: watched TV, laughed together and even managed to go to the pub and have a conversation about nothing at all of any importance. Until Charity said, after a gulp of lager and lime, 'Jed, do you think we should have a more open relationship?'

Jed was a bit shocked.

'I thought we already had one.'

'No. I mean more open in the sense of,' she hesitated, 'less married.'

'Are you suggesting a divorce?'

'You know I'm not.'

He didn't return her smile.

'Well what *do* you mean?'

'I dunno, we become more . . . *separate* . . . as *people*.'

'You're having an affair.'

'No . . .'

'It's that doctor.'

'I'm talking about us becoming two separate people again, that's all, being more ourselves. We hardly see each other and when we do we're not even friends. Our marriage is getting in the way of that. I'm just saying let's give each other some more space. And stay friends.'

As Jed contemplated her adultery his mind wandered momentarily to himself and Miranda.

The whole idea became more agreeable.

'It probably is worth trying,' he said.

She went to the bar to get some more drinks.

'To friendship,' they toasted when she came back and fell to talking about pleasant matters of no importance again, like furniture, debts getting paid and TV programmes.

That night they were more friendly in bed. Charity lay on her stomach instead of on the side which faced her away from him, and Jed curled towards her, his knees lightly touching her bare leg. As sleep neared, Charity asked, 'Do you still love me, Jed?'

To which he replied (old style), 'Of course I do,' and didn't return the question.

He never did.

If he had, Charity would have said, 'I *think* I do,' causing Jed to feel insecure enough to want to make love immediately.

It was the next day that Miranda disappeared.

She didn't turn up to work, neither was she to be found at her flat. Jed and Charity argued over who would do her shift that night.

The next day there was still no sign of the young nurse and the whole system began to show signs of strain.

At first neither Jed nor Charity supposed the absence would continue for long and though they said nothing they both suspected it was a protest, to let them know just how indispensable she had become. It was less than a week before the television crew would turn up.

For days a pall of gloom cloaked the house as the residents realised how much *they* relied on the young nurse, how much they liked her. She had a way of

197

making each one of them feel special and somehow when she was around life was all the more worthwhile.

'Physiotherapy of the heart,' Rose called it once.

By the end of the week Jed was beginning to realise that Miranda might never be seen again and he was numbed by the thought.

Charity seemed to be even worse affected than Jed. A fact which Jed put down to their girls' talk. 'She's got no one to tell tales on me to now,' he said to Lilly one morning.

It was Jed's turn to work that night (again) and he went to bed early to watch TV and feel sorry for himself, that is drink whisky. He'd have to get up later and do the rounds before finally sleeping but bed seemed the only consolation. Bed and whisky: an especially toxic mix.

He felt like a jilted lover.

At the same time he was worried that Miranda had abandoned a sinking ship – perhaps they really were being careless. The prospect of prison occurred to him again. Why hadn't he listened to her? Perhaps the television crew *would* unearth some of their secrets. Maybe it *was* a set up. He cursed Charity for having accepted the offer without consulting him.

He slurped from his bottle and wondered where Miranda had gone. He wondered if she would find an older man who would let her do whatever she wanted without question and with whom she would eventually fall in love and stay with him in his nice apartment whenever she wanted.

Gulp. Gahh.

Then the door of the staff living-quarters opened and in she walked. A big smile broke over Jed's face. He could hardly summon the wit to greet her before he realised she wasn't smiling.

Miranda just managed to blurt, 'Jed . . .' before a great sob welled up and choked her speech. Then she dashed across the room, flung herself on the bed, buried her head in his chest and they were both engulfed in her distress.

*F*or months now Mrs Prior-Pointment had occupied her time perfecting her disguise, her new self.

The racy haircut had been the first step. From the looks on their faces she suspected some of the ladies thought her overcome by mischief, but she reassured herself that she had copied the close-cropped style from fashion magazines; that the ladies were out of touch – a bunch of fuddy-duddies some of them, without a flicker of life left inside.

Next came the clothes and the make-up.

She needed a complete outfit. Several of them. Including a swimming costume and hat for the beach. And jewellery – extravagant earrings and bangles, the sorts of things no one would have dreamt she'd wear.

The thing was to make herself look younger.

The loss of weight helped of course, but she needed toning, so she took herself down to a local gym and joined the aerobics class, went out jogging and did exercises every morning.

She sat in town and watched younger women to see how they moved and dressed, copying them later in front of the mirror.

The make-up was more of a problem.

She didn't want to look like a young Barbara Cartland, her face cracked with flaking, dried foundation, her eyes those of a corpse. In the end she opted for sunglasses of a different shape for the day and a pair of flamboyant fake glasses for the evenings, coupled with earrings. She would wear blusher only and hold her mouth in a different way. She tried a different perfume. This was her breakthrough.

With the sharp new perfume she felt like a different person. She instantly found the character she wanted to create, with a new walk, a different stance, even her features seemed to change. It all fell into place with the fresh scent.

Mrs Rodgers, that would be her name.

She pranced around the house for a couple of days like a girl whose mother has gone away leaving her the freedom of the house.

Then she was packed and on the plane to Gibraltar.

She first saw Arthur when 'Mrs Rodgers' was sitting on the balcony of the hotel dressed in her swimming costume and a long cotton dress unbuttoned at the front. She was watching their apartment across the square, looking through a pair of binoculars.

It was her first morning and she was really only trying out her position, checking that she could not be seen, practising adjusting the focus on the binoculars, when suddenly he was there. Her heart leapt and she nearly dropped the binoculars over the balcony.

Until that moment it hadn't seemed real.

Seeing her husband there as a stranger, strolling pleasantly across the plaza she felt a new wave of desire for him. She hadn't intended to follow him on the first day, rather to keep an eye on the apartment, check the timing of his movements to and fro and get used to the idea of seeing him and not being with him. But when he stopped and chatted with some old men sitting on a bench in the shade, she yielded to her feelings and, with a sense of exquisite excitement, gathered her things and ran out of the room. She buttoned herself up while pattering down the stairs.

When she came out into the dazzle, she caught a glimpse of him disappearing down one of the narrow streets off the square and ran after him with a hand on her hat and a thumping in her chest.

She followed him for about ten minutes before she lost him. She had been over-cautious, skulking out of sight, far behind; he had been too quick, the streets too winding.

She would have to be bolder.

When he emerged that afternoon, she was sitting at the table of a cafe in the square, feeling nervous, but determined. She left her money on the table with the bill and skipped after him.

This time she stayed close. Sometimes as close as a few yards behind as he walked jauntily through the bustle. There were postcard-stands and tourist shops in plenty so it was easy to stop when he did and hide behind some display, while all the time keeping an eye on his progress.

He looked so happy and calm and contented there in the shade of the busy street, dressed in his light summer clothes. Perhaps she imagined it, but it seemed to her that a lot of people smiled at him, admired him as he passed grandly by and in a peculiar way she felt proud to be his wife.

She followed him to a cafe where he met some very ordinary-looking men.

After dithering for a moment on the pavement opposite, she daringly sat at a table a little way off, behind him, in the same cafe.

She noticed one of the men had a scar down the side of his face. It was hard to see it at first because it was buried in his healthy, tanned wrinkles. It was him – she recognised him from the detective's photographs – he was one of the 'heavies'. 'Rodriguez', he called himself now. Not very original, she thought, not as good as 'Mrs Rodgers'.

At that moment another man walked in and joined them. Her heart stammered. It was Eddie whoever-he-said-his-name-was. Dash it. This Eddie fellow was sharp and cunning (unlike Arthur); she cursed herself for having been too bold on the first day.

Without recognising her, Eddie settled himself down at the table. The disguised wife realised she was trembling.

As she watched, Rodriguez slid a briefcase across the floor, under the table, so that it ended up by Arthur's chair. When she looked up Rodriguez was looking directly at her. He smiled and gave her a flirtatious wave with four fingers.

All the men looked round at her, presumably to see who Rodriguez was waving at. From behind her sun-glasses, she looked right into Arthur's face. She thought she would pass out.

After checking her out for the briefest of moments, with a faintly disdainful look on his face, which betrayed not the slightest recognition or surprise, or even interest, Arthur turned back to the table and muttered something. There was a raucous kind of laugh among them.

It was time to make her exit.

Just as she was about to make a move Arthur stood up and left with the briefcase that had been passed to him.

Rodriguez was still leering dangerously at her, so she gathered up her things quickly and stumbled self-consciously for the door. She realised halfway out that she hadn't paid her bill and blushing furiously had to go back. She placed a large note on the table and flew out of the cafe, another peal of raucous laughter behind her.

She followed Arthur a little more cautiously now. He was moving more quickly than before. He was more business-like altogether.

She was still trembling, but reassured herself that not even her husband had seen through her disguise.

She saw Arthur dip suddenly into a tourist shop.

She followed him in.

He was talking loudly and in a very friendly way to a

202

large fat man, with filthy dirty hair and a big moustache – obviously the owner, who she also recognised from the detective's mug shots.

There were a few other people in there. She browsed discreetly behind the sun-glasses stand.

Arthur placed the briefcase by the side of the counter and walked out of the shop briskly. She stayed long enough to see the man place the briefcase out of sight behind the counter.

She followed Arthur to the beach then.

His young woman was waiting for him. .

She kissed him and he took off his smart clothes to reveal swimming trunks. The young woman folded his clothes, putting them neatly in a bag.

From the beach cafe, Mrs Rodgers, spy, watched the couple play Frisbee and swim and talk and laugh.

At one point the young woman came into the bar and ordered a couple of beers with a husky 'Hello sexy' to the barman.

Yes well you can afford to drink beer at your age, thought the poor wife. As she listened to the foolish conversation and watched the silly flirting she thought the girl was exaggerating her huskiness. Yes well she probably has little else to offer – a proper little madam.

After one or two G&Ts and three or four stabs of jealousy the good woman left Arthur and the girl to their beach games.

'Enjoy yourself while it lasts, dear,' she said aloud as she walked back up the path to the town.

A man smiled at her and she nodded.

'You want company?' he asked in a foreign accent.

'No thank you,' she smiled. 'I'm doing fine by myself.'

It was the perfect time to be in Gibraltar. The temperature, though very hot, was not oppressive and though the crowds had thinned out for the end of the season there were still enough people to cover her espionage.

She had been there for five days now. Originally she decided she would watch Arthur and his associates for two or three days at most but, when she realised how easy it would be to go undetected and how exciting it felt to act the part of a spy, she decided to stay incognito for a little longer. She wanted to get a bit of sun too, before showing herself, so that when she and Arthur sat on the beach together she would not have to skulk under an umbrella and be a nuisance with her sun block. She would walk boldly with him and swim when he wanted to. And play Frisbee.

On the fifth night, when she was sure Arthur was home alone, she bathed, dressed and assessed herself in front of the mirror. She was proud of her achievement. She looked fit. She *was* fit. She looked modern – not flighty, but elegant. She was a mature woman, wifely in the best sense, capable of womanly suffering, yet able to make her own demands and assert herself.

Tonight she would prove it.

She left the bulky luggage in the hotel when she checked out, with instructions for it to be stored until further notice. She took a smart overnight bag with her, walked briskly over the square and pressed the buzzer to the apartment.

There was a *Crrrr*. 'Hello?' Arthur's voice.

She said with exaggerated huskiness, 'Open up, naughty boy.'

He said, 'Hello, sexy.'

There was a buzz, she pushed open the door and went up the stairs.

As Miranda lay in his arms sobbing convulsively, Jed lay perfectly still except for his hand which smoothed the hair on her forehead.

As he did this he realised he had never touched her before other than for a moment and generally by accident. She seemed to generate static electricity.

He was moved to the most abject sympathy and yet at the same time he was electrified and uplifted. He felt so big and full he could feel the concrete foundations of the building pressing down on the earth underneath.

His arm had gone dead by the time she stopped sobbing, but there was no way he would have moved even if his whole body had gone dead and been cremated.

When she began to speak, without looking up, or wiping her eyes, to Jed her voice sounded as if it were in another time.

'I just had to go. My head went. It happens sometimes, when I feel like I'm losing control of things. I don't know why. (A pause.) I felt like I was getting in the way . . .'

Jed blinked. 'Getting . . . in the way? . . .'

'Jed, it was terrible. I went to Manchester. I knew what I was going to do. I went straight there. It was like I *had* to.'

He couldn't take it in properly. He thought he should tell her she could never be 'in the way', but he couldn't interrupt. What did she *have* to do? What did she know she was going to do?

There was silence for a while, even the cars that drove past on the road held their breath.

She tightened her grip on him.

'I was going to come straight back, but as soon as I'd used it – I only smoked it – I had to get more.'

Jed's head was spinning. 'Only smoked what?'

'I lost it completely, Jed. I was straight back where I was before I moved here – worse. Just like that. I spent all my money in a couple of days – everything I saved working here – fucking everything. I'd saved loads.'

'Where did you stay?'

She shook her head, choked.

'You should've come straight back.'

'I couldn't . . .'

They were quiet again for what seemed like hours, the space of a minute or so. Jed could sense Miranda was trying to tell him something.

She was.

'Jed, I ended up on the corner waiting for someone to pick me up.'

Another clump fell from Jed's heart. 'On the corner? . . .' His voice wobbled. 'Did . . . did anyone stop?'

'I've never done that before, not like that, not on the fucking corner.'

Jed was breathing heavily.

'And afterwards I went and scored and went straight back again. On the fucking corner.'

She cried some more then. Jed stared at nothing and ground his teeth and held her more tightly. He was angry. What sort of world was it when such things could happen to a young woman like Miranda?

He pictured her there, on the corner, waiting.

With a stab of self-loathing he found he was getting an erection and that he wanted to make love to her himself.

Vile.

She told him how even on the first day she'd bought hundreds of pounds worth of 'rock' – she explained this was crack cocaine – which had made her want heroin all the more. In the end she'd slept with one of the dealers – 'a dirty horrible bastard' – and ripped off the money he had lying around and some of his supply.

'I couldn't believe how quickly it got bad. It was instant.'

In the end she'd just got back on the train before it

was too late – or the guy caught up with her. She didn't know how she made herself do it.

She cried more and told Jed she'd brought some heroin back with her and showed it to him and he suggested throwing it down the sink in the corner. She agreed but he had to do it because she couldn't. It was embarrassing because Jed had to get across the room to the sink while concealing his ridiculous arousal.

When she'd recovered from the shock of the drug going down the sink, which took a few minutes of trembling and cursing, she said, in a smaller voice than Jed had heard before, 'What do you think of me now?' and hung her head.

'Huh. What do you mean?'

'Do you still like me after I . . . you know.'

'Of course I do. I . . . feel just the same.'

'I thought you wouldn't like me any more if you knew.'

'Don't be stupid. It doesn't make any difference. It couldn't make any difference.'

'Will you still be my special friend.'

'All the more so.'

Jed was stunned by this exchange. It made him want to tell her that he loved her like he'd never loved anyone ever before. What was that she'd said about feeling like she was getting in the way? In the way of what? Could she mean in the way of his relationship with Charity? He hoped so.

They lay for a long while and she helped him drink his whisky and eventually cheered up slightly. She started to laugh about some of the men she'd been with, telling Jed what they'd said and the crazy things they'd wanted, saying, 'Men are such a bunch of weirdos.'

Jed decided to tell her about his trip to Preston as she perched on the edge of the bed, sipping away.

'What you didn't black out for two days?'

'I did black out, but not for two days.'

She was calmer now, definitely.

'So what did you do?'

'I met a woman.'

'Fuck, where?'

'Oh, just in the hotel.'

'What, a prostitute?'

'*No*! She was staying there, some conference.'

'Did you shag her?'

Jed nodded.

'Was it good?'

'It was alright.'

'Was she horrible?'

'She was alright.'

'You naughty man. And there's me thinking you were happily married.'

'Well, married, anyway. We had a talk the other night. The night before you disappeared. We've decided to have a more open relationship.'

'Oh yeah? What does that mean?'

'It means I don't get to feel so guilty.'

'About feeling women up at parties and going with prostitutes?'

'She wasn't a prostitute! I told you . . .' he laughed like a liar.

'What about Charity?'

'She gets to do her own thing.'

'What, you mean you don't mind if she goes out and gets laid?'

'If she wants.'

'And you won't get jealous?'

He was scratching his ear. 'She doesn't want to go out and get laid.'

'Really?'

'She just wants a bit more freedom.'

'Freedom to do what?'

He shrugged. 'Whatever it is she wants to do.'

'So long as it's not going out and getting laid.'

'That too if she wants.' He laughed. He was embarrassed by the conversation. 'I just can't imagine her doing that. It's not her way.'

'You want to keep an eye on that doctor.'

'She's not interested. She told me.'

'Bloody hell. I'm never getting married.'

'You're not the type,' he laughed, a bit harshly, 'Not dishonest enough.'

'You'd be surprised.'

'"Honestly dishonest", that's you.'

She smiled and gulped more of the whisky and he noticed how tired she looked and wanted to wrap her up safely in his arms forever. He saw the two of them as some kind of bizarre father and daughter. Very bizarre.

She said 'Jed can I get in with you? I need to sleep.'

'Of course you can,' his mouth replied of its own accord.

She tugged her clothes off leaving on only her T-shirt and pants. When she took her top off, her T-shirt almost went with it and Jed caught a glimpse of her breasts.

It must have shown on his face because she said, 'Don't worry, I won't rape you.'

As she climbed in he remembered he still had to do the rounds, so he stooped awkwardly into his trousers and ran round the house throwing pills at residents and turning lights off.

Then he was back and they were in bed.

'That was quick.'

'I don't hang about.'

'I hope you're not neglecting your patients, nurse,' she laughed.

Jed had to suggest that she curl up into his back because the bed was so small, but really it was because of his twitching.

When they snuggled down it felt as if his back was being kissed by angels.

Miranda said, 'Jed, don't let me go off in the morning, whatever I say, don't let me go off . . . *please.*'

He promised.

He knew he wouldn't sleep and lay feeling her every

209

breath, mentally savouring every square inch of contact, where their legs touched, where at one point her hand rested lightly on his stomach (which was almost too close for comfort).

He roamed in verses of deranged poetry and such was his anxiety that, without carnal contact of any kind, he felt the experience was as exhilarating as any sex he'd ever had.

After an astonishingly beautiful period of silence when he thought she'd been asleep for ages – during which time his stomach began to ache from the pressure of a suppressed fart – she shuffled infinitesimally and said, 'So you do still like me then?'

A few moments later Jed managed to say:

'I love you, Miranda.'

She was asleep.

He was awake all night. He may have fallen asleep towards morning, but he couldn't be sure.

In the morning he felt her wake up.

Contrary to his expectation she clung hold of him and moved closer.

'How do you feel?' he asked.

'Don't ask.'

'That bad?'

'I feel like going out and taking some heroin.'

'You're not going to?'

'I wouldn't have told you if I was.'

After a couple of minutes she grumbled an, 'You alright?'

To which he replied, 'Well the whole of the left hand side of my body is paralysed, but apart from that I'm fine.'

She laughed. 'Here turn over then.'

'No, no – I'm only joking.'

She nudged him. 'You've got a stiffy, haven't you.'

'No!'

'Don't lie.'

210

His whole body blushed. 'How can you tell?'

'All men wake up with stiffies: it's the pressure of the bladder pressing on the prostate gland.'

'Oh.' He was disappointed with the explanation.

'What's the time?' she croaked.

'Shit. They'll be wandering about in a minute.'

He waited for her to say something like, 'Stay and make love to me,' but she let him down.

So he lay there for a little longer, delaying. 'Are you asleep?'

'I won't sleep for days now.'

'Will you be alright?'

'I'll raid the medicine cabinet for some trancs.'

Jed reluctantly began to climb out of bed, when Miranda said, 'Just check everything's OK and come back for a bit,' which, however he took it, had the effect of propelling Jed out of the room at top speed.

A few minutes later he stumbled back in, ashen faced, saying, 'I think old Mrs Prior-Pointment's dead.'

 The apartment door was open so, in the role of Mrs Rodgers, Mrs Prior-Pointment walked straight in.

Arthur shouted merrily from the kitchen when he heard the footsteps, 'Come in, take your clothes off . . .'

He appeared, sleeves rolled up, carrot in one hand, vegetable knife in the other, wearing a bright yellow apron.

She stood defiantly in the middle of the room, overnight bag on her shoulder, looking directly at him.

'Hello, naughty boy,' she said.

He looked at her, blinking, taking in the meaning of her words.

It was so quiet as they stood there looking over

the mountain that separated them, that Mrs Prior-Pointment noticed the *week-week-week* of the *cicadas* in the square, and Arthur's heavy breathing, through his nostrils.

The look on his face betrayed resignation at most. He seemed amused rather than anything.

'Hello Sylvia. Whatever have you done to your hair?' he said, at last. And 'Good Lord, very extravagant earrings. Not like you at all.' Then he disappeared into the kitchen with a 'Help yourself to a drink; you look like you need one.'

'Mrs Rodgers' had only foreseen his being aghast and spluttering apologies, or sulking, or at least his being ashamed – she had rehearsed bold first lines like, 'Don't gawp, Arthur, you'll swallow a mosquito' and 'Don't worry, I'm not armed'; instead Mrs Prior-Pointment had to struggle to stop her hand fluttering to her throat.

Arthur was right. She poured herself a large sherry and sat on the sofa.

She would go straight to the business.

'What on earth have you done with Mother?' boomed out of the kitchen. Then he appeared without his pinny and with his whisky glass. 'I suppose you've *off-loaded* her onto someone? I do hope she's all right.'

'Sit down, Arthur.'

Her tone took him by surprise.

He just about managed to restrain his impulse to obey and topped up his drink from the mini-bar in the corner.

Then he sat down.

'So,' she said.

'Cheers,' he said.

She raised her glass.

He was quiet now. Yes, he was definitely subdued.

She sipped her drink more confidently, took the envelope given to her by the detective from her bag and tossed it onto the table.

There was no conversation while he looked through

the series of photographs. There was no tell-tale twitching at the corner of his mouth, no awkward shuffling in his seat. He did though raise his eyebrows slightly when he came to the compromising pictures of himself and his lover, which Mrs Rodgers had planted, rather dramatically she thought, at the end of the series.

When he was done he tossed the snapshots back onto the coffee table disdainfully.

'Is there any more, or is that the end of the show?' he said harshly.

'Oh the curtain is just going up, Arthur.'

He sighed heavily. 'Oh dear, how tiresome.'

'Don't sulk, Arthur, it makes you look old,' she found herself saying.

His eyebrows went up again.

'And don't gawp. You'll choke on a mosquito.'

He laughed. 'Have you been drinking? You've had a few on the plane.'

'No dear, I've been here for five days. Staying in the hotel across the square.'

That one wiped the smile off his face. He looked like he was replaying scenes from the last five days.

'You've been busy, haven't you Arthur? I've been watching you.'

He stood up. He wanted to take control again. Mrs Rodgers crossed her legs with a flourish; Mrs Prior-Pointment hovered somewhere in the background.

'Well then, you've discovered my secrets.'

Mrs Rodgers smiled.

He took a large gulp from his glass and shrugged his huge shoulders. 'So you want a divorce.'

Her sherry nearly jumped out of the glass. 'No, Arthur!'

'Oh come on dear, drop the game. What are your terms?'

She was in turmoil now. He was so casual. 'I have no intention of going to court.'

213

'I won't fight you, Sylvia. You'll get everything you need. Everything you deserve.' He sounded like he was discussing next year's holiday 'I've been rotten. You're absolutely right. It had to come to this. It couldn't go on forever. I'm sorry, Sylvia, I really am.'

She said firmly, 'A divorce is not one of the options.'

'Darling, be serious.' He hoped she wasn't going to start being silly.

'I'm your wife.'

His laugh was ironic. 'I know dear. As I said, I'm terribly sorry. I've behaved badly. I don't deserve a wife like you. I never did.'

'I intend to remain your wife.'

He looked at her again. He wasn't used to this tone. Or perhaps it was just the look of her that was strange.

'What *are* you suggesting? That we keep up some ridiculous pretence? I suppose you're worried about what the ladies will say.'

'I'm worried about you, Arthur. About us.'

'Sylvia – "us"?' He was shaking his big, round head. 'There's no such thing. "We" don't exist. We haven't existed for a long time.'

'Oh but we do.'

He had an 'oh dear how tiresome' look about him again. 'What *are* you talking about?' he sighed.

'I'm talking about our *family*.'

His laugh was getting harsher. 'Oh yes. "the family", the Great Family. You still believe in all that poppy-cock? . . .' He flopped a hand towards the photographs.

'It's only now I realise how much it really does mean, Arthur.'

He was shaking his head again.

'It means more now than ever.'

His laugh was hopeless. 'You *are* suggesting a pretence. Or should I say "no change"?'

'You're not getting the hang of this at all, are you Arthur?'

214

He had an idea which changed his tone for the better. 'Is it your work? Will it make a difference to your "career"?' He shrugged. 'If it's that, I suppose – huh. That is an important consideration.'

'I'm talking about love,' she said, firmly.

His eyebrows were back in play. There was a faint whistle in his nostrils.

And some silence. The *cicadas* outside. More sipping of whisky. (He was drinking rather a lot of it.)

There was shouting in the square.

'I'm your wife,' she repeated.

Arthur was choosing words.

Not very carefully.

'Darling, it's impossible.'

Those words again.

'*What* is impossible, Arthur?'

'Our marriage, for God's sake!'

'Of course it's not impossible. What *are* you be talking about?'

'I'm talking about *another woman*, dear. The one in your "snapshots".'

'And I'm – that is *we*, are talking about a *marriage*. A lifelong commitment. I'm talking about real love, Arthur, not some . . . *infatuation*.'

His shoulders caved in. There was an 'oh dear *dear*, how very *very* tiresome' kind of slumping and a sigh that was like a glacier creeping down an ice-age valley.

Then the words, 'You're deluding yourself, Sylvia. Don't be a fool. I haven't loved you for a long time.'

She tried not to let this pronouncement hurt her but failed.

She resorted to a prepared speech, her voice wobbling as she spoke. 'Love is not something that just happens, Arthur. It's something that is built over time. Something that requires *work*. Something you don't find until you look, until you make it happen.'

He was getting cross now.

215

'You didn't imagine you were going to confront me with a lot of sordid photographs and have me fall into your arms, surely? I credit you with a little more intelligence than that. For God's sake, what do you *want* of me? You wouldn't have come all this way if you didn't *want* something.'

'I want you to love me,' she said simply.

He looked at her as if she were an impossible child. 'You're being ridiculous. You can take what you want. The house, everything. Only don't be ridiculous.'

'I can make you love me,' she said.

He tutted.

She went on. 'If you want to love me, you can and you will love me.'

By the look of him he was too exasperated for words.

'Please don't *make* me *make* you,' she added in a small voice.

The hook scratched him.

'What are you saying, Sylvia?' There was an aggressive note in his voice suddenly.

'You were right,' she said, 'About me not coming all this way for nothing. I didn't go to all the trouble of hiring a detective and following you round Gibraltar just for the fun of it – although I must say I did rather enjoy some of it. You've no idea how close we've been these last few days. Really you're very unobservant . . .'

He couldn't contain his anger. 'You're going to "turn me in", is that it? What? Unless I declare love . . . and presumably get rid of Sandra . . .'

Sandra, so that was her name.

'. . . You'll go running down to the police with a lot of photographs and tell them your husband is working for the mafia?'

Taking her silence to mean 'yes', he went on, becoming more abrasive as he spoke:

'You imagine you have some hold over me do you?

216

You imagine yourself going to the commissioner of police with those . . .' Again he threw a careless arm at the photos. 'Huh. I'll come with you. Why don't we go tomorrow? You can explain that your adulterous husband is laundering money for drug cartels. What do you think? Oh and mention the Khmer Rouge . . .' He was sarcasm personified. 'Or perhaps we could try the newspapers. We could make a day of it. We'll have lunch with my friends at the Governor's office – you can tell them the story over an *aperitif*.'

He was more or less huffed out by the end of this, but added for good measure, 'How terribly naive you are Sylvia. You always were a silly little school girl.'

The buzzer went.

'Ah, that'll be Sandra.'

'Tell her you're busy.'

'I'm not busy. You were on your way out.'

He was leaning against the table. Insouciant, defiant. And a bit drunk.

She gathered the photographs, silently putting them back in her overnight bag.

He held the door open, waiting.

'You can let Sandra in on your way out. I don't want a scene on the stairs.'

As she closed her bag and walked across the room to leave, she said, 'Very well. I may as well warn you before I go, Customs and Excise will be paying your 'Mr Rodriguez' a visit before morning. They'll know who he really is by then. I know just the officer. He's very keen. Young and very ambitious . . .'

Arthur closed the door before she reached it.

'Arthur, Sandra's waiting!'

He was looking at her through eyes that had narrowed. She thought he looked shrewd like that, and cunning. And handsome. He was summing her up afresh.

She tried not to look too pleased with herself.

He said, 'Sandra can wait.' And then, 'Please. Sit down.'

She thanked him and did so.

*T*he old matriarch had been ill for a couple of weeks.

When Dr Haggarty came to see her he recommended a transfer to hospital or a geriatric unit.

'She won't go,' announced Lilly who was sitting next to the bed holding the old woman's hand.

Old Mrs Prior-Pointment was able to communicate on a seismic level when Lilly held her hand.

Dr Haggarty's brow took up its customary position over-hanging his eyes in a great corrugated heap. 'Humm,' he resounded.

Rose was standing behind the doctor, the better to intimidate him. 'She's perfectly *happy* here,' she said, at which pronouncement the doctor inadvertently flinched. Rose had her reasons for wanting the old woman around.

'Is it *necessary* to transfer her?' asked Charity. She was thinking of the accounts. They didn't want to lose anyone right now, especially not their first fee-paying resident.

'It would be better for her to go.'

'She doesn't want to go,' insisted Lilly. Lilly was thinking how lonely the old woman would be elsewhere and how she might not survive another upheaval.

And indeed old Mrs Prior-Pointment seemed to be munching for dear life, her eyes flicking around the room desperately. 'She won't go,' Lilly repeated, at

218

which words the old matriarch undeniably munched
in the affirmative.

'Well, I'm sure there's nothing I can say of any
influence here,' boomed Doctor Haggarty on his way
down the stairs, the ploughed flesh of his forehead
rumpling and re-rumpling with each downward step.

He was right.

Mrs Prior-Pointment was moved to a room on the
top floor so as to be closer to the night staff in case
of emergency and put on a strict course of medication.

Now, two weeks later, Jed had found her dead.

'This is not the kind of stiffy to wake up with!'
Miranda said.

Jed's laugh wasn't very hearty.

'You'll have to get used to this you know,' she said,
'There's gunna be a holocaust when they put that
hard-core porno channel on satellite TV.'

But it was no good. Jed had never seen someone dead
before and no amount of tickling would have made
him laugh. Death, he knew, was inherent in the job,
but nothing could have prepared him for the sheer
anti-climax of the real thing.

No matter how hard he tried he couldn't find anything as harrowing in the sight of the body that was
even remotely as terrifying as the idea of death itself.
He was transfixed.

'Aren't you supposed to shut her eyes, or something?'
he asked.

'Why? You gunna do something she wouldn't want
to see?'

Still no smile.

'Doesn't look all that bad, does it?' he murmured.

'You wait till you have to clean up under here,' said
Miranda pulling back the bed sheet. 'This is the real
horror of death.'

As Jed took in the meaning of this gruesome lesson

Miranda picked up the pill bottle from the bedside table.

'Jed? Are these the pills you gave her last night?'

'Er – yeah, I think so.'

'Are you sure?'

'. . . Let's have a look. Yeah, that's them.'

'Shit.' Dead serious.

'What's the matter?'

'These are the wrong pills! Oh my god . . . these are lethal for someone in her condition!'

'No.'

'Jed, you fucking killed her!'

Jed stood staring at the corpse for a moment then went over to the sink and vomited.

Rose was generally first up in the mornings.

Isolation had taken its toll and she was often heard muttering to herself now, seen making faces she was unaware of and disappearing on her own into her room for long periods. The thin line of her lips had begun to resemble Mrs Crotchley's lemon-puckered pout (which was lately tasting sweeter fruit.)

In her loneliness, Rose had taken to sitting with and chatting one-sidedly to old Mrs Prior-Pointment first thing in the morning, especially since the famous matriarch had been taken ill.

It was during her early morning vigils that Rose would rummage in the old green holdall and slip her neat IOU's into the side pocket. As old Mrs Prior-Pointment snoozed, Rose would quietly stand on a chair, open the top cupboard, exchange notes for chitties and then resume her steady mumble of conversation.

Like everyone else in the house, Rose assumed that old Mrs Prior-Pointment was incapable of speech. It was something of a revelation therefore, when, the day before the old woman died, she saw fit to speak to Rose.

Thinking that old Mrs Prior-Pointment had nodded

off, Rose had begun to scribble an IOU for ten pounds, when she heard the words, 'I know you've been taking money out of my bag . . .'

Rose was so embarrassed she felt dizzy. She crumpled up the IOU she was writing and blushed awfully.

But the old woman said, 'I don't mind . . . You've been very good . . . I watched you . . . and you've always made a note, I've seen those . . . I know where it's gone, I've seen what you do.'

They looked at each other then, the older woman breathing heavily but munching heartily, wearing a crafty smile which reminded Rose of the canny old woman she had once been, who had seemed old to Rose even all those years ago. She seemed to be telling Rose that as well as speak she could even climb up on a chair and look into the top cupboard!

The old matriarch, tired out by her speech, withered, melting back into the pillows.

'It's near the end,' she said. But she wanted to give Rose a word of warning. She'd seen Mrs Crotchley searching her room one day when she thought she was asleep. 'I've become very good at watching. She's after an inheritance. Dreadful woman. She's always been jealous of me. She thinks I'm hiding something. Hee. And I am, aren't I? That's all I've got in the world. You'll look after it won't you? See that it does some good when I'm gone.'

The old woman winked at Rose several times that day as Rose popped in and out of the room but as far as Rose could tell she never said another word.

The next morning Rose made her way as usual to old Mrs Prior-Pointment's room.

As she got to the top of the stairs she heard voices inside the old woman's room.

She stood outside the door, trying to work out who was in there, reluctant to enter and expose herself to unnecessary conversation. She resented the intrusion into her only social hour. She was sure she could hear Mr Green and, yes, Miranda.

Then she could have sworn she heard Mr Green being sick. Surely not. And again, yes. He must be vomiting. Into the sink she hoped.

Rose was puzzled to the point of concern.

She did a little indecisive two-step. She wanted to march into the room and find out what was going on, but there was something stopping her. The voices in the room were agitated. She strained to hear what was being said. She heard the voices getting clearer, moving towards the door. On impulse she blustered along the corridor and hid herself in the cleaning closet opposite the stairs and the lift.

The door of Mrs Prior-Pointment's room opened and the noise of voices flooded onto the stillness of the dim landing. With a shiver of excitement Rose pulled the door to.

Miranda said, 'I'll be an hour at the most. Make sure no one finds her.'

Jed said, 'What shall I tell them?'

'For fuck's sake you'll think of something. Just keep them away.'

'Be quick won't you?'

'Clean her up as best you can. And make sure you get Charity down here.'

'What shall I tell her?'

'Tell her the truth.'

'Can't I tell her it was Edith?'

'Shh. No. She needs to know. She'll be more careful that way.'

Jed didn't sound too sure of this. There were a few moments of silence before he said, 'OK, go on.'

Miranda said, 'And cancel the television.'

Jed said, 'No! . . . I thought you said everything was going to be OK.'

They were talking in hissing whispers.

'Yeah, but it might not be by eleven o'clock.'

'Well if it's not we'll cancel it at eleven when they arrive. Don't look at me like that – its the only chance we've got to get some publicity. It'll only a take a few more of them to kick . . . to die and we've had it, we've got to get some proper fee-payers soon.'

'You've gone completely fucking mad!'

Rose heard Miranda run down the stairs and Jed go back into Mrs Prior-Pointment's room.

'*T*urn over.'

She obliged. He wished she could be a little more obliging.

He knew this part of the examination wasn't strictly necessary, but he wanted to get as complete a picture of the patient as possible.

'Is that strictly necessary, doctor?' a voice behind him asked.

Why did the young women round these parts have to bring their mothers along? Even into the surgery itself! Didn't people trust doctors any more?

He turned to face the protector sitting by his desk. 'I want to get as complete a picture as possible', he said shortly, leaving his hand in place on the patient's leg as he spoke, before slowly returning to his examination.

He sized up the femur – it really was an excellent specimen – gave it a little squeeze and somehow restrained himself from patting her on the bottom as he said, 'That's fine. You can get up now.'

When mother and daughter had escaped, he buzzed reception and said, 'Give me ten minutes, nurse, no interruptions at all please.'

Doctor Stayne (as he now called himself) lay down on the examination couch where the young woman had just lain – she was no more than a girl really –

and, having pulled down his trousers, gave himself up to the limited pleasures of his imagination.

He imagined all the harmless little complaints the young woman might have come to him with, *sans chaperone*, and imagined the delicious quack remedies he would surprisingly administer; how she would be nervous at first and then, suddenly seeing the sense of it, become ardent and demanding, loudly issuing instructions, but not too loudly . . .

He didn't want to get into trouble again.

Perhaps the consultation would take place at his home.

Difficult to arrange.

Impossible.

No, the consultation would take place here, but quietly.

She would simply walk in and demand sex, stripping off her clothes there and then. Or when she took off her clothes to show him her complaint she became hopelessly aroused and begged him to teach her how to masturbate. Yes that was a good one.

Perhaps he would apply a blindfold so that she could strip off without self-consciousness.

No. She was timid and shy. He needed a realistic scenario.

That was the bloody problem round here.

Shortage of realistic scenarios.

He thought about Charity.

She really was a beautiful woman and she had accepted his invitation to dinner, and charmed him all evening but declined his invitation to have sex afterwards.

He began to replay this scenario with a happier ending, but soon found himself worrying about the nurse he'd seen at the centre – he'd forgotten her name now, but not her face – he knew she had recognised him.

He didn't want to be reminded of the old days, so he resorted back to this morning's young patient and the old anaesthetic routine: somehow he was obliged to administer an anaesthetic. It was one of those minor ops and she told him she was too scared for a local so he volunteered to put her to sleep properly.

For safety's sake all he did was take off some of her clothes and have a good look.

But as he played out this scene in his mind he accidentally thought back to his former life in Manchester, how he had allowed himself to sink into the swamp.

As soon as he had become known as a 'bent doctor' who would write 'scripts', the antiseptic stillness of the waiting room had been contaminated by a plague of rogues and strumpets. It had been standing room only at morning surgery and poor Mrs Temperance, who believed in the advancement of humanity through the virtues of thrift, honesty and the Roman Catholic rite of confession, was suddenly required to perform the role of bouncer at a festival of sick junkies.

He had been lucky to escape prosecution.

Once he had dipped his foot into the river he had been amazed to find how polluted the water really was, how widespread drug abuse had become and how quickly he had become embroiled in crime.

He recalled his old anatomy lecturer's comparison of the country to a human body, with the cities as the major organs. He had realised during the period of his debauch that the body's major organs were riddled with cancer in the form of drugs. It was surely only a matter of time before it spread to the minor organs, before the whole body was infected.

He was one of the mutant cells.

No! He was reforming.

Healing himself. Going straight.

He had drifted badly away from the matter in hand.

He quite liked the anaesthetic routine and returned to the image and played around with it until he was grunting and straining away.

Then before he knew what was happening the door to

225

his surgery opened and in walked Miranda. Which was embarrassing enough bearing in mind his position, but the blush potential was compounded by the fact that his receptionist followed immediately in her wake.

'Sorry, doctor, she just marched in! – oh!'

His receptionist retreated trying not to remark upon the condition of the good doctor's dress, only leaving the young woman in his 'capable hands'.

When the doctor had resuscitated a little of his dignity by seating himself grandly behind his desk, he said, 'I can't help you.'

To which Miranda replied, 'Oh, but you can.'

*R*ose opened the door to Old Mrs Prior-Pointment's room and stood looking at the scene.

Jed was bent over old Mrs Prior-Pointment's naked body dabbing at it with a face-cloth. He looked almost as bad as the corpse.

Jed hurriedly realised the obscenity of the picture with which Rose was presented and covered up the old woman's body. As he did so the feet were exposed at the other end. He fussed over these details as he spoke.

'I'm afraid something awful's happened . . . er, something awfully *sad*.'

Rose simply looked at him.

'Poor thing's died, I'm afraid. She passed away in the night. Quite peacefully we think. She wasn't well. But I think she was happy here, while it . . . she . . . er lasted. Hum. Miranda's gone to fetch the doctor . . .'

'Wouldn't it have been easier to telephone for the doctor?' Rose asked.

Jed flinched at this remark.

'Erm, yes. Yes. Probably . . .'

226

Rose said, 'Would you like me to break the news to the rest of the house?'

Jed had to pretend to be too preoccupied to answer while he thought of a reply to that one.

Eventually he said, 'Rose, please sit down.' Then, 'Oh perhaps not,' and after some unpleasant hopping and dithering he sat down himself on the chair by the bed, thinking he should have locked the door. 'Rose . . . something . . . very unfortunate has happened.'

Rose seemed to be looking at something over Jed's head. He followed her gaze but there was nothing there, only the old built-in wardrobe.

Rose said in a sympathetic voice, 'Are you alright, Mr Green, you look terribly upset,' which was the first friendly remark Rose had ever made to him.

Jed noticed this and felt extremely grateful. 'Yes. No. Rose, it might be better if we . . . that is . . . didn't *mention* any of . . .' he flapped his hand over the sheet, 'It might not be in everybody's best interests for residents to know . . .' He stopped.

'You'd better explain what's happened Mr Green. I might be able to help.'

'Yes. Yes. Edith . . .'s been up to her old tricks . . .' There were all kinds of itches to be scratched and uncomfortable little folds in his clothing that needed to be adjusted as he spoke. 'It seems . . . last night . . . that Edith . . . apparently – though we're not *exactly* sure yet . . . administered the wrong . . . medication. A fatal dose.'

'I see,' said Rose. She did now. From what she'd heard on the landing she knew it must have been Jed. *Blame it on Edith.*

Jed said, 'We don't want to upset anyone unnecessarily and the doctor might – that is he might be able to help us . . .'

Rose said, '. . . And we certainly don't want to draw attention to ourselves in the current climate do we?'

227

'Er . . . no. Absolutely not.'

'It really would be a shame to lose everything over an unfortunate incident like this.'

'Yes, yes, exactly.' Jed could hardly believe it.

'Poor Edith,' Rose said.

'Yes, poor Edith. And poor old Mrs Prior-Pointment.'

Rose had a distinct air of bustle about her now.

'Yes, and of course once people begin talking – there's no end to it until it's over.'

Jed was slumped in the chair looking at Rose with an expression of incredulity, filled to the brim with gratitude.

'The best thing,' Rose said, 'would be if nobody knew at all. Not at least until the doctor has been consulted and we've had a proper think . . .'

Jed nodded a little vaguely.

'Perhaps we'd better leave now, in case anyone decides to pay a visit. I know Lilly usually comes at this time.'

'Yes! . . .' Jed stood up quickly, looking anxiously at the bed.

Rose gently took hold of his arm and said, 'Come along, leave things as they are for now. We can sort that out later.'

She led him out of the room, kindly, in the manner of a nurse leading a sick patient.

'Let's lock the door behind us shall we?'

Jed allowed the stout old woman to take charge of this task as he recovered himself on the landing. When she was done Rose placed the key in her pocket, took Jed by the arm again, murmured a 'Come along' and led him to the stairs.

The lift door opened. Lilly, Edith and Mrs M rolled out.

The procession was halted by Jed's shins.

Rose said, 'The old dear's taken a turn.'

Jed was in too much pain to speak.

Lilly said, 'Oh dear, the old lady's taken a turn,'

228

to Edith. And, 'We'll have to look after her, won't we, dear?'

Jed said, 'The . . . doctor says she's not to be disturbed.'

'Oh we won't be disturbing her, will we dear?'

'She's not to be disturbed on any account,' Jed added.

'Nonsense, she'll need someone by her in case she takes another turn, or gets worse.'

Rose spoke firmly. 'Lilly, dear. The doctor was quite clear. He said, on no account is she to be disturbed. I asked him, what about her friends and he said, not by anybody. He gave her an injection and said he'd be back shortly.'

Lilly stood there obstinately, her head shaking slightly from side to side. 'I can't see what harm it could do.'

Rose said again. 'Doctor's orders.'

Then to help settle the matter Rose took hold of the side of the wheelchair and began to 'help' the threesome turn around, which caused some confusion and giddiness. Before they knew where they were they were all in the lift and Rose had pressed the button for the ground floor.

As they piled out at the bottom Rose twisted the key which turned off the lift and put that in her pocket too.

When they were alone in the office, Jed asked Rose whether she could see herself taking over as chair of the residents' committee once again.

Rose inflated slightly and said that it would very much depend on the voting.

'**A**h yes, deadly. Definitely the cause of death.'

Doctor Stayne rattled the little brown bottle. 'Lethal.'

Miranda and Charity were in attendance, and the late Mrs Prior-Pointment. The two breathing women exchanged a glance which said:

MIRANDA: Told you so!

CHARITY: You'd better leave us to it.

Miranda didn't so much back out of the room as melt away. Jed was waiting anxiously on the other side of the door. He and Miranda exchanged another mini-series of glances which basically said:

MIRANDA: You did kill her.

JED: Oh fuck.

Miranda nodded at the stairs and they slipped away.

Charity watched the doctor as he quite literally performed his role. There were cheerful little flourishes as he probed the corpse and a distinct spring in his step as he skirted the death-bed. There was an occasional 'Um-hum', and the odd 'Ah-ha'.

Charity waited for negotiations to commence.

Miranda had explained it to Charity like this:

'He owes me one.'

Charity was angry with her. 'Why didn't you tell me you knew him?'

'I didn't think you'd want to know.'

'Why not!'

'It was a long time ago.'

'So?'

'So I didn't think it was worth mentioning.'

'You slept with him?'

'No.'

Charity's face didn't.look very convinced.

'I did him a favour, alright.'

'What *kind* of favour?'

230

'I got him out of a bit of difficulty.'

'What kind of difficulty?'

'The difficult kind.' It wasn't very convincing. They both knew it.

Charity's eyes narrowed. 'You should have told me.'

Miranda had pressed her arm. 'Trust me, OK.'

'I did trust you.'

'I'm *sorry*. (Sigh.) Trust me again. Just explain the situation to him.'

'I thought you'd already explained.'

'He'd like to hear it from you. He'd enjoy that.'

The doctor had to open the bidding. He said: 'She was very old.'

Charity nodded. She tried to smile.

'It says on her file you refused to let her go.'

'She refused to go *herself!* She was very *happy* here!' Charity sounded angry. She was frightened.

'Hum. I'd better make sure I make that clear on the file.'

'Yes. Please.'

'It's a bit of a difficult situation, really,' the doctor declaimed, taking the chair next to the bed and speaking to Charity across the lumpy sheet.

Charity couldn't swallow properly.

He didn't miss that.

'It's Haggarty's territory. He moans about the place constantly, but he won't give up the responsibility.'

Charity looked terrified and helpless. The doctor thought it charming.

'I think he's got a little soft spot for your nurse.'

Charity nodded.

So did the doctor, thoughtfully. 'She was very old,' he repeated, nodding at the corpse.

'It wasn't – *exactly* unexpected,' Charity managed.

'No. No. Not unexpected at all. Quite . . . *expected*, indeed. Natural, even.'

Charity nodded again, uncertainly.

231

'There can't have been more than a few days in it.'

'Really, do you think so?'

'There's no doubt about it.'

He sat staring at her. Charity looked at the sheet – she had the distinct impression the old matriarch would sit up and protest.

'So, exactly what happened, in your opinion?' The doctor's tone was very reassuring.

'As far as we can make out, our old nurse . . . Edith . . . administered the pills to her by mistake.'

'Hum. When exactly did she do that?'

'In the afternoon. I think.'

'Are you sure?'

'Fairly certain.'

The doctor hummed. 'I think it must have been . . . later than that; the effects would have been felt fairly quickly.'

'Possibly tea time?'

'Might she have delayed taking them?'

'Erm . . . *possibly.*'

'The old nurse, you say?'

Charity nodded.

The doctor thought about something, while Charity felt herself drifting further under his influence (perhaps a consequence of the power he held over their future at that moment, no doubt enhanced by the subtle twinkling of his eyes and the practised, reassuring tone of his voice).

'Is there anything you can do?' she asked at last.

'I'm afraid she's stone dead.' He patted a lump in the sheet that must have been the old woman's shoulder.

Charity looked down to stop herself grinning.

The doctor was excited by Charity's blushes and by her apparent naivety. 'I think it's wonderful what you do here,' he said. 'You're doing some really important work. Breaking new ground. It would be a tragedy to spoil the whole thing over an incident like this.'

232

'Do you really think it was just a matter of a few days?'

He nodded gravely. 'She should have popped it years ago.'

Charity looked guiltily at the sheet.

The doctor spotted this and recomposed himself.

Mustn't become too irreverent. He needed to appear responsible and commanding. 'I think we can avoid a scandal.'

'Do you really?'

'Have you informed – the relatives.'

Charity shook her head guiltily.

'Then don't. Not just yet.'

'I'll see if there's a way I can take over from Haggarty here. Once he's out of the way, I just have to sign a death certificate and Bob's your late uncle. If Haggarty finds out, you've had it. Maybe he's up to something. I'll do a bit of rooting around. Meanwhile I'll embalm the corpse – I'll do that this afternoon – then lock the door and keep her in here as if nothing's happened. No one must know.' He looked at Charity sternly. 'Do you understand that? No one must know.'

Charity nodded like a frightened child.

'We're taking a risk. A big risk. There could be serious consequences . . .'

He realised Charity had welled up and stopped.

She thought she was expected to say something, but when she opened her mouth she lost her cool and spluttered. Tears fell; she couldn't stop them.

Stayne cursed himself for being insensitive and took great pleasure in coming over to where she sat, going down on his haunches before her.

She put a hand over her eyes and sobbed. 'I'm sorry . . . I'm scared . . . I . . .'

'Shhh . . .' Calm, reassuring.

'Everything's falling apart suddenly . . .'

'Nonsense. Everything's going to be fine.' He'd taken her hands in his now.

233

'It's not our fault . . .'

'No one said it was anyone's fault.' His voice was super-sincere.

'We've had to fight for this.'

'Well then – you have to fight a bit longer.'

He took the bold step of holding her chin in his hand and summoned his most reassuring voice. 'Trust me.'

She nodded.

'You'll do as I say?'

She nodded again.

'I'm in it with you now. We're in it together.'

She was blowing her nose and smiling shyly.

'So. We lock up and pretend everything's the same until I can get Haggarty off the case?'

He was waiting for her to give the go ahead.

She could see it, and after enough time for her conscience to make the appropriate adjustments – which was largely a matter of envisaging the consequences of the real cause of death and the real perpetrator becoming known – Charity looked straight at him and said:

'I'll do whatever you say. Please don't let anything happen to us.'

The residents were in a state of excitement that morning, as two days of filming for the documentary were to begin. Consequently the news of old Mrs Prior-Pointment's 'turn for the worse' went largely unremarked.

What *was* noticed was the change that had come over Rose.

That morning she bustled round the house offering advice to residents who were wasting time and energy unnecessarily and lending a hand to any residents who were having difficulties.

The old trade unionist spent over an hour with a surprised Mrs Crotchley going helpfully through the budget, making useful suggestions on where money could be saved and respectfully pointing out where it could be better employed. Not only was her advice useful, Mrs Crotchley remarked to Charity afterwards, but Rose had been polite and even friendly.

Lilly wasn't her usual self, either. She was hovering uncertainly in the entrance hall when Charity saw the doctor out. The two of them clattered down the stairs and at the door Charity took Stayne's two hands in hers, saying, '*Thank* you. I really don't know what would have happened . . .'

She stopped dead as the doctor glared warningly at her, nodding infinitesimally towards the passage.

Charity turned and saw Lilly, who the moment Charity caught sight of her seemed to freeze and then act as if she was just minding her own business.

'No problem, said the doctor.' And then in a louder voice, 'Now, as I said, *absolutely not to be disturbed.*'

Charity mimed that the old woman was blind and the doctor, first checking the coast was clear, turned and contorted his face at Lilly, pulling his mouth wide and waggling his tongue. Charity giggled – a little harshly for her.

At that moment Lilly recoiled as if in fear and made her way hurriedly back down the corridor, groping her way along the wall.

Charity checked that the coast was clear and, going up on her tiptoes, pecked the doctor shyly on his lips.

In the office later that morning Jed and Charity were shouting, or at least talking very loudly at each other about something (the word 'stupidity' was used once or twice and 'irresponsible' was clearly audible).

Jed stormed out, slamming the door behind him.

He'd just finished hunching his shoulders at the crash, when he realised Lilly was standing there.

'Who's there?' she called, seeming to cower away from him.

Jed softened himself to reply, 'It's only me, Lilly.'

Lilly didn't say anything, but stood, poised like a bird on the lawn, listening intently for further signs of movement.

Jed slinked back into the office to make his peace with Charity.

A little later Rose found Lilly on the landing of the second floor wheezing for breath looking like she was about to begin an ascent to the third floor. 'Who's that? Who's there?' demanded Lilly.

'It's Rose. What are you doing up here? You'll do yourself a mischief on those stairs.'

'Get your hands off me!' said Lilly sharply when Rose took hold of her arm.

A very unfriendly frown appeared on Rose's brow.

Both women stood glaring angrily at one another. Lilly's gaze actually fell on a faded print of a pastoral scene hanging on the wall, but the meaning of the look was clear.

Rose was cast back in time suddenly and remembered that other Lilly – the Lilly who had led the striking women from the factory floor and who had been willing to take the thing to its bitter end when the will of others, including that of the unions, was failing. Lilly had been despised alike by the Prior-Pointments and by those trade unionists who wanted to make a deal, those who had eventually formed the new union. In those days Lilly and Rose had been proud allies.

Lilly had that same, unmistakable air of a woman who would not be moved.

Rose resorted to her sternest tone, 'Mrs Prior-Pointment is not to be disturbed. Doctor's orders.'

'What harm will it do? To have a friend nearby.'

'Doctor's orders,' was all Rose could say.

'Something's going on. Why isn't the lift working?' said Lilly.

'The lift is broken down.' replied Rose.

'It was perfectly alright this morning.'

Charity came by and Rose with a facial expression appealed for help.

'What's Lilly doing here?' chirped Charity.

'She's been climbing up the stairs on her own,' said Rose with a significant nod at the stairs going up.

'The lift's not working.' said Lilly.

'You're going to do yourself an injury,' Charity said, nicely. 'Come on, I'll make you a cup of tea. We'll fix the lift, don't worry.'

Lilly allowed herself to be led downstairs and guided back into the morning room, where she sat cup-of-tea-less, her head shaking slightly, not saying a word for the rest of the morning.

'Poor dear, she's out of sorts,' Rose said, back in the office. 'Quite out of sorts.'

Most of the residents had expected a truck the size of a removal van with GRANADA TV emblazoned on the side, a bank of lights from a Hollywood film set, make-up caravans, wardrobe assistants buzzing around, and perhaps even the odd celebrity materialising during the day to see what was going on.

Instead nothing happened at all until twelve o'clock, by which time the residents had given up their vigil in the front dining room, which had been maintained since nine, and returned to the morning room to watch television and bemoan the unreliability of the modern generation.

Just as the day's kitchen staff were preparing to cook lunch, a blue Sierra Ghia pulled up in the car park containing two large men, both dressed in leather jackets with expensive and somewhat strange-looking boots.

They unloaded a single camera and tripod out of the back and began to film the front of the house without introducing themselves or even attempting to make contact with anyone inside.

In the end, prompted by curious residents, Rose ambled out shyly (for her) and attempted to strike up a conversation.

'Would you like a cup of tea?' seemed a likely opener.

One of the men looked at her disinterestedly and shook his head. The other, who was peering through the camera with one eye said, 'No thank you.'

Rose was left standing there. Her arms took up their defensive position over her bosom.

'Are you from Granada Television?' she tried.

'Yes, luv,' said the first man with the tired attitude of a person who feels they are always talking unnecessarily to the public.

'Is that everyone?' she asked.

'No, luv, the woman who runs the show's coming tomorrow,' he said, meaning: 'Sod off and leave us alone, will you.'

Rose beat an indignant retreat to make her report which concluded with a condemnation of the manners of the modern generation.

'Who cares,' someone said, 'at least they're here.'

When the two men finally did enter the building to begin filming (still, Rose noted, without making contact with anyone or asking permission of any kind) there was an electrification of the house.

Suddenly everyone was busy doing the job allotted to them for the day, whilst at the same time trying to stay on camera. Everywhere the men turned there was a job being done. At one point the laundry was being sorted, the dinner loaded on to the trolleys, the dishes cleared away, the tables laid, the clean bedding arranged and the bins emptied all at the same time – which might not have been so bad except that, impossibly, it was all being done in the entrance hall where the cameramen happened to be at that moment, trying to get footage of the ornate Victorian tiling.

Everywhere the men turned someone was there working and pretty soon the whole place was in chaos. The dinner was ruined, the laundry was covered in ketchup and the overall impression was of old people left *by* themselves, trying to grab the limelight *for* themselves and generally making a mess *of* themselves.

One of the men told Miranda that they could sort it all out in the edit and would she like to come and see his collection of celebrity stills that evening when they were done.

Later in the afternoon the filming of a residents' meeting was proposed.

It was a bit awkward really as Jed was chair and he didn't want to show himself on camera because of the bankruptcy business.

It was the ideal opportunity for Rose to take over the chair once again. It would look better too if residents were seen to be making decisions independently.

Jed explained the situation to Rose and Mrs Crotchley – fudged it really – saying he had tax problems. It was agreed that voting would take place that very afternoon.

'I think she's ready,' Mrs Crotchley said. 'She's become personable. Hasn't she Tink?'

The meeting was called and the cameras set up.

As secretary Mrs Crotchley read the minutes of the last meeting in her usual pert tone and then put forward a motion calling for a new chair. She proposed Rose to nods all round.

But when she asked if there were any other proposals Lilly struggled to her feet.

'Yes. I'd like to propose myself,' she declared boisterously. Then to Edith, 'I said, I'm putting myself forward for the chair, dear.'

Edith said, 'Oh yes. Good idea.'

There was some murmuring now as residents realised there would be a clash of loyalties.

They were all happy that Rose had come back to herself so suddenly. They had been pleased to see her bustle around busily. She had been very good with the men from the TV, showing them around and introducing them to people even when they looked as if they might not otherwise have been interested in meeting people; and most of the residents felt grateful to Rose for some favour she had done them over the past months regarding petty cash.

But Lilly was very popular. Her consistent good humour and generosity were irresistible. She stood for something, too. Lilly's philosophical acceptance of her fate, her huge body with its scars and cuts and plates, her chuckling in the face of blindness, were a source of strength to others: she was the living embodiment of hope, of misfortune withstood, of cheerfulness in spite of everything. She was the very soul of the house.

Voting was swift and brutal.

Rose received only four votes in favour, fingers really — those same fingers that had tended to rise in support of Mrs Crotchley for the sake of her feelings.

The first item on the agenda was Lilly's. 'What the bloody hell has happened to the lift?'

The second item was her suggested visiting rota for old Mrs Prior-Pointment, at which point Rose had to repeat the doctor's orders and refer residents to staff.

The rest of the business was conducted without fuss and with some gaiety.

The lift was 'fixed' by Jed later that afternoon.

*E*dith felt Lilly shaking her arm.

'Oh! Time for bed?' she said. Then, 'Oh! Is it morning?'

But she could see that it wasn't morning, the curtains were still drawn and through the gap she could see that it was dark outside. Mrs M was sitting in her chair looking very pleased with herself. Lilly was leaning on the handles behind her.

'We're going on a *mission*, dear,' Lilly whispered.

'Pardon?' Edith shouted.

Lilly made her way round to Edith and put her mouth close to Edith's hearing aid. 'I said, we're going on a mission, dear. We have to be very *quiet*.'

'Night fishing?'

Lilly bent patiently to Edith's hearing aid once again. 'A *mission*, dear. We're going to the third floor. To see our friend. We have to be quiet.'

'Oh.' Edith seemed to have got the message. 'Oh.'

Lilly made the 'shh' sign to make sure.

Edith wasn't blind, but she was no eagle eye and in the dark, resonant entrance hall the passing of The Terrible Trinity was sonorous to say the least.

Quite how the fire-extinguisher found its way into the path of the wheelchair as Edith guided it through the murk is unclear, or how, when the clatter had died away and Lilly had pulled it out from under the wheels of the chair, Edith managed to remove the pin, which normally even in the heat of an emergency people can't find the knack of twiddling out, remains a mystery.

The fact was, that by the time the lift doors banged noisily open, the entrance hall was flooded with water and the air had been filled with a loud, wet, whoosh and several 'Oh!'s as the jet caught one after the other of the women with its cold force.

It wasn't until they were in the lift itself that it became apparent that Mrs M's glasses had fallen prey to the jet.

241

It wasn't until the lift door closed and there was a crunch that they realised where Mrs M's glasses were.

When Mrs M heard the sound she demonstrated the eternal good humour for which she was renowned by craning her neck and beaming at Edith, who of course hadn't heard a thing. Poor Edith had a soggy strand of hair splattered over her face now, which impaired her vision still further.

When she complained to Lilly, Lilly forgetting herself said, 'I expect you look like a mop *without* a hairnet on!' then pressed the button for the third floor.

'Pardon?' Edith nearly shouted.

Lilly frowned, squeezed Edith's arm and repeated the 'Shh' sign with great emphasis. They couldn't afford to make a sound on the third floor – the lift was just down the corridor from the staff room.

The door banged open. The clang echoed, sounding like an explosion to Lilly.

The wheelchair got stuck against the door on the way out and the door closed on it causing an 'Oh!' from Edith. Lilly groped for the 'OPEN DOOR' button and accidentally pressed the button marked 'ALARM'. The bell sounded right over their heads making Lilly gasp, but the noise only lasted a split second before she whipped her finger off the button.

When she hit the right button, the door opened; she gave Edith a shove, the wheelchair unhooked itself from its snare and the three women went flying (almost) out of the lift, zoomed (well . . .) across the corridor and only came to a halt in the cleaning closet opposite. It was a tight fit, but somehow all three of them squeezed in.

It was lucky because the moment the lift door closed, the door to the staff room opened and the sound of quiet music drifted into the corridor.

In the dim light that accompanied the music Edith again saw Lilly signal a 'shh'. Lilly reached for the

242

closet door and silently pulled it towards her to conceal them a little better.

Edith gripped hold of Lilly's arm.

'I definitely heard something.'

It was Miranda's voice.

She could be heard padding about on the landing.

Lilly wondered who Miranda was talking to. As far as she knew there was only one member of staff on at night. Perhaps the young nurse had a boyfriend with her.

'Probably her bloody ghost,' Miranda laughed.

Edith looked at Lilly who detected the movement and squeezed her arm reassuringly.

Then they heard Charity's voice.

'If it is a ghost it'll get more of a shock than you. Come and put some clothes on.'

'I'll just check her out in there. Not that she'll be having a party.'

'Hurry back,' said Charity.

They heard Miranda pad across the landing, coming closer.

'Urrh,' called Miranda, 'The floor's all wet here.'

But Charity had gone back into the staff room out of earshot.

Lilly heard Miranda unlock a door which must have been to Mrs Prior-Pointment's room and go inside. Why was the door locked?

After a few moments Miranda came back out of the room, padded back across the landing and slipped back into the staff room. Lilly was certain she hadn't re-locked the door behind her.

They waited for a minute before backing clumsily out of the closet and making their way along the landing.

Again there were bangings and clatterings, exaggerated in Lilly's mind by the anxiety of the moment.

Lilly had mixed feelings. Unlike Rose, Lilly had great respect for doctors and their orders and it was foremost in her mind that the doctor's orders were that Mrs Prior-Pointment was not to be disturbed.

Yet she had not been told this by the doctor, not by the usual doctor, just that other man that she had overheard talking to Charity.

Why should their friend be isolated? If there was some danger from a contagious disease they would have been told or perhaps even examined themselves.

The staff were acting strangely.

Lilly liked the staff, but life had taught her to be wary.

She was suspicious, but she was not sure of what.

They had to be careful. They didn't want to disturb the old woman they had befriended, but at the same time Lilly had the feeling that there was something going on, something dreadful, something they might even regret having discovered.

When they found the door, which was unlocked, Lilly took great care that the wheelchair was guided gently and quietly into the room and carefully shut the door behind them.

Edith's 'Oh!' and her sudden stiffening made Lilly fear the worst.

'What is it dear? What can you see?'

But Edith didn't answer. She held on tightly to Lilly and the blind woman could feel her shaking.

Lilly disentangled herself, groped her way along the bed, dismally feeling the stony bumps. She had just felt the terrible, cold flesh of the old woman's face when she heard the sound of someone on the landing.

There was nothing that could be done except wait.

A few moments later Miranda, having remembered that she had forgotten to lock the door, corrected her error, trapping the three women in the room with the corpse.

It was the most beautiful week Mrs Prior-Pointment could ever remember.

She had been right. Arthur had quite returned to himself. He had been loving, kind, sensitive and, above all, a gentleman.

It only went to show that, if you have the will to love and make the effort, love will blossom, no matter what.

She had been careful not to rub Arthur's nose in it. The most important thing was the relationship. It didn't matter who was right or who was wrong, so long as one understood one another. One had to be prepared to forgive.

The night she confronted him at the apartment, Arthur had been quick to understand her position. He carefully explained to her that if she tipped off Customs and Excise about the identity of any of his 'junior partners' and especially Rodriguez, she would be placing him in great personal danger, possibly endangering his life.

He listened carefully, too, when she explained that she understood the situation perfectly, but that as far as she was concerned he had already died, her life had been shattered and she could not continue to live while he was 'carrying on' with another woman. She told him about her dream (she called it a dream) in which he had died and how, after the months of turmoil, the vision had brought her peace.

She also took the trouble to explain that unless she made a telephone call to a certain number in England at 9am and 5pm every day, an accomplice would telephone Customs and Excise and do her business for her. A ruse which Arthur swallowed.

After that it hadn't been long before he took her in his arms and explained that he had never wanted to hurt her; he was weak; the young woman had thrown herself at him; he hadn't been able to resist; she meant nothing to him.

Mrs Prior-Pointment, or Mrs Rodgers (she was no longer very sure *who* she was) demonstrated that, as his wife, she understood. Men found it difficult to resist feminine guile. In the long run it may even have been for the best – through his dalliance she had come to know the strength of her feelings for him and the importance of their marriage.

That night they went for dinner at a traditional Spanish bar, and ate *tapas* with the fishermen. Arthur told her the story of how he had come to be involved in crime.

After the family business was sold, which had been unavoidable, as she knew, he had joined in the 'overseas investment scramble', as he called it. It was a cut-throat world and he had come close to losing everything. Through his ordinary business, he had become friendly with Eddie who had 'know-how but no-way' – ideas but no money (or not enough money). They had become partners and gradually built up from there, getting more and more daring as time went on.

'Easy money makes money easily' he explained.

She understood. They left the bar and walked round the bay gazing at the lights on the mainland, feeling the warm breeze from the Mediterranean and recalling times long gone, old friends from the tennis club, reflecting how they could never have imagined then the way it would all turn out.

He took her hand in his and at the end of the harbour, to the sound of the water lapping against the fishing boats and the bobbing of the yachts, he held her to his chest, sighed heavily and said, 'I'm so sorry I called you a silly school girl.'

She said, 'You were right.'

He laughed. 'You're an *overgrown* school girl, but you're not silly.'

She squeezed him.

He squeezed her back.

'It's a beautiful night,' she said. 'One of the most beautiful nights I can ever remember.'

'Yes,' he said.

There were tears in her eyes.

'I want to make love,' she said.

'Yes,' he said. 'Yes of course.'

She thought there were tears in his eyes too. In fact it was the breeze.

They played Frisbee on the beach every day.

She didn't fuss around with the sun creams, or mention his drinking, there was hardly any need.

She discreetly abandoned her earrings and jewellery, but kept going with the scent. Arthur complimented her on it.

They drove through the Spanish mountains to Seville. The hills, tinted with opaque blue that had fallen from the sky, filled the wife's heart to the very brim, so that Arthur had to stop the hire-car to comfort her tears. He spotted a chameleon by the roadside then and held it against the car while they watched it change colour.

In Seville that evening they paraded with the Spanish in the evening shade and, while he was buying ice-creams, she was approached in a friendly way and complimented by no less than three men, one of them in his thirties.

'It's my Roman nose,' she laughed.

That night they stayed in the best hotel in the city and swam in the pool at midnight. They passed three dreamy days among the cobbled streets and Classical facades of the great city, and every day made love during the siesta. Then they drove back through the mountains to the Rock – the distances, the impossible blue of the sky and the endless parched scrub quenching the good woman's heart as the bottled spring water quenched their thirst.

That night as they sat on the balcony of their apartment, drinking wine and watching the stream

247

of evening life below, Mrs Prior-Pointment looked at her husband longingly. She wanted to ask him if he really loved her, or whether all this had been a show, put on to save his skin and his business.

There was no point in putting the question, she knew, it would have to linger unanswered in her heart. She must have sighed because Arthur turned to her and gave her a warm smile and raised his glass to her.

'Here's to our new life,' he said.

If he was acting, she thought, smiling at him, he was good enough even to rival Mrs Rodgers.

'Cheers.'

The day after they got back to Gibraltar, Sandra appeared on the beach to make a farewell speech.

The break had been made over the telephone before Seville.

While his wife listened Arthur rang Sandra at her 'little apartment'. It was done firmly, without betraying the slightest appearance of regret, or hint that it might be a temporary arrangement. He would transfer a 'generous sum' to her account that morning and did not wish to see her again. He thanked her and apologised for any inconvenience, but pointed out that it had always been a temporary arrangement. There had been some argument on the other end but Arthur had been firm to the last.

When he saw Sandra approaching them on the beach Arthur turned to his wife and said, 'Oh dear,' and 'I'm sorry dear.'

She said, 'You're my husband, I love you.'

Sandra's was a 'You barstard', type of speech, with an 'I thought you might like to know the truth about your husband' thrown in.

From which Mrs Prior-Pointment learned: that the arrangement with Sandra was an older one than she had been led to believe – it had gone on for five years; that Arthur had declared Sandra his true love; that he often said his wife was a bore, called her The Powdered

Hag and boasted that he only kept her on to baby-sit his mother, who he loved ten times more dearly than his wife.

Arthur waited patiently until Sandra was done and then pointed out as politely as he could that she was not walking away empty handed, which seemed to make matters worse. Eventually the jilted lover wildly kicked sand in Arthur's face, spat at him furiously, announced to everyone within earshot that he was a gangster and an international drug dealer and stormed off across the beach.

Secretly Mrs Prior-Pointment was impressed. The young woman – who was, it could now be admitted, very attractive – had obviously loved Arthur very much, despite the difference in their ages. He was a man to be reckoned with indeed. And he was hers.

As he wiped his face on a towel, Arthur said, 'I'm sorry dear. I've behaved despicably.'

She smiled sadly. 'I'm afraid she's right, Arthur. I have become something of a terrible hag, especially compared to Sandra.'

'Nonsense, dear, you've aged beautifully,' was the reply.

She cried again then.

Later, as they tidied up their beach things and made their way slowly over the warm sand for an early drink at the hotel before supper, she thought to herself, 'Such a shame all this has to end.'

 *J*ed burst into the entrance hall at *Newfoundland* to find Charity mopping up water.

'What's going on!'

'Someone let off a fire extinguisher in the night,' said Charity. 'What's the matter with you?'

'Bloody Lilly and Edith are in Old Mrs Prior-Pointment's room, that's what's going on!'

'What!'

'I've just seen them hanging out of the window. Lilly's waving a sheet or something – she looks like she's trying to attract attention.'

'Oh my God!'

'Where's Miranda?'

'Out.'

'We'll have to get them out of there.'

'But they'll . . .' Charity lowered her head. 'They'll *know*.'

'We've got to get them away from the window!'

Charity said, 'I'll phone Stayne.'

'What for?'

'He'll know what to do.'

Jed glared at her as if to say, 'So I don't?'

Charity returned his stare. 'Well what do you suggest?'

Jed shook his head and sighed. 'Phone him.'

Jed was standing outside the door of old Mrs Prior-Pointment's room dithering when Charity arrived.

'They've barricaded the door. I don't believe it . . .'

He saw the look on Charity's face.

'What did Stayne say?'

'He said, give them a sedative. He's on his way.'

They looked at each other.

'A sedative?'

Charity nodded.

'What? An injection?'

250

Charity nodded again.

They stood there, looking at one another. Grim faces. Ashamed.

Then they heard Lilly's voice, shouting out of the window – 'Hello? – Hello, excuse me – Hello? . . .'

Charity said, 'There must be someone out there!'

Jed ran into the next room to look out of the window.

'No, there's no one.'

'Let's get it done.

'They've got the bed in front of the door.'

'Jed, if two old women can move a bed in front of the door, you can get the bloody door open!'

'I didn't want to make a big noise!'

Charity called to them through the door in a friendly voice, asking Lilly to open up saying, 'Don't worry, everything's going to be fine,' and 'Come on, what are you doing in there?' but Lilly ignored her, so Jed had to push the door with his shoulder. It wouldn't budge.

'They've jammed the bed against the wall; we'll never get it open.'

They heard Lilly again, shouting out of the window.

Jed became frantic and bashed against the door with his shoulder.

Charity said, 'That's not going to do any good. Try moving the bed.'

Cursing away, Jed opened the door as far as he could, stuck his arm through the gap and tried to move the bed – still with old Mrs Prior-Pointment lying on it. 'Done it,' he said at last.

When they entered the room, Lilly turned away from the open window and groped for Edith's arm. Fear was etched on the old women's faces. Jed and Charity felt like monsters.

They were surprised and dismayed to see Mrs M there too, though Mrs M didn't seem sure of what was going on and smiled broadly at them – until she looked at Lilly and Edith, when her expression became puzzled.

'Why are you hiding her? Why did you say she was ill when she's dead?' said Lilly in an angry voice that neither Jed nor Charity had ever heard before.

Charity said, 'Come on, Lilly, you've had a nasty shock.'

'Take your hands off me!' Lilly said. 'What's going on? Why are you keeping her here like that?'

Charity put her little bag on the bed and began to prepare a syringe. When Edith saw it – her emerald eyes cold with fear – she let out a little whimper.

Lilly said to her, 'What is it dear? What are they doing?'

Jed said, 'We didn't want to upset everyone, not while the television are here . . .'

Lilly said, 'Nonsense! You don't keep people locked up because – not unless something's happened. Something . . .'

Charity nodded at Jed who took hold of Lilly's arm.

'Take your hands off me!' said Lilly again.

But Jed kept a firm hold of her. 'Come on, Lilly, sit down. You've had a nasty shock.'

'You're bloody right I've had a shock. Let go of me!'

Lilly was resisting, but although he was surprised at the strength of the huge old woman, Jed was firm. After a bit of a tussle Lilly reluctantly allowed herself to be sat down.

Edith stood staring at the syringe with a hand at her throat.

'Are you alright, dear?' Lilly asked, groping hopelessly for Edith with her free arm.

'I'm going to give you a little sedative,' said Charity in as friendly a voice as she could muster.

'I don't want any sedative!' said Lilly. She was trying to pull her arm away from Jed as he rolled up her sleeve. Jed was following Charity's mimed instructions.

It was quite a struggle for Jed to hold Lilly's arm steady. He didn't want to hurt her, but at the same time

252

she was pulling away for all she was worth, which was quite a lot.

Jed was saying, 'Come on, now, don't be silly; we're not going to do you any harm,' as gently as he was holding tight.

Lilly was saying, 'Let go of me,' and even, 'Help,' once or twice,

Charity was saying, 'This'll calm you down.'

Lilly had to submit when she felt the steel of the needle touch her arm and Charity said, 'Careful, now, you're going to hurt yourself.'

Edith accepted the sedation gratefully after that.

Mrs M smiled as usual.

When Doctor Stayne arrived Lilly and Edith were transferred to wheelchairs (with some difficulty in Lilly's case). The three women, all staring glassy-eyed into the middle distance, were then moved into separate rooms for the first time since Edith's retirement.

Rose, asking no questions about Lilly's 'little turn', organised a game of bingo in the morning room.

Back in the office, Stayne said, 'We'll keep them sedated for a few days – until I've found a way to get Haggarty off the case. It's perfectly safe. Sedation's normal where there's been a nasty shock. (Here he was troubled by a dry cough). We'll explain everything to them properly when the danger's passed and they've recovered. They'll understand.'

'I wouldn't be so sure,' said Charity.

The doctor looked at her. 'Everything's going to be fine,' he said, quite sternly. 'When they come round the old woman will be safely cremated. People aren't going to start listening to some cock and bull story about a body in the attic.'

Jed laughed – a little too easily. 'Course they aren't.'

'Lilly will just have to accept your story. It's a very good one,' he said, and Jed could have sworn the doctor looked at him oddly.

While Jed pondered this, the doctor softened his voice and looked at Charity, 'You're going to be OK, aren't you? Not going to start worrying yourself unnecessarily?' He was telling her. Firm but gentle.

'I'll make sure of that,' said Jed.

The house was subdued that day, glum, despite the expected arrival of the woman from Granada Television who was going to do interviews with people.

That Lilly could have vandalised the first floor and broken Mrs M's glasses and then given old Mrs Prior-Pointment a nasty, potentially fatal shock in the middle of the night – not to mention bullying Edith and Mrs M into delinquency – shook the self-confidence of even the hardiest residents. If senility could bless even Lilly with its terrifying grace, carry her away so quickly . . .

It was like the death of hope.

As if a breath of stagnant air wafted through the house, sighing, 'Who next, who next . . .?'

Only Rose and Mrs Crotchley bothered to look out for the arrival of the cameramen and the woman from Granada, only they seemed worried that the atmosphere in the house might put them off including *Newfoundland* in their documentary.

At half-past ten Rose marched into the morning room and clapped her hands, saying, 'Come along ladies, what's the matter with everyone.'

She received glares and a 'Well!' for her trouble.

Nobody seemed to want to do their job properly. It was very worrying.

At quarter to eleven Miranda turned up.

Jed dragged her into the office.

'Where have you *been*!' he said.

Miranda looked at him indignantly. 'I've been out.'

'You were supposed to be here . . .'

'I told Charity!'

254

'I know, but . . .'

He noticed that Miranda didn't look too well. Her eyes were red; she looked tired.

'What's the matter?' he said, 'Are you alright?'

'Fine!'

It was the first time he'd ever challenged her. 'Where have you *been*?'

Miranda glared at him. 'If you must know, I had to go and see a guy. Someone I'm shagging.'

Jed realised his mistake with a stab. He apologised and explained what had happened.

She said, 'Fuckin'ell. I thought I heard something . . .'

Jed looked at her. 'You were *here*?

She shook her head. '. . . No. I mean . . . this morning. When I arrived . . . before I left again.'

Jed didn't see her blushing. He said he didn't want to be around when the woman from the TV turned up. They were in enough of a mess without complicating things any further. He wanted to get away.

Miranda reassured him that they would look after things, they would make sure no one said anything about his involvement at *Newfoundland* and Jed made for the front door.

He'd just got there when Charity called him back.

'You're in a hurry.'

Jed hopped awkwardly. 'Yeah.'

'Where are you going?'

'Anywhere.'

'Yeah, leave us to carry the can. Thanks.'

'It's dangerous for me to hang about – with the cameras and that.'

'You were alright with the cameras yesterday.'

Jed was getting annoyed. 'The woman who runs the show's coming today.'

'So you thought you'd go out and get pissed.'

Jed was too irritated to answer this, mainly because it was true.

255

It didn't stop him going out to get pissed though.
It just stopped him saying goodbye.

At eleven-thirty the woman from Granada turned up.

Her suave Tahiti green (metallic finish) convertible Escort Cabriolet swooped into the car park.

The woman climbed out, wearing a pair of sunglasses, despite the clouds, puffing a cigarette in the manner of a 1930s *dame du cinema*.

Her protuberant blouse open to the limit of decency, she stepped majestically over the gravel in a fawn suit, came to a halt before the steps and raised her sunglasses to her forehead, apparently to take in the effect of the great Victorian frontage.

As she did so Rose came out onto the steps to greet her.

There was a moment of recognition.

'Hel-lo . . .' beamed the woman from Granada putting out a hand for shaking and letting out a deep, throaty laugh.

A her her her.

Rose said, 'You're the journalist who covered the demonstration?'

'I've come up in the world since . . .'

A her her her *hurr*.

Rose nearly curtsied.

While Rose and Mrs Crotchley – the only two residents that seemed unaffected by the tragedy that had befallen Lilly – guided 'the woman from Granada' around *Newfoundland*, Jed, armed with a half-bottle of whisky, climbed a hill alone.

As soon as the alcohol hit his blood a fury was

unleashed. He relived over and over his having to hold Lilly's arm while Charity injected her with a tranquilliser.

It was vile. What kind of a person had he become?

He blamed the mess on Charity. On Eddie. On both of them together. On the government. On society. Why couldn't you just go out and make a reasonable living and live in a nice ordinary way he asked himself. But as he did so a picture of frills and flounce jumped into his mind that made him curse again.

He stomped to the top of the hill where he threw himself down on the grass and looked out over the moors.

He ran through the arrangements concerning Lilly and Edith and old Mrs Prior-Pointment, checking them for flaws. Thank fuck the family didn't give a damn about the old woman. What if they'd come to visit regularly? Huh. If they'd been coming to visit regularly the old dame probably wouldn't have been there in the first place.

Gradually he calmed down.

Thinking about Miranda did the trick. And drinking.

He thought back to their night together. He hadn't even had time to think about it all properly.

Surely she would fuck him soon.

He lay back on the grass in ecstasy at the thought.

But as he retrod the details of the night they had spent together, he stumbled on the morning – the discovery of the old woman, dead.

He sat up.

What a mess.

Then, right on the furthest point of the horizon, he caught a glimpse of something he recognised.

Himself a few months previously.

He and Eddie.

Eddie talking, Jed listening, feeling smug and safe.

Shit, what had happened in between?

He remembered his fantasy about a little apartment of his own.

He wondered what Eddie was doing.

But he didn't want to be Eddie.

He wanted to be himself in a nice apartment.

With Miranda.

Eddie could never have fallen in love with Miranda, not like he had.

He wondered if he really did want Miranda.

Perhaps not.

Perhaps he just wanted to be by himself and 'stay friends' with her.

He wanted to be pissed.

Jesus.

The thought occurred to him that he was becoming an alcoholic.

Which made him want a drink.

He shuddered as he swallowed a great mouthful and tried to imagine life without drink.

Horrible.

The fact that he found this prospect horrible was horrible too.

He never used to drink, not much anyhow.

Then another thought plopped into his head.

He was ashamed that it had been missing from his reflections so far.

Charity. His wife.

She hardly even figured in his thinking anymore.

It was impossible to picture her clearly.

There had been a time when she was the constant feature in his life. His wife and his work. With a shudder he remembered her seeming like part of the drapery of the house.

He remembered the last sex they'd had and their subsequent philosophical discussion about a more open marriage. He thought about her and the doctor.

Hadn't the doctor said he'd be back later?

The thought of Charity and the doctor together always made him want her again.

He was probably there at *Newfoundland* now!

It was time to put in an appearance.

He set off with a feeling of unease.

Not about the old woman lying dead on the third floor whose daughter-in-law was influential in Elderly Services; nor the three women who'd discovered the truth, now suffering from shock and illegally sedated to the point of delirium; nor the blackmail and fraud that if discovered could bring disaster.

Jed hurried down the hill with the uneasy feeling that the doctor would use the opportunity to chat up Charity or make a move on Miranda.

Stayne was indeed at *Newfoundland* chatting to Charity.

He was about to 'check out his patients' upstairs when he bumped into his older partner Dr Haggarty in the great ornate entrance hall.

Both men were embarrassed.

'Haggarty! What are you doing here?'

An 'Oh er hu-humm,' rebounded from the great tiled walls and 'just a routine duty call', before the old doctor recovered himself and realised he had every right to be there. At which point all the skin on his head collected in a mat on his forehead formulating the reverse question well before the rumbling of the enunciation proper could begin.

'I was just passing,' Stayne said quickly. 'I'm a friend of the owners . . . Jed and I play golf, I'm just trying to fix up a game. He's not in.'

'Humm.'

The older man seemed satisfied. He had no reason to be suspicious after all. Besides he felt a little guilty himself because he knew very well that he never made duty calls and that really he had come to have a word with that pretty young nurse he was so fond of.

Taking his rumpled partner by the arm and leading him to Charity and Miranda, Stayne said, 'The television are making a documentary about the place.

259

Perhaps you could make a contribution . . . ah, Nurse Jones, would you be good enough? . . .'

Stayne stopped and examined the uncomfortable look on the young nurse's face as she looked at Dr Haggarty. He noticed that Haggarty too was flustered.

'I'll introduce you to the producer,' said Miranda.

'Oh, hu-hum. Ums (meaning "yes")' replied the great ploughed field (his crumpled suit was the perfect complement to his forehead).

The old doctor's contribution to the documentary was: 'Usm, hu-hum well, I really do think some of their ideas are, frankly, crackpot and the care verges on the dangerous, but you know old people, they're like children, they never listen to a word you say.'

The 'producer' gave the man a generous smile (a her her) and Haggarty was hustled out of the front door as quickly as possible.

His contribution was edited out at an early stage.

Jed was sucking an Extra Strong Mint when he arrived back at *Newfoundland*.

He found the three of them in the office. Charity, Miranda and Dr Stayne. There was – in mid-flow – a great roar of laughter as he opened the door. Paranoia was prompted by its sudden death on his appearance.

'How's it gone?' he asked.

'Easy,' said Charity.

'You should see her, Jed!' Miranda laughed, 'The woman from the TV.'

'She's *awful*,' winced Charity.

'She's got a top car, but . . .' Miranda pulled a face. 'You should hear her laugh! . . .' Miranda did an impression. A her her her *hurr*! Charity and the doctor laughed at it.

Jed froze.

'Is she still here?' he gulped.

Charity said, 'Yeah. We told her you were a volunteer worker in case anybody mentioned you.'

Miranda said, 'She's been here before, Jed, re-member . . .'

She didn't have time to finish her sentence before Jed sprang for the door.

But as he poked his head out he saw Virginia striding down the corridor from the morning room, heading straight for the office.

He gasped and sprang back in the room. All he could do was pretend to be a pillar of salt.

It didn't work.

When she saw him, in full view of Charity, Miranda and Dr Stayne, Virginia gave him a huge smile and said, 'Jed! Hel-*lo*. Don't tell me *you're* the volunteer worker!'

A her her her *hurr*!

The tone made Jed feel that they were still writhing on the dusty wooden floor of an old church hall in Manchester with everyone present watching.

'How *marvellous*!' Virginia went on as Jed broke down into his constituent chemical components and evaporated into the atmosphere.

Charity, Miranda and the degenerate doctor gazed with amusement and curiosity at the spectacle of this improbable friendship.

Jed was the colour of the condemned.

The great fawn-suited celebrity saw everyone gawp-ing and said, 'Oh, don't worry, we're *old friends*' (a her her), and 'Oh *please* can I borrow him for a minute. Jed, you can show me round upstairs, what a *marvellous* building!'

Without waiting for permission she dragged Jed (whose legs did an impression of the Straw Man in the Wizard of Oz) out of the office and up the stairs.

As soon as they got to the top of the stairs and were alone on the first landing, Virginia squeezed his arm feverishly.

'Jed! Thank God it's you!'

It was impossible even to read Jed's lips.

'How well do you know them?' she whispered.

'Who?'

'The staff, the owners?'

'. . . I don't. I mean – not very well.'

She seemed pleased.

Jed's head was spinning. He couldn't admit his connection to the place, but he didn't want her to think she could safely advertise their history either.

'. . . It's probably best that they don't know about you and me though,' he added quickly.

'There's not very much for anyone to know,' she scolded.

'I'm sorry . . .'

'Don't worry about that. Is there anywhere we can be alone?'

'What! Here? Now?'

'I need to talk to you.'

'What about?'

She looked about. 'I can't tell you here. Isn't there anywhere we can be alone?'

Jed realised that Virginia wasn't being 'sexy'. She was being furtive yes, but serious too. What was going on? It crossed his mind that she might have stumbled on something.

Did he dare to take her into the staff room?

Her, 'I think there's something going on, here, Jed,' clinched it.

Up they went.

Down they sat.

Out it came.

In it sank.

She sighed. 'Honestly, I'm exhausted. I've been *ac*ting all day.'

Jed looked puzzled.

'Acting the drama queen, *dhar*ling – putting on a big show downstairs so that everyone'll take me for an idiot. I'm very good at it.' A her her her!

As she spoke her eyes began to shine with the evil light of righteousness.

'I'm really *on* to something, Jed. It's a real stroke of luck you being here. You won't believe it . . .' She stopped herself, fixing him with a look. 'You don't have anything to do with them downstairs do you? I mean you're not *married* to any of them or anything gruesome like that, are you?'

Jed shook his head.

She was apparently trying to assess the truth of this.

'You're not *involved* with any of them?'

'. . . The woman . . . Charity . . . knows my wife vaguely, that's all.'

'Nnn, well, good. Listen . . .'

She flapped her hand to indicate that she'd start at the very beginning.

'I don't know if you heard – you might not have been around at the time – a while ago there was a demonstration outside?'

'. . . I did hear something.'

'Well I was working for the local rag at the time – doing stories about weddings, charity functions, that sort of thing, dead interesting – a her her – and then suddenly there's a bunch of *grannies* sitting in the road outside here singing *We Shall Not Be Moved*, so I decided to *check out* what was going on behind the scenes. I mean you don't get a bunch of *grannies* sitting in the road *protesting* unless something pretty *weird* is going on, right?' A her her.

Jed was all ears. (And some blood.)

'*Anyway*, to cut a long story short, I think the whole thing's a bloody great fraud.' She put her hand

263

on his knee and leant forward. 'And guess what? There's *blackmail* involved. You wouldn't believe it, in a nice quite seaside town like this!' A her her *her*! 'You know that awful woman, Mrs Prior-Pointment or whatever her name is – "Mrs Butter-wouldn't-melt-in-her-bloomers" (a her), "Mrs Up The Family", "Mrs I'm backing Britain in my Honda Legend"?' Virginia, took a breath, 'She's being *black*mailed – I'm sure of it. It's all to do with this place.'

She was glowing.

Jed sort of waggled his head. 'Uh – how do you know?'

She gave him a professionally laden look of mock modesty.

'I wanted to get something on her as soon as I got here. I mean at first I just hated her – I mean no one's that squeaky clean, right? Then I bumped into this detective who told me some sordid stuff about her husband and business arrangements he's involved in, in Gibraltar. I thought – right! I'm gonna get you, bitch! The detective wouldn't tell me much. I had to *wrestle* the information out of him.' A her her.

Jed ummed as best he could through the exposition.

'So anyway. It turns out that there's another guy involved in Gibraltar who used to be an accountant. I mean he's posing as a doctor over there, but he used to practise as an accountant – until he was arrested and jumped bail. Turns out he was acting for the parties who bought this place! That woman downstairs and her husband.'

She laughed. 'It's all so bloody obvious when you start looking at it.'

Jed said, '. . . The *husband*?'

Virginia nodded. 'The husband. Used to own a business that went bankrupt. I don't know much about him yet, but I think he's the real owner. He's either blackmailing Mrs Prior-Pointment or they're in cahoots – I mean they bought this place for nothing, Mrs PP practically gave it to them. Do you know him, Jed, the husband? The mysterious "Mr Green"?'

'Er – no, I've never met him.'

For a moment Jed thought she was testing him. She had written to him at Eddie's office – Fuck! Surely she'd made the connection. He hadn't used his real name, but *Greenhouse* was pretty damn close.

'I don't know anything about him, yet,' she was saying. 'I was just going to start following them round. But, I mean I'm a bit conspicuous. I've got to be careful. I don't want to spoil the whole thing by giving myself away. You'd be ideal. You could be my *inside man* (a her her) . . .'

'Uh. How sure are you of all this stuff?'

'I'm totally convinced. I just need more info and proper evidence. But that's just a matter of time. Jed you've *got* to help me.'

'Why are you . . . doing the documentary?'

'It's a set-up, Jed. I want to give them a bit of publicity. I want everyone to know Mrs Prior-Pointment's involved. Have her on film talking about it. I've got a great interview I did a few weeks ago where she claims the credit for the whole thing.'

She sat back looking very pleased with herself.

'I'm going to make a name for myself, "female investigative journalist of the nineties". They might have to invent a special award.'

Jed's face must have been saying something because she added. 'You didn't think I was just doing some poxy story about a bunch of old fogies who think they're fantastic because they get to do all the work, while someone makes a load of money out of them, did you?'

'No, no, I . . . who else . . . knows about all this?

'Look, it's my story, I'm not going to let someone else get hold of it and ruin it. Absolutely no one knows – my boss knows I'm working on something good, but not what, I don't even trust *him*. You've got to watch your back in this business, Jed. It's every woman for herself.'

'I bet you've . . . got a big file of evidence tucked away somewhere?'

She tapped her forehead. 'I've got it all up here. It's safer. I'll get the documents together at the right time.'

She had her hand on his knee again.

'You've got to help me. It's so corrupt the whole thing, it's brilliant. I mean only today I discovered the nurse downstairs, what's her name?'

'Miranda?'

'Jones. Nurse Miranda Jones. I've been watching her all day. I'm certain she's a heroin addict – I worked on a documentary about heron addicts earlier in the year. Her eyes – little pin dots – I know the signs. Doing this to your nose (gesture of squeezing) and itching and scratching like this. She's been "stoned" all day, I'm sure of it. She's probably robbing them all blind.'

This really was news to Jed.

'So it's . . . only . . . you who knows the story?' Jed asked.

'You're the first person I've told. Jed, you'll help me won't you?'

Mrs Crotchley was making Rose a cup of tea in the kitchens. Rose was putting out a morsel for Tinkerbell and fussing over him.

Tinkerbell, whose memory was apparently longer than Rose's, growled viciously and tried to bite the old trade unionist's finger as she put the food in front of him.

Rose ignored the slight.

The two women settled down over one of the huge metal working tops to a cup of tea and a piece of

Madeira cake and fell to talking about the events of the day.

'I must say, you excelled yourself,' Mrs Crotchley remarked. 'I mean you put that dreadful woman in her place. Wasn't she awful!'

'Oh they're all like that at the television,' said Rose, as if she'd spent her life in the industry. 'And I must say, you covered the book-keeping very well indeed. Even I understood.'

They wholeheartedly agreed that it was a shame the rest of the house had been so miserable, but that it was understandable under the circumstances. It was just as well there were people to represent residents who understood the importance of the media to the survival of their way of life and who were capable of presenting themselves in a normal way no matter what the state of their personal feelings on any particular day.

And so on.

Eventually, encouraged by the delicious cake and the self-congratulation, the two women fell to talking about the past.

The old strikes had been caused by belligerence and bloody-mindedness on both sides, they agreed. Rose granted that the unions had been bullied by hard line elements and Mrs Crotchley conceded that the company had been harsh and even foolish in being determined to win the battle at all costs.

They agreed that if both sides had been able to talk things out properly and sensibly things would have been different. If only everyone thought the way they did society wouldn't have degenerated into violence and crime.

It had never been like that when they were young, had it. (Apart from the war, of course, but that was different.)

Regarding *Newfoundland*, Rose allowed that they had been hasty calling the second demonstration and Mrs Crotchley acknowledged that some good had come of it in the end, albeit indirectly. The new system was of benefit to all and would have to be defended in new ways.

'It's only a shame you weren't voted into the chair at yesterday's *débâcle*,' Mrs Crotchley said.

Rose generously waved away the compliment. It was only a matter of time, she felt.

'It's only a matter of time, dear,' Mrs Crotchley said. 'I mean, *really* when you look at Lilly's behaviour . . .'

'Poor old dear,' said Rose.

'It just goes to show, you never know who's being voted in these days . . .'

At that moment, as if as a contribution to the conversation, Tinkerbell was sick.

'I really do think we need sensible leadership at a time like this,' Mrs Crotchley said, as she went to mop up the little dog's vomit. 'It's essential if we're going to maintain standards.'

Jed saw Virginia to her Tahiti green Escort Cabriolet after an extravagant series of kisses and goodbyes around the house.

Jed had arranged to meet his executioner in a fortnight.

She was to spend the week editing the documentary for transmission the following Saturday.

'It's got to be *per*fect,' she said, 'I'm going to do practically the whole programme about this lot. I want to put them right up on a pedestal. From where . . .' here she mimed a flick. A her her her.

After transmission she was going away for a week.

Jed was to 'do some snooping around', and report his findings on her return.

'Phone me at my hotel. And *don't* expect to get back to your wife!' A her her. 'At least not in one piece.' A her her her *hurr*!

He must have looked sheepish because she leaned on his arm in that way of hers and added. 'Jed. Don't *worry.* I'm only *joking.*' She shrugged. 'You can stay if you like, of course. But you don't *have* to.'

A her. A her her. A her her her.

Miranda was the first to collar Jed when he came back into the building.

'I know who *that* was!' she whispered furtively.

Jed looked at her eyes. Little pin dots.

'*She*'s the one you felt up at that *party*, isn't she?'

Jed flushed. In anger mainly.

Miranda took a step back. 'What's the matter with you? Wouldn't she give you a feel?'

Jed shook his head and mumbled something.

Next thing Charity was there too.

'*So*, "old friends" are we?'

Jed's eyes flashed. 'I used to know her at college. I met her at that wedding in Manchester last year,' he said and before Charity could even raise her eyebrows he added, 'The night Eddie tried to seduce you.'

'*I* remember.' Charity was indignant. 'Was she that friendly at the wedding? Surely not, or you'd have mentioned her.'

Jed bunched his face into a fist. 'Fuck. Off,' he said and left the building.

Charity said, 'Fuck you, too.'

Miranda was probably the most shocked of them.

That night Rose waited patiently for the house to settle down for the night before taking the key to the room on the third floor (out of the locker in the office where she'd been keeping an eye on it) and getting into the lift.

Jed was on duty and he seemed to have gone to bed early. She was sure he smelled of drink when he came in, so she didn't think he would be about.

She wasn't sure what had been going on that day, but she knew there had been some commotion in the room with the body in it. She wanted to make sure everything was in order in the top cupboard.

She listened at the staff room door, or as close to the staff room door as she dared to stand – nothing.

She made her way quietly along the corridor and slipped into the makeshift mausoleum.

She shuddered as she shuffled round the bed. It all looked very spooky in the dark – the cold metallic light from the moon throwing shadows over the gruesome mounds in the sheet on the bed.

She pushed the bedside chair against the old built-in wardrobe, climbed plumply up, opened the top cupboard, just as she had on mornings when she thought old Mrs Prior-Pointment was asleep, and groped inside.

She had just realised that the cupboard was empty when there was a scuffling and a scratching behind her. Tinkerbell was sniffing around! The dog followed her scent to the chair then growled and bared his teeth at her.

Rrrr-*wiff*! Rrrr . . .

Rose was stranded.

Next thing the light came on causing Rose to pucker her eyes and squint. Mrs Crotchley was holding up the battered green holdall.

'You had your own key made too, did you? Is this what you're looking for, dear?' she asked holding up the bag. 'I found all your little notes. It was awfully good of you to keep a record.'

When Jed left *Newfoundland* after his shattering interview with Virginia and his brief row with Charity, he stormed off across the sand dunes that hid the old building from the town.

He was drunk with rage.

As he kicked his way through the whirling columns of crisp packets and dried grass, growling and furiously booting odd pieces of what looked like cork, or gnarled knots of petrified wood (but which were in fact dried pieces of shit) his mind railed against his misfortune and he cried hot bitter tears.

270

It was so clear now how naive he had been, how smug and pathetic.

He cursed himself as he kicked at the sand and found himself again replaying the horror of holding Lilly's arm while she struggled against him.

There was nowhere to run, no one he could turn to. He was sitting at the bottom of the barrel with the dregs. Where he belonged.

He'd go to prison. It was certain now. He pictured himself in a cell. For how long? 'Nine years' came into his head from somewhere. Miranda had said it. Jesus! Who with? Do you get locked up two and three to a cell like he'd read in the papers? And what was it . . . 'Slopping out'? . . .

Nine years! *In a tiny cell*!

He couldn't do it.

It was absolutely impossible.

He marched up the sandy slope, grinding his teeth, stomping his feet into the soft sand, gasping for breath.

There had to be a way out of it.

There was *no – way* – that he was going to go to jail. *No way*.

He was standing on the top of one of the highest hillocks now. From here you could see into the bedrooms of the drab grey billets of Pontins further down the beach; see out over the Estuary; see in the distance the endless houses of the resort town, which looked so safe and organised and ordinary.

As he stood there cut by the sharp breeze from the beach – the tide was miles out – he felt as if he was being slowly pierced by a rod of cold, rusty iron.

Cruel determination rose up in him.

There was no way he was going down without a fight.

He was going to go to war.

To save himself.

*T*wo nights and some calculation later, Jed was sitting up in bed in the staff room about to get drunk when there was a tapping on the door.

He'd successfully avoided human contact for a couple of days. He and Charity hadn't exchanged a word; he'd hardly seen Miranda. He assumed they were both avoiding him. He was glad.

It was Miranda.

She whispered, 'Can I come in?'

It was the first time Jed could remember not being pleased to see her. He didn't even bother to conceal the bottle of whisky as he would normally have done.

She sat on the bed uninvited. 'Where have you been? I've hardly set eyes on you. What's going on?'

Stumm.

'Are you still not talking to each other? She wasn't really jealous of the TV woman, you know. Huh. Who could be jealous of *that*!'

Silence. Miranda tried to penetrate him with her eyes.

She knew it was serious when she failed.

'Are you worried about Lilly? She'll understand. No one wants the place to close. We all need it too much.'

She rubbed her nose and scratched her arm.

Jed snorted cynically when he saw this, but he didn't comment because he didn't want to communicate at all.

He wasn't going to give anything away from now on.

That was it.

Stumm.

He knew what it meant now. He'd learned how to do it.

He twisted the top off the bottle.

She said, 'You're drinking too much.'

He had to laugh then. 'Fine coming from you!'

'Yeah. And look where that got me.'

He just sat there. Ashamed of his drinking after all. Then she grinned. 'Well, give us a slug then.'

He took a gulp and handed her the bottle.

When she'd had a go she handed him the bottle back and said, 'Can I get in?'

He laughed without feeling amused. Resignedly. 'If you want.'

She stood before him, as she had so many times in his imagination and removed her clothes. All of them.

As he tried not to watch she hopped over to the door and turned off the light.

She was climbing in beside him.

He was still wearing his old T-shirt but he could feel the bareness of her legs next to his.

She took the bottle off him, took a drink, offered him another slug, which he took, then she put the bottle on the bedside table and tugged at his T-shirt.

He took it off.

They slid down into the bed and pressed against each other, front to front.

Miranda was kissing him and breathing loudly, making little noises – gently touching him, with light, expert fingers.

Jed was a million miles away. On another planet. He felt like an alien in his own body. Fuck, it was really going to happen.

He didn't want it to.

At the same time he was stiffer than he could ever remember being.

Cold, dry lust: he was sick with it.

He found himself squirming to avoid her touch for fear of coming off there and then.

She took his squirming for a desire to climb on top of her, so hastened his journey with a shove, a nimble swivel of the hips and a clamping of the legs.

His mind racing, he tried to delay entry by holding

off, holding his bottom in the air. But she soon put paid to that with a firm finger in the right place, causing him to gasp and thrust and – oh-my-God.

He knew immediately that he was close to coming. Very close.

Shit.

Maybe he'd come ice.

He tried to move as slowly as possible to prevent . . .

He was holding his breath – more than his breath, holding his being, trying not to . . .

But she was moving, as vigorous as he was hesitant.

'Keep still,' Jed hissed. And, 'Slowly . . .'

But she was having none of that. She heaved and ground for all she was worth.

He fought her for a while (seven or eight seconds), tried to hold it off, tried not to think about what he was doing so as to prolong it. But . . .

Shit, shit.

In the end he sort of went rather than came.

A splut, rather than a spurt.

A holding on rather than a letting go.

He apologised.

She said, 'Shh . . .' and, 'It was nice,' both of which made him cringe.

He lay there feeling putrefied.

Emptied, rather than fulfilled, thinking that he didn't want her to stay the night and wondering at the change. How he would have died to be where he was now even two days previously.

Then he fell to thinking of the general situation again.

How to get out of it.

The various options.

It had been all he thought of since Virginia had left.

'What are you thinking?' she asked.

He rolled off and they settled down with her head on his shoulder.

He felt a little more comfortable like that.

'There's something you're not telling me.'

'It's nothing, honestly – I'm not getting on too well with Charity, that's all.'

'You were getting on OK the other day – before *she* came.' She shook him slightly. Reassuringly. 'It's stress, that's all.'

'Yeah, yeah. I know. Just stress.'

They lay for a while, Jed thinking how the bed was too small. Miranda nipped to get a fag from her jeans and they started gulping from the bottle again. She told Jed about a film she'd seen and Jed cheered up slightly with the fresh influx of alcohol, started to care less about . . .

All that.

After a couple of minutes, during which they sat listening to the infrequent passing of cars on the road outside, Jed said, a little haltingly, 'If you were going to do away with someone, what would you do?'

She laughed. 'That's easy. Give them an overdose.'

'Huh. What if they don't take drugs?'

'A machine gun.'

He laughed. 'No, if you wanted . . . to get away with it.'

She looked at him. 'Thinking of getting rid of me are you, now you've fucked me.'

'I'd just give *you* an *overdose*.'

She thought for a moment. 'You've definitely got to make it look like it was an accident.'

'That's what I reckon.'

'Or make it look like suicide.'

'Yeah.'

'Push them under a train or something.'

'Um.'

Miranda explained to Jed about how junkies are always being murdered by people giving them overdoses. 'When someone's already out, just bang a few extra grammes in – nobody bothers because it happens so often.' Simple. 'Like old people really,' she added.

Ten minutes later, Jed suddenly and urgently wanted to steer the conversation back to sex.

Miranda must have sensed this because she snuggled back down under the covers and pulled him down that way.

When they were front to front Miranda said, 'Jed, I hate to ask but – could you lend me some money? Please.'

There was a little clink somewhere in the corner as a penny dropped.

'. . . How much?'

'About . . . a hundred.'

There was a pause while he adjusted his calculations and worked out how he could get the money.

'As long as it's not for drugs,' he said at last.

'It's not for drugs,' she said, sliding her hand onto his stomach, and then lower.

They both knew it was for drugs.

He felt her shaking him gently.

It was early. Even the light was sleepy – steely grey and dim.

'Jed . . .'

It was a hiss.

'Jed.'

'Um.'

'Can I borrow that money?'

'Um.'

Hand shaking him. Sensation of his whole being hurting.

'What?'

'Jed. Can I borrow that money?'

He allowed himself to be really annoyed with her for the first time.

'What the fuck's the time?'

'It's early. I've got to go.'

'I'll get it for you later.'

'I need it now.'

'It's the middle of the fucking night!'

He looked at her through a sleep-encrusted eye.

She was dressed and ready to go.

'I haven't got a hundred quid right now, believe it or not.'

She was brandishing his cash card.

He was even more annoyed now, because she'd been through his trousers.

'That's Charity's.'

'Isn't it the one you use?'

'I'll get it for you later.'

'I need it now. I've got to get it to someone. I owe them. They need it.'

Silence.

'I wouldn't ask if it wasn't important.'

Silence.

'Tell me the number Jed. I'll go to the cash machine and I'll come straight back and give you the card. It's my shift.'

'*Fuck*in'ell.'

'*Please*, Jed.'

An angry sigh. Then:

'Twenty-seven, thirty-five.'

Her slight smile.

Footsteps.

Door handle.

'Thanks.'

'You'd better come back.'

Click.

Gone.

There was a steely grey light in Jed's head when he finally crawled, later and more painfully than usual, into consciousness.

He didn't want to leave the staff room yet and stood staring out of the window for a while thinking about the sex of the night before.

Not how he had expected it to happen.

He had expected to wait longer.

He had expected a passionate, gentle, loving experience that would project him into a new future. He had expected to feel an overwhelming sense of caring for the girl. He had hardly dared to expect it at all.

He certainly hadn't expected to end up paying for it.

He knew that was what he had done.

With his wife's credit card.

But what was more surprising was the fact that he had enjoyed it so much more the second time, when he knew he was paying for it.

It had been cold, calculating and excellent. Or hot, calculating and excellent. At least that's how it seemed in the light of the morning – now she was gone and all that remained was the replay. And the smell on his fingers.

He found himself making steely grey calculations.

Could he sustain this with Miranda? If so, how long for?

He decided it was possible to sustain it for about two weeks. Until he'd sorted out the biggest problem. He wouldn't want to be messing about with Miranda after that.

After that they'd get everything straight again.

Mrs Rodgers took the table next to Eddie and Rodriguez.

Arthur was safely ensconced at the apartment with a copy of *The Times* and a glass of whisky, under instructions to have a thoroughly lazy afternoon.

He didn't need to be persuaded.

Rodriguez saw her immediately and smiled his crooked smile.

This time she nodded boldly and smiled cheekily back.

The old crook stood up at once and came over to her table. The first of her calculations had been correct.

Would she like to join them for a drink? Oh yes, that would be lovely, thank you.

Eddie nodded vaguely when she sat down at their table, he seemed a little distracted and carried on reading the paper. Rodriguez made up for Eddie's self-absorption with a broad and friendly charm and a very attractive accent, making the good woman think how pleasant he was for a criminal, how personable and intelligent. It was only when the man took hold of her hand and commented on the smoothness of the skin, pressing it to his lips and complimenting her mature beauty, while at the same time gazing unflinchingly into her eyes with no regard for Eddie, or for that matter anyone else in the cafe, that it occurred to her that as far as Rodriguez was concerned they were only a hop and a skip away from bed.

'Would you like that we take a little (pron: leetle) walk?' he said when he was done with his flattery.

Mrs Rodgers was a little flustered. She had miscalculated the speed with which Rodriguez would pass from the social to the sexual.

She glanced a little nervously at her watch with something of her old primness and then at the door, perhaps a little obviously.

Eddie seemed to notice this step out of character and gave her a new and searching look, checking over his shoulder to see what she had been looking at.

Mrs Rodgers said that she would like to go for a 'little walk' just as soon as she'd finished her chocolate which made Rodriguez smile so broadly that a gold tooth she had not previously noticed came into view. The suntanned pirate oozed charm now and as he did so the seductress saw Eddie peering at her. She knew he was on the verge of recognising her.

Again she was looking at the door. Where *were* they?

She knew it the moment Eddie 'sussed' her. It was written all over the way he flinched. And frowned. And checked again over his shoulder. The way his lips twitched. The way he looked like he wanted to tell Rodriguez but wasn't sure whether or not it was a good idea.

He had identified her as Arthur's wife – the prim, frightened woman he had had the misfortune to have to put pressure on all those months ago – now apparently transformed into . . . God!? . . . transformed anyhow – into the strange woman who had sat on the next table watching weeks ago, making eyes at Rodriguez. Hadn't Arthur been there then? What was the hell was she doing now, flirting with Rodriguez? . . .

Eddie had heard that Arthur's wife had turned up in Gibraltar (from Sandra), but he had not been introduced and had so far managed to avoid her.

Eddie knew something was about to happen.

Mrs Rodgers knew that he knew.

At that moment the two men she had been waiting for walked into the cafe and Mrs Rodgers visibly relaxed.

Rodriguez was too wrapped up in his seduction to notice anything but mature beauty.

Eddie spotted the two men and when he saw the disguised woman giving him the sort of look you would expect to see on the face of a person that you had been holding at gunpoint but who had now turned the tables and was pointing the gun at you, all he could do was try to smile, wonder whether Arthur had betrayed him and await further developments.

Mrs Rodgers caught the eye of the two men who had come into the cafe and then nodded at Rodriguez.

Rodriguez was at last distracted from his soft focus, hand-kissing daze and turned round just as the two men approached the table and the youngest and most smartly dressed of them produced his identity card. He was from Customs and Excise. The man then discreetly informed Rodriguez that he was under arrest and that, in case he was thinking of causing trouble for himself, the other officer was armed.

Rodriguez nodded politely, if curtly, at the enthusiastic young customs officer then turned a cutting look on Eddie that, had it had material form, would have sliced clean through his windpipe.

Swallowing, Eddie said, 'Nothing to do with me.'

While Rodriguez held the visual knife to Eddie's throat, Mrs Rodgers said. 'Allow me to introduce myself. I'm Arthur's wife.'

At which Rodriguez swivelled his head in her direction altering his expression automatically, if only slightly, to take into account the gentleness of her sex, so that as the look metaphorically cut through the good woman's jugular it also, as it were, apologised for doing so and made a sympathetic 'there there' kind of sound.

'Touché,' said Eddie when the intruders had departed and the waiter had served the coffees.

Mrs Rodgers sipped lightly at her drink, blowing on the froth to cool it down. She was enjoying herself again now.

'So, you decided to spare me.'

'Oh, yes,' she said, 'We have – "unfinished business" you and I. Besides, your position is unassailable – as far as I can tell you have the full protection of the Governor's office and police department.'

He laughed, good humouredly. 'You seem to have a firm grasp of the subtleties of international finance.'

'You were my first teacher.'

His hand made the acknowledgement. 'I presume you're acting independently.'

'Of course.'

'Huh, at first I thought maybe Arthur was up to

something.' He grinned. 'I should have known he was too stupid.'

She nodded, graciously allowing the slight against her family.

'As I was saying – *your* position was unassailable.'

Eddie sat back. 'Yes, yes.'

'Not so Rodriguez, unfortunately.'

'Yes, he's wanted by Customs. That was always our weak spot.'

Mrs Rodgers smiled.

Eddie said, 'I presume you know that Rodriguez will have Arthur and I killed? Probably before the day's out.'

'Customs will hold him for forty-eight hours before allowing him any contact with the outside world. It was part of the deal.'

'Rodriguez was not the only mug involved here . . .'

'Yes, the tourist shop. They'll be calling there about now.' She looked at her watch rather theatrically. 'They'll hold the fat man in isolation for the same period.'

Eddie grinned. 'Huh. Very thorough aren't you?'

'Very.'

He sat back. 'So. Forty-eight hours. Just enough time for you to . . . conduct your "unfinished business"?'

She smiled.

They understood one another.

'I presume you have something in mind, or else . . .' He made the sign of having his throat cut.

'It doesn't occur to you that I might have had humanitarian motives for "sparing you"?'

'Nice idea, but . . . no.'

They both laughed.

'Quite correct.' Despite everything she found herself drawn to this Eddie who-ever-he-was. He seemed perky, even as she was ruining him. 'If you don't mind me saying, you seem very relaxed for someone

282

whose business is collapsing round his ears,' she remarked.

He flapped a hand. 'I had an excellent day yesterday because I thought to myself, "tomorrow all this is going to come to an end". And I had an excellent day the day *before* yesterday because I was thinking "tomorrow all this going to come to an end" . . .'

'Good Lord, really?' Mrs Rodgers found this a bit extreme. 'And what about today?'

'Today it all came to an end.'

She was fascinated.

Eddie was as philosophical as ever. 'Do you know what? I almost think I'm glad. Huh, I'd been thinking it was time to settle down. I might take this as my final warning. Unlike Arthur I *do* have contingency plans.'

She would have liked to talk a little longer, but they only had forty-eight hours if they wanted to avoid having their throats cut.

A few sips of coffee and down to it.

'Arthur tells me you're the money-man.'

'He never could keep his mouth shut.'

'How much is there?'

'Not a penny.'

She nodded. 'As I thought.' She sat back and folded her arms staunchly.

Eddie said, 'Are you going to show me your hand? I assume you've a deadly weapon concealed about your person.'

They still understood one another.

'How well do you love your friends at *Newfound-land*?' she asked.

Eddie was puzzled. '*New* . . . what?

'The old people's home.'

'Ah.' He leaned his elbows on the table. 'I love them very well indeed. But you're going to need something better than that. You're up to your own neck there.'

'I've retired from politics.'

283

Eddie blinked. 'What about your beloved Party? It would cause a lot of trouble if it came out.'

She laughed generously. 'The party will survive.'

Eddie took a few moments out to search her impenetrably affable face.

'You're bluffing. You wouldn't . . . you're in too deep.'

She feigned disappointment and stood up. 'Oh dear. Love means that little to you, does it? Your poor friends. You'd gamble with their happiness.' She sighed as she proffered her hand for shaking. 'Who knows – perhaps you're right to call my bluff. I mean I've entirely misread the rest of the circumstances . . .'

'Wait.' Eddie was grinning. Broadly. 'Sit down. Er . . . Please.'

She did so.

'You're a very foxy lady.'

'*Thank* you.' She made herself comfortable. 'Now. How much is there?'

He shook his head. 'How much did you have in mind?'

Touché.

 **M**iranda didn't come straight back from the cashpoint.

She was due to start her shift at eight thirty and at nine thirty Jed was still waiting for her to take over from him.

By ten o'clock it was obvious she wasn't going to show up and Jed reluctantly decided to phone Charity.

No reply.

He was quite relieved because he didn't want to have to speak to her, but he did wonder where she was, whether she hadn't been out all night.

Stayne.

He stuck it out until lunch time and tried her again. 'Hello?'

'Oh, hi. It's me. Uh, Miranda hasn't shown up.'

'Oh.'

'I've been trying to get you all morning.'

'I was out.'

Yes I know. 'Could . . . will you come in?'

'It's my day off.' She was very cold sounding.

'Yeah, I know. It's just . . . I'm tired.'

'So am I.'

'Yeah, yeah I know.' *Tired*! 'Look I'm sorry about everything, I've been a bastard,' he said without even convincing himself.

Silence.

'. . . Who's on tonight? Is it you?' he asked.

'Miranda.'

'Shit.'

She said, 'I'm not doing tonight. I've got something arranged.'

Oh yeah? 'I did last night!'

Charity said, 'Get a temp, then.'

'I thought we'd agreed not to do that at the moment.'

'Well do it yourself.'

Silence.

He sighed.

More silence.

Why didn't she put the phone down if she wasn't going to say anything?

Why didn't *he* put the phone down?

Oh fuck. 'Charity?' Extra sweet.

'What?' Flatter than flat.

It hurt him to open his mouth. 'I really *am* sorry – I've been out of my mind . . . with worry. I'm sorry I said fuck off the other day. And I'm . . . I'm sorry.'

'Have you got something to be sorry *about*?'

'No! For f . . .' He stopped himself.

Conciliation.

'No. I've . . . just let it all get to me. I lost my temper because I was embarrassed . . . because . . . Virginia's so horrible and I was embarrassed – to be associated with her. I was cross that you thought something could have happened between us.' (That was a good one.)

Still the damn silence.

'So I took it out on you. I'm sorry. I've been acting badly. It's the bloody stress. I'm worried sick.'

'We're both under stress, Jed. It's an awful situation.'

'Yes.'

She softened. At last. 'But it really is going to be over soon. Stayne's going to sort it all out. We'll be straight again.'

'Yeah. Yeah.'

He felt sick. He had that old feeling again. Of her innocence and his guilt.

He gave in. 'Look, you have your day off. I'll have a kip this afternoon. If she doesn't show I'll do tonight as well.'

'Thanks Jed.'

'You can reward me another time.'

'See you tomorrow.'

'Yeah.'

'Oh, Jed . . .'

'Yeah?'

'Did you go to the bank this morning?'

He came very close to spluttering. '. . . Yeah . . . yeah, I nipped out first thing.'

'It's none of my business, but what did you need two hundred pounds for?'

'Two h . . . Oh . . . Miranda wanted to borrow some . . . fifty . . . she asked me yesterday . . . I thought I'd save myself having to go back . . . You know I can't write my own cheques – I'm sick of running backwards and forwards to the cash machine . . .'

'Hum.'

'. . . Is everything OK?'

286

'Yeah. Yeah . . .'

Charity was being cagey now.

'What is it?'

'Uh . . . well . . . Miranda borrowed fifty quid off *me* yesterday.'

'Oh.' *Humm* '. . . She must be broke.'

'Yeah.'

'See you tomorrow.'

Jed waited for Miranda to show up that night.

She didn't.

It was her day off the next day.

The next night, while Charity worked, Jed paced round the house, kicking things. Miranda still had the credit card. He wasn't allowed one himself by the bank, so he used Charity's account, borrowing one of her cards. He'd had no money all day but had to pretend to Charity he had. At one point he'd had to steal ten pounds from Charity's purse.

He was just dressed for bed when the door bell rang.

He was immediately turned on.

'Hiya.' Miranda was sheepish. She handed him the card.

'Come in.'

'Are you in bed?'

He nodded.

She walked straight to the bedroom.

Jed stood there blinking.

She was forgiven.

She was taking off her clothes when he got into the bedroom. 'I owe you one,' she said.

'You owe me several.'

The following night Jed spent a very pleasant night with his wife.

Charity had done the business. He was obviously forgiven.

Meal, video, wine – his favourite Jack Daniels for after

– which in the end he didn't touch. They hardly ever treated themselves to wine.

He knew within the first ten minutes that they would make love that night.

He felt calm and in control.

Contented.

Uxorious, even.

He had made his plans; he was going to carry them out. The trouble seemed very distant in the glow of homeliness.

Everything was going to be all right.

They didn't talk much, but the silence was a contented one and when they did communicate they talked about the past, holidays they'd had and their friends, whom they agreed they had neglected. Charity had seen one of her old friends and filled Jed in on odd bits of gossip about people they hadn't seen in ages.

They watched a trashy film and Jed looked around the cosily-lit room with some relish. There was a soft femininity about it which was reassuring.

It was the first time they'd made love since . . .

Since that time.

Very soft and gentle it was too.

They kissed and held on to each other tenderly, each of them trembling slightly.

Charity whispered, 'It's been so long, I'm nervous,' into his ear.

Jed laughed, gently. 'Me too,' he said and it was true.

Jed was surprised by how warm and close it felt. How new. How lovingly she kissed him.

There was a part of Jed that was wickedly comparing the sensations with those of the sex he'd been having with Miranda. It made it all the nicer to be with his wife.

He was transported. He gave himself up to to her completely, made her feel as special as he could, told her how special she was to him. And then . . .

Oh my God, no!

She was Going On Down South.

No. Not tonight. *Please.*

He took hold of her shoulders and stopped her at his belly button.

'Don't,' he whispered. 'Don't do that.'

'OK,' she whispered.

Then she crawled back up and lay her head on his chest, shyly, lying there on top of him.

'I don't like it,' Jed whispered.

She looked at him through the benign shadows.

'You don't like it?' she repeated.

He shook his head bashfully. 'I don't really like it.' He laughed. Embarrassed.

She drew herself level, dug her elbows into his chest, mock-maliciously, looking down on him, smiling.

'You mean to tell me we've been married all this time and you've just got round to telling me you don't like me sucking you off?'

He grinned. Very embarrassed, now. 'I'm . . . not very good at . . . communicating.'

She guffawed.

Then she kissed him on the lips and said, 'Thank you,' looking like she meant it. She grinned wickedly. 'Would you mind telling me exactly what you *do* like?'

He smiled, again feeling bashful.

She said, 'Please Jed,' in such a way as to convince him to open up. When he'd told her (in a whisper) she said, 'You naughty man!' kissed him and did it. Later she told him what she liked best, or at least what she wanted to try and he did it.

They carried on making love until they were exhausted and fell asleep in each other's arms, Jed thinking as he drifted off that he wouldn't even mind if Charity did get pregnant.

*T*he following night Jed was back with Miranda.

Though he *was* relieved when she got up and left in the middle of the night with the fifty quid he'd withdrawn from the bank that morning.

Now, worn out by his exertions, Jed was asleep in the office at *Newfoundland*. His head was on the desk and he was dribbling like you do when you fall asleep on the train.

He felt someone shake him.

'I keep telling your wife: you're overworking yourselves.'

He spluttered and pain shot through his eyes as he took in the scene.

Dr Stayne was standing in front of him.

'How are the patients?'

Lilly, Edith and Mrs M were still sedated.

'. . . Not a peep.'

The doctor sat down. 'We need to talk.'

Jed found it difficult to look on the doctor without contempt. As they sat there, he tried not to say, 'So you want to fuck my wife, do you?' and succeeded largely because the doctor spoke first.

'How well do you know your nurse?' he asked.

'. . . How do you mean?'

'Well, for example, do you know anything about her past?'

I see.

'Possibly not as much as you.'

The doctor nodded, sagely.

'So you know she's a heroin addict?'

'*Was* a heroin addict.'

The doctor made one of those 'Oh come now, do you really believe that, or are we playing some kind of game' expressions.

'I think she's having it a bit, now and then,' Jed said, a little weakly. 'She came here to get away from it. She'd been doing quite well until . . . until just recently, I think.'

He felt as if the doctor were examining him for symptoms of an anti-social disease and that there were large red blotches all over his face.

'She had a bit of a . . . (what was the word) . . . *scare* recently,' Jed continued. 'But she seemed to get over that.'

The two men looked at each other, until Jed's gaze sagged and he had to struggle not to fidget like the perfect specimen of deceit.

Stayne said, 'Why are you defending her?'

Jed opened his mouth but realised too late that there was nothing to come out of it, so it gaped idiotically for a moment. 'I suppose . . . I think she deserves a chance,' he managed eventually, with some truth. 'She's done well . . . until recently.'

Something in the doctor's eye stopped him.

'Did you know she'd been hitting Doctor Haggarty for drugs?'

Jed's face answered the question.

'I only found out myself the other day. The day the television were here. He came here looking for her – said he was on a routine call. Huh, he hasn't *got* a routine; he never makes routine calls. I knew what was going on as soon as I saw her face. The very next day I spotted her coming out of the surgery as I was going in. I went straight into Haggarty and told him I knew – bluffing of course – I described the likely circumstances, in some detail . . .'

'What, from experience?' Jed said. The doctor ignored him, only faltering slightly,

'. . . as if I knew all about that sort of thing. Haggarty fell right into it. Admitted it right out. She's been at him for some time. She's had a regular supply for months.' He sat back. 'Not what you'd call "doing well" at all, in fact.'

'Not for months, surely.'

291

'Haggarty cut her off immediately. So she's going to get pretty desperate.'

Jed thought about the 'business' of the last few days. Then the doctor said, quite casually,

'Is she blackmailing you?'

Jed's reply to the simply-put question was supposed to be 'What! Don't be ridiculous, of course she isn't blackmailing me,' but it came out as, 'Pffwhatt, dumpt besstupt,' and ended with, 'budda budda – blackmail? What – I mean of course she's not,' which was altogether counter-productive as a reply and had a levitational effect on the doctor's eyebrows.

Jed calmed himself under the stern gaze and summarised his outburst with, 'I've got nothing to hide.'

There was a mildly scornful mutation of the doctor's gaze and a clinical, 'Humm.'

Jed waited as long as he could. He felt surrounded. By eyebrows. 'Whatever gives you the impression she could be blackmailing me?'

'It's one of her specialities.'

'And you'd know about that would you?'

'I'm afraid so. Yes.'

Jed was pleasantly surprised by the frank admission, said, 'Oh, urh,' and visibly relaxed.

Prematurely.

'I thought she might be blackmailing *you* over poisoning the old dame.'

If the doctor had needed more proof of Jed's guilt than he already had, Jed's face gave it to him.

'It was obviously you,' he went on. 'The timing was all wrong. If it had been – the old woman, what's her name . . .'

'Edith . . .'

'She would have had to have been on the night shift. By all accounts the latest possible time she could have administered the drugs is still four hours before they could have been taken . . .'

He stopped.

'And the only person who could have administered a drug like that to a person in her condition was someone who had no idea what they were doing.'

He looked at Jed squarely.

'Now Nurse Jones may well be a fraud, but she does know what she's doing.' The scornful look reappeared. 'Not so, your good self, unfortunately. It was you who was on duty, I believe.'

Jed was suddenly struck by the notion that the whole world knew what was going on at *Newfoundland*. Was there a sign outside the building he wondered: Blackmail, Bribery, Corruption. Fraud. Apply within.

'. . . And if it *had* been the old nurse why would you have panicked like that when the old women discovered the body, surely you would have been able to explain the situation to them. You said one of them was the poisoner.'

It was bloody obvious.

Jed said, '*You're* not going to blackmail me, are you?'

There was a distinct atmosphere of 'Ah, now we're getting somewhere'.

'What do you want?' Jed asked.

'I want out. That's all. I came to this God forsaken town to get away from this sort of thing. I'm a respectable doctor now (the word 'now' was more or less swallowed), with a nice respectable practice. I intend to keep it that way.'

Jed was cautiously relieved.

'This nurse Miranda is endangering all that. She's got to be got rid of.'

'Miranda's alright. She's . . .'

'Dangerous.'

'She's got problems.'

'She's not to be trusted.'

'She won't . . . she wouldn't . . . she's not going to harm anyone. She's not the type. I trust her completely.'

293

Stayne calculated his pause just right. So that Jed had started to feel uncomfortable when he spoke.

'If you think she's so trustworthy, tell me this: she knows we have to get Haggarty out of the way if we're going to cover up what happened to the old woman. She knows how much depends on it – she knows what would happen to you if it gets out – the whole place could close down for God's sake – and you could go to . . . you could be in very serious trouble. Very serious. And all the time she could have just told you he was bent. I mean now I've found him out he's talking about retiring at the end of the week, just like that. Why didn't she say something?'

Jed couldn't answer.

Stayne went on, 'It's because she'll do anything to protect her supply. She'd rather see the whole thing go down – see you go to jail. It's the only thing that matters to her.'

Jed sat there, denying it to himself.

'By the end of the week Haggarty will be gone – we don't want this Miranda hanging around after that.'

'What can we do?'

'Get rid of her.'

Jed huffed. 'Impossible.'

'Difficult perhaps . . . impossible?'

'Very difficult.'

'Where there's a will . . .'

That was the problem.

There was a gruesome smile on the doctor's face now. 'You never know,' he said, 'she might even take an overdose and save you a lot of trouble.'

Virginia did indeed do a good job on the documentary.

Rose and Mrs Crotchley were very impressed. They watched it on the new television in Mrs Crotchley's room and just before it started Mrs Crotchley produced a very grand-looking bottle of wine.

'I had it delivered,' she said, giggling happily. 'Tinkerbell's got smoked salmon.'

Rose looked at the dog who was scoffing something from a bowl in the corner.

Griffle-ruffle-ruffle. (Slobber-slobber . . .)

'I ordered the wine from Dominic of London – they delivered it yesterday. It's their best House claret. It's thirty years old. Father used to order it on special occasions when I was a girl. I used to have half a glass . . .'

The wine was served in crystal goblets that Mrs Crotchley produced from a blanket drawer and they settled down to watch the programme.

Rose thought the wine tasted like Sainsbury's best, but she didn't say anything.

The way the documentary was edited made life at the centre seem highly organised – the residents seemed lively, energetic and full of life. Rose and Mrs Crotchley both came across as highly articulate and well-adapted women, which of course they were. So did Miranda and Charity.

There was a lot of time devoted to *Newfoundland* and their way of doing things, and there was a long interview with Mrs Prior-Pointment (the younger) in which she praised herself and the Party and especially the new spirit of private enterprise. *Newfoundland* was a symbol of the future, she said, and even though residents were, most of them, entirely without family in the nuclear sense, it was generally agreed that a traditional family feeling lay behind the success of the venture. There was caring and sharing. And after all wasn't that what family life was all about.

At this point Mrs Crotchley's lips tightened into a thin smile and she raised her glass to Rose.

'Bottom's up,' she said.

The documentary was very well received elsewhere.

It went out at seven o'clock Saturday evening and by ten o'clock that night Charity had in front of her a list of thirty people of both sexes offering substantial sums to take up immediate residence. She couldn't get out of the office all evening.

On about the twentieth call Charity mentioned that they already had a waiting list and the anxious caller doubled his offer on the spot.

At some point in the evening Doctor Stayne called to offer his congratulations. Charity told him about the flood of callers.

'There are a lot of rich, lonely people out there,' he said, 'Do them a favour and take their money.'

'We're full already,' Charity lamented. 'But I took their details anyhow.'

Jed watched the show with Miranda.

Or, rather he had intended to. She didn't show up until it was all over.

'How was it?' she asked.

'You're a star.'

'Wish I was. They get the best cocaine.'

Monday Edith and Lilly died.

Jed and Charity were in the office when doctor Stayne came in and made the announcement.

'Both of them? What of?' asked Jed his legs nearly giving way beneath him.

The doctor's 'I'm ... not sure,' made Jed's heart miss a beat.

Charity burst into tears. Jed stumbled across the room

to comfort her with an awkward arm on her shoulder. She was sitting in the old chair which *eeked* in time to her sobs. Jed hovered over her as best he could for a while, staring at the doctor who was busy moving small items around in his bag. Jed wanted to say something but he couldn't even swallow.

Charity looked up, her face soaked. 'We've killed them!' she blurted and renewed her outburst of grief.

After a few moments she looked up again. 'We've killed them,' she repeated.

It was an appeal.

'Of course we haven't . . .' Stayne inclined his head awkwardly instead of finishing his sentence. 'They've suffered some kind of viral infection; it's very common in people their age.'

Both Jed and Charity stared at him in horror.

'Both of them?' Charity said.

'I'm afraid so.'

'What the fucking hell kind of viral infection?' asked Jed, at last able to speak.

'The fatal kind,' said Stayne.

Jed was quiet again then. All he could do was stare as the suddenly demonic-seeming doctor took out his pad and generally fussed over his equipment.

'But they've both *died*,' murmured Charity.

'It's really very unfortunate,' agreed Stayne. 'But these things happen. You're a professional, you understand that.'

At this point Rose came in.

The threesome froze.

Rose took in the expressions one by one and stood looking at them for a moment.

'Oh, I'm interrupting something,' she said and left.

As the door clicked shut the atmosphere changed instantly.

Galvanised.

'It's very unfortunate. Very sad indeed,' the doctor said, in a firmer tone, feeling for something behind his ear and noting the change that had come over his audience. 'And I do think the sedation may have had *something* to do with it. It certainly weakened their resistance to . . . the infection.'

He paused, statesman like.

'But we must remember these were *very old women*. It was . . . a miracle they were alive at all. Most people their age would already have passed away.'

They were sickening words. All of them knew it.

'It's a tragedy but there's nothing we can do about that now.'

There was silence for a full minute as the three human beings allowed themselves to feel the weight of the circumstances. During which time both Jed and Charity shocked themselves by feeling at least a twinge of relief. At least they wouldn't have to explain to Lilly why they had done what they had done.

Stayne resumed. 'I think it would be a mistake to involve Haggarty at this stage. He's leaving at the end of the week . . . as you know . . . and . . . in *my* opinion it would be inadvisable – and indeed unnecessary – to involve him. That is bring him down here. At this stage . . .'

There was a tap on the door.

Rose popped her head round and said, cheerfully:

'We're going for a "family walk" over the dunes. It's a lovely day. Everyone's coming. We'll probably be gone all morning.'

There was a milling about in the entrance hall and a few minutes of kerfuffle while coats were put on and people nipped to the toilet.

The three sat watching tensely through the glass door.

'I've – locked the door to the two rooms,' the doctor said, reading the common mind.

When the last echo of the hullabaloo had died away, the three rose and without a word, transferred the two

298

deceased (with difficulty in Lilly's case) to a little box-room on the top floor, down the corridor and round the corner from the Prior-Pointment mausoleum.

Jed and Charity wanted to be together that night.

Unfortunately Miranda didn't show up for her shift so Jed had to stay over at *Newfoundland*.

It occurred to him to ask Charity to stay over with him, but, thinking about it, he decided not to. It was possible Miranda would show up sometime during the night.

'She's getting worse,' was Charity's comment.

Jed looked at his wife to see if she knew anything more than he imagined. He nodded. 'She is pretty . . . *unreliable* lately.'

Charity scoffed at the understatement.

'She's getting worse,' she repeated.

Jed tried not to look guilty.

They parted reluctantly, with a tender kiss and a knuckly squeeze of the hand.

*J*ed was right.

At about midnight there was a tapping on the staff room door.

His mood was grim.

He was ready to be angry with her.

But when he saw her he was shocked at her appearance.

'Jesus, what happened to you?'

Miranda had a black eye and looked drawn and distraught.

She came running across the room and buried her head in his chest, as she had once before, sobbing helplessly, too upset to speak.

Jed was already in a state and as she shook in his

299

arms he was engulfed in a new wave of emotion.

She was like a child shaking with grief, howling her distress. As he held her he noticed how thin she was, and how lank her hair had become. It didn't look like it had been washed for a week. Jesus. He wasn't sure she didn't smell.

She did smell.

The smell set him off. He was reminded of a time he'd travelled to Morocco and befriended a couple of street urchins for the afternoon. Or rather had been befriended by them. They'd had the same musty smell, and their little faces were encrusted with dirt, yet they had seemed like little old men too, wise as Magi. As he'd watched them they'd transformed from one moment to the next from one state to the other, back and forth, child/man, man/child.

Now here was Miranda. Same smell, same impression – woman/child, child/woman.

While she lay on his chest he gently stroked her head and soothed her.

He was gutted by pity. And remorse.

What had he done?

He had paid this child for sex.

He had taken advantage of her when what she needed was love.

He'd given her money for drugs.

The thoughts of the sex suddenly revolted him utterly.

How could he have done that?

He felt as monstrous as she was pathetic.

He held on to her tightly – while trying to avoid her hair going in his mouth.

He smoothed it down as best he could.

When she stirred he reached her a tissue from the bedside table and she blew her nose.

'I've been ripped off!' she spat angrily. 'They kicked me to fuck and took my gear. I'm withdrawing to fuck now.'

300

He didn't know what to say. He wasn't entirely sure he knew what she meant.

'Fucking bastards stole my gear!'

She was an angry, dishevelled woman again.

She looked at him evenly. As evenly as she could, bearing in mind she was 'withdrawing to fuck'. Her face looked haggard. She looked ten years older.

'Do you want a fuck?' she said.

He was dumbfounded.

He never wanted to 'fuck' her again.

'No,' he said. 'I want to help you.'

She laughed in his face. 'Huh. Well give me fifty quid then.'

He was stung. But he indulged himself by thinking he deserved it. 'I don't mean help you like that.'

She stamped her foot, angrily, like a child. 'Jed, I need it!' Almost shouted.

He was trembling now.

'You've got to get *help.*'

'I've got to get heroin,' she said, 'And quickly.'

'We can get you help . . .'

This time she did shout. She stood up to do it. Went red in the face. Screamed. 'Don't tell me what I do and don't need! You don't know me, right! What I am, who I am, nothing! – You haven't got a fucking *clue what I need!*'

They were staring at each other. It was Jed who looked like a child now.

'Give me fifty fucking quid. Now!'

He just sat there, hoping words would come.

'I haven't got fifty quid,' was all he could say.

She flashed him a look he didn't recognise from her repertoire and which made him think that perhaps she had been right in her outburst: he had no idea what she was, who she was – nothing.

The look was pure hatred.

'Jed.' She was threatening. Trying not to shout now. 'Jed, don't make me go and talk to Charity. Please.'

301

It was said.

At last.

'I haven't got fifty quid.' He sounded sad, as well as scared.

She didn't have time for nuances of tone. 'How much have you got?'

He shrugged.

She was picking up his trousers. 'Where is it?'

'Back pocket.'

She searched the trousers feverishly, finding about twenty quid. A bit more. 'This'll do,' she said and made for the door.

At the door a little bit of her humanity returned. She looked back at his saddened face.

'I'm sorry Jed,' she said. 'I'm really sorry.'

The next morning Miranda turned up for work as usual.

Jed couldn't believe his eyes.

She'd disguised the bruising on her eye far more effectively than Jed had been able to disguise the bruising he felt inside. She was chatting to Rose in the office when he lurched in, having stumbled out of bed three quarters of an hour late.

He wondered if she could feel him staring at her in amazement. She didn't show it if she did.

Throughout the morning though he detected little worried glances in his direction as he and Miranda went about their business, aiding the loosely-ordered chaos.

At eleven o'clock she took his arm and diverted him into the laundry.

Now he could get a good look he saw that, under the thickish layer of foundation or something that was smattered all over her face, she still looked rough.

Hardly surprising.

Was she going to ask him for money again?

'Jed, I'm *so sorry* about last night.'

He shrugged.

She took hold of his arm imploringly. 'I mean it. It was really shit. I didn't mean it that I'd go and talk to Charity – it was a dirty trick. Real snide.' She was pulling his arm. 'I won't let you down. You know that don't you?'

What could he say?

It was the old Miranda again. But he didn't believe in her anymore. He was still thoroughly revolted by what he'd seen the night before.

Especially as it was only a reflection of himself, of the person he'd become over the past few weeks.

Months.

The doubt was written all over his face.

Miranda could see it. 'I'm going to stop, Jed.'

'Yeah.'

'I *am*.'

'I'll help.'

It didn't sound very convincing.

Neither of them were very convinced.

Jed looked at her. 'Will you do the shift tonight?'

'Yeah, OK.'

'Promise? I need a night off.'

'Yeah, no problem.'

'Will you be – OK?'

'Yeah. No problem.'

Which was easy for her to say at eleven o'clock in the morning.

Miranda didn't show up for her shift. It was obvious she wouldn't be there for the night shift either.

Money was missing from petty cash.

When Jed phoned her, Charity said, 'Get a temp.'

'I don't think that's a very good idea right now.'

'Jed, we've got to talk.'

'It's not safe to leave . . . everything overnight.'

'Lock all the doors properly, hide the keys, make sure everything's OK. I want you here tonight. I need it.'

He sighed. 'I need it too.'

There was a pause during which both of them wanted to say 'I love you.'

'See you later,' they said. 'Bye.'

*I*t all happened very quickly for Arthur in the end.

One minute he was sitting on the sofa with his wife sipping whisky, wondering when the hell she was going to get fed up and leave him on his own again (whereupon proper life could recommence) but lacking the means to raise the subject in even the most oblique manner for fear of stirring up suspicion; the next minute Eddie arrived at the flat and broke the news that Rodriguez had been arrested by Customs and Excise, that Customs had been tipped off by Arthur's own wife and that they had three hours left to leave Gibraltar to avoid death by strangulation. Or worse.

Arthur went purple and tore his hair.

Eddie said, 'Careful mate, you haven't got a lot of that to spare!' But it didn't make any difference.

Arthur erected a great monument of abuse in honour of his wife, who didn't flinch, or blush or show any sign of ladylike modesty for a full minute, after which she stepped up to him and slapped his face with such force that even Eddie flinched.

Rubbing his cheek, Arthur fell back onto the sofa and shivered like a child just out of the bath. Eddie handed him a briefcase full of money.

'What's this?'

'It's the loot, dear,' said his wife.

Arthur peered into the bag, then at Eddie. 'Where's the rest of it?' he snapped.

'That's all there is for you, mate.'

'You . . . mean that's all you could get?'

'No, mate. I mean that's all you're getting.'

Arthur's eyes narrowed sharply, but before he could operate his vocal chords Eddie said (in a colder tone than Arthur had heard before): 'You're lucky to get that. I could have cleared out and left you with bugger all . . .'

'The goodness of your heart made you stay, did it?' Arthur was naturally suspicious of generosity.

Eddie stumbled slightly over his reply and gave Mrs Prior-Pointment one or two awkward sideways glances as he spoke. 'We've been partners a long time and . . . I thought . . . well . . . I didn't want to just leave you.'

Mrs Prior-Pointment coughed significantly.

Eddie hung his head.

'What's been going on?'

The good woman spoke. 'I've got a hold over him, Arthur.'

While his mouth gaped Arthur took in the fantastic story of his wife's friendship with his partner, spanning time, blackmail, and revenge. As it sank in Arthur began to understand that he had been outwitted, outclassed and out-foxed by his wife. His shoulders began to sag and blotchy patches appeared on his face.

'. . . So there's your quarter of a million, mate.'

'It's a drop in the bloody ocean!'

'I thought it was rather a handsome sum, dear . . .' the wife put in.

Arthur turned on her again. 'It's none of your damn business!'

She said simply, 'On the contrary, dear, it's what's left of the family business,' which shut him up properly.

Arthur fell into a trance until the words 'We'd better be going,' shocked him back to life.

'Where will I go? he spluttered, frightened again.

'You'll come home with me, Arthur.'

'I can't!' He blinked. 'Can I?'

Eddie reassured him. 'We've been careful enough. No one knows you. You *have* been careful haven't you?'

'Yes . . . yes. Oh my God!' His poor hair again. 'Sandra! Sandra knows me!'

Eddie was able to reassure him on this point too. 'Sandra's coming with me, mate.'

Even his wife felt a bit sorry for Arthur now, he looked so dismayed. His face seemed to shrivel up and when he spoke his voice had shrunk too and risen a few semi-tones higher in pitch.

'Where will you go?'

'Home, mate. England. I'm going to start a little practise somewhere – retake my professional exams under a new name – make a new start. Keep myself out of trouble.' He laughed merrily. 'Sandra'll make a nice little secretary, don't you think?'

It didn't look like Arthur did think so.

'Where . . . abouts exactly . . . will you go?'

Eddie's face said, 'You know me better than that, mate.' He smiled nicely. 'I might even start a family.'

By the time his wife spoke, Arthur was no more than a lapdog.

'We'd better go and pack our bags, dear.'

'What about the tickets? We'll have to get a flight . . .'

His wife was calm. 'I've got the tickets here, we fly from Malaga at nine. We're flying to Switzerland for a nice little holiday. You can go to the bank. Come on now – tidy yourself up. Let's keep up appearances, shall we? We'll soon be back to normal.'

*I*t was as if Jed and Charity had been apart for months.

It was a falling-into-each-other's-arms-on-the-doorstep.

They stood holding and swaying each other, conscious of their knees touching.

Charity whispered an 'Oh, Jed.'

Still they stood there.

God knows what the neighbours would have thought if they'd seen it. Husband and wife? Unheard of. Mind you he is a bit peculiar, and who's that young woman who's been visiting at all hours. I've seen her leaving first thing in the morning.

Next thing she was pulling him by the hand to the bedroom.

On the bed there was a clinging entanglement of the kind where need and lust become one, a frantic struggle to get inside the other. There were teeth-touching kisses and moanings on both sides, grappling caresses, clutching, grinding, gripping and groping.

Jed gave himself up completely to the tussle.

He looked down on his wife (who was staring wide-eyed up at him) as on shelter in a bombardment. As on sanity. And safety. And longing. And love. As on something clean and soft and pure. She was someone who loved him and needed him and wanted him and – please, oh my God please, God the exclamation, Jesus the swear word, *please* let everything work out all right.

What they did wasn't what they'd done the other night when they'd swapped their little secrets. It was more simple than that. And beautiful.

It was an expression of mutual fear.

Of pure need.

To get away from it, into each other.

It sounded like anguish when they came.

Staring into each other's eyes.

307

Then they crashed, exhausted and wet.

Jed on top.

Impossible to move.

God knows what the neighbours would have thought if they'd been listening in the garden.

Charity cried and said 'I love you,' and Jed smoothed her hair.

Her clear, clean locks, soothing her like a woman that he loved.

They lay there for a long while, listening to the starlings fighting outside and a lawn mower in the suburban distance.

Late summer evening.

With a surge of emotion Jed realised as he lay there that he would do anything he had to to protect this . . . this safety, and love. This was what was important. His wife. And his home. He made a promise (with his jaw clenched) to make sure they survived. No matter what.

As he did so he started thinking about what exactly it *was* that needed to be done: the dangers that scratched so grittily the flesh of human comfort, like sand in the suntan cream.

He alone knew the real danger, the full story. Only he knew what he had to do.

He became hot with anxiety and felt the desire to roll over.

Charity said, 'Don't go,' with a squeeze of her arms and started to say something. 'Jed, I . . .'

He became aware of her breathing. And hesitating.

'Jed, we need to talk.'

Anxiety prompted him to prop himself up on his arms and look into her face.

She stopped him, pulled him back down, so that her face was hidden from view.

His body tensed.

So did hers.

Fuck. Something was wrong.

Then he knew.

He knew before she spoke what the words would be.

'I've been having an affair.'

He felt a surge of anger. Against the doctor.

Bastard!

He had to roll off now. He sat up.

She grabbed him. 'Jed! It's not Stayne.'

'What!' He glared at her. 'Who the fuck is it then?'

She blushed, looking away.

It was Miranda. He knew before she said it.

'We've only had sex once,' Charity said. 'But we've slept together quite a few times.'

Strangely he was relieved. It would have been terrible – appalling – if it had been the doctor. He couldn't have taken that. But Miranda?

'It's over now,' she said.

They looked at each other like people who were no longer married. Jed was struck by the peculiar notion that he was sitting on the bed with a naked woman who he didn't really know.

Which was exciting actually.

He made the uncomfortable discovery that the idea of Charity sleeping with another woman was quite sexy.

There was hardly room in his head for it all.

Especially bearing in mind his own infidelity.

He noticed that her face was a picture of fear.

He took hold of her hand and squeezed it reassuringly. He was thinking about telling her his secret. *One* of his secrets. Now was the time surely. Get it out in the open.

But he was terrified to open his mouth. His hand was shaking.

Charity thought it was because he was upset. 'I'm sorry, Jed. I probably wouldn't have told you but . . .'

Her head shaking.

He was suspicious again.

'Wouldn't have told me but for what?'

'. . . she threatened to tell you about it.' Before he

could react she said, 'Jed, she's a heroin addict. She's been . . . she . . .'

'. . . She said if you didn't give her money she'd tell me about you and her.'

'More or less.'

He sighed and stood up.

'Where are you going?'

'I'm going to run a bath. Then we're going to do some more talking.'

They'd done a lot of their talking in the bath in the old days.

It was a tradition that had died out.

It seemed appropriate again now.

He was sat at one end with the taps either side of his ears and she was squashed at the other.

'Are you angry with me?'

He shook his head and burnt his ear on the hot tap. He spoke while readjusting himself into a more comfortable position. 'No darling. No I'm not.'

'Aren't you jealous?'

'Yeah. Yeah I am a bit.'

'How jealous?'

He sighed.

'Charity I slept with her too.'

It hadn't occurred to Jed until he opened his mouth that his sleeping with Miranda wasn't exactly equivalent sin-wise to Charity having slept with her – it didn't translate exactly. It was more like her sleeping with the doctor in fact. What made him realise this was the look on Charity's face.

So he added, 'We only had sex once.' As it came out they both realised how unlikely it sounded.

'You bastard!' she said. 'You fucking bastard!' Jed noticed the pronunciation of the word 'fucking' – with the 'g' at the end – loud and clear, because the word was so unusual coming from her.

'I probably would never have told you, but – huh,

310

she threatened to tell you about it.'

She stood up.

'Where are you going?'

She said, 'I don't know!'

'Are you jealous?' he asked stupidly.

'I'm fucking *angry*!'

He didn't know what to say to that. But he didn't need to say anything. He needed to defend himself.

Charity kicked water at him and started screaming and slapping him. 'You bastard!' Then she was out of the bath and had hold of the glass shelf from over the sink and in blind rage threw it at him. It shattered, cutting him and crashing loudly all over the place. Then she was piling anything she could find on him: laundry, the chair, anything she could lay her hands on.

He was too shocked to react. He looked at the blood on his arm and struggled to get out of the bath without cutting himself but the glass was everywhere and he cut his foot too.

Charity had run into the bedroom. He followed.

She was lying on the bed crying.

He was checking the cuts to see if there was glass still in them. Negative. As far as he could tell he was just bleeding.

He approached her, touched her lightly on the shoulder.

He was in tears now, too. Almost.

'I'm sorry.'

She turned over quickly. She was trembling, or shivering, neither of them were sure which.

'Is it over?' she asked.

He nodded. 'Well and truly.'

She reached up and took his hand, pulling him gently onto the bed beside her, where they lay shivering and wet and he bled all over the place, staining the ruffles and flounce of the bedspread and the winceyette sheets.

He said, 'We sure made a mess of the bathroom.'

She said, 'We've made a mess of everything.'

They stayed very close that night.

When one of them left the room the other followed. They cleaned the bathroom, bandaged Jed's hand and put a plaster on his foot. They even went to the toilet together.

Two very scared people.

In bed they held each other tenderly, kissing occasionally, reassuring kisses.

They made further confessions, too.

Charity said that she'd made the mistake of telling Miranda the whole story. Everything. To which he said, 'Hum,' and, 'We'll have to be very careful.'

Jed admitted he had a drink problem.

'I know *that*,' said Charity, then checked herself. 'But it's good you've admitted it.'

Then with some difficulty Charity said, 'Jed, you don't . . . think we . . . did . . . kill . . . Lilly and Edith do you? I mean you don't think *he* did . . . because . . . because he thought I wanted him to?'

'Don't be stupid. Of course not.'

'Really? You do think it was an infection?'

'Yes, of course. Definitely.'

'Do you, really?'

'Yes.'

'Even though he didn't want anyone else to see the bodies?'

'Yes.'

They were quiet for a few moments.

Then Jed said, 'Do *you* think he . . . did?'

She shook her head in the dark. 'No.'

'Really?'

'Really.'

'Even though he didn't want anyone else to see the bodies?'

She shook her head again. Or was it a shudder. 'He was just being careful.'

It was the last time they ever mentioned the subject.

Charity put her hand to her temples then and admitted to Jed that a part of her had been relieved when Lilly and Edith had died and Jed admitted that he'd felt the same.

'I loved Lilly,' Charity said, 'But I was scared.' She began to sob. 'Jed, I was scared because she was a *good woman.*'

Jed patted her shoulder in the dark. He wanted to say 'Don't worry,' but it wouldn't sound right.

'What does that say about me, Jed?'

Jed didn't know what to say.

In the end he decided upon, 'It'll all be over soon. We'll get back to normal. Believe it.'

They were quiet then for a long time. Staring wide-eyed into the night and lying close.

During the darkest part of the night Charity said, 'You won't ever do that again, will you? Sleep with someone?'

'No.'

'Never?'

'Never.'

After a moment he said. 'What about you?'

She said, 'No.'

'No what?'

'No I won't ever do that again.'

In some tiniest, darkest, corner Jed was disappointed.

At Malaga airport Eddie left Sandra with the bags and went off to buy a postcard.

He selected a suitably tacky shot of some semi-clad bronzed bathing-beauties, but changed his mind, opting instead for a nice conservative picture of the Rock of Gibraltar standing out against a gorgeously blue sky and seascape.

He was about to address the postcard to 'Charity and Jed', then he remembered to put Jed's name first.

He wrote the words, 'Every Mother for Himself', stuck on a stamp and went to post it.

Just before he let it go, he stopped himself, thinking, 'Hang on, I just spent two hundred and fifty grand on those guys!'

The thought occurred to Eddie that he wasn't such a selfish bastard after all. It had always been a central tenet of his philosophy on life that he was just that. That he and everyone else in the world were out for whatever they could get.

It must be, he thought, that once you've got it, plenty of it, you can afford to give a bit of it away.

He took out his pen and added the words, '. . . and his best mates':

Every Mother for himself and his best mates.

Then he wondered it he'd really only spent the two hundred and fifty grand on them because he fancied the pants off Charity.

The idea certainly fitted in better with his philosophy.

But in the end he decided he *was* being generous. He missed Jed too.

He tore up the card.

'Leave them. Let them live happily ever after.'

Yes, he was definitely a generous guy.

 The next evening Jed called at Miranda's flat.

She didn't look too pleased to see him.

He'd called there several times that day, in vain.

She just stood there.

'You can't come in.'

'We've got to talk.'

She fixed him with a cold stare. 'Are you trying to sack me?'

He could see that this was the new Miranda.

'We've got to talk.'

She hesitated. Then submitted and nodded a reluctant, 'Come in.'

In the passage he said, 'Is anyone at home?'

She said, 'I'm waiting for someone.'

The place was a tip. A vile bedsit. Filthy, or at least grotty. Piles of unwashed dishes, full ashtrays, grime and a sticky floor by the door.

That musty smell.

She didn't seem to want to apologise for it.

She hovered around the kitchen unit.

He wasn't sure how best to create a 'let's talk,' atmosphere. It seemed impossible.

'*Are* you trying to sack me?'

'I'm not *trying* to do anything,'

'Do you want sex?'

'No thank you.'

Squalid was the word that came to mind.

When he'd recovered from her question he said, 'I thought I'd try bribing you,' and produced an envelope from his inside pocket.

He tossed it on to the worktop that separated the kitchen from the tip, separated him from her.

It made an impressive thump.

When she heard this she looked at him sharply.

'How much is there?'

'How much would it take?'

She picked up the envelope, peeped inside.

Grinned.

'What do I have to do?'

'Get out.'

'What, out of the area, out of your life? What?'

'Completely away.'

The doorbell went and she snapped into action.

She went to go to the door, stopped herself and threw

315

the envelope back on to the worktop. After which she dithered, picked it up again, took out a couple of notes, tossing the rest, still in the envelope, back on to the working top and hurried to the door.

Jed heard some conversation, heard the front door being closed and she was back.

She went straight to a drawer and spoke to Jed as she placed a spoon, a syringe, and other evil looking items on the counter.

Jed watched, listened and spoke without expressing amazement. She spoke without looking up from what she was doing.

'How much is there?'

'Sixteen hundred.'

'When do I have to go?'

'Now. I'll give you a lift as far as Manchester.'

She was concentrating on what she was doing.

'That keen to get rid of me, eh?'

He laughed a hollow laugh. She clinked and clicked: lighters, knives, spoons, needle. A Jiff lemon?

He did well not to gawp.

When she was sucking the finished product up into the syringe, with a little difficulty of some kind, she said, 'What makes you think I won't blow the gaff?' She looked at him. 'I could get you into a lot of trouble.'

He returned her stare and said, 'You've got enough problems of your own,' which unsettled her slightly.

It seemed for a moment that she was on the verge of tears.

Jed said, 'Anyway, I trust you,' and it was her turn to laugh a hollow laugh. One harsh, 'Ha!'

Then she came and sat on one of the chairs and did a very expert-looking thing with a belt round her upper arm, holding it tight in her teeth. She took it out for a moment to say:

'The gear's shit round here, anyhow.'

*   *   *

316

As soon as she agreed to go Jed began to feel for her once again.

After she'd had her 'dig', as she called it, and Jed had watched her slump back in the chair where she let her eyes roll back for ten minutes or so with a trickle of blood running down her arm – during which time she didn't move a muscle and neither did he – Miranda packed a single, tatty-looking bag and said, 'OK, let's do it.'

She even left the door open.

And she certainly didn't look back.

By the look of it, he felt more wobbly than she did.

It was just over an hour to Manchester.

Not far at all really.

It was getting dark as they set out. Miranda put a tape in the car stereo, a dirgey thing Jed didn't recognise. She said it was the *Velvet Underground* and he had the feeling he should have known it.

'Your era, ain't it?' she said.

Pretty soon they were on the M61. The motorway lights sweeping over them out of time to the music.

Jed was overcome.

He wanted to say something appropriate, something loving, but felt that he didn't deserve to. Events had destroyed any possibility of that, he thought bitterly.

But he couldn't help revisiting his affection for the girl, the times they'd spent, him in rapture, her unaware (he thought), talking, laughing, teasing him, telling him her tales from another planet. To where he was now returning her.

Then he wondered if he had ever really known her. Surely she hadn't been taking drugs all that time as Stayne said. Stayne was probably exaggerating to scare him. Hadn't everyone loved her? Hadn't she loved them? She'd brought the house back to life, brought *him* back to life.

Surely there had been *something* between them. Was it all rotten? There had been times when he thought he

317

loved her more than anyone he'd ever known. Hadn't there? Fuck, he didn't even know anymore.

He slapped the steering wheel in frustration.

Miranda reached over in the dark and took hold of his hand, holding on to it.

'I'm sorry, Jed.'

He couldn't believe it. 'I'm the one who's sorry!'

'It's a fuck-up. It's always been like this for me.'

'Haven't you had enough?'

'Oh, I've had enough alright.'

'Can't you get help?'

'They always say I've got to want to stop.'

'I thought you did.'

'I do. Huh. Just not yet, obviously.'

They were quiet then. But she kept hold of his hand.

Somewhere along the way, when he was almost consumed by the darkness, Jed said, 'Would you believe it if I said I loved you?'

Miranda said, 'No.'

Jed was embarrassed. He thought she was probably right.

He was glad it was dark to hide his discomfort.

Then they were in Manchester.

Miranda hadn't said another word. They'd agreed the area to which she was to be delivered before they left.

As they drove down one of those endless, desolate roads that connect Manchester to Greater Manchester, lined by ancient warehouses and squat modern factory units, Miranda said:

'You're a good man, Jed.'

Another of his hollow laughs later, she continued:

'You are. You've got a lot of good in you. I've seen it.'

He wondered scornfully where.

Then she said, '*I've* got good in *me*,' and Jed could go along with that. He told her so but thought he sounded insincere.

318

He saw her nod and turn her head away, facing it out of the window.

He caught a sideways glimpse of her in the yellow intermittent light. Her cheek shone with tears. He saw her wipe them surreptitiously on her shoulder.

'Don't lose yours.' She spluttered slightly. 'Keep hold of it. Keep hold of the good. It's worth fighting for.'

All he could do was drive.

'Here'll do,' she said suddenly.

'Where? Here?' He pointed to some large Victorian houses, back off the road.

'No, just here.'

'What, on the pavement!' He thought she was joking.

'Here's fine.'

Fuck.

He was pulling up. He felt like someone else.

She was getting out.

It was too quick.

'. . . Where will I contact you?' he said.

'You won't,' she replied.

'Hang on . . .' He fumbled in his pocket. Took out the rest of his money. Proffered it. 'It's all I've got.'

'Is this supposed to be symbolic?'

He felt despicable then.

'We could have parted on a finer note,' she said, taking the wad and pocketing it.

Then there was her smile. And her freckles.

'See ya,' she said.

Jed's hand waved itself and she was gone. The door had slammed shut.

He wasn't sure which way she'd gone and looked round and about for a last glimpse. But she was nowhere to be seen, as if the pavement had swallowed her.

He'd driven a couple of miles before he realised the tape was still playing.

319

He cried his eyes out then. And cursed the way it is. Cursed the reasons it's like that. Cursed his own role in it all.

Then he turned the music up, gritted his teeth and drove into the darkness.

'*I* think this is taking conspiracy a bit far, Jed!' A her her her.

It was somewhere they could both find.

He arrived last.

Their two cars were parked in a lay-by half way in the middle of nowhere (West Pennine Moors), one of those wagon-stops-off-a-dual-carriageway-with-a-tea-caravan. Virginia could hardly make herself heard over the roar of passing lorries accelerating away from the traffic island and the cars overtaking them.

'I hope you're not going to suggest a *haute cuisine* candle-lit dinner,' she shouted pointing at the caravan. A her.

'Let's go somewhere quieter,' he shouted. 'Follow me in your car.'

'You haven't joined MI5 in the meantime by any chance?'

'I've got some news for you.'

Her eyes sparkled. 'Good man.'

He took a step away.

She pointed at his feet. 'Jed, your feet . . .'

He looked down at them.

'They're enormous! I never noticed before.'

Jed didn't know what to say. He looked very flustered.

She had spotted it. 'Well, you know what they say about men with big feet,' she purred to soften it.

320

He was grateful and tried to say that the shoes were a size too big . . . he'd bought them ages ago and left them in the boot . . . he'd come out in his trainers by mistake and put them on instead, but it sounded convoluted and stupid so in the end he just stood there blushing. Like a liar.

'Are you alright?' Virginia asked.

He tried to smile. Succeeded mostly. 'Shall we go?'

They drove around for what seemed like ages while she followed in her Tahiti green convertible boudoir. She had the roof down and in the mirror he could see her red hair flapping into her eyes as she drove along.

He thought. 'Maybe she'll kill herself on the way there.'

They drove down winding lanes, between hedgerows, over squashed animals. He could see her grinning to herself behind him.

He pulled up somewhere familiar to him, where there was space enough for the two cars.

'It's very beautiful round here, Jed, but where's the restaurant?' she said when she stepped out of the cat-mobile.

'This is one of my favourite spots. I was going to show it to you and then I thought we could go back to your hotel for dinner and sex.'

A her. A her her her. She looked about. 'Yes, well it's very beautiful.'

He crossed the road towards a stile.

'You're not suggesting going for a *walk*!' she said, as if it were the sort of thing done only in laboratory conditions, by the lowest life-forms.

'It's not far. It's a lovely night.'

'But I haven't got the right shoes!'

'Haven't you got anything else?'

'Only a pair of old pumps I use for aerobics.'

'Well then.'

'Jed, in case you haven't noticed I'm wearing a tight, sexy skirt. I'll look a complete idiot with those things on.'

'There's only cows to see you. Come on.'

She gave him a mock sultry look. 'You can be quite *forceful*, can't you.'

'Slow down, Jed, I can't keep up.'

He was trying to avoid speaking to her.

He didn't know how to do what he had to do.

So he just plunged on.

'Jed! I've got brambles all over my skirt!'

He stopped.

'I'm going to rip that off you later,' he said.

Virginia grinned.

'You can rip it off me now, if you like.'

'We're going to play a game first.'

Jesus. He was getting turned on. Which made him feel really perverse. He turned round, sharply and walked on, pointing. 'If you look up there – see over those trees – that house? – you can just make out the roof. It used to belong to a friend of mine.'

'You must have some rich friends.'

She was struggling to keep up again.

They passed the rusty iron stile where Eddie had nearly ripped his £600 trousers and where Jed had ruined his own later.

They arrived at the bridge.

'Here,' said Jed.

'What?'

'I'm going to test your nerve. If you pass the test, I'll tell you my news.'

At that moment there was a thunderous roar as a train hurtled under the bridge, causing the grass under their feet to jolt with the change of air pressure. Virginia screamed with fright and exhilaration.

When it had passed, he sat her on the wall and explained Eddie's game ('What, no holding on at all!') and when he was finished she gave him a calculating look. 'So you want to make me wet my pants, do you?'

Jed said, 'Believe me, it's a big turn on,' felt sick and forced himself to smile. 'There should be another train in about ten minutes.'

They sat.

Waiting.

Virginia had to do all the talking.

Jed was sitting there desperately trying to think, and not think at the same time, wondering whether or not he was embroiled in a murder plot.

Certainly that had been the original idea, all those years ago, a fortnight previously, when Virginia had told him what she knew.

Every time he examined the overall situation it was there as the obvious solution.

The *most* obvious thing was to tell her the truth, try to persuade her not to do anything, but then if she refused it would become infinitely more difficult to get rid of her, if not impossible.

Unfortunately, so far the plan had gone like a dream, passed without the slightest hitch.

As the moment approached he wished there had been more in the way of hitches.

He'd thought it all out.

He decided for example that if they bumped into someone – a potential witness – en route to the bridge, he would abandon the mission, and somehow bring her back a few days later, or perhaps look for other means.

But he knew they hadn't been seen.

The path was invisible from Eddie's old house and no cars had passed when they parked up.

He had considered the smallest details.

His footprints for example.

He thought if someone did suspect something they might check out foot prints in the area. Details like this were important. Or could be. So he bought a new pair of shoes two sizes too big, which of course she'd spotted immediately. He'd throw them away later.

He'd thought about the details of actually pushing her off the bridge, too. What if she went through the windscreen and killed the driver? Apart from not wanting to be a multiple murderer he thought that maybe there would be a more thorough investigation if two people died, or what if the train crashed with the driver dead! Perhaps the train company would pursue an independent investigation.

One day he'd checked the timing of the drop by carefully dropping stones, (which he reckoned would take the same time to fall as Virginia) so that they landed just before the train arrived at the point of impact – note the technical sounding term. He didn't want to give her enough time to jump or crawl clear, if she was in any position to do so after her fall from the bridge.

The other thing was: what if she fell and the train went over her without touching her because she was lying in the middle of the track?

To reassure himself he'd filled a sack with sand and placed it on the track in such as way that it stood the best chance of being missed. To watch the result he hid in the bushes by the side of the track. But it was obvious as soon as the train came by that nothing could survive under there, there was such a rush of air that even at a distance of ten metres he was physically shoved back by it.

This was an Intercity 125, travelling at over a hundred miles an hour – the force was colossal.

No problem.

These experiments – carried out within a couple of days of Virginia's revelations – had been a light-hearted affair. The extreme measure, though available if all else failed, would not, he believed, necessarily be required. Something would turn up.

At first the idea of 'doing away with Virginia' had been a distraction from the main issues of his guilt over Mrs Prior-Pointment's death and the sedation of

Lilly and the others. It was a macabre game he was playing. Neither Death nor Murder were being seriously contemplated.

But after a few days, especially after the doctor had revealed just how obvious his role was in Mrs Prior-Pointment's death, the seriousness of the situation re-presented itself.

So he decided to weigh up the odds properly and see what was at stake.

He phoned a solicitor he knew and even though the man was obviously busy, dragged him into a conversation about a film he said he'd seen – about a doctor who'd prescribed the wrong medication. Jed said he was sure the film had been mistaken about the offence and the sentencing and what did *he* think – oh and by the way a friend of mine is being prosecuted for fraud and what do you think he'd be looking at sentence-wise.

His acquaintance obviously thought he'd gone off his rocker but Jed got the information he needed.

If there was clear evidence of negligence the charge could be manslaughter and the sentence would be 'five to fifteen(!). For the fraud he was looking at – 'five to ten.'

These two were enough without the various minor deceptions for which it looked like you could still do up to five years for.

He knew very little about parole and concurrent sentencing and so he thought he was basically looking at life imprisonment anyhow.

Five fucking years was bad enough.

After this there was less zest and more science involved in his calculations.

He remembered something Miranda had once told him in one of her speeches about life on the other planet – in which people took drugs, committed crimes, got arrested, wounded, raped and murdered. That it was very rare for anyone to be convicted of a murder unless it occurred within the family.

Most murders, she had told him, took place between members of the same family, and of the rest only a tiny percentage are ever 'solved'.

'The bizzies don't give a shit,' she'd said, 'They don't even bother to investigate properly. Especially not if they think it's suicide. They make a stink sometimes if there's been a gruesome murder and it's in all the papers, but then they either arrest the first person they get their hands on and fit them up, or as soon as it's out of the news forget about it.'

Jed could believe this but, bearing in mind the stakes, he wanted to check it out. So he went to the library and found it in black and white in the crime statistics and inbetween the lines of one or two reports to parliamentary select committees on the subject.

Every event of the fortnight had brought a new perspective.

Every day brought him closer to the climax.

Now suddenly he was there in the flesh.

They were both there, sitting on the wall where he'd conducted his experiments, where Eddie and he had sat and Eddie had scoffed, where he'd even thought of throwing himself off once. (But not for very long.)

He was no longer the schemer, the bankrupt, the manslaughterer, the negligent, the fraud, the husband, the adulterer, the failed businessman.

He was just plain Jed. Exhausted, frightened, doubtful.

And in the distance was a train. The track was very straight. You could see for miles.

'There's one,' Virginia said laying down, making excited little noises to go along with the game.

It was as if he had awoken from a dream that he'd been in for the whole of his life so far. It was as if things were happening in slow motion and that he could see everything more clearly than he had seen it before. The leaves, the earth, the wall. Virginia, lying there, a young woman, a woman in the prime of life. Himself.

'I'll crouch down here, ready to grab you just in case,' he heard himself say. (This was a detail he'd thought about: what if the driver saw two people on the bridge? He had to make sure he was out of sight.)

'If I wet my pants, you're eating them!' Virginia laughed.

Everything was in place.

Rose's restoration to the chair of the committee had never been an official appointment, she had not been voted back in following the announcement of Lilly's death, she had simply begun to act the part.

Indeed the announcement of Lilly's death had been the start of it:

Shortly after Doctor Haggarty's sudden retirement, Rose was summoned into the office by Jed and Charity. They explained the bad news and Rose was so overcome that Jed and Charity both thought she was about to drop dead on them.

The poor old woman's head span as her eyes swam. For a moment she too thought she was about to pass away. And when she managed to regain her breath she was struck by the crazy notion that Lilly and Edith had been killed because they had refused to go along with the deception surrounding the death of old Mrs Prior-Pointment . . . that perhaps they had discovered the old woman's body and threatened to go to the authorities. She recalled the conversation she'd overheard on the landing between Miranda and Jed: 'Blame it on Edith' . . . she remembered the scene in the office the morning Lilly and Edith were taken ill and moved upstairs: Charity in tears, the two men looking very frightened – frighten*ing*. Miranda herself had suddenly disappeared . . .

It all hit at once, preposterous, frightening – possible.

'Both of them?' Rose asked – partly to steady her thinking.

'I'm afraid so, sadly,' said Jed.

'It's impossible . . .'

'Unfortunately not.'

It was too much. Grief and fear united in a great wave and Rose sobbed pathetically.

As she did so, the old trade unionist was struck by another terrible thought: that what had happened was her fault, that she was partly responsible for the death of her two old friends. Rose had been suspicious when Lilly and Edith had been moved upstairs, but had ignored her suspicions. Why had she turned her back on her friends like that? Why hadn't she listened to her heart? She knew about what had happened to old Mrs Prior-Pointment and hadn't spoken out . . .

'What about Mrs M?' she spluttered.

'She's been very poorly also. But she seems to have made a recovery. She's out of danger. She's doing very well.'

Jed and Charity explained very kindly about the illness and about how Lilly and Edith would be dearly missed and how they had both been very fond of Rose. Charity was offering Rose a handkerchief to blow her nose.

Rose looked again at the kindly faces smiling sadly at her, especially Charity who had her arms around her now, rocking her gently. She felt herself relax. She thanked Charity, said yes, she would like a little something to calm her down and began to think how silly she was being, how she was upsetting herself because she had suffered a nasty shock.

Mrs Crotchley joined them and was told the news. She took it very well.

A few minutes and a warm cup of tea later, Rose agreed with Mrs Crotchley's suggestion that they should call a meeting of residents and make the announcement themselves. It was only yesterday that they had broken the news of old Mrs Prior-Pointment's death.

Rose said 'Yes of course I'm sure and don't be silly, I'm fine. I've had a bit of a shock. Poor Lilly. Poor Edith. And poor old Mrs Prior-Pointment, it's all come at once.'

Twenty minutes later Rose convened a meeting and made the dismal announcement.

And there, right at the front, was Mrs M, sitting in her wheelchair looking at her with a bewildered and, Rose thought, frightened expression. As Rose spoke she thought Mrs M was shaking her head, objecting in some way to the news, that the poor dumbfounded woman was about to stand up and declare to the world that a foul crime had been committed and that she, Rose was responsible because she had stood by and not listened to her heart and let it all happen, that she would burn in hell for her sins.

It was a most vivid and frightening hallucination and for a moment Rose was forced to stop speaking and steady herself against a chair. As she did so, it occurred to her that she had been given a tranquilliser and that she was beginning to feel the effects, really it was quite peculiar.

She looked again at Mrs M and saw only the familiar, if dazed, expression that the woman always wore, with perhaps slightly less of her usual cheer. She *had* been very poorly.

It was all very upsetting.

Rose was very upset.

It was all over in a few moments. The news was communicated, Rose awaited people's response and prepared herself to comfort the worst effected with tributes to the deceased or other kind words.

But she needn't have worried.

329

When she was done the scene was as tranquil as when she had begun. The residents had all been given a little something themselves by the new nurse – rather a large little something – and the weight of the medication pressed down on them now as they took in the meaning of Rose's words.

'Very sad.'

'She was a good woman.'

'They both were.'

'Yes.'

'We'll miss them.'

'Poor Lilly.'

'Poor Edith.'

'Oh, and poor old Mrs Prior-P . . . ? . . .'

'Prior-Pointment.'

'Yes.'

'That was yesterday.'

Soon the babble of daytime TV cloaked the scene, Tinkerbell snoozed quietly on Mrs Crotchley's knee and Rose settled down in an easy chair with the rest of them.

Some months after their return from Gibraltar, Mrs Prior-Pointment received an important phone call at home.

'Sylvia? It's John. John Stingham.'

'John, how *are* you?'

Glory be to first name terms.

They exchanged pleasantries for a moment, then the man said, 'Sylvia, are you going to the selection meeting tonight?'

'I wasn't going to, John, why?'

'I won't beat about the bush. We want you in The House with us. We've been watching your progress and . . . we like your ideas. The Cabinet are behind you all the way.'

Mrs Prior-Pointment tried not to sound too flattered. 'That's very kind of you John, but you know as well as I do it's a matter for the constituency party. It depends on the voting.'

He laughed, heartily. 'Yes, and you know as well as I do the constituency party votes the way the Cabinet wants it to. Excepting of course when the *ladies* are opposed.'

It was her turn to laugh. 'It would certainly help, John, if a Cabinet Minister were to personally . . . make a recommendation.'

Arthur, from his chair, was listening intently.

'That's exactly what I've just done. The only serious opposition has been persuaded to stand down, the result's a foregone conclusion. Can you make it to the meeting? I'm sorry it's short notice.'

Arthur said he was pleased when she told him.

'So I suppose that means you'll be travelling back and forth from the capital every week,' he said sulkily.

'I'm sure you'll manage,' she said.

He was positively petulant when she told him she was off to a meeting in half an hour.

'What will *I* do? You *promised* we were going out for *dinner.*'

Mrs Prior-Pointment sighed unhappily.

Sometimes it was difficult for the good woman not to compare her husband to a neutered cat now that he'd become fat and fussy. Arthur was a changed man. He hadn't adjusted at all well to retirement and had taken the news of Mother's death very badly indeed. He tended now to mope around the house, refusing to take an interest in anything.

He was always complaining that the house was being watched, and, on the rare occasions when he ventured out, that he was being followed.

He didn't look happy at all.

'Oh well, I'll just stay in and watch television,' he moaned. 'Who knows, I may even see you on it.'

When Mrs Bullmore arrived fifteen minutes later to pick up the leader and take her to the meeting, she was keen to say hello to Arthur, not having set eyes on the man for such a long time.

She still remembered Arthur from the days when he had heartily pinched her bottom at the tennis club all those years ago, even while he was courting Sylvia.

She marched into the room, stood to attention and presented her hand to him for shaking as if it were an extended military salute.

'Terribly sorry to hear about your mother,' she said smiling sympathetically. 'She had a jolly fine innings. We'll all miss her.'

Mrs Bullmore noted how Arthur had shrunk in stature, seeming to be swallowed by the armchair from which he didn't return her eye contact. He had aged terribly, his handshake was limp.

By the time the meeting was over that night the trusty lieutenant had duly informed the ladies' caucus that Arthur Prior-Pointment had given up on life and decided to drink himself to death.

When the two women left the house Arthur went upstairs to his old study, now taken over by his wife. He went over to the window and peeped furtively through the curtains, up and down the road – what little of the road you could see from the window. He was transfixed for some minutes before he left off and opened the little compartment of his old bureau, took out a little brown bottle, extracted a green and black pill and washed it down with the rest of his brandy.

He poked around in the office for a while, glancing at papers marked 'confidential', but which contained nothing of any interest to him, then went downstairs, put on his golf jacket and his tweed cap and went out into the back garden.

It was just beginning to get dark.

The garden was badly over grown.

He stumbled down the weedy shale path, under the

canopy of tall, imposing trees through which no ray of light ever penetrated, between the overgrown rhododendrons, past the ornate stone bird-bath, pausing for a moment to gaze at the hideous shapes suspended in the black water of the stagnant pond, surely not fish, and went on up to the imitation rococo summer house, shuttered up now.

He opened the sliding door with some difficulty – it needed oiling – and unfolded a collapsible chair.

'Winter's upon us,' he muttered as he did so.

He opened one of the shutters slightly, took out a packet of cigarettes he kept hidden from his wife and settled down for a crafty smoke, staring dejectedly out over the ornate gloom of the old Victorian garden.

*W*hen custody of old Mrs Prior-Pointment's legacy passed irrevocably over to Mrs Crotchley, Rose had very little left to bargain with.

At first Rose's claim to a share of the booty had carried some weight. The two women anticipated a confrontation over the money with the younger Mrs Prior-Pointment when the bad news about her daughter-in-law became known. She and Rose had agreed to deny all knowledge of the hoard and for a time had made common cause. Mrs Crotchley had been generous to a fault.

When the moment arrived for the younger Mrs Prior-Pointment to collect her mother-in-law's effects and settle up the outstanding bill, Rose volunteered to assemble and sort through the late matriarch's scant belongings. It was agreed with Mrs Crotchley that Rose would place the (empty) green holdall in a position of prominence.

When everything was ready Rose and Mrs Crotchley

333

lined themselves up by the bed which had been the old woman's and awaited the entry of the terrible daughter-in-law.

When Charity showed Mrs Prior-Pointment into the room she was a little surprised to see Rose and Mrs Crotchley there.

It was all achieved with facial expressions of the kind that are so subtle and at the same time expressive of clear and precise meaning that only women with a lifetime's experience of reading the impenetrable faces of men and communicating in secret across men-filled rooms could have understood.

Mrs Prior-Pointment's almost-Roman nose immediately shot an arrow at the old green bag and then pointed accusingly at Rose. Then it sniffed out Mrs Crotchley.

There had been no communication between the two relatives for years, Mrs Prior-Pointment was unaware even that Mrs Crotchley was resident at *Newfoundland*.

Within the space of a few seconds she *knew*.

It was all there in the look of pleased defiance and in the tiny adjustments of the two old women's features as Mrs Prior-Pointment looked back and forth between Rose, her relative and the battered green holdall.

Mrs Prior-Pointment stiffened, marched to the bag, felt it's (lack of) weight looked sharply back at her adopted enemies and sniffed.

She knew it would be useless to protest.

She was a little ashamed of her conduct now Mother had actually passed away. She still felt a little guilty. She knew that the two old women were playing on that, that it would be impossible to raise the matter with dignity.

Mrs Prior-Pointment's only problem was how to conduct her business and leave the room while maintaining a modicum of decorum.

Mrs Crotchley understood this.

'Come along dear,' she said to Rose and left the room without further telepathy. Rose bustled out in her wake. Charity stood there blinking.

Two days later Rose was dropping hints that would have flattened Birmingham about needing a few pounds, when Mrs Crotchley abruptly explained that 'the legacy' was now 'tied up' and that they'd 'both had a good run'.

From which Rose deduced that from now on, financially, she'd be walking alone, if not standing still altogether.

Newfoundland had changed almost beyond recognition in the months since the documentary.

The building itself looked different with its improved disabled access and colourful new railings and window surrounds, but the biggest change was to the social composition.

There were only Rose and Mrs Crotchley left of the 'old generation': while the rest had either passed away or passed on to 'more suitable accommodation', their places taken by a new, more robust generation of fee-paying 'guests' (as they were now called).

Rose didn't like all these newfangled expressions. Even Charity now referred to the residents as 'guests', but this term was infinitely preferable to 'clients' which was the term Mr Green used.

The new residents were younger and more forceful and paid Rose less heed than their predecessors. As their numbers had increased, so Rose's influence around the house had declined. Her chairpersonship of the residents' committee had been an early casualty.

At the first meeting (after Rose was deposed) of the newly-named members' forum, a rule was passed that only those members who could make it to the dinner table of their own accord would be permitted residence, others would be 'found more suitable accommodation elsewhere'. All the new members were in favour. The majority was slender but adequate.

This decision consolidated the process of change.

Mrs Crotchley seemed happier and more contented

335

among the new generation and would occasionally deign to invite members to her room for a glass of vintage claret. The new members respected her as a community elder, sought her advice on personal matters and generally spoiled her with cups of tea, letting her off lightly work-wise.

Rose, on the other hand was very unhappy and, without even the comfort of her uneven interviews with old Mrs Prior-Pointment, fell back into the most appalling isolation.

She retreated into the office, and confined herself to 'interfering' (as Mrs Crotchley called it) – opening letters, prying into the filing cabinets and answering the phone, stubbornly refusing to leave the room when she knew privacy was required.

She wasn't sleeping well and when she did drop off, usually, with the aid of a pill, she was visited in her dreams by awful scenes in which Lilly and Edith would be drowning, or suffering unspeakable torture of the kind she had heard stories about in the war, while Rose stood by, able but unwilling to help. She would then be condemned to suffer herself, at which point she would wake up feeling scared and lonely, occasionally soaked in sweat and often in tears.

'Mrs Green, I've a message for you, from Dr Stayne.'

'Rose please, call me Charity, you make me sound like – I don't know what!'

It was said nicely.

'The doctor said to ask you if you are going to – what was it? "Are you going to go south tonight, as usual" or something.'

Charity's face fell. 'Thank you, Rose.'

'He said will you phone him when you get back.'

Charity said she would and Rose left the room to give Charity a chance to make her call. As soon as Rose was sure the connection had been made she bustled back into the room.

Rose had a dislike of Dr Stayne which, when added to her traditional mistrust of the medical profession, qualified as loathing.

Rose hovered about the office pretending not to listen to Charity's end of the conversation.

She knew that Charity was uncomfortable; it was obvious from the stilted way she spoke.

'Erm, I got your message.'

'Well?'

'Yes. Rose gave it to me – *didn't you, Rose?*'

Stayne took the hint. 'Ah, the little spy's listening in, is she?'

'. . . That's correct, yes.'

'Well? Can you make it tonight? I've got somewhere very special in mind.'

'I'm afraid I'll have to cancel that appointment.'

He was disappointed. 'I thought we had a regular commitment.'

'Will next week be alright?'

'Oh I suppose so.' He was exaggerating his regret. 'I was so looking forward to that little trip to the South Downs you promised me.'

Charity put her hand over the mouth piece. 'Rose, would you excuse me for a moment? Please?'

Rose pretended to be surprised – 'Oh, of course,' – and left the office.

But Rose had developed a special way of closing the office door – with a bang and a rattle of the handle – that left the door open slightly for just such occasions.

Through the crack, from outside in the entrance hall, Rose overheard the following:

'Nick! Please don't leave messages like that with Rose. It's not funny. If Jed had been there when she

337

gave it to me he'd have cottoned on immediately . . .
It's all right . . . Yes, next week. Something urgent came
up for tonight, I'm sorry . . . No you don't, you liar, you
just want me for sex, now shut up.'

Rose was in the office with Jed a little later when the
phone rang.

Rose said, with a faint air of malice, 'It's Mrs Prior-
Pointment, MP, for you, Mr Green.'

Rose knew that Jed didn't like speaking to Mrs Prior-
Pointment, especially since the good woman's election
to Parliament. The discomfort was written all over his
face as he took the phone off her.

'Thanks,' he said miserably, preparing his extra polite
telephone voice. 'Can I help you?'

'Mr Green?'

'Speaking.'

'Mr Jed Green?'

'Er – yes?'

'Mr Jed Green, *sycophant*?'

'!? . . .'

'A her her her.'

'Ah.' Jed heaved a sigh. 'Yes?' Jed knew he'd have to
act now, for Rose's benefit. So did Virginia.

'What a lovely telephone voice you have when you're
grovelling to an MP, Jed, I'm very impressed.'

'I see, yes. How can I help?'

'You know, I really enjoy making you squirm, Jed. I
can just see you standing there with Rose listening in
and you acting your little heart out.'

Cough. 'Is that so.'

'I must be a vindictive little bitch.' A her her her.

Jed had to communicate to Virginia without communicating to Rose. 'I'm afraid . . . *that*'s been can-
celled . . . uh . . . tonight, that is . . . until next week.'

'Oh Jed, now you're disappointing me. I'd bought
some special underwear, too.'

'Something urgent came up.'

338

'Something urgent usually *does* come up in my experience.' A her her her.

'So I'll look forward to that next week, shall I?'

'A her her her.'

'Thank you. Goodbye.'

'Oh, Er . . .'

Jed put the phone down and left Rose to it in the office.

So Jed didn't murder Virginia in the end.

The whole thing was ridiculous.

Understandable given the stress.

As she lay on the wall and he crouched down, with the train still a little way off up the track she turned and gave him an intense, searching look.

She said, 'Jed, I *know*, you know. I know it's you. You're the mysterious "Mr Green" It was right under my nose all the time, well – in my address book to be precise – you crafty bastard.'

He blinked.

'I sussed it the day after I saw you at *Newfoundland* . . . It was the accountant's address – your name . . . well, near enough: "Greenhouse".'

She had a victorious kind of gleam in her eyes. But not malicious.

His mind raced. 'Aren't you going to "grass me up"?'

She laughed. 'What do you think I *am*?'

'Why didn't you tell me?'

'You ruined my story you bastard – I wanted to make you sweat a bit. It could have been quite big you know . . .'

The train took them by surprise. They both screamed and shouted at the thunderous bridge-shaking roar beneath them and Virginia nearly held on it was so frightening, but managed not to.

'Fucking hell!' (She pronounced the "g") I nearly *did* wet my knickers!'

Then they had it off, right there on the bridge and Virginia ruined her tight, sexy dress.

Afterwards she said, 'That's the first time I've ever done it in stockings *and* plimsolls.'

On the way back to the cars she stopped, gave Jed another searching look and with a suspicious frown said, 'You weren't thinking of pushing me *off* that bridge, by any chance, were you?'

He laughed. 'Course I bloody wasn't! What do you think I am!'

It was lunchtime.

Grace had been said. Rose, as usual, had pointedly refused to participate. Tucking in her serviette, she reached for the ketchup.

But her hand stopped dead in its tracks, hovered for a moment and quickly withdrew to the safety of her lap.

There was no ketchup on the table.

Rose glanced over at the sideboard to double check. Nothing.

Mrs Crotchley's face gave nothing away, yet Rose knew that from now on there would be no ketchup at mealtimes, not even in bowls with a little teaspoon for those who wanted the wretched stuff. She also knew that everyone else on the table had seen what had happened, and that they knew their message had been received.

There would be no debate on the subject. There would be no scene.

Those days were gone.

After lunch Rose left the table early, saying she was tired and wanted to take a nap in her room.

In the entrance hall she came across Tinkerbell who was no longer permitted in the dining room and confined at meal times to a basket under the stairs where one of old Mrs Prior-Pointment's tartan blankets now made a cosy (if smelly) bed.

Tinkerbell was sitting by the front door *hit-hit-hitt*ing to be released, presumably to create havoc on the road outside.

As Rose kindly opened the door for him, he wagged his little knob of a tail enthusiastically and dashed through the car park with a lively *wiff- wiff*.

Rose shuffled up stairs muttering something to herself about taking an extra pill.

Jed and Charity had both cancelled their arrangements.

It was a special occasion. By coincidence they both had 'little announcements' to make and had agreed to 'do the business' that evening instead of having their regular weekly 'night out on their own'.

'Are you sure you don't mind, Jed?' said Charity as she poured herself a glass of wine.

'No, I'm fine with this,' he said pouring himself a glass of sparkling apple juice. Jed had stopped drinking and started going to AA.

'I'm not going to have much.'

'Don't worry. I'm fine. Cheers . . .'

There was a little *ching* of glass on glass.

They were in the kitchen, preparing food together. It was getting dark outside. Jed was putting a salad he'd made onto the nice, solid wooden table.

'Shall I get the candles out?' he said.

'That'd be nice,' said Charity, nicely.

As he did so he said, chattily, 'I'm sure Rose is getting worse. She was hovering round in the office today when I was trying to use the phone. I couldn't get rid of her.'

'Did you have something you didn't want her to listen into?'

'*Para*noid! . . .'

Charity laughed.

'I sometimes wish she'd suddenly be "unable to make it to the dinner table of her own accord",' he said.

'Oh, Jed, Don't be unkind, Rose has been very good to us. She doesn't mean any harm. She's getting old. I think she misses . . . the others sometimes.'

'She's a very difficult client,' Jed said and thought for a moment. Quite grave.

Then he said 'No, you're right. I'm being unkind.'

He raised his glass.

'Here's to being more kind.'

Ching.

So the table was laid, the candles lit, the scene set.

'How's the salad?'

'Um, fine. Nice.'

Jed sighed contentedly. He liked the kitchen. The living room was better now he'd added a few touches of his own. The bedroom was still pretty awful, but he was trying to be more tolerant. The bedroom was Charity's room, he told himself. He concentrated on the cosiness of it now, rather than on the design itself. It was comfortable. In a frilly kind of way.

'What's that book you've been reading?' Charity asked. 'Didn't look like your usual style.'

They were trying to chat their way through the main course and save their announcements for after, like they would the crackers at Christmas.

It was a little awkward, Jed was glad of something to say.

'Um. I'm enjoying it actually. It's a Jackie Collins. It's really quite good. Absolutely filthy. I was surprised – every combination you can imagine, and I'm only on page sixty!'

Charity smiled.

Jed went on, 'It made me a bit sad, though. There's an inscription to Miranda on the inside cover. I found it in the staff room – it must have been one of hers.'

'What does it say?'

'The inscription? Erm . . . Oh, "To Miranda, Yours was the best of them all, love Baz", or something. I nearly cried when I saw it.'

They ate in silence for a while, until Charity put down her knife and fork. 'Oh, for God's sake, I can't wait any longer. Let's tell.'

Jed grinned. 'OK, you go first.'

'No you. *Please*, Jed.'

'OK,' He smiled broadly. 'I got that job.'

'Which one?'

'The management consultant . . .'

'Really? That's wonderful.'

'It's better than I thought . . .'

He explained all about it for a few minutes and Charity smiled and asked questions. He said how it would mean a fantastic salary – they'd probably be able to afford a new house.

'They were very impressed with what we've done at *Newfoundland*; they want to see more of the same,' he beamed.

A few more congratulations and it was Charity's turn.

'Well?'

She hesitated.

'What?' he grinned, a bit embarrassed for some reason.

'I'm pregnant,' she said.

In his surprise, Jed went up to the roof of the house, came down through the central heating pipe, squeezed through the boiler, went back on his past life and relived his birth.

He must have looked pretty shocked, because Charity asked, 'Are you alright?'

He went to say 'Yes, I'm fine,' but said 'Yuzmfn,' instead, and 'Bloody hell!'

'Aren't you pleased?'

'Huh . . . of course I'm pleased. I'm just . . . a bit . . . surprised. Shocked . . . Fucking shocked.'

343

He said, 'Ffff,' a few more times and puffed his cheeks once or twice and then pulled himself together. 'Well that's fantastic!' he said. 'Marvellous. I mean I'm really happy. It's fantastic.'

She smiled then. She was convinced.

He was still shaking his head. Smiling now, though. Broadly. Then he stopped and said, 'Oh my God! How are you? I mean, how does it feel?'

Charity grinned. 'Beautiful.'

'Can you *feel* it?'

She tutted. 'No, of course not. It just, I dunno, feels beautiful.'

He groped for his glass. 'Cheers.'

She grinned, picked up her own glass and said, 'Cheers.' And, 'To the future.'

'To the future.'

Ching.

He sipped his apple juice, racking his addled brains for a toast. 'Here's to the past,' he tried.

There was a slight curl at the corner of Charity's mouth at that one.

'. . . I mean . . . good riddance to it.' Jed frowned, a bit embarrassed. 'Oh, I know . . .' He raised his glass, solemnly. 'Here's to . . . *getting away with it.*'

Charity laughed. 'Yeah. Getting away with it.'

Ching.

Jed was getting into the swing. 'And here's to our *children* getting away with it . . .'

Charity said, 'No. Here's to our children not *having* to get away with it because they're not in trouble!'

'Yeah.'

Ching.

Jed smiled. 'Here's to *all* the children.'

'Huh. Let's not get carried away, Jed. We'll have enough on our plate.'

'Yeah. Good point.'

'I've got one,' Charity said. 'Here's to Eddie.'

'*Eddie*?' Jed didn't sound too pleased.

344